Her expression, as she gazed up at him, was chagrined. "Ah'm sorree."

The sound of her voice was beginning to have the oddest effect on him. He wanted too much to hear it. "You don't have to be," he began, but she shook her head.

"Ah'm stup-hid."

"Lily." He covered the hand she held on his arm. "No. I won't have that."

She made a sound—a husky chuckle that shivered all the way through him, turning his brain to mush. Her smile flashed up in the dim lantern light "Fool-*ish*," she amended. "L-Lord Grah-don, you are so g-hood to m-he. Ah'm so gr-ate-ful."

Gad! he thought, staring down into what he knew was the most riveting countenance he'd behold in his lifetime. Grateful! If she had any idea of what he wanted to do to her at that moment, she'd probably think he was nothing but a perfect swine!

Dear Reader,

We are delighted to be the first to bring you a Regency by Susan Spencer Paul, who also writes mainstream historicals as Mary Spencer. Touted as one of the top historical writers today by *Affaire de Coeur,* Susan will captivate you with *Beguiled,* the heart-wrenching story of a mute noblewoman who is the unsuspecting party when a much-sought-after earl is blackmailed into marrying her. The charming earl soon learns the power of unspeakable love.

Claire Delacroix returns this month with *My Lady's Desire,* the awe-inspiring sequel to *Enchanted.* In this thrilling medieval tale, a blade for hire and an exiled noblewoman marry to reclaim her lost estate, and together find an unexpected passion. Another surprise match results in Liz Ireland's adorable new Western, *Prim and Improper,* when a prim young spinster falls for a very improper cattle rancher who she believes is in love with her sister.

Rounding out the month is *Malachite* by *USA Today* bestselling author Ruth Langan. In the final book of her popular THE JEWELS OF TEXAS series, long-lost Jewel brother, Malachite, emerges from the wilds of Montana to confront the father he never knew, and finds love in the arms of a gentle widow and mother.

What a terrific lineup we have for you this month! Whatever your tastes in reading, you'll be sure to find a romantic journey back to the past between the covers of a Harlequin Historical®.

Sincerely,

Tracy Farrell
Senior Editor

Please address questions and book requests to:
Silhouette Reader Service
U.S.: 3010 Walden Ave., P.O. Box 1325, Buffalo, NY 14269
Canadian: P.O. Box 609, Fort Erie, Ont. L2A 5X3

Susan Spencer Paul

BEGUILED

Harlequin Books

TORONTO · NEW YORK · LONDON
AMSTERDAM · PARIS · SYDNEY · HAMBURG
STOCKHOLM · ATHENS · TOKYO · MILAN
MADRID · WARSAW · BUDAPEST · AUCKLAND

ISBN 0-373-29008-X

BEGUILED

Books by Susan Spencer Paul

SUSAN SPENCER PAUL

lives in Monrovia, California, with her husband and two young daughters. She started her first novel when she was in her early teens but eventually put it aside, unfinished, in favor of more important interests...such as boys. Now happily married and—somewhat—settled down, she's returned to her love of the written word and finds it much easier to finish the books she starts.

To the wonderful ladies at The Book Rack in Arcadia, California, who have so kindly supported me over the years and kept my bookshelves at home well stocked, this novel is dedicated with all my thanks and appreciation.

Chapter One

It had often been said among those who should know that the Earl of Cardemore was not quite human, that he was, in fact, a devil who had managed to escape from Hell and take on human form. Some argued that his unnatural size was proof that he wasn't a native of this world, while others contended that the vivid scars mapping his harsh features gave testament to the fierce struggle he'd made while grasping and clawing his way out of the eternal pit of fire. Anthony Harbreas, the Earl of Graydon, had never given merit to the ridiculous rumorings. Until now.

The summons he had received from Cardemore an hour earlier—although he used the word *summons* out of polite habit, as it had really been a threat—was the least of the surprises he'd met with that night. The gloomy interior darkness of Cardemore's immense and elegant town house, Wilborn Place, located in the midst of London's most fashionable district, had certainly given him a turn, as had the sight of a number of carriages belonging to some of England's highest-ranking nobles parked outside that same house. The fact that all of Cardemore's servants appeared to possess the ability to fade rapidly into shadows had been cause for some question, as well. Lord Daltry, who'd been present when the summons arrived and had subsequently insisted upon accompanying Lord Graydon, murmured as they followed Cardemore's ominously silent butler down a darkened hall, "If I'd known we'd be surrounded by ghouls, I would have brought along a priest."

But the most potent shock by far had been the sight of Cardemore himself, when he had at last come through the doors of the study in which Graydon and Daltry awaited him.

Unkempt, unshaved and dressed in the coarse manner of a dockside laborer, appearing both aggravated and weary, the man walked into the room, looked down at his guests from his superior height and commented gruffly without preamble, "Brought a friend along to hold your hand, did you, Graydon? Just as well. I can't abide most of you sorry young dandies, but at least Daltry knows how to fight properly."

"Not against you, however, my lord," Daltry remarked with a slight bow. "The last time I had the honor of matching you at Jackson's you nearly knocked all my teeth out. I was obliged to eat boiled oats for a week."

With a rare chuckle, Cardemore stalked past them, reaching for a decanter of brandy set near the impressive desk that took up one end of the room. "Sit down," he said, pouring himself a drink. "I haven't long before I must return to more important matters."

"No thank you, my lord," Graydon replied, his gaze following Cardemore's movements as the man settled into a large chair behind the desk. "As it happens, Daltry and I are expected at Lord and Lady Hamilton's shortly. We only stopped here first because your missive was so urgent."

"Urgent," Cardemore repeated, his dark eyes taking in his guests' elegant evening clothes with clear amusement. "Oh, yes, Graydon, it is indeed an urgent matter that brings you here tonight. But I have less use for fine manners than I do for young dandies, so let's dispense with them and speak plainly. You came because I told you to come. Because I've bought up every debt you owe, every marker you've pledged and every deed you've mortgaged, including the one to St. Cathyrs.'' He paused long enough to sip his drink, his eyes holding Graydon's over the rim of the glass. "That was foolish of you," he continued pleasantly in a moment. "Didn't you realize how vulnerable your family estate became when you used it to secure such a large loan?"

"It was an unfortunate but necessary action," Graydon replied quietly, warily. "It was to be repaid this coming quarter. Indeed, if what you say is true, if you hold the note to the mortgage, then you will receive the outstanding amount due. In full."

"No." Cardemore set his glass on the table. "I won't accept payment in money for the outstanding amount. I won't accept money for any of your debts. What I require," he said, sitting forward and tenting his fingers beneath his chin, "is payment of a different kind."

Graydon gave not the slightest indication of surprise. "You bought all of my debts in order to put me beneath your hand? May I tell you, my lord, that such as that is blackmail, and more than likely to end with you in Newgate?"

Cardemore's lazy smile widened. "Oh, no, my boy. That's not one of your options. You don't know enough about me to even begin to understand what I can do to you without fear of reprisal. I vow I wouldn't lose so much as a moment's sleep on your behalf. If you don't want to find yourself ruined and your dear mother and charming sisters thrown out of your ancestral home, then I suggest that you sit down and listen to what I propose. There will be enough opportunity for you to rant and rave after, if you wish."

"Might as well sit, Tony," Daltry remarked with practical resignation, adding, when Graydon looked at him sharply, "Unless you want to stand here all night while you argue with the man."

When they were both seated, Cardemore said, "Let me tell you plainly what I want and we can save ourselves the effort of playing cat and mouse. My sister, Lily, and my niece, Isabel, are coming to London next month to have their comeout. I want you to dance attendance on Lily while she's here and make certain that both she and Isabel are fully accepted in society.''

A stark silence followed these words as Cardemore looked from one man to the other, at last saying, ''Never thought I'd see the day when one of you frippery young lords could be shocked speechless, but I suppose here it is. It's a nuisance to put my own sister into such a man's care, but you'll treat her well enough or suffer the consequences. That's the best I can do, short of buying Lily a husband.''

With an effort, Graydon found his voice. ''My lord, what you suggest is preposterous.''

''You won't think so when you're corresponding to your family and friends from debtor's prison,'' Cardemore assured him.

''But why should you wish to do such a thing?'' Graydon demanded. ''And why me? I can't suddenly start squiring a girl I've never even met before.''

''Why not?'' Cardemore gave a shrug of his massive shoulders. ''Like the rest of your kind, you've been taught from the cradle how to manipulate others. There's very little you can't manage if you put some effort to it. And don't think I don't know it. I come from the same sort of people, with all their ancient titles and ancient blood and ancient emotions.'' He sat back comfortably in his chair. ''The Walfords go back to before the days of the Romans, so far back you'd think we'd have water in our veins by now instead of blood, we've been stretched so thin. Some of us are half-mad,'' he said with a grin. ''Some of us are nearly inhuman. I happily abandoned my family when I was fourteen and never would have gone back if my brother hadn't had the bad manners to get himself killed without leaving a son to inherit the title and estates, and if Lily hadn't needed me. I've loved few souls in my life, Graydon,'' Cardemore said softly, intently, ''but Lily is the most precious among them. I've held her safe from every harm these past many years, keeping her in the country, as far from fashionable society's vultures as possible, but now I think perhaps I've done her a disservice. She's twenty-one years of age and as vulnerable as a newborn babe. Coming to London is as a dream to her. An answer to all her prayers. I'll not allow her to be disappointed. Understand that." His expression took on a hint of menace, as gentle and firm as his voice. "Lily will have all the things she's dreamed of. Exactly as she's dreamed of them. You'll make certain of it or lose everything you hold most dear. I give my word of honor on it."

"Why?" Graydon asked, shaking his head. "There must be dozens of better men you could have chosen."

"Hardly," was the casual reply as Cardemore opened a desk drawer and pulled out a single sheet of paper, which he scanned. "I've been informed by my sources that you're a notable sportsman, a leader of fashion, highly admired among the nobles as a rising power in Parliament, considered the catch of the ton by the mothers of marriageable females and, according to my mistress—" Cardemore glanced up at him "—handsome enough to make young girls faint should you happen to smile at them. Not that I want you felling Lily, of course, but she's far too level-headed for that sort of nonsense." Leaning, he offered the paper to Graydon, who read it through with narrowed eyes.

"Is it all correct?" Cardemore asked.

"Quite thorough." Graydon passed the paper to Lord Daltry. "Right down to the name and location of *my* mistress." He smoothed his fingers in a relaxed gesture over the folds of his cravat. "I'd ask how you came to know so much about my sisters, even their dates of birth, but I'm afraid I wouldn't like the answer much."

A chilly smile lifted the corners of Cardemore's mouth. "No, I'm afraid you wouldn't."

"Dear me," said Daltry, tossing the paper onto the desk. "Even my name's listed as one of your frequent compan-

Beguiled

ions. Never knew you'd be such a dangerous fellow to associate with, Tony.''

"There's one pertinent bit of information missing from your collection, however," Graydon said. "I spent most of last season openly courting Miss Frances Hamilton, and it's well-known among the members of the ton that she and I have an understanding, despite the fact that I've not yet made her a formal offer. I cannot possibly do what you ask without starting a great many unpleasant rumors flying, perhaps driving Miss Hamilton away even if I should be able to explain the matter to her.''

Cardemore's expression sharpened. "You'll tell no one of the understanding between us. Either of you." His dark gaze fell briefly on Lord Daltry, who smiled cheerfully at him in turn. "If Lily should ever hear of it I would be most displeased. I don't care what you do with Miss Hamilton. In my mind, she doesn't exist as a problem. The only thing I'm concerned about is that Lily enjoy her first season in London and that she be spared any unkindness on the part of fashionable society. If she wants to attend parties, you make sure she attends them. If she wants to dance, you make sure she dances. When she leaves London to return to Cardemore Hall, I want her doing so with a smile on her face.''

"If you love your sister so dearly," Graydon remarked, "then why don't you squire her yourself?''

Cardemore stood, setting his hands palms down on the desktop. "That's a foolish question, Graydon, even for you. If I took Lily about she'd be treated with respect for no other reason than simple fear, while behind her back all those sharp-tongued matrons of the ton would gleefully wreak havoc. If the most notable gentleman in London shows a keen interest in Lady Lillian Walford, however, society will welcome her with open arms." From his great height, he gazed down at them much as a waiting panther might look with satisfaction upon its helpless prey. "Lily and Isabel will be arriving in three weeks, with my sister-in-law, Lady Margaret. Their first outing will be to Almack's, where I have already secured vouchers for them. I advise that you make yourself known to Lily then, Graydon, for a month after that I'll be holding her and Isabel's comeout here at Wilborn Place and I'll expect to see you leading Lily out for the first dance." To Lord Daltry he added, "If you bear your friend any affection, then do what you can to aid him in his endeavors. Otherwise you'll find yourself lending him comfort as he serves his time in debtor's prison. It will be, I promise you, a lengthy period of time in which to prove the mettle of your friendship."

Chapter Two

"That can't be the girl, surely." Lord Daltry frowned. "I didn't expect her to be beautiful, what with having Cardemore for a brother, but I didn't think she'd look more like a man than a woman. Are you sure there isn't any way for you to get out of this?"

"I'm sure," Graydon replied grimly, clasping his hands behind his back as he contemplated the tall, dark-haired young woman standing at the other side of Almack's. "Cardemore headed off every attempt I made to retrieve my debts. He's evidently got his own personal army of cutthroats. My tailor was so upset when I tried to pay him personally that I thought the poor man would have a seizure. It was the same everywhere else I went. People, it seems, are rather in awe of Lord Cardemore."

"You're going to go through with it, then?" Daltry asked, eyeing the young lady doubtfully. "With her? Only look at those shoulders. Looks like she could take on every man in the room and come out the easy winner. Gad. She gives new meaning to the notion of country girls being healthy."

Graydon chuckled. "She's not that bad, Matthew. Perhaps not beautiful, certainly nothing like Miss Hamilton, but handsome enough. As long as she's well mannered I don't suppose I'll mind escorting her about London."

"Handsome," said Daltry. "Huh. If that's what you like in a female."

"I rather fancy tall women, and she looks to be even taller than Miss Hamilton. And look at that smile. Stunning. See how she's charming old Hanby there? Don't think I've ever seen him laugh before. Wonder what she's telling him?"

"Probably 'Laugh or I'll give you a black eye, you skinny whelp,'" Daltry suggested dryly. "God's feet, there goes Curtis taking her a glass of punch. The chit's got more men fluttering around her than a horse does flies. Whatever was Cardemore worrying about? Doesn't look like she needs helping. You ought to go back to that hell house of his and tell him that his sister's doing fine on her own. What?" He looked over as Graydon's hand gripped his sleeve. Seeing the expression on his friend's face, he repeated, "What?"

"There." Graydon nodded across the room. "Sitting right behind where Cardemore's sister is standing. See her?"

Tilting his head to see through the swirl of dancers on the floor, Daltry looked, and after the initial shock wore off, announced, "She's mine. You've already got Lady Lillian to look after, as well as Miss Hamilton to keep happy."

"She's fantastic," Graydon murmured, staring. "I've never seen hair that color, so blond it's almost white. She looks like a painting of an angel come to life. Who do you think she is?"

"Doesn't matter, old boy," Daltry assured him, smoothing both hands over his elegant black coat. "She's all mine. You go take care of Lady Lillian. I'll take care of the angel. Do you think she's been given permission to waltz?" He looked about. "Where's one of the patronesses?"

"There's Lady Jersey," Graydon said, smiling at that lady in his most charming manner as he sketched her an elegant bow. "Ah, that did it. Here she comes."

"There you are, Graydon, at last," Lady Jersey said

without preface as she neared them, adding in a lower voice, "I've been waiting an eternity. I assured Lord Cardemore that his sister would be well taken care of even before you arrived, but, try though I might, none of the gentlemen I've introduced her to will ask her to dance. I don't know what Cardemore expects if it's not a miracle. Of course, if you'll dance with the girl, the rest will follow. Come and be introduced to her sister-in-law. You, also, Daltry."

Exchanging glances, the two men obediently followed as Lady Jersey led the way.

"Lady Margaret!" Lady Jersey greeted enthusiastically, holding out a hand to a tall, elegantly dressed woman who stood in the midst of a group of similarly aged ladies, chatting amiably. She was a stunningly beautiful woman, with dark red hair and large green eyes, and Graydon found it impossible to gaze at her without a surge of masculine admiration.

"My dear," Lady Jersey said, pulling her forward, "I want to introduce you to two favorable gentlemen. Anthony Harbreas, the Earl of Graydon, and Matthew Rowling, Viscount Daltry. My lords, this is Lady Margaret Walford, the Countess of Cardemore."

They exchanged polite greetings before Lady Jersey confided to Lady Margaret, "Lord Graydon has expressed a desire to dance with your sister-in-law. If it is acceptable to you, I'll introduce them and give her my permission to waltz."

Lady Margaret's steady gaze fell upon Graydon, so cool and contemplative that, after a moment of silent perusal, he began to feel uncomfortable. He realized that she must wonder at the normally inflexible Lady Jersey's obsequious behavior. He was rather amazed, too. In the wave of self-pity—and rage—that had engulfed him during the month since his meeting with Cardemore, it hadn't occurred to Graydon that others might be affected by this peculiar nightmare. But here was Cardemore's animated, red-cheeked sister, his angelic niece, his beautiful, wary sister-in-law and even the indomitable Lady Jersey, all caught up in the same roiling mire that Graydon was. All victims of Cardemore's whim and power.

"I should be grateful, my lady," he found himself saying, feeling a sudden kinship with the woman. The idea of having his revenge at the expense of Cardemore's sister had appealed to him a time or two, but now, staring into Lady Margaret's green eyes, all such thoughts permanently fled. It wouldn't do to take out his anger on these innocent women.

Lady Margaret's gaze didn't waver, but she nodded and said, "If Lily is willing, then I give my approval. You shall have to ask her, of course." To Lady Jersey she added, "I'm grateful, my lady, for your kindness."

And so Graydon found himself following both ladies, with Daltry in tow, across the room. When they were nearly there the buzz of gentlemen surrounding the dark-haired girl parted and the young lady herself emerged, coming at them with such a charming, dazzling smile that Graydon felt a sudden shock of appreciation. She was tall and, as Daltry had said, healthy. Her smooth, tanned skin was dotted with freckles, her eyes sparkled like blue sapphires. Her hair, which Graydon had assumed was black, was actually a deep auburn, with a multitude of shining red strands glimmering beneath the light of Almack's chandeliers.

"Mama!" she cried, clasping one of Lady Margaret's hands. "It's the most wonderful thing! Lord Hanby's brought several of his best hunters to town, and he says we may go riding with him one morning, whenever it would please us to do so!"

"That's very kind of him, my dear," Lady Margaret agreed, adding, when the girl opened her mouth to say more, "Isabel, I'd like to introduce you to the Earl of Graydon and to Viscount Daltry. My lords, this is my daughter, Lady Isabel."

"My lady," Graydon greeted with a polite calm that was

fully at odds with the way his head was spinning. Bowing over the sturdy hand Lady Isabel offered, his gaze fell upon the young woman sitting almost directly behind her. That, he realized, was Cardemore's sister. The very beautiful Lady Lillian Walford. And he was the lucky man who was going to have the pleasure of escorting an angel about London for the next three months.

Oh, no, Lily thought with a groan. *Not him. Anyone but him, please, Aunt Margaret.*

She wished she'd never come to London. What had ever possessed her to think that she would be able to fit in here, among people who didn't allow themselves or their families to acknowledge, let alone associate with, someone like her? Aaron had tried to warn her what it would be like, and Aunt Margaret, too, but Lily had been stubborn. And foolish, she thought now with deep regret. How naive she'd been! Dreaming of London, of parties and beautiful clothes and dancing with handsome gentlemen like the ones who had so politely found reasons over the past hour to excuse themselves and walk away.

Oh, help. He was smiling at her now. The handsomest man in the room, the one every woman was looking at with open admiration—she wouldn't be able to hide her humiliation this time. She had managed it with all the others, somehow, but when this man's face filled first with realization, then with revulsion, Lily knew she wouldn't be able to keep the pain at bay.

Clenching her trembling hands together, she stood when Aunt Margaret brought him forward, just as she had stood to be introduced to all the others. It was harder to make herself look into his face. She'd seen him the moment he'd arrived—indeed, everyone in the room had turned to look at his tall, blond figure, so elegant in the blue satin evening clothes that matched the color of his eyes.

"My lord," Aunt Margaret was saying, although Lily barely heard her above the buzzing sensation in her head.

She wondered if she was going to faint, and thought perhaps it might be a blessing if she did. "May I present my sister-in-law, Lady Lillian Walford? Lily, this is the Earl of Graydon."

He gave her a smile so charming and appreciative that it made Lily's toes curl in her slippers. If she hadn't already been unable to speak, that smile alone would have robbed her of the ability. Her hand seemed to lift of its own accord, and she felt the warmth of his fingers closing gently about her own, pulling them up to his mouth as he bent to briefly press his lips against the silk of her glove.

"My lady," he said, his voice as caressing as his blue-eyed gaze, "I'm honored."

When she was a child, Lily had spent hours on her knees praying for a miracle, but never, not even in those tearful, pleading moments, had she wished more than she did now that she could speak as others did.

He kept smiling, holding her hand, waiting for a response, and Lily realized that she was simply staring. Giving a slight nod, she looked expectantly at Aunt Margaret, who only said, "Lord Graydon has asked for permission to dance with you, Lily, and Lady Jersey has given you her permission to waltz."

Lily's eyes widened, and, as if in league with her misery, the musicians suddenly began to play the music for the next dance—a waltz.

Lord Graydon looked as pleased as if he'd just received a boon from heaven itself. "Indeed, if you are not already spoken for, I should be grateful for this dance, my lady."

She couldn't. Never. She'd rather be humiliated on the spot than have the memory of dancing in his arms to think about for the rest of her life. Lily began to shake her head, to tug at the hand Lord Graydon insistently held, all the while looking pleadingly at Aunt Margaret, who gazed back with calm encouragement.

"You came to London to dance, my dear," Aunt Margaret said in a low voice. "You must dance."

She wasn't going to tell him! Lily realized, feeling the shock jolt vividly through her limbs. Aunt Margaret had told all the others. Why wouldn't she tell him?

She turned to Isabel for help, only to be met by the younger girl's pleading expression. Isabel had refused to dance until they could both do so. She had wanted this time in London just as much as Lily, herself, had. *Oh, help.*

Lord Graydon's handsome face began to fill with bewilderment. He would realize the truth in a few moments. He would feel like an utter fool. Lily cast one last pleading glance at Aunt Margaret, who only motioned her toward the dance floor.

It happened, somehow. Lily couldn't remember whether she had walked into Lord Graydon's arms or whether he had pulled her. One moment she was merely standing, and the next she was with him, gliding across the dance floor. She didn't know how it was that her feet managed to make all the right steps, but somehow they did so. Lily felt as stiff as a stick of dry wood, and just as unreliable. Lord Graydon seemed to think so, too, for he said after a few rigid turns, "It's very crowded, is it not? Is it much worse than what you're used to in the country?"

Lily couldn't bring herself to look at him. Keeping her eyes on her feet, she shook her head.

"I'll not let you trip, Lady Lillian," he said gently, much nearer to her ear so that she felt the warmth of his breath. She lifted her head to find that he was smiling down at her with an expression as innocent and unthreatening as a schoolboy's. He tightened his grip on both her hand and waist and spun her about in a rapid turn, causing Lily to gasp aloud before he returned their movements to a more normal pace. With the same smile on his lips, he added, "You dance very well, my lady."

The kind lie was so blatant that it almost made Lily smile in turn. She *could* dance well when the circumstances were right. At the moment, however, she didn't doubt that she was dancing with all the grace of a lame cow. Fortunately,

Lord Graydon was capable of pulling her along with enough ease to keep her from appearing too clumsy to the onlookers in the room. In the morning, the gossiping would start. Aaron had told her it would, but the idea hadn't particularly distressed Lily before tonight. Now, having had her first taste of the ton, she was fully grateful that polite society wouldn't be able to add "ungainly" to her list of shortcomings.

"Are you enjoying your visit to London this season, Lady Lillian?" Lord Graydon asked.

She shook her head. *No.*

A flash of surprise lit his blue eyes, though his features betrayed nothing more than polite interest.

"Have you only recently arrived? I disremember seeing you before at any other functions."

Lily shook her head once more, and could see that he was becoming slightly wary. It would only be a moment more before he finally understood the truth, before his admiration turned to distress. He would be too much of a gentleman to desert her in the middle of their dance. She would have to endure the hellish moments of his dismay until the music ended.

"Perhaps," he began hesitantly, "we should find a way to make your stay in town more enjoyable. I would be honored if you would allow me to bend my efforts to the task, my lady."

Lily felt as if her heart had dropped all the way from her chest and into her feet. If he could only know how she had longed for a man to say such sweet words to her. If he could only know... But realization was dawning as he gazed questioningly into her eyes. Little by little, as they danced without speaking, she could see that he understood. He was stunned for a few moments, and then, as her vision blurred with tears, he began to look angry. His hands tightened on her once more, and he released a hard, taut breath as he twirled her about sharply. He was more than angry, she realized. He was furious. People were watching them, had been watching since they'd begun to dance. He must have suddenly realized how foolish he appeared at having tried to converse with her—with a woman who didn't speak. He would feel as if he'd been duped by Aunt Margaret, perhaps even by Lady Jersey, perhaps even by Lily herself, into dancing with a freak.

"Don't cry," she heard him command tersely. "The dance will be over soon. For pity's sake, don't let them see you in tears."

Lily tightly shut her eyes, but he said, "Look at me." And again, more firmly, "Look at me, Lady Lillian. Into my face. Yes, just like that. Keep your eyes on mine. Now...smile." He smiled into her stunned expression as if to show her how it was done. "Smile," he said again. "At me. As if I'm the most charming, witty fellow you've ever known. If they're going to talk, let's give them something worth talking about."

Something worth talking about? she thought incoherently, unable to fathom what the words meant. He wanted her to *smile* at him?

"Not like that, as if I've just sprouted two horns," he chided. "You're supposed to look as if you're enjoying this. Aren't you enjoying it? I am. You're the most beautiful woman in this room. In all of London, for that matter. And you're dancing in my arms. Even if you are looking at me as if I were a horrible apparition."

Lily didn't believe him. He couldn't mean what he said, for she'd never seen anyone who looked as if he was enjoying what he was doing less than Lord Graydon did at that moment.

He spun her about again until Lily began to feel breathless, then he leaned closer and whispered, "Let's give the gossips something to talk about. Shall we?"

She didn't care what his motives were. If he could pretend to enjoy himself to save face, then so could she. With a definitive nod, she lifted her chin and gifted him with her most dazzling smile. He blinked at her, then his own smile widened. "Very well, then, my lady."

The remainder of the dance was pure enjoyment. Lily relaxed and matched Lord Graydon's daring movements step for step. By the time it was over they were both flushed and grinning. Lord Graydon bowed over her hand with a gallant flourish, kissing her fingers grandly as the rest of the assembly looked on.

"Thank you, Lady Lillian. You're a marvelous partner. I'm honored to have been allowed to lead you out in your first waltz."

Lily replied with an elegant curtsy.

With unhurried and deliberate care, Lord Graydon returned her to Aunt Margaret's side, and then, with Lady Jersey beaming and Isabel fluttering and everyone in the room watching, he said, "May I call on you one day soon, my lady, with the hope that I might have the pleasure of your company for a drive?"

He was still furious. Lily could hear his anger clearly beneath the gentilesse of his words. He was doing what was expected of him, what was necessary to keep from appearing foolish. She should tell him no and release them both from the burden of any further pretense, yet when he gazed into her eyes she found herself nodding.

Lord Graydon bowed, gently kissed her hand again, then took his leave of Aunt Margaret and Lady Jersey. He spoke to no one else as he made his way to the assembly room doors, ignoring the stares and whispers of all those who watched him depart.

Chapter Three

He walked for some time, aimlessly, neither knowing nor caring where he went. The night air was cold, and his harsh breathing coupled with it to form a painful, icy knot in his lungs. He tried not to think of what had just happened, of what he had almost done. Instead, he let his anger dwell solely on Lord Cardemore, and on what he would do to that man if he could somehow manage to get his hands around his thick neck.

The idea pulled Graydon to a stop, and he stood where he was and stared thoughtfully into the darkness. *Cardemore.* He was more than half tempted to go to the man's house and bid him to the devil. Or personally send him to the devil, more like. The man had claimed to love his sister so well. *Love!* Graydon thought with silent disdain. The inconsiderate swine wouldn't know what love and care were if they walked up and bit him on the...

"Good evening, Lord Graydon."

Graydon turned to face the owner of the voice that hailed him. He recognized at once the slender, well-dressed man who'd repeatedly appeared in various corners and side streets during the past several days while Graydon had attempted to repay his debts. He'd been hesitant, at first, to believe that the fellow was one of Cardemore's minions, but it had become clear, despite the gentleman's obvious

civility and manners, that he was fully adept in the business
of being an efficient shadow.

"Your master must pay you well, sir," Graydon stated,
his voice low and calm. "Day *and* night, is it?"

"I'm paid well enough for services rendered." He made
a slight bow, never taking his eyes from Graydon's.

"I see. Do you intend to accompany me to my mistress's
home and wait for me until I've finished with her? Will
you watch over my house while I'm sleeping? Surely Cardemore doesn't expect me to flee the country in the middle
of the night."

"You'd have to ask Lord Cardemore what he thinks, my
lord," the man answered evenly. "I don't make a habit of
questioning my employers."

"Certainly you don't. Dogs are obedient to their mas-
ters."

A thin smile curled the man's lips. "Wise dogs are, my
lord, which is a lesson I recommend you learn to live by
until you've regained your debts. I was curious to see that
Lady Lillian left Almack's shortly after you did. Perhaps
you'd best tell me what transpired, as I shall need to know
what to report back to Lord Carde —"

Graydon shoved the man up against the wall of the nearest building, easily lifting him by the collar until they were
eye to eye. "To Lord Cardemore? You need to know what
to report back to your demon master?" He thrust the man
harder into the bricks. "You tell him that he should've
warned me beforehand that the sister he claims to love so
well is mute. You tell him, you filthy cur, that I very nearly
humiliated that same sister tonight because I wasn't prepared, because of my shock. I can only thank a providential
God that my mother taught me so well never to embarrass
a female in any event, else Lady Lillian surely would have
found herself dancing alone on the floor at Almack's.
That's what you tell him. Understand?" He hauled the
smaller man a few inches higher for emphasis.

"Put 'im down, m'lord."

Graydon glanced briefly to one side, seeing the two burly men who stood nearby.

"Ah, so the shadow has shadows of his own, does he?" His lips pulled back into a feral smile. "How very convenient."

"Now, if you please, m'lord. We don't want to make you do it."

"Don't you?" Graydon asked softly, lowering the other man slowly to his feet. "But *I* should like very much to see if you could." To his captive he said, "Remember the message I want you to give your master. Word for word, you understand? And remember, too, that if I ever see you sneaking around and about me again I'll make you very sorry indeed." Then, raising one fist, he deftly sent the man flying into the arms of his guardians. "Now," Lord Graydon said as his assailants stared at him in disbelief. "Shall we do this one at a time or all together?"

"Guess we'd better teach 'im a lesson, Bill," the taller of the two said as he carelessly tossed Cardemore's insensible minion to the ground. "You hold 'im, and I'll school 'im."

Smiling, Graydon began to pull the gloves from his hands, but stopped when he heard Lord Daltry's rather bored voice emanating from the darkness.

"I'm very sorry to interrupt," said Daltry as he strolled into their midst, "and I know you'll not forgive me for spoiling your fun, Tony," he added affably, placing his large, muscular person companionably near his friend, "but out of respect for your dear mother, I fear I must. I would appreciate it if you...*gentlemen*—" he drew the word out meaningfully "—would take your friend and leave."

"Your timing is unfortunate, Matthew," Graydon said. "I was going to enjoy this."

"I know," Daltry said apologetically as the two ruffians took in his size with some dismay. "But, devil take you, can't you confine your amusements to more conventional venues, like gambling and drinking and women?" With a nod at the man lying on the ground, he repeated, "Take him and go before I change my mind and let my friend vent his ire on you. I can assure you that his temper is dismally volcanic."

Exchanging glances, the men clearly decided that they'd be better off doing as they were told. When they had dragged their companion away, Daltry turned to Graydon with a sigh. "You," he said, "are getting to be an exhausting fellow to know. Here." He pushed a dark garment at him. "You left your cape at Almack's, along with your coach. I think tonight must be a record of some sort. You've managed to set London's tongues wagging, send your coachman into a state of apoplexy wondering whether he should wait for you to return to Almack's, and expose yourself to a deathly chill all in an hour's time. Quite exceptional, even for you."

"Yes, Mama," said Graydon, setting the elegant cloak about his shoulders.

"Never seen you look so thunderstruck on a dance floor before," Daltry continued pleasantly. "Was it the angel's beauty that put you in such a state, or was it something she said?"

"The angel," Graydon replied, leaning wearily against the wall, "didn't say anything. She can't speak. Either that or she won't speak. She's mute."

Now it was Lord Daltry's turn to look thunderstruck. "*Mute?* Cardemore's sister? Are you certain?"

"I'm certain. Didn't you wonder why such a beautiful woman wasn't being fought over by every man in the room? Lady Jersey said that none of the men she'd introduced her to had asked Lady Lillian to dance. I can't say that I wouldn't have found some excuse to keep from asking her myself, if I'd known. Fortunately, she seems to be able to hear well enough. She must, for she clearly understood what I was saying to her, and she was able to dance in time to the music. But unless she's profoundly unable to make simple conversation, I can only conclude that she is mute.''

"But surely Cardemore would have said something."

"One would think so," Graydon agreed. "Any decent, normal, civilized man would have. But not Cardemore. I can't begin to fathom why he kept it from me, but it was a disastrous omission, especially for his beloved sister. I was so surprised when I realized the truth that I very nearly humiliated her, and disgraced myself." He leaned his head against the bricks, staring up at the sky. "What was she thinking all that time while I chattered on? I don't even remember what I was saying…some idiotic talk about London, I think. It must have been a nightmare for the poor girl. The way she looked when she knew I'd realized why she was silent." He groaned and rubbed his forehead. "I can only pray that we finished the dance cheerfully enough that the vultures will be somewhat tempered on the morrow."

"You recovered well," Daltry assured him. "And if that look you had on your face when she smiled at you was an act, then you should take up the stage, my boy, and stop depriving the world of your talent."

Graydon remembered with some discomfort how thoroughly Lady Lillian's smile had stunned him. She was one of the most beautiful women he'd ever seen, but when she smiled she was something else again. Just the memory made him feel slightly dazed.

"Was she all right after I left?" he asked. "I should have stayed, but I was so angry that it was either leave and take my tongue with me or stay and bid Cardemore to the devil in front of too many of the ton's best gossips."

"She seemed a little embarrassed, if that's what you mean," Daltry confided, "but no damage was done. A few other fellows approached her. Seaborne Margate, for one. I suppose, having seen you come out of the experience intact, they decided she was safe."

"She danced, then?"

"No. She evidently didn't appear safe enough for that. But it didn't matter. Lady Isabel declared that she was tired and wanted to leave. They make a habit of keeping country hours in the city, or so the chit informed me."

"Lady Isabel?" Graydon grinned at his friend. "Did you dance with her, Matthew?"

"If you could call it that." Lord Daltry gave a wry chuckle. "It was more like a wrestling match, trying to lead her about. Gad, she's got more muscle on her than my younger brother. And when she got excited, which was every five seconds, she squeezed my fingers so hard I can swear that they'll be bruised in the morning." He shook the hand in question as if to drive the painful memory away. "They go riding every morning, she and Lady Lillian, sun, rain or snow, and she wanted to retire early so that she might rise before the dawn. Lady Lillian looked thoroughly relieved to go."

"I'll wager she did." With a sigh, Graydon turned and began to walk back in the direction of Almack's. "A woman without a voice. What does Cardemore expect of me? She'll be accepted only so far in society, to the point where her muteness doesn't make those around her uncomfortable, but beyond that..."

"I don't know why she should have any trouble," Daltry put in. "A beautiful woman who can't chatter a man half to death sounds like the ideal female to me. I should think every unmarried man in Christendom would want to wed her." He grinned at his somber friend, who didn't share his attempt at humor.

"It's a damned shame," Graydon said, "for a remarkable beauty to be cursed with such a frailty."

"You make too much of it," Daltry argued. "So she hasn't got a voice. That doesn't mean she can't make herself understood, perhaps even well enough to manage a house and be a hostess and raise a herd of children. A man doesn't want more than that in a wife, does he? And who needs a voice to listen to when you've got a face like that to gaze at across the breakfast table?''

"Would you marry a woman who couldn't speak, Matthew?''

"Me?'' Lord Daltry sounded as shocked as he looked.

"I thought not,'' Graydon said. "You see how it is. And that's not the worst of it. You know what people think of the deaf and mute. She'll be labeled a lackwit, or demon-possessed.''

"I suppose that's so,'' Daltry put in more thoughtfully. "I've read Sir Benjamin Hatton's treatise on deaf-mutes. He claims they're essentially amoral, and under a curse from God. Born that way, they are. But Lady Lillian isn't deaf, you said.''

"It doesn't matter. She'll still be labeled as more animal than human. Only those of us blessed with voices evidently possess souls. Sir Benjamin's been quite influential in spreading such opinions. Lady Lillian will have far more than her lack of speech to combat if she wishes to make her way in polite society.''

"You're going to tell Cardemore that what he wants is impossible, then?''

"Not at all. I'm going to do exactly what he asked of me. His sister wants to enjoy her stay in London, and enjoy it she shall. I doubt she knows what she's asking for, but for the next three months I intend to make certain that Lady Lillian Walford has the time of her life.''

Chapter Four

The Earl of Cardemore disliked change, especially when it involved his own home. He disliked having the place lit up so that even the least used hallway was as bright as day in the middle of the night, and having more servants about than he required for his lone care, with maids and footmen constantly cleaning and scrubbing and carrying and fetching.

He felt exposed in the light. The scars on his face were more readily visible and it was impossible to hide his over-large, bulky self. Even when dressed in the most elegant and gentlemanly of fashions, he felt society's eyes upon him, staring with the kind of revulsion that made him feel more like a beast than a man. Not that he gave a damn about what society thought, but there were a few people whom he didn't care to distress with his ugliness, and having the most significant among them residing in his home for several months was, for Cardemore, an acutely unpleasant sensation. Every time Lady Margaret looked at him with one of her steady gazes he wanted to put a hand up and cover his face. She was the only woman—the only person—who had the power to make him wish he was something other than what he was.

He had left his home at the age of fourteen and hadn't returned until the day of his brother's funeral. He'd had news of his family over the years, and had been aware that George had married, but he'd never actually seen Lady Margaret until that day. There, standing at George's graveside, he had set eyes on a woman so perfect that his knees had nearly given way from the shock. The remainder of the service passed as something of a blur; he'd been too busy trying to force the workings of his brain into some semblance of order to pay much attention to the proceedings. But it had been of little use. Whatever spell had befallen him at setting sight on Margaret Walford had taken hold, and had maintained its iron grip since. Every time he saw her the passion he felt seized him anew, as if it were the first time all over again. Even now, as she reclined before the warmth of the library fire, her head tilted lazily against the heavily cushioned chair, her eyes closed with weary languor, he stood in the shadows, watching, his heart pounding more frantically than it would ever do for any spectacle that his mistress, or any other woman, might perform for his pleasure. In her sleepy, slightly disheveled contentment, Margaret Walford wielded more power to stun than an avalanche.

"You had a pleasant evening, then?" he asked, wishing that he knew how to be comfortable with her, how to sit near her and converse the way another man might do. "Lily seemed happy enough."

Opening her eyes, she smiled. "She did, didn't she? I was so relieved when she finally danced. Before Lord Graydon arrived I thought the evening would be a complete disaster." More thoughtfully, she added, "It wasn't what she'd been hoping for, just as we knew it wouldn't be, but she was so happy afterward. Having the handsomest man in the room for a partner in her first waltz must have been exactly like one of the dreams she's so often told me about." Lady Margaret's smile grew wistful. "Like the dreams every girl has, I imagine. I only wish you had seen them together, Aaron. They made an enchanting couple, and Lily danced with perfection. You would have been so proud.''

"I'm always proud of Lily," he replied, taking a sip from the glass of whiskey he held. "Graydon observed the proprieties?"

"Oh, yes. He's everything that a young lord should be, quite perfect in every detail. I doubt there was a girl at Almack's who wasn't eaten alive with envy at his asking Lily—and only Lily—to dance."

The sadness in her tone caused Cardemore to stiffen instinctively. "You disliked him, Margaret?"

"Of course not, Aaron. I hardly know the boy enough to disapprove of him. But I worry about Lily. I don't want to be such a dismal naysayer, but—I know you'll understand what I mean when I say this—I almost wish we could have gotten it all over with tonight instead of giving her a reason for hope. Even if Lord Graydon should follow through on his promise to take her driving, I'm afraid she'll still be terribly hurt, perhaps during our next outing. Not one man who was introduced to her tonight would ask her to dance before Lord Graydon did. And then she was so afraid to dance with him that I had to make her do so."

"She seems to have come through the experience well enough."

Lady Margaret suddenly sat forward. "Yes, but—"

"We have to give her this chance, Margaret," he said firmly. "We warned her and she didn't want to listen, but experience is a far better teacher. After tonight she knows what she's up against, and it's her decision if she wants to go on or go home. Lily's not a quitter. Or a weakling. If she were, I'd never have let her leave Cardemore Hall."

Lady Margaret pinned him with the sort of tightly angry expression that always made him want to kiss the breath out of her. "Lily isn't you, Aaron, or even remotely like you. She's a naive, sheltered young woman. She wouldn't be able to go through the kind of 'experiences' you've had and come out intact."

Cardemore couldn't repress the laughter her words caused. "My dear Lady Margaret, I hardly think you can compare a season in society to spending fifteen years in the company of pirates, thieves and murderers. I admit there are some daunting similarities among the main actors, but at least Lily need never worry that Mrs. Drummond-Burrell might stick a dagger between her shoulders if she doesn't make a proper curtsy."

"Words and deeds, Aaron, can be just as painful as a physical attack. In the hands of a Mrs. Drummond-Burrell, perhaps even more so."

"Mrs. Drummond-Burrell," remarked Cardemore, "attacks Lily at her own peril. You needn't worry over the matter."

Lady Margaret shook her head with clear dissatisfaction. "So we just let Lily go on until she meets with disaster, is that it? Tonight wasn't humiliating enough. We must let her continue until polite society brings her to her knees?"

He'd been acutely in love with Margaret Walford during every minute that had passed since he'd set eyes on her, but there was something about moments like this, when she gave way to her hot Irish temper, that always made him think about what it might be like to take her to his bed and make love to her. Her unbound mahogany hair would be a glorious sight against the purity of snow-white sheets.

"Society won't bring Lily to her knees," he assured her with as bland a tone as he could muster. Walking out of the shadows, he set his empty glass on a nearby table with stark finality. "I'll not allow it."

Lady Margaret pushed to her feet and stood full height, her chin lifting stubbornly. "My lord, I understand a little about the power you wield, perhaps too little, but even you can't make all of society obey you."

"I don't require that all of society do so. Only those few whom I deem necessary. And you're quite right. Despite whatever I'm able to do in smoothing matters over, Lily must find her own way. I didn't want her to come to London any more than you did, but we couldn't very well bury her in Somerset when she didn't want to be buried."

"She wasn't buried," Lady Margaret countered. "She has friends there who love and accept her, and days filled with activities she enjoys. Her life has been full and happy."

"Not enough, evidently, to keep her from dreaming of London," he remarked quietly.

She gave a long sigh and, although he wasn't watching, Cardemore could almost see the softening in her stance. She moved toward him, so near that he could hardly hear her speaking over the thunderous pounding of his heart in his ears.

"I know you're right, Aaron. I only wish I could find a way to stop worrying on the matter. It's been a long time since we've argued about Lily." He heard the smile in her voice and felt an answering smile form on his own lips. "Do you remember how we used to fight over her?"

"I'll never forget," he said, chuckling, "The only times I've ever known real fear were when you greeted me with the words 'My lord, I *must* speak with you.'"

They'd argued countless times about Lily, especially in the beginning, when he'd returned to Cardemore Hall after an absence of fifteen years to find himself responsible for not only his family's titles and estates, but also for a small, pale, silent child who was brought to him by a serving maid only a few minutes after he'd arrived home. He'd never before seen the sister to whom his mother had died giving birth, although he'd learned about her, also about his mother's passing, several months after both had occurred. His father hadn't known what to do with a mute girl child, George had probably been too busy with his own affairs to give his young sister much thought, and Margaret hadn't been allowed to interfere. Lily had been given into the care of the servants and, as long as she was kept clean and fed and out of the way, was mostly ignored. Despite the fact that her inability to speak in a normal voice had been

caused by an unfortunate incident when she was but a tiny
child, she was treated as if she'd been born an idiot. But
Cardemore had known, from the moment he'd looked into
her lively blue eyes, that an intelligent mind hid behind her
silence.

For her part, Lily had taken in her elder brother's dark,
scarred face, his hulking size and his filthy clothes, and had
smiled a smile of beguiling, welcoming sweetness, unwittingly making the first crack in a heart that had long since
been pronounced unassailable. It had been his intention,
until that moment, to see his brother buried, gain the title
that he'd always disdained and promptly sell every thing
of value before taking his spoils and returning to the life
he'd chosen. As he stared into the trusting little face that
reminded him so much of his mother's, the idea evaporated
as quickly as if it had never existed. He'd hated his father
and his rigidly perfect brother and everything about the
nobility that had made his mother age with such cruel rapidity; he'd come to hate everything associated with the
name Cardemore; but perhaps he and Lily could make
something out of the wreckage they'd inherited from their
ancestors. They could certainly try.

Margaret made it easier when she insisted upon moving
into Cardemore Hall with Isabel to run the household for
him and to take over Lily's care. She turned off the servants
who found it impossible to treat their new master with respect and quickly put the fear of God into the rest. She
loved Lily with a mother's tender care, as well as with a
mother's vigilance. They'd fought over everything, from
doctor's opinions about Lily's inability to speak to which
teachers and methods would profit Lily the most. And when
they weren't arguing with each other, they were arguing
with the doctors and teachers.

"Was I so fearsome?" Margaret asked in a low voice,
so near to him that he could feel the heat emanating from
her tall, elegantly curved form. "I have to admit that I
didn't trust you overmuch in the beginning. I was afraid,

for years, that you would disappear the way you had when you were a boy. Lily adored you so much, she would have been badly hurt if you'd left. It was hard enough when you finally did go, although she was old enough then to understand how many duties you must perform as the Earl of Cardemore, and why you had to come live in London.''

He didn't give a damn about his duties as the Earl of Cardemore and never had, which was a truth he devoutly hoped kept all his sainted ancestors continuously spinning in their respective graves. It had been she, Margaret, and the torture of being with her every day, loving and wanting her and not being able to bring himself to do so much as touch her, that had driven him away from Cardemore Hall five years ago. "I've tried to visit as often as I'm able," he said. "If I thought Lily needed me, I'd stay for as long as necessary.''

"Oh, Aaron, I know that." Gently, she set a hand over the one he pressed against the table. "You've been wonderful to Lily, and to Isabel and me. I've long since learned to trust you completely.''

He couldn't speak. He could barely draw in breath. All he could do was stare at the cool, smoothly feminine hand pressed over his own ugly, hairy paw and feel a tingling sense of wonder.

"We've missed you, Aaron. Lily and Isabel and…me. All of us.''

Some long-honed instinct made him realize that the library door was about to open only a moment before it did. Pulling his hand free, he turned in time to see his butler enter the room.

"The gentlemen you were expecting have arrived, my lord. I've put them in your study.''

"Thank you, Willis. I'll be there in a moment.''

Margaret was already gathering her things. "I'll leave you to tend your business, Aaron. You do keep the strangest receiving hours." She stopped at the library doors. "One night while we're here, you must put a few hours aside and play a game of chess with me. Do you remember how we used to play?''

He nodded. ''I remember that you generally beat me.''

She laughed. ''My only area of victory over you.'' She put her fingers on one of the door handles. ''Good night, Aaron.''

''Margaret,'' he said, stopping her. ''Don't worry about Lily. Everything is going to turn out very well, I promise you.''

She gazed at him for a searching moment. ''I know better than to ask that you accompany us to any of the outings the girls have been invited to, but I would make one request of you.''

''Anything.''

''Will you dance with Lily at the girls' comeout ball? I know it's been a great many years since you had your lessons as a boy, but surely you remember enough to partner her in a country dance? It would mean a great deal to her.''

He let out a groaning sigh, knowing full well that if anyone else had asked this of him he'd have dismissed them without a thought.

''One dance,'' Cardemore told her. ''Only one.''

The warm smile she gifted him with before she left the room was more than worth the regret he felt at giving the promise.

Chapter Five

The early-morning air was bracingly cold, and the two lone men mounted on horseback in Hyde Park shrugged more closely into the warmth of their coats while their steeds moved impatiently beneath them.

"I hope you won't mind me saying this," said Lord Daltry, the words puffing small clouds into the air, "but this is the damnedest idea you've ever had."

"I didn't ask you to come along," Lord Graydon replied calmly "And I'm not keeping you here. Go home to your warm bed, if you like."

"And leave you to the mercies of two country-bred females?" Lord Daltry asked with mock dismay. "What sort of friend would I be? Besides, you need me to occupy Lady Isabel while you make your apologies to Lady Lillian. I can't see the chit keeping her mouth closed long enough for you to so much as say good-morning unless I keep her otherwise engaged."

Lord Graydon smiled. "You're a good fellow, Matthew, but I'm perfectly capable of managing two young females without any help, thank you."

"You might be able to handle Cardemore's sister," Lord Daltry agreed affably, "but I'd wager a pony you can't handle Lady Isabel Walford, even if you could catch up to her long enough to get her attention, which is unlikely."

He shifted in his saddle and scanned the horizon. "The girl rides like a demon. Not even the grooms can keep up with her."

Lord Graydon looked at him with surprise. "You've seen her ride?"

A stain of color crept across Lord Daltry's handsome face. "Ah, well…yes, I have. Yesterday, as it happens." At his friend's accusatory grin, he added insistently, "Cerberus needed exercising."

"At this ungodly hour?" Graydon asked, laughing. "Matthew, in all the years we've been acquainted, I've never known a mere horse to get you up so early. Certainly not when you could just as well send a groom to exercise him." Leaning toward his discomfited friend, he added in a conspiratorial tone, "Lady Isabel's caught your interest, has she?"

"That mannish female?" Lord Daltry was indignant. "Have you lost your senses? The very idea makes me shudder."

"I found her to be quite charming," said Graydon.

"Charming," Daltry grumbled, "is not the word Lady Isabel brings to mind. God's feet, here she comes. Look! Do you see?"

Graydon saw, and gave out a soft whistle as a slender, sapphire-clad figure, bowed low over the neck of a magnificent black steed, raced full out across the empty park.

"What did I tell you?" Lord Daltry demanded angrily, pulling up his horse's head. "Dratted female's going to break her neck."

"She's magnificent," Graydon declared with admiration. "What a seat—she must've been born in the saddle."

"Seat, my eye," Daltry said. "What her seat needs is a good paddling. Of all the foolish, brainless— Damnation! She's not going to take that fence?"

Graydon opened his mouth to reply that, yes, indeed, she was, but never said a word. Daltry had already taken off after the girl, presumably to rescue her from harm. The effort would prove a needless one, Graydon imagined, as it was obvious that Lady Isabel was a skilled rider. Returning his attention to the direction from which Lady Isabel had appeared, he was greeted by the sight of Lady Lillian, followed by two grooms, riding at a more sedate, ladylike pace. She had seen and recognized him and now was gazing at him warily, clearly uncertain as to whether she should continue on or turn back.

"Lady Lillian," he said when they'd neared each other, "what a fortunate occurrence. Good morning."

God's mercy, he thought as his senses registered her beauty anew. She was almost too good to look at. The proper black riding outfit she wore only served to accentuate her white-blond hair and crystalline eyes. Such beauty would certainly gain her favor in the eyes of any normally blooded gentleman, while with the ladies of the ton…well, some of them were bound to be obdurately jealous. He began to ponder how he would manage to get around those particular ladies when he belatedly realized that he and Lady Lillian were simply sitting in silence, and that her expressive face had taken on a look set somewhere between caution and embarrassment. She lifted one hand suddenly toward her wrist, as if to grasp hold of something—her glove, he thought, or perhaps a bracelet—then stopped, biting her lower lip with obvious distress.

With a mental shake, Graydon smiled too brightly and said, in an equally bright tone that made him inwardly cringe, "What a pleasurable accident to have met you here."

Oh, gad, he thought as her eyes filled with bewilderment. He'd already said something like that. He'd never known, until that moment, how much he always depended on women to make conversation.

He was about to speak again, to say only heaven knew what, since he didn't have an idea, when she lifted one gloved hand and touched her lips, tentatively, with her forefinger. She hesitated as color mounted in her cheeks, and then she pointed at him, then at some flowers beneath a nearby tree and then at herself. Pressing her hand flat above her left breast, she made a slight bowing motion with her head.

"Oh," said Graydon, mortified that he was unable to understand whatever it was she was trying to tell him. This was horrible. He felt like an idiot. "Uh...yes."

Her face was flaming now, but she drew in a breath and repeated the motions, pointing first at him, then the flowers, then herself. By the time she finished, realization had blissfully struck.

"The flowers I sent?" he asked. "You liked them?" When she nodded he uttered a laugh, relieved. Unable to keep the grin off his face, he said, "I'm glad if they brought you pleasure."

She placed her hand over her heart and made the bowing gesture again, and he said, "You're very welcome."

Her answering smile made him feel dizzy, as it had on the floor at Almack's, and a flood of reassurance waved through him. Perhaps this wasn't going to be quite as bad as he'd thought.

"I have a confession to make," he said, and she tilted her head questioningly. "It isn't by accident that I met you here this morning. I knew that you and Lady Isabel ride here every day at this time, and I purposefully came and waited, hoping to meet you." The wariness was back on her face again, mixed with surprise. "I owe you an apology for my behavior at Almack's two nights ago, and I wanted to make those apologies without anyone else present. I was afraid that perhaps you might be further distressed if I expressed such sentiments before others."

Her brow furrowed, as if she didn't understand him, and then, pointing at him, she shook her head slowly and firmly.

"No?" he asked. "It wouldn't have distressed you?"

A silent laugh crossed her lips and she shook her head again, making it plain that he hadn't understood. For a moment she was thoughtful, then, she set the reins she held in her lap and lifted both hands, smiling at him in a manner that invited him to join her world of silent symbols. Graydon nodded, leaning forward in his saddle to watch what she did.

Entwining the forefingers of each hand, she rotated her hands in smooth, swirling motions.

"Dancing?" Graydon guessed, and she nodded.

"Us, dancing?" he asked. She shook her head and mouthed the word *Almack's*.

"Ah, Almack's. I see."

One forefinger fell away, leaving the other alone. Making an exaggeratedly sad face, Lady Lillian pointed at herself and gave a sigh. The lone forefinger bobbed over to one side and bent into what Graydon assumed was a sitting position.

"There you are, sitting alone at Almack's, while others are dancing?" he ventured.

Lady Lillian nodded again, and gave another hefty sigh. Turning her head suddenly, she gave a look of surprise at the sight of her other forefinger, which she'd lifted high and straight some distance from her other hand. This time she made a gasping sound. When Graydon began to laugh she gave him a stern look and poked the straightened forefinger at him.

"Oh, that's me, is it?" he asked, still chuckling.

She nodded very firmly before resuming the surprised expression as the straight forefinger marched across the air to the sad, sitting forefinger. The straight finger bowed politely, to which the sitting finger reacted with shy reluctance, all of which Lady Lillian deftly reflected through her facial expressions coupled with her hand movements. Graydon watched, fascinated, as the two fingers enacted with precision their encounter at Almack's. He found it difficult to tear his gaze away from her animated face, which so rapidly and easily expressed the changing emotions of both characters in her little play. She was kinder to him than he deserved, he thought, since his character seemed to be a mainly noble being possessed of stoic expressions and gentlemanly behavior. By the time his finger-figure marched out of the imaginary Almack's, he had somehow managed to transform her sadly sighing little finger into a happily sighing finger. Dropping her hands, her face suffused with a blush, Lady Lillian looked to see if he understood.

"My apologies," he said slowly, "evidently aren't necessary?"

With obvious relief, she shook her head.

"You are very kind, Lady Lillian. I was afraid, perhaps, that my indecorous behavior had embarrassed you or given you the wrong impression. It is true that I didn't realize you are mute until we were dancing, but I assure you that my distress at the knowledge was in no way directed toward you. You were a delightful partner in every way. It is my fondest hope that you will be kind enough to gift me with many more such pleasures during your stay in London."

The blush bloomed more brightly, and Lady Lillian's lovely features took on a childlike mixture of embarrassment and delight that charmed Graydon right down to the soles of his feet.

The sound of angry voices signaled the approach of Lady Isabel and Lord Daltry, and Lady Lillian and Graydon turned their horses about.

"My lord," Lady Isabel said without waiting for Graydon to greet her, "will you please tell this mutton-headed acquaintance of yours to return the control of my horse to me?" As an afterthought, and having given Lord Daltry a withering glare, she added, "Good morning."

"Good morning, my lady," Graydon replied calmly, noting that Lord Daltry did, indeed, hold the reins to Lady Isabel's mount in his hands. "Taken to horse stealing, have we, my lord?"

The look Lord Daltry set upon him could have melted a polar icecap. "Any female who rides the way this particular female does shouldn't be allowed to get within ten feet of a horse.''

Lady Isabel's gloved hands curled into fists. "Oh! You ignorant, jealous…''

"Jealous!" Lord Daltry repeated.

"…*rude* idiot! You're only angry because I was able to outride you so well," Lady Isabel charged hotly, tugging on her reins to no avail. "Yes, jealous!"

"Will you kindly keep your voice down?" Lord Daltry demanded. "You're unsettling the horses. I realize it's probably beyond your country-bred abilities to act like a gentle lady, but you can at least strive to *speak* like one.''

"Ahem.'' Graydon loudly cleared his throat. "I believe you're the one who's shouting rather over loudly, old man.'' He indicated the two grooms who sat on their horses at a proper, albeit within hearing, distance. "And from what I observed earlier, Lady Isabel is an excellent rider.''

"Thank you, my lord," Lady Isabel put in with satisfaction, lifting her chin in Lord Daltry's direction.

"Don't you think you should return the control of her mount to her?'' Graydon suggested.

Lord Daltry scowled darkly. "Not that I'd care if the little fool broke her neck, but I think it might be wisest if I escorted her back to Wilborn Place and had a word with Lord Cardemore. He should be apprised at once of his niece's reckless behavior.''

"Much good that will do you," Lady Isabel stated. "My *uncle*'s the one who taught me to ride.''

"Somehow," Lord Daltry said tightly, "that doesn't surprise me. You certainly ride like the devil's daughter. Or niece. If it were up to me—''

"I beg your pardon, Lord Daltry," Lady Isabel interrupted in icy tones, at last wrestling her reins from his grip while her horse danced confusedly beneath her, "but it is *not* up to you.'' She moved her steed a safe distance away from him before adding, "I should like to return home now, Lily.''

Lady Lillian responded with several fluttering movements of her hands, too rapidly for Graydon to make any sense of.

"Apologize?" said Lady Isabel, clearly having no difficulty in understanding what the other girl was saying. "Absolutely not. Never. Ever."

Lord Daltry made a huffing sound. "Probably doesn't even know how to."

Lady Isabel pinned him with a hot glare. "If Lord Daltry has been insulted and requires satisfaction, he may challenge me to a race and determine for himself which of us is the better rider."

At this, Lady Lillian made more hand movements, drawing Graydon's fascinated gaze. It was her way of talking, he realized, but it was so fluid, so rapid—like the fluttering of hummingbird wings. How did Lady Isabel manage to interpret it?

"We *are* from the country, Lily," Lady Isabel said in terse reply, "and if Lord Daltry wishes to tease us about that fact then he's not the sort of gentleman that Lord Graydon obviously is." She graced Graydon with a stunning smile. "If I must apologize, it will be to him for causing him to endure such an unfortunate scene. I do apologize, my lord."

"Please don't worry over the matter, Lady Isabel," Graydon replied. "I always strive to enjoy Lord Daltry's mad fits, often as they occur."

"Most wise," said Lady Isabel, while Lord Daltry glowered at his friend.

"We'll not detain you further," Graydon said, including both women in a charming smile. "If it's convenient, may I have the pleasure of calling upon you ladies this afternoon to take you driving? I should deem it a great honor to show you something of London."

With a delighted enthusiasm that Graydon found both touching and amusing, Lady Lillian and Lady Isabel assented, and the two men were shortly riding away.

"Fits?" Lord Daltry asked. "*Mad* fits?"

Graydon shrugged lightly. "I don't know what else you'd call chasing after a perfectly happy female who had her mount under complete control and treating her like the veriest child. Really, Matthew, you astound me. Why didn't you just grab Lady Isabel by the hair and drag her about the park like a heathen cave dweller?"

Lord Daltry straightened in his saddle. "I don't want to talk about that female, if you please. I don't even want to hear her name. Never met a more pestilential woman in my life. She'll have London on its head before the season's done, mark my words. Did you make any headway with Lady Lillian?"

Graydon gave an assenting nod. "I think it's going to work out quite well. She's a charming girl, and can make herself understood more ably than I'd expected. Whatever her upbringing was, it must have been good enough to give her the confidence to express herself. I may try to engage Miss Hamilton's aid in the matter," he added more thoughtfully. "She's always been tenderhearted to the less fortunate, and if she'll befriend Lady Lillian, I've no doubt matters will proceed much more smoothly."

"That's not a bad idea," Daltry said approvingly. "With Miss Hamilton for an ally, none of the other comeouts will dare be uncivil. But what," he asked directly, "will you tell her?"

"She's already aware that I've undertaken to introduce two young ladies from the country into society. I needn't tell her anything more, although Miss Hamilton is such a gentle soul that she wouldn't turn them away even if she knew the full truth."

"Please," Daltry said, "don't tell her. I don't fancy spending the next ten years visiting you in prison. And I doubt Miss Hamilton would care for it, either."

Graydon laughed out loud. "I've no intention of giving Cardemore a reason to be displeased. Never fear, Matthew.

Lady Lillian will enjoy her stay in London. I'll devote myself to the task entirely.''

"It may be harder than I first thought," Daltry admitted.
"I didn't understand any of those hand movements she
made. Looked like a sorcerer's trick.''

"I didn't, either," Graydon said, "but before you and
Lady Isabel returned she used a different method of communicating that was quite charming. If I can somehow convince her to use it with others, I believe she'll readily con-
quer even the most unforgiving members of the ton.''

"You sound more confident than you did two nights
ago.''

"I am. All I need to do is make certain she's out and
about town as often as possible, meeting the right people
and making the right friends. Her beauty and Cardemore's
power should do the rest in securing Lady Lillian's place
in society.''

"I hope that's true, my friend," said Lord Daltry.

"As do I. Most fervently.''

Chapter Six

Graydon spent the remainder of the day making plans and visits. The plans, he knew, were only as good as upcoming circumstances, or the Fates, might make them. He wrote his steward at St. Cathyrs with instructions to proceed with the land improvements they had agreed upon. Having met and, to some degree, successfully communicated with Lady Lillian, he at last felt comfortable in taking such a step. To his mother and sisters he wrote a determinedly lighter, more entertaining missive, striving to erase any fears they might have taken from the steward's behavior. Not that Graydon believed his competent employee would have spoken of or shown his concern regarding the warnings of impending doom that Graydon had recently sent him, but the ladies of St. Cathyrs were remarkably sensitive, and Graydon, having spent a lifetime drowning in their well-meant concern, had learned early on to nip such worries in the bud. In addition, he wanted his mother in London. It was true that Countess Graydon rarely came to Town, and his sisters seldom more, if they could avoid it, yet his dainty, slightly lunatical mother still welded the respect and power claimed by only the staunchest of the ton's matrons to ably launch a young lady, regardless of the particular young lady's imperfections. If Lady Lillian could weather his mother's and sisters' peculiar brand of coddling, she'd have nothing left to fear in the way of making her way through the ton's treacherous waters.

The visits were, on the whole, more predictable. Frances and her mother, Lady Hamilton, received him in the usual fashion, making him feel exactly like what he knew he was: an extremely eligible, highly titled, unmarried peer of the realm. The prize of the season's marriage market, just as he had been the season before, and the season before that, and even the season before that. He'd had more young women thrown at him during the past four years than he could either remember or give count to, but had successfully managed to escape wedded bliss, or even the consideration of it, until the right woman had finally been thrown at him.

Frances.

She was as delightful in her own right as she was in her physical form, and he had realized, shortly after having met her, that she was the ideal wife for him. Graydon had very nearly decided to make her an offer this season. Nearly. He wasn't altogether certain what it was that held him back. He was fairly sure of the depths of his own feelings—if he didn't actually love Frances, he certainly admired and held her in great affection—and he had good reason to believe that she felt similarly toward him. She had given him every indication that if he should ask her to become his wife, her answer would be a positive one.

And yet he held back, waiting for something that he couldn't define. Something foolish, he often told himself, chiding. Something ridiculous. A bolt out of the heavens when he looked at her, perhaps, or a light-headed feeling when he kissed her lips—as he had already done twice without feeling even the least bit dizzy—or some kind of heart-pounding sensation, anything, that would tell him he would never regret making her his wife.

His visit with her this afternoon only served to confirm to Graydon how foolish he was to hesitate. Frances and he were ideal for each other, both in mind and spirit, and he would surely never find another such lady, so sweet and intelligent and understanding.

He presented himself at Wilborn Place at half past four, and was informed by the earl's dour butler that the earl wished to speak with him before Graydon took Lady Lillian and Lady Isabel on their planned drive.

The study to which Graydon was taken was by now familiar to him as that place where Cardemore carried out most of his dealings. This time, the earl was already in the room, waiting.

"You're here," Cardemore said, glancing up from the papers on his desk as Graydon walked through the door. "Good. Sit down." He nodded to the chair Graydon had occupied on his earlier visit. "I suppose you already know what I want to discuss."

"I can guess," Graydon replied, staring down at his host from behind the chair, where he continued to stand. "Your minion took no permanent damage, I hope. I shouldn't want to have the man out of the way of useful employ. Such a one shouldn't be allowed to live off the largesse of the workhouse."

Cardemore smiled in an unpleasant way. "Perhaps you'd prefer to make him the responsibility of the jails? Never fear. I take care of all those in my employ, one way or another."

Graydon didn't doubt that in the least. He wondered if the little man who'd made such a pest of himself, having made a muddle of his assignment, was even still breathing. "I'm glad to know it," he replied evenly. "Send another such a one to shadow me and I can promise I'll not leave so much to care for."

Cardemore gave a grunt of amusement. "You'll not be bothered again, I give you my word. Little though you may credit it, my word is as reliable as death." His attention still given to his papers, which he was neatly piling into different stacks, he added tersely, as though Graydon were an aggravating and misbehaving servant, "I offered you a chair."

With an effort, Graydon didn't react with so much as a raised eyebrow. "You may take your chair, my lord, and go to Hell. If you wish to speak with me, then I advise you to speak. Otherwise, I'll not keep Lady Lillian and Lady Isabel waiting."

With an abrupt movement, Cardemore sat back and regarded his guest. "It isn't so much what I might say to you, Graydon," he stated with cool intent, "but rather that I believe you have something you wish to say to me."

The muscles in Graydon's jaw tightened painfully, and for a moment his anger was so white-hot that he thought he would say something truly unwise. But he remembered himself, and remembered the sort of man Cardemore was—one not to be dealt with lightly, or, worse, foolishly.

"If you received the message I gave your minion, then you already know my sentiments. I should be curious to know, however, why you neglected to tell me that Lady Lillian cannot speak, and why you seemed to find such information irrelevant."

A look of irritation crossed Cardemore's scarred features, and he replied, gruffly, "Lily can speak. She chooses not to do so for reasons of her own. As you say, I find the fact irrelevant, both in regard to Lily and in regard to your seeing to it that she enjoys her time in London. However you may view the situation, whether Lily speaks or does not speak has no bearing on the task set before you."

"So you say," Graydon replied. "Because of your lack of care, I very nearly humiliated her. At *Almack's.* Even you, with your disdain of the accepted social customs, must realize what that would have meant to her."

"It would have been unfortunate," Cardemore admitted, "especially for your mother and sisters. You may think me an unconscionable swine for subjecting Lily to such a chancy situation, but I felt assured of your response. You and your kind are too well-bred to so readily fall on your faces. You'd shatter before you'd crack. Isn't that so, Graydon?''

"You," Graydon said quietly, "take much for granted."

"Aye," Cardemore concurred with a thin smile. "There is often little other choice for a man in my circumstances, which is why planning for any eventuality is so needful. If you had, by chance, brought Lily sorrow, you would know by now how unfortunate a mistake it was."

"Your threats, sir, grow wearisome. I find it difficult to believe that Lady Lillian is in any way related to you."

At this, Cardemore uttered a laugh. "I find it the same, and ever have. Lily's a beauty, isn't she? Charming, well-mannered and thoroughly delightful. She's so unlike the rest of my family that I'm often tempted to believe the fairies left her, rather than that my father, especially, had any part of her. But that is neither here nor there." He waved one hand outward. "You want to know why Lily doesn't speak, is that not so?"

"It would be helpful."

Cardemore gave him a measured look before saying, "She was born in a perfectly normal state, despite the fact that the birth was complicated and my mother died a few hours later. She was an extraordinarily quiet baby, seldom crying, which evidently led my thick-skulled fool of a father to believe that she was somehow mentally deficient. I suppose if she had squalled night and day as my brother and I probably did, he would have assumed she was perfectly hale. As you have seen for yourself, she is."

Graydon inclined his head.

"When Lily was three years of age, so some of the older servants tell me, she had only just begun to speak, later than most children, perhaps—" he gave an indolent shrug "—but not so extraordinarily late as to give proof to my father's belief in Lily's mental failings. She was, these same servants insist, a bright and clearly intelligent child. If allowed to progress in her own manner, I have no doubt that even my stubborn father would have at last admitted his mistake. But it was around this time, shortly after Lily's third birthday, that one of the serving maids lost her own young child, an unfortunate event that subsequently caused her to madden. For some reason, she decided that Lily would be better off dead, and to that end she mixed lye into the milk in Lily's silver cup and served it to her with her dinner in the nursery.''

"God in heaven," Graydon murmured, horrified.

"Indeed. She nearly died from ingesting the poison, most of which, fortunately, she spat out, else she never would have survived. A long illness and high fever followed. To my father's credit, Lily was surrounded by the finest doctors and given every care. To his discredit, he refused to believe these same doctors when they insisted, after Lily recovered, that her sudden inability to speak or even utter a sound was due to the inflammation that had severely scarred her vocal cords. He was convinced that she was an idiot, just as he had been convinced of it before, and as she could no longer even make a human sound, he refused to have anything more to do with her. She was given over to the care of the servants, who learned to keep her out of my father's and brother's way, and had not, until I inherited the title, even been given the benefit of a tutor. Lily could not read or write a word until she was twelve years old. She couldn't speak a word until two years later, when she was fourteen.''

"But she *can* speak?" Graydon pressed.

"She can, although it is painful for her to do so, and she grows weary after a brief effort. Also, it is very…difficult. Lily dislikes the sound of her voice. The scarring makes it impossible for her to achieve anything remotely feminine, although, for my part, I find her speech delightful. Still, she prefers the sign language.''

"The sign language," Graydon repeated more thoughtfully. "This morning, in the park, she and your niece, Lady Isabel, were communicating in such a way, with their hands.''

"It is the same method that is taught in France at the Royal Institute for Deaf-Mutes, by Abbé Sicard, of whom I am sure you've heard tell. One of Sicard's most ardent disciples, Mr. Charles Cassin, has established a school here in England using these very methods, modified, of course, to English. Before doing so, however, he lived at Cardemore Hall for five years, serving as Lily's tutor, also as mine and the rest of my household's. Every one of us, including the servants, learned the sign language for Lily's benefit."

His words presented Graydon with a baffling picture of the Earl of Cardemore, very different from the one he presently held. The man must care for his sister if he went to so much difficulty, going so far as to require even his servants to learn a language that they would most likely only ever use with Lady Lillian. He realized, suddenly, why she had been so confident in coming to London. Cardemore, for all his wickedness, had given her that.

"But there are other methods of training deaf-mutes, are there not?" Graydon asked. "Better methods? The French sign language has not been widely used here."

"Not here in England, no, although it has been widely accepted in other parts of the world. Here the oral method is the approved manner of dealing with deaf-mutes, although it seems to be a method better suited to those who can hear and speak than it is for the deaf-mutes. We tried that with Lily, at first, but since she is not entirely deaf, she can hear the sound of her own voice and, as I have said, dislikes it. Eventually she became so unhappy that my sister-in-law, Lady Margaret, insisted that we find an alternative. Charles Cassin came to us after that, and the change in Lily was both rapid and remarkable. She's made up for a good deal of lost time with Mr. Cassin's help."

"Remarkable," Graydon agreed. "You said that she is not *entirely* deaf? I had not realized she was deaf at all, for she seemed to hear perfectly during our time at Almack's, also this morning in the park."

"She hears well enough, save for in her left ear, which was affected during her youthful fever and has since only been partly useful. Her right ear seems to have escaped damage. Her lungs were also scarred, although to a lesser degree. She's taken ill several times with an inflammation, and nearly died of it twice. I advise you, however, to avoid the topic of health altogether whenever you're in Lily's hearing. Unlike a good many other females who rely upon their wilting frailties to produce conversation that never fails to bore one and all, if Lily ever thought you considered her of delicate health, she would most likely break your nose to prove the matter to you otherwise."

Graydon could barely suppress the smile Cardemore's words wrought. The notion of the sweet creature who had so utterly charmed him only a few hours ago launching a fist at his nose was laughable.

"You're taking Lily and Isabel driving?" Cardemore asked. "They'll be rather more awed by the experience than other ladies of your acquaintance. Thus far, London seems to have made a grand impression upon them. It's understandable, of course, being their first visit to Town. They'll need close watching, however. I shouldn't like either of them to seriously misstep."

At that, Graydon did raise an eyebrow. "Am I to understand that I now have the care of *both* Lady Lillian and Lady Isabel? Who will there be next? A male second cousin from Brighton who fancies a tour of London's most notorious hellholes? How far—*exactly*—must I go to repay my debts?"

For the first time that Graydon had ever seen, the warmth of sincere amusement touched Cardemore's features. "If any such person existed," he said, "I believe I could despoil him better than you, and certainly much more quickly. As to Isabel, I believe I made myself clear when we first spoke on the matter that I expect you to make both her and Lily's way clear into fashionable society. As far as Isabel is concerned, that is all I require. Although I do have a bit of advice to pass on to your friend Daltry, who seems to have elicited Isabel's particular dislike. He'd do best to go lightly with a female like that. She's much more dangerous than she looks, and as you've seen for yourself, she looks deadly."

"I believe it's too late for warnings, my lord," Graydon said. "I should like to leave you one of my own, however."

"Would you?" Cardemore sounded mildly interested.

"I'll tell you this only once. I am not a frippery young lord, and it is to your own folly that you mistake me for one. I'll do what I must to smooth Lady Lillian's and Lady Isabel's way into society, and I shall make certain, as best I can, that your sister enjoys her visit to London, but I will not do so under threat by either yourself or your minions. You will leave me in peace to fulfill my word of honor. If you cannot, then you may burn St. Cathyrs to the ground now and we'll have no more to do with each other."

"Well said," Cardemore returned without a pause. "A better speech than even Wellington can lay claim to, I imagine. I am not, however, as you might realize, a man who much admires speeches. Prove yourself, and I will do what you ask. As to being followed, I've already given you my word."

"Then we have an understanding," Graydon stated with a nod. "I'll bid you good-day, my lord."

After the door closed and he was alone, Cardemore spent a full silent minute shuffling through his papers again before shoving his work aside and saying, "Come out, Porter."

A closet door opened on the other side of the room and the man who had served as Graydon's shadow walked out.

"Ah ooh thatithfied, mah ord?" he said.

Cardemore rose from his chair. "Don't speak, Porter. It's painful to hear. And sit down before you fall." He moved to the room's lone window, pushing the drapes aside just enough to keep an eye on the street below. "Am I satisfied? Aye, I am. Very satisfied, indeed. He's better than I could have hoped for. Perhaps not the man I would have chosen for a brother-in-law, but he'll be a good husband to Lily or live to regret it." A thin smile played on his lips. "Somehow, I doubt it will ever come to that."

He turned to his minion, who sat nursing his aching head in both hands.

"I want you to proceed as planned with the kidnapping. Lily's comfort is to be of utmost importance. I won't have her harmed in any way. You can do as you please with Graydon, so long as he isn't permanently injured. And make certain everyone involved understands that the blame is to be laid at Saxby's door. I don't want Graydon or Lily ever discovering who's truly behind their brief imprisonment. Certainly not until they're married. There are to be no slips. No mistakes. Do you understand, Porter?"

"Ess, mah ord," Porter replied obediently.

"Make certain of it. If anything should go wrong, you'll have more to worry about than a broken jaw. Much more."

Chapter Seven

At night for the past three years, just before she fell asleep, Lily had lain quietly in her bed and let herself dream of all the exciting things that a young lady having her first season in London might experience. Being driven through a London park at the fashionable hour of five o'clock in the company of a handsome gentleman had been among her favorites, but Lily had been realistic enough never to let herself believe that the event would actually happen. The closest she would get, she had told herself with all practicality, would be in coercing her brother to take her out one afternoon. But Aaron disdained fashion almost more than he did the ton, and, although he would dutifully perform the task, Lily had too often envisioned the constant scowl he would wear, and the dark comments he would make, and had given up on the idea long before she and Isabel had ever even set foot in London.

But God must have heard her prayers, for here she was, not only rolling through Hyde Park in the most elegant barouche imaginable, but escorted by a gentleman whose handsomeness far exceeded even her most willfully exaggerated dreams.

She glanced down at the simple day dress she wore and felt foolishly plain. The dark rose gown, with its lighter-colored pelisse and satin trimmings of cream and pink, had been the height of fashion in the country. But here in London it was at least two years behind, no matter what Aunt Margaret said about it looking perfectly lovely. Lord Graydon had been effusive in his compliments, of course, but that was to be expected. A man of his good manners wouldn't speak the truth about such matters, even though he himself was dressed to perfection. Aaron would call him a dandy, or a frippery young lordling, or, worse, a man who let himself be managed by his valet, but Lily knew what the rest of fashionable society must think: that the Earl of Graydon was clearly a pink of the pink. A man who dressed with impeccable taste, wearing clothing cut of the finest quality.

He was sitting beside her in the elegant barouche, looking inhumanly perfect in buff-colored pantaloons and a dark blue coat. He appeared very relaxed, almost indolent in his posture, tapping his long fingers in a rhythmic motion over the top of his walking cane and grinning like a boy across the carriage at Isabel, who was entertaining him with humorous stories of all the scrapes the two of them had gotten into at Cardemore Hall. Lily found it hard to believe that he found such tales so interesting, but it must have been so, for his delight and laughter seemed genuine. He glanced at her, as if feeling her gaze upon him, and his smile softened from amusement to gentle interest.

"Are you enjoying the ride, Lady Lillian? What do you think of this mad crush?" He gestured with one hand toward the crowded lane.

She thought it wonderful, although it was, in all truth, quite silly for so many people to go parading about in the late afternoon, day after day after day. They'd been hailed and stopped by a number of elegants since they'd entered the park, some of them riding horseback, some of them perched high upon their fashionable phaetons, some riding in open carriages of varying elegance and size, and all of them desiring to be introduced to Isabel and her. Most of them had looked at her with dismay upon discovering that she didn't speak and had quickly thereafter made their excuses and left, but Lily was used to that. Simply meeting such a variety of fashionable people had been an event, and she imagined herself back in Somerset, holding court before her awestruck friends while regaling them with memories of her time in London.

He was waiting for a reply, and Lily opened the little gold case that dangled from a bracelet at her wrist. She had forgotten to have it with her when she'd gone riding that morning, but had made certain to bring it for her drive in the park. Extracting one of the tiny sheets of paper and the small gold pen, she wrote, *Wonderful. Better than Hassim's Traveling Circus.* She underlined *circus* twice and handed him the note, grinning with satisfaction when he burst into laughter.

"Dear me," he said, chuckling as he passed the note to Isabel. "I shall have to see what I can do to give you ladies a much more favorable impression of Town. Tell me, are there any particular places in London that you should enjoy seeing?"

"The Tower!" Isabel said at once, while Lily scribbled another note.

"Vauxhall," he read, slanting an amused glance at her, "and Madame Tussaud's."

"Oh, everywhere," Isabel told him, her face filled with childlike earnestness. "We decided that long before we came, isn't that so, Lily? If this is to be our only season in London, we want to see all there is to see, and do everything there is to do."

"That's quite a challenge, but I should be very glad if you would allow me to assist you in the matter," Lord Graydon replied, "at least so far as I am able, when Parliament isn't in session. Perhaps tomorrow, if you're free, might I escort you both, and Lady Margaret, if she would enjoy such an outing, to the Tower of London? I should deem it an honor."

"Oh, yes!" Isabel said with open delight. "How very

kind of you, my lord! I'm certain Mama will wish to come.''

''Then it's settled. I'll speak with Lady Margaret when we return to Wilborn Place.'' A rider on a magnificent black horse neared their carriage, and Lord Graydon raised a hand in greeting. ''Hello, Daltry. I wondered if we might meet you here.''

Lord Daltry, handsome in tan trousers and a black coat that hugged his large, muscular person to perfection, looked tense and uncomfortable as he brought his steed alongside the barouche. He made a slight bow in his saddle. ''Good day Lady Lillian, Lady Isabel.'' The glance he sent Isabel's way was greeted with a frozen stare. ''Graydon,'' Lord Daltry continued stiffly, ''I hope the day finds you well.''

''Quite well, I thank you,'' Lord Graydon replied casually. ''Despite the crowd, the park is rather pleasant this afternoon, don't you agree?''

Lord Daltry didn't seem interested in the park. He glanced at Isabel again and when she pointedly lifted her chin and looked away, he replied, ''Yes.''

''If I'd known you'd be parading today I would have invited you to come along with us and make a foursome. I'm sure the ladies would have enjoyed having your company.''

Lily nodded and smiled. Isabel tapped the bottom of the carriage with her parasol and made a sound of disdain.

''As it happens...'' Lord Daltry said, clearing his throat. ''Ahem. As it happens, I've been reconsidering some of the remarks I made to Lady Isabel this morning, and it has occurred to me that...perhaps...an apology is in order.''

Isabel stopped tapping her parasol and looked him full in the face.

''*Perhaps?*'' she asked.

''Ahem,'' Lord Daltry said once more, looking so uncomfortable that Lily felt sorry for him. ''No, not perhaps, exactly. I certainly owe you an apology, although you will admit that you provoked the situation and that we both made remarks any normal person would regret—''

Isabel cut him off. "I beg your pardon, my lord, but I do not, as it happens, regret one word that I said to you this morning. And I did *not* provoke the situation."

"You most certainly did," Lord Daltry returned more heatedly. "Riding your horse so recklessly that you might have broken your neck *and* lamed the animal. A more nit-witted display of horse handling I've yet to see."

Isabel stamped her parasol so solidly on the barouche's floor that Lily thought she'd poked a hole through it. "I had my mount completely under control, sir, and would have continued to do so if you hadn't come charging out of nowhere and frightened the poor beast half to death!"

"That poor beast was already frightened," Lord Daltry insisted. "If I hadn't stopped you when I did—"

"Ah, Hanby," Lord Graydon greeted loudly as another rider on horseback joined them. "Good day. Please, come and join our fracas." His mild tone caused Lily to smile, as the situation was so ridiculous, and he turned back to her with a conspiratorial wink that nearly sent her into whoops of laughter.

"Good day, Graydon. Daltry. Fracas?" Lord Hanby repeated, lifting his tall hat from his nearly bald head just long enough to make his bow to the ladies. "I wished to greet Lady Isabel and Lady Lillian. Good day," he said to Isabel, only briefly including Lily in his smile.

"Good day, my lord," Isabel replied politely, ignoring Lord Daltry's immense scowl as she leaned past him to smile at Lord Hanby. "My, what a fine mare. She looks wonderful to ride."

Lord Hanby flushed with obvious pleasure, and sat up straighter in his saddle, although it did nothing to heighten the look of his short, slender person. Beside Lord Daltry, Lord Hanby looked almost elfin.

"She is indeed," he agreed with unabashed pride. "She's but one of the finest in my stable that I brought to

Town for the season. One day you must allow me to take you riding, Lady Isabel. I should be very happy to provide you with a mount that I believe you'll find quite exceptional.''

"I wouldn't, Hanby, if I were you," Lord Daltry muttered.

Isabel glared at him before replying to Lord Hanby sweetly, "Lily and I would like that exceedingly, my lord. Thank you."

Lord Hanby glanced at Lily, their eyes meeting for the briefest of seconds before he turned back to Isabel. "Will you be at Lady Pebworth's ball tonight, Lady Isabel? I would very much like to reserve a dance with you, if I might."

"Hah," Lord Daltry remarked as if he'd never heard anything more foolish.

Isabel gifted Lord Hanby with her most dazzling smile—the one that had slain more men in Somerset than Lily could keep count of. Lord Hanby fell beneath its effect at once, leaning toward Isabel on his saddle until he met with Lord Daltry's hard elbow.

"You honor me, my lord. Lily and I would both be very glad to reserve a dance with you, if you would only tell us which dances you prefer."

Oh, Isabel, Lily thought with a groan. She couldn't tell who was more red-faced, she or Lord Hanby, who was suddenly at a loss for words. Beside her, Lily saw Lord Graydon's hand tighten upon his walking stick, and she wondered, with a sinking heart, if he was embarrassed to be seen in her presence. She was used to being treated as though she were invisible, but to others, especially to a person with a kind heart such as Lord Graydon possessed, the experience might seem terribly unpleasant.

"Why, I…" Lord Hanby began, clearly flustered.

"I've already reserved a waltz with Lady Lillian," Lord Graydon said suddenly, tightly, "as well as the supper dance."

"And I've reserved a waltz and a quadrille," Lord Daltry put in. "You'll have to make do with what's left over."

"Oh, well," Lord Hanby said, looking at Lily uncomfortably. "Perhaps, then, if you'll save me the first country dance, my lady?" He turned away before Lily could do so much as nod at him. "Lady Isabel, I was hoping that you might not yet have reserved the supper dance?"

"She has," Lord Daltry answered, not giving Isabel a chance to speak. "With me. You can have a quadrille. Now please be a good chap, Hanby, and shove off."

"Well, really," Lord Hanby said, affronted by this glaring lack of good manners.

Lord Graydon covered his mouth with his hand and coughed. He glanced at Lily and she had to look away to contain her own amusement.

"I have *not* reserved the supper dance!" Isabel insisted furiously.

"Yes, you have," Lord Daltry countered firmly. "Hanby, do I have to tell you twice, or would you rather serve as my next sparring partner at Jackson's?"

Lord Hanby's eyes widened, taking in Lord Daltry's massive person, and then he said meekly, "A quadrille will be quite acceptable, Lady Isabel. Good day." He nodded nervously at Lily and Lord Graydon. "Good day, my lady. Graydon. Daltry."

"Why you ill-mannered, conceited swine!" Isabel said after Lord Hanby had ridden away. "How dare you lie about such a thing."

Lord Daltry looked down at her from his greater height and said, "I rather like Hanby, at least enough to protect him from an underbred country chit who'd probably run some of his finest horses into the ground before she was done turning the man into a simpering fool by merely batting her eyelashes at him."

Isabel lifted her parasol with the obvious intent of smashing it upon Lord Daltry's head. Lily sat forward with a gasp to stop her, but Lord Graydon's hand pressed reassuringly on her arm.

"Ah, Lady Hamilton and Miss Hamilton," he said as another carriage pulled up beside them in the long line of slow-moving vehicles. "What a pleasant surprise."

"Lord Graydon!" the handsome, middle-aged woman in the other carriage greeted. "Indeed, it is. Frances and I were just hoping that we might see you here." The lovely young lady sitting beside her smiled first at Lord Graydon, and then at Lily. "Won't you introduce us to your companions?"

"With pleasure," said Lord Graydon, and Isabel lowered her parasol.

Within fifteen short minutes, Lily found herself strolling arm in arm with Miss Frances Hamilton through the colorful paradise of Kensington Gardens, with Lord Graydon escorting Lady Hamilton beside them. Somewhere not far behind, Lily could hear Isabel and Lord Daltry arguing hotly, but, thankfully, not overloudly.

Frances Hamilton was close to Lily's age, and very much like the friends that she and Isabel had left behind in Somerset. With curling, golden hair and warm brown eyes, she was a pretty, easygoing girl, open and kind and utterly unfazed by Lily's inability to speak. She accepted the notes Lily wrote without a pause in conversation, just as if Lily had spoken, rather than written, the words, and she was quick to understand the hand signals Lily usually found it necessary to make.

"I do so hope that you and Lady Isabel will be able to attend the small party my mother is giving next week, Lady Lillian," Miss Hamilton said. "It will mainly be a literary gathering, but we'll have music and cards, and I'm sure you'll both find it most entertaining. Of course, it will be nothing compared to the sort of ball that Lady Pebworth is giving tonight. Will you and your cousin be attending? Oh, how lovely! Do tell me what you're going to wear. I'm so grateful that I don't have to wear white this season, as I did last year. I'm mortally weary of it."

Miss Hamilton had the kind of voice that Lily had always been envious of, clear and bell-like, musical when she chattered on, as she was at the moment, so feminine and pretty that Lily had to tamp down the bitter jealousy that so swiftly rose within.

"Please tell me, what color will your gown be?" Miss Hamilton asked. "It won't matter, of course, for you're so beautiful that any color will look lovely. Every man who sees you must fall in love with you."

The compliment made Lily's cheeks burn, and she smiled at Frances Hamilton and shook her head.

Miss Hamilton pressed her arm and said earnestly, "Well, it's perfectly true. Don't you agree, my lord?"

"Indeed, I do," Lord Graydon replied.

Lily hadn't realized that the other couple had come so close. She pushed away in her embarrassment and strode to a nearby rosebush, which possessed flowers of a light, pinkish white hue. She fingered one of the soft petals and lifted a small handful of her skirt.

"How lovely," Miss Hamilton said approvingly. "And aren't you clever, choosing such a beautiful shade? White, but not quite white. I wish we had thought of such a thing, Mama, when I had my first season, rather than buying only white gowns."

Lord Graydon smiled down at the girl, possessing one of her dainty hands. "I liked you very much in those gowns," he murmured, his gaze intimate. "You look beautiful in white." Lowering his head, he gently kissed the hand he yet held, and then gazed into Miss Hamilton's eyes for a long moment before releasing her.

Miss Hamilton's cheeks grew pink and her expression filled with pleasure, while Lady Hamilton looked on with smiling approval.

Lily stood very still, watching the scene as if she were, in truth, completely invisible, as if she had no part in any

of it. They were in love, she realized. Lord Graydon and
Miss Hamilton. And she realized, too, that it couldn't possibly have been a coincidence that they had met here like
this, or that Miss Hamilton had been so friendly to her.

Did they think her an idiot? she thought with sudden
fury. Or that because she was mute, she wouldn't be able
to reason the matter out? It was bad enough for Lord Graydon and Lord Daltry to lie about having asked her to dance,
but this…this well-intentioned pity, this forced kindness…she *hated* it! The only thing she hated more was not
being able to tell them how much she resented being treated
in such a way, as if she must be handled differently from
anyone else.

But you are different, she told herself silently, her fingers
unwittingly crushing the delicate petals in her hand as she
stood there, invisible, watching. *You don't even exist most
of the time.*

She should be grateful that Lord Graydon had made such
an effort on her behalf, she thought, but she wasn't. Why
had he done it? What on earth had ever made him do it?

"You," she heard Isabel's angry voice say as she and
Lord Daltry neared, "are an obstinate, thick-headed and
stupid swine."

"Yes, but at least I can ride a horse without half killing
it," he replied, adding acidly, "*Lady* Isabel."

Lily had never been more grateful for her relative's hot
temper, and when Lord Graydon said, with a chuckle,
"Perhaps we had better go before war breaks out in Kensington Gardens," she readily let him guide her back to his
waiting carriage and hand her in.

Chapter Eight

Something was wrong, Graydon thought as he watched Lady Lillian Walford from across Lord and Lady Pebworth's ballroom floor. Very, wretchedly wrong.

She was ethereally beautiful in her airy pink gown, which was indeed similar in color to the roses that she had so charmingly compared it to earlier in the day. He remembered perfectly the moment when her gloved hand had fingered the tiny petals—it was the last time she had smiled at him, the last moment she had gazed at him with the open friendliness he had found so refreshing. It seemed like an eternity ago.

She'd been misleading about the dress, however. It wasn't simply a pink ball gown; it was a creation that had clearly been fashioned to suggest the dawn of a perfect new day. The net overskirt was fixed with what must have been hundreds of—what?—diamonds?—so that every movement set off a sparkling that looked like early stars fading against the blush of a clear morning's light. The effect was eye-catching, and enchanting. Not that Lady Lillian needed such a gown to gather attention. She could have been dressed in a grain sack and every man in the room still would have been eyeing her with admiration. The trouble was that admiration, at this point, was the only sort of attention she was getting. The ball had been in progress for more than two hours, and she'd not once danced, not even with him.

Somewhere between the delightful afternoon they'd spent together and tonight, Lady Lillian had ceased to be an angel and had turned into a frigidly unapproachable ice maiden. He'd stood before her, having gone to claim his waltz, with his hand outstretched and his most charming smile frozen upon his face, both looking and feeling a fool, not knowing quite what to do. He had never before been turned away when he had requested a dance, and she—*she* had done nothing but stare at him as if he were something disgusting. She hadn't even written him a note from her little golden note case, as she had done so often during the day, but had disdainfully communicated through Lady Isabel, who had clearly been highly embarrassed, relating that Lady Lillian had said it was not necessary for him to dance with her.

Not necessary, he thought angrily, watching her across the floor. What in the name of heaven was that supposed to mean? He'd gone to a great deal of trouble on her behalf, and now, for no good reason, she threw it all back in his face. Just thinking of what he'd had to do to assure her a few dances made him clench his fists. Seaborne Margate had even had the gall to insist that he would only dance with the silent Lady Lillian if Graydon would sell him the black hunter he'd purchased last year. Now he'd lose the hunter for nothing; she'd turned Sea away just as coldly as she had the rest of them. Not that it hadn't been amusing to see the handsome, lofty Sir Margate refused for once in his charmed life—the man had looked positively thunderstruck, a circumstance that Graydon knew Daltry wouldn't stop taunting the man over for days to come—but Graydon still felt like wringing Lady Lillian's ungrateful little neck.

She was standing near her sister-in-law and Lady Isabel, much as she had been at Almack's a few days before. At Almack's, however, she had at least looked approachable. Now, Lady Lillian looked like nothing better than an impenetrable fortress. Even Frances, who had been so generous in her friendship that afternoon, had been coolly rebuffed, and Lady Jersey had been sent scurrying away with little more than a chilly glance.

Both Lady Margaret and Lady Isabel looked as if they were lost, exasperated but completely unable to reason with their beautiful relative. Lady Isabel had tried to refuse to dance as well, clearly waiting for Lady Lillian to join the gaiety before she did, until Lord Daltry had finally refused to be put aside and had forced that formidable young woman into a waltz by practically carrying her onto the dance floor. When it was finished he carried her back to her mother and strode purposefully to Graydon's side.

"She's unhappy," he said in a low voice. "Lady Isabel, that is. Seems as if Lady Lillian spent the rest of the day locked away in her bedchamber after we took them home. Cardemore went in and spoke with her after an hour or so, and when he came back out he didn't look very pleased."

"Damn," Graydon muttered under his breath. "Something's gone wrong, somehow, although I can't imagine what it is. She was perfectly content this afternoon."

Daltry accepted a cup of burgundy from a passing footman.

"She was silent on the way back to Wilborn Place," he commented. "Not that she isn't always silent, I suppose, but...you know what I mean."

"I'm beginning to think that I don't know anything," Graydon told him. "Save that I spent all of this morning making visits that have clearly been a waste of time, and that I won't lose St. Cathyrs because a pretty female has suddenly taken leave of her senses."

With that, he began to make his way across the dance floor.

A momentary surprise possessed her features when she saw him stalking toward her, to be covered almost at once by the chilly expression she'd worn for most of the evening.

He made his second greetings of the evening to both

Lady Margaret and Lady Isabel before turning to the object of his wrath.

"The supper dance is about to be played, I believe, Lady Lillian. I should be honored if you would allow me to be your partner."

She lifted one white-gloved hand and made a sharp, negative gesture. Behind him, he heard Lady Isabel say unhappily, "She said 'Thank you very much, my lord, but I'm afraid that I don't feel quite up to dancing at the moment.'"

Proficient in sign language he was not, but Graydon knew very well that Lady Lillian hadn't said anything quite so nice.

"Then perhaps you might enjoy a walk in the gardens? The evening air is comfortable and I understand that Lady Pebworth has decorated the walkways with Chinese lanterns."

Her clear blue eyes glittered with what Graydon recognized as a fury that matched his own, and her hand came up again. Before she could consign him in her silent language to the place to which her expression had already condemned him, Graydon took her hand and held it very firmly.

"Thank you most kindly, my lady," he said, forcibly placing her hand upon his arm. To Lady Margaret, who was somewhat distracted by the spectacle of Lord Daltry carrying her daughter off onto the dance floor again, he said, "I shall make certain to return your niece in time for supper, ma'am."

Getting Lady Lillian out into the gardens was like dragging an anchor across the room and out the French doors. Once outside on the terrace, she tried again to gain her freedom, but there were several other couples sitting there, enjoying the cooler night air, and what Graydon had to say to Lady Lillian required a much greater privacy. He clamped his hand even more firmly over hers, nodded in greeting to his various acquaintances on the terrace, and resolutely led her down the stairs and into the relative darkness of the garden.

"Here," he said as they neared a bench in a private alcove. "This will do."

She wrenched herself free.

Glaring at him, she opened her mouth, and said, *"D-hon't!"*

The word stunned him, momentarily, for it was spoken in such a deep, strangled tone that his brain registered it as a man's voice. Or rather, a young man's voice. It was misplaced, coming out of her beautifully feminine mouth, as if some other person, not she, had said it.

"Don't?" he repeated, drawing in a long breath, striving to keep the shock from his features. "Don't what, my lady?"

She turned away from him.

"Touch you?" he offered. "Speak to you? Ask you to dance?"

She made a scoffing sound, and he moved to stand in front of her.

"Forgive me for speaking so boldly, Lady Lillian," he began, clinging to the civility that had been bred in him from the day of his birth, although he wished to heaven that he could send his manners to perdition and speak to her plainly—which was to say, he would have liked nothing better than to grab and shake her soundly. "I seem to have in some way offended. If this is so, I pray that you will tell me what I have done."

She was fuming, staring at the ground, but she said, "Ah m-hay n-hot spheak verrey well—" at this she had to stop and draw in a long breath "—bhut th-hat dhoes n-hot mean I am an idee-yot."

The effort it took for her to say the words was great; he could see how difficult, almost painfully so, it was for her to force her deep, grating voice to work. Even more could he see how the sound of her own voice disgusted her. She was terribly angry, and hurt, else she never would have spoken, and the knowledge softened his wrath.

"Certainly you're not an idiot," he said. "I can't think that I have ever given you reason to believe I've thought so." She lifted her head suddenly, and he was taken back by the accusation in her glare. "*What* have I done to offend you?"

She went to sit upon the bench, flipped open her gold note case with the ease of long practice, removed a sheet and her tiny pen and began to write furiously, squinting in the darkness to see. When she had finished, she held the note out to him.

"I lied to Lord Hanby?" he said after he had read it, then laughed. "I never lied to Lord Hanby. What a notion! I should never do such a..." It occurred to him, suddenly, what she meant, and he felt the shock of disbelief. "You can't mean about having reserved dances with you?"

She nodded, and he was filled with affront. Why, the ungrateful little shrew! He'd merely behaved as any decent gentleman would, saving a lady from being openly humiliated. If she was going to be angered, it should be with Hanby for treating her as if she were some sort of dreaded disease that he didn't want to touch, let alone dance with. Graydon remembered the moment perfectly; he'd wanted to smash the swine's face in.

"I'm terribly sorry if that chivalrous action was so displeasing, my lady," he said from behind set teeth. "The next time you're treated to the sort of ungentlemanly behavior as Lord Hanby gave to you this afternoon, you may be certain I'll not interfere."

Even in the darkness, he could see the hot color rising in her cheeks. She scribbled another note and held it out. He took it, read it and felt his heart drop into his feet. Oh, gad.

"Yes," he admitted stiffly. "Miss Hamilton and her mother met us at the park at my request."

She'd found out. Graydon stood there with her note in

his hand, all of his careful plans crumbling like chalk beneath the hammer of her blow, and felt utterly helpless. He saw St. Cathyrs being taken away; his family estate, his home, being put into the hands of strangers. How would he ever explain it to his mother and sisters?

She wrote another note. *The dances, too? Sir Margate?*

He drew in a long breath and nodded. "They are all good friends of mine. I asked them to dance with you."

It had never occurred to him that Lady Lillian would realize what he had done, or, perhaps, if it had occurred to him, he'd assumed that she would be grateful. That she would be glad to receive the kinds of attention that a perfectly whole young lady would receive.

She was staring straight at him, not boldly, but as if her icy facade was about to crack. The straight line of her mouth trembled; the effort it cost her to keep from crying was obvious from the tension in her body, which was held as stiffly as a board, and in her hands, which were clenched upon her lap.

"*Why?*" she asked, her deep voice harsh and uneven. "Pah-hity?"

She tried to say the last word again, to make it more clear, but it only came out as an unintelligible croak, and she drew in a breath and lowered her head.

Pity. Merciful God. She believed he pitied her. He knew what she was feeling now. Ugly, and unapproachable, and unwanted and different. As if she would never be able to fit in the way others could. She had come to London with all her dreams, and he had been the one to break them. So soon. It would have happened eventually. He knew the truth of that; she probably knew it as well. But it shouldn't have been so soon, and it shouldn't have come from him. It might have been enough if he could have given her even a few weeks of pleasure, of being a diamond of the first water enjoying her first season in London. It was all that she had wanted, and not so very much to give. Watching now as she struggled to keep from crying in front of him,

Graydon wished, with all his heart, that he had been able to give it to her.

"It wasn't pity," he murmured. "I know what it looks like, but it wasn't that. I pray that you'll believe me."

Her head still bowed, she wrote another note.

A jest, then? A wager?

"God's feet, no!" he said vehemently. "Lady Lillian, I realize what you must think of me, but I would never insult you, or any other lady, in such a way. I give you my word as a gentleman."

Still she wouldn't look at him, so that he couldn't see what her reaction to this statement was. Perhaps she didn't think him a gentleman. Perhaps she thought his word utterly worthless.

"Why?" she asked again, pleadingly this time.

It was an awful moment. The worst that he could ever remember. He had no experience in hurting people, and little idea of how to make it all better. He couldn't tell her the truth. Even if Cardemore hadn't put such a restriction upon him, knowing that he had been blackmailed into being her escort was bound to hurt her more than she already had been.

"Your brother," he began slowly, trying to find his way among the treacherous rocks, "is an...acquaintance of mine."

She lifted her head slightly, sniffling.

"I daresay he's never mentioned me to you," he went on, wishing that he were better at making tales. "But he has mentioned you...to me...on a number of occasions." Two was certainly a number, he told himself. He wasn't quite lying to her. "When he mentioned that you were coming to Town, I knew that I must certainly do whatever I could to...smooth the way for the sister of my...dear friend." At this he coughed, trying not to choke upon the words, and prayed to God that he wasn't damning himself to Hell for all eternity. "He did not, however, explain that

you do not speak. Usually speak, that is. You can imagine
my surprise when we danced at Almack's.''

Her head lifted a little more, and with the back of one
hand she wiped both of her cheeks before looking at him.
The hopefulness in her expression seared him with guilt.

"Why d-hid you n-hot men-shion Ah-rhon?"

He stared at her, trying to comprehend what she'd said.
For the life of him, he couldn't figure it out.

"Uhm," he said, grasping his hands behind his back and
praying for inspiration.

She took pity on him, and wrote a note.

You never mentioned before that you knew Aaron.

"Well, no...no, I didn't," he said, fumbling desperately
for an excuse. Of course he would have mentioned her
brother to her, if they'd been good friends. It would have
been one of the first things he would have told her, once
they'd been introduced. Any kind of fool would have realized that. "I suppose...that is...I didn't want you to think
that I was merely doing your brother a favor. Perhaps that
was my original intent, but I quickly found you to be a
charming companion, and wished to pursue the acquaintance for my own selfish reasons."

That only served to make her look suspicious.

"Surely you know that you're an extraordinarily beautiful young woman, Lady Lillian," he pressed on. "I'd be
a liar if I didn't say that I'm honored to be seen in your
company. If you find that impossible to believe because of
your lack of speech, then I can only try, to the best of my
ability, to assure you that I do not now find, nor have I
ever found it unpleasant. I realize that my attempts to ease
your way into London society have deeply—and under-
standably—offended you. My only excuse is that I wanted
you to enjoy your time in Town. It is difficult to make a
successful entrance here for any young lady, but even the
smallest imperfection will make the task that much harder.
I wanted to make your way easier. If my methods were

wrong, I pray that you will believe my intentions were well meant.''

She was still for a long moment, gazing up at him, clearly thinking all of this through.

"If my presence has become distasteful to you," he said more softly, "I certainly understand, and will no longer distress you with it. I would ask that you be kind to Miss Hamilton. It's true that she and her mother met us at the park at my request, with the intention of making your acquaintance, but surely you realize that their behavior was sincere. Frances—that is, Miss Hamilton—has truly hoped to make a friend of you.''

She released a shaking breath and looked down at her hands again, and he stood there waiting, waiting, feeling his future all held there, so precariously.

She wrote another note, longer than the others, hesitating one moment before going on. She handed it to him.

I did not understand, and was wrong to judge you so harshly. If you will forgive me for my part, I gladly forgive you for yours.

He was so deeply relieved that he felt momentarily weak.

"You are very kind, Lady Lillian. Thank you.''

She smiled a little, giving him hope, so that he plunged ahead, needing to know whether there was yet a chance for him to save himself, his home.

"We've not had a good beginning, for which I fully accept the blame. But I spoke the truth when I said that I should like very much to show you some of London. Is there any chance that we might begin again?''

He wasn't quite certain, but she looked relieved, too.

Yes, she wrote upon a tiny scrap of paper. *I should like that.*

And then she smiled at him in that brilliant way and he knew everything was going to be all right.

"As would I," he said sincerely, holding out a hand to raise her from the bench. "More than anything.''

Chapter Nine

"Well, Tony, Cardemore won't have any reason to complain," Lord Daltry remarked as he stretched lazily beneath the shade of the tree that the two men shared. His gaze was fixed upon Lady Lillian, who, with another member of their picnic party, was strolling slowly along the bank of the Thames. "Lady Lily's certainly had a successful season so far. I doubt there's another woman alive who can say that she's ever had Sea Margate looking so pathetic."

Graydon chuckled softly, smiling after the two figures near the water. "He does seem smitten. Never thought I'd live to see the day. But who can blame the man? She's utterly beautiful."

"Hmm," Lord Daltry concurred, lifting a sugared almond from his plate and regarding it closely before popping it into his mouth. He swallowed before adding, "It's not just that. Lady Lily has nice manners. Quite a pleasant female, all around. If it weren't for the idea of being related to Isabel Walford through marriage, I might take an interest in the girl myself."

Graydon laughed outright and suffered Lord Daltry's withering glare before finally stopping, his mouth set into a wide grin. "I suppose this means that I should remove my bet from White's books about you and Lady Isabel becoming betrothed by summer's end?"

"As soon as you pay me for losing the wager, you mean," Lord Daltry told him.

"I think I'll let it stand a while longer," Graydon said. "It's such a lonely, one-sided wager. Me against half of London. I can't resist the idea of the winnings I'll make if you two should get leg-shackled."

"What you'll get is empty pockets and a reputation as a fool. Look at her." Lord Daltry nodded toward where Lady Isabel held court over half a dozen members of her ever-growing court. "The forward chit has every man in Town slobbering over her like a pack of hairy hounds. I'm less than nothing to her. Worse, she *hates* me." He took up his wineglass and drained it. A nearby servant silently moved forward to refill the cup. "You're throwing your money away for nothing, Tony."

"Don't give up hope yet, Matthew," Graydon advised kindly. "At least she hates you with devoted consistency."

"Grand," Daltry muttered. "A thing to cherish when I'm old. You'd best keep an eye on your protégée before Margate gets her all to himself in that grove of trees."

Sitting up, Graydon craned his neck to see toward where Daltry had nodded. "Lady Lily knows better than to let him try something like that. She's not a child." He reclined upon the blanket again. "And she's not my protégée."

"Your charge, then," Daltry amended. "Your baby chick. Your season-long bundle of blackmail."

"Perhaps," Graydon said, idly toying with an orange upon his plate. "I can't say, in truth, that I've minded. It's been the least dull season I've weathered yet." He smiled. "A thing to cherish when I'm old."

Daltry shook his head. "I'm beginning to think you're half-mad, Tony."

"Admit it. You've enjoyed taking Lady Lily and Lady Isabel around Town just as much as I have. Remember the day we took them to the Tower?"

"Certainly I do. How could I forget? Lady Isabel said she'd like to see my head upon the chopping block."

"And you replied that if *her* head had ever been severed from her body, it would float away rather than fall into the basket." Graydon made a tsking sound. "Naughty, Matthew. Such an interesting courtship you two are having. Now, Lady Lily," he pressed on quickly, not giving his indignant friend a chance to retort, "being a much more typical female, found the place to be thoroughly romantic. I've never quite understood why that happens with women. You'd think they'd find it to be ghastly."

"I doubt they'd find it so curst romantic if they were the ones who'd been locked up."

"Perhaps," Graydon agreed. "And I shall never, in all my life, forget the afternoon we escorted the ladies to the museum. Lady Isabel's remarks about the Elgin Marbles will live forever in my memories."

"She nearly had us thrown out," Daltry said heatedly. "I can't think how Lady Margaret managed to raise such a shocking chit."

"Oh, I don't know." Graydon lifted a tiny egg tart from his plate to inspect it before setting it aside again. "I thought it rather amusing, hearing you compared to a block of stone." He smiled. "Lady Margaret actually laughed."

"What about her behavior in Bond Street? You didn't find that amusing, I'll vow."

"No," Graydon agreed more seriously. "That wasn't amusing at all. Certainly not for Lady Margaret. Seeing Cardemore with his mistress was bad enough without Lady Isabel shouting at them to stop and speak with us. Quite unfortunate, that."

"Cardemore clearly thought so. Looked as if he'd take the girl over his knee then and there."

"Lady Isabel couldn't have known who the woman was," Graydon said. "She and Lily were raised in the country, remember, and haven't been much exposed to the kinds of happenings that pass as the usual in Town. I imagine she still doesn't realize that her uncle keeps a mistress."

"Due entirely to the fact that the Cyprian in question

was mannerly enough to keep her mouth shut and let Cardemore do all the talking. I don't suppose he'd ever keep a dim-witted female. Fortunate thing. Did you see the look on Lady Margaret's face? Positively thunderstruck, she was."

Graydon nodded slowly. "She must have been shocked to find herself staring at her near mirrored image, save that Cardemore's mistress is a rather dull copy of Lady Margaret's beauty."

"I didn't see that they looked that much alike. The hair was nearly the same shade of red, but otherwise..." Daltry gave a shrug, finishing off the last bite of cold salmon on his plate.

"But there was enough of a similarity to make the occurrence quite odd," Graydon murmured. "One can only wonder at what Cardemore is about, keeping a woman who looks so much like his sister-in-law. Lady Lily was terribly upset by it later."

"Was she?" Daltry asked around a mouthful of food. "At Vauxhall?"

"Yes. When we went for a walk just before the fireworks began, she told me how troubled she was by the event. She even asked me if the woman was her brother's mistress, and I didn't know what to tell her."

"How would you know who his mistress is?" Daltry said. "You hardly know the man."

"Ah, but you forget. I am now his 'very dear friend.'"

Daltry snorted. "Oh, yes, indeed. And stiffer friends I've never seen together. I can't believe Lady Lily fell for such a bouncer."

"What I can't believe is that Cardemore ever agreed to attempt the ruse."

"Well he had to, didn't he, to keep Lady Lily from discovering how he's blackmailed you. So what did you say to her about the lady seen in the company of your 'very dear friend'?"

With a sigh, Graydon pushed his empty plate away and

rolled over onto his back, gazing up through the branches of the tree to the sky above. "I told her the truth. What else could I do? She's too canny to lie to about something that she's already seen for herself. There are times when I think she's reading my thoughts, she's so often beforehand in what I'm about to do or say, and I can't believe she still accepts the reasons I gave her for making her acquaintance. If she weren't so ready to find the best in everyone she meets, I don't doubt that she'd set me on my ear and send me on my way. Fortunately, for me, she's blessedly naive."

"Not for much longer if you gave her an earful about Cardemore's ladybird. What did she think of it?"

"She understood," Graydon lied, closing his eyes against the brightness of the day. "She accepted that her brother is a man of the world."

It wasn't even close to the truth, but Graydon wasn't about to tell anyone, not even his closest friend, of how deeply hurt Lily had been. He'd told her the truth, as gently and kindly as he could, and had watched all the color drain from her face. She had stared at him and then scribbled a furiously fast note.

But why?

The tiny page had joined the myriad others in his pockets, although it had been crushed in his fist first. She watched his face anxiously, waiting for his reply, and all he'd been able to say was "I'm sorry."

She moved to sit on a bench, and he joined her there, taking her hands in both of his.

"Lady Lillian," he began, and she pulled her hands away so that he forgot himself and said, "Lily."

She wrote another note and gave it to him.

She looked like Aunt Margaret.

"Yes," he admitted. "She did, rather. But it was merely a coincidence."

Lily shook her head firmly.

"I'm sure it was," Graydon told her. He took her hands again and held them tightly, feeling her unhappiness as if it were his own. "Lily," he said softly, "we shouldn't be speaking of such matters. It is considered to be very unacceptable. You should ask your aunt Margaret to explain these things to you."

"N-ho," she said insistently, surprising him, for although she had used her voice in his presence before, if they were alone, it was still quite rare. "If ah can-nhot sp-heak with you, there is n-ho one ehlse."

He might have smiled at the words, or tried to correct her, but he didn't. Because she was right. There was a communication between them. A bond. At least for as long as she was in London, where she had become so unwittingly—he might almost have said unwillingly—dependent upon him. There was no one else she could turn to. Only him. He seemed to be the only person in this foreign land, save her relatives, who understood her.

He should have told her again that he was sorry, that he couldn't possibly discuss such things with her, but instead he ran his thumbs lightly over the backs of her glove-encased hands and said, "Tell me what you want to know."

The conversation that followed hadn't cheered her any. She wasn't upset at the idea of her brother keeping a mistress; it was the general nature of men she hotly deplored. *He should marry that poor woman!* she'd written.

Graydon had made the awful mistake of laughing out loud and replying, "Good heavens! My dear girl, it would be impossible for a man of your brother's standing—for the *Earl of Cardemore*—to marry a woman of her station."

Lily had set her lips in a straight line and looked as if she'd like to strike him. She wrote another note. *Then he should marry Aunt Margaret.*

This sentiment surprised Graydon so much that he said, before he could think better of it, "Marriage isn't necessarily a solution, my lady. A great many married men keep mistresses, even when they claim to love their wives."

Her mouth fell open and she stared at him as if he'd just

pronounced some unfathomable evil, and Graydon, angry
with himself at speaking with such a lack of tact, stuffed
the note into his pocket and abruptly stood. "I apologize.
I've upset you. We shouldn't be discussing these things.
We'd best return to the others before the fireworks begin."

"Whait." She put a hand on his arm to still him, after
he had pulled her to her feet. Her expression, as she gazed
up at him, was chagrined. "Ah'm sorree."

The sound of her voice was beginning to have the oddest
effect on him. He wanted too much to hear it. It was too
pleasurable, knowing that he was one of the few allowed
to do so. "You don't have to be," he began, but she shook
her head.

"Ah'm stup-hid."

"Lily." He covered the hand she held on his arm. "No.
I won't have that."

She made a sound—a husky chuckle that shivered all the
way through him, turning his brain to mush. Her smile
flashed up in the dim lantern light. "Fool-*ish*," she
amended. "L-hord Grah-don, you are so g-hood to m-he.
Ah'm so gr-ate-ful."

Gad! he thought, staring down into what he knew would
stand as the most riveting countenance he'd behold in his
lifetime. Grateful! If she had any idea of what he wanted
to do to her at that moment, she'd probably think he was
nothing but a perfect swine.

"Fireworks," he mumbled desperately. She was much
too near—he could distinctly feel her warmth through both
their layers of clothing—and if she didn't stop gazing up
at him as if he were some divine hero he wouldn't be held
accountable for what occurred. "Uhm." He cleared his
throat and stepped away. "The fireworks are about to begin."

He'd led her away, then, because there was nothing else
he could do. It was impossible to seduce her. She was the
daughter and sister of an earl, as well as an innocent. But
he had a much better reason for leaving her intact.

Something strange had happened during the past few weeks—something he'd never foreseen. Lillian Walford had begun to mean something to him. More than a burden, or a charge, or even an acquaintance. He'd told himself innumerable times that it was merely a brotherly sort of concern he felt for one less fortunate, that he only wished to keep her safe from hurt and harm, to make her understood by others, to give her this time in London just as she had wanted it. But he was starting to fear that it was more than that.

He was uncomfortably aware of her as a woman; worse, he was beginning to feel obsessed. She was too beautiful. Too desirable. He contemplated her mouth so often that he *knew* the activity was unhealthy. And contemplation wasn't where it stopped. His imaginings were completely out of hand, not stopping at the thought of that mouth merely kissing him, but of being occupied in a much more alarmingly personal manner. That led to other, even more shocking ideas, which pursued him even as he slept, so that Graydon would often wake, hot and cold and sweating all at once, certain that such wickedness was condemning him to everlasting Hell. It had to be sinful to dream such things about an innocent, *mute* female. And if Cardemore, in all his omniscience, ever discovered what his sister's escort was thinking, Graydon had no doubt he'd find himself delivered to Hell's fires rather more quickly than he'd generally expected.

It was a wretched predicament, wanting to help her, wanting her. She trusted him, which was no small attainment. It had taken a full week before she'd allowed him to interpret for her, even with his meager ability, for he didn't think he'd ever understand her sign language, and relied solely upon her notes and her ability at playing charades, and he recognized the honor for what it was. She trusted him to be her friend, to guide and speak for her, to know when it was all becoming too much and take her away to a quiet place, where they might simply sit together in comfortable silence.

"I don't know how it is that you talk to Lady Lily at all," Daltry remarked, not unkindly. "If it weren't for you being able to understand the girl, I doubt I'd have the nerve to so much as say good-day to her."

"It only wants a bit of practice," Graydon said. "Not difficult at all, really, which you'd know if Lady Isabel didn't keep you so fully occupied every moment of the day, and which the rest of the ton would realize, as well, if it weren't so afraid of anyone and anything so far out of the usual."

"I doubt it," Daltry said. "It isn't fear of Lady Lily's lack of talk that keeps some of them away. Cardemore's reputation isn't exactly cheering, and there are those theories about the deaf and mute being cursed. And I'm *not* occupied with that hellacious female every moment of the day. Fiend's foot, I'd probably lose my mind if I were." Gazing at the female in question as she sat near the river, surrounded by admirers, he gave a long sigh. "Oh, well. Is your mother, the countess, coming, then?"

"No, not yet." Graydon gracefully pushed up into a sitting position, squinting across the wide expanse of green to where Lily and Sir Margate were seated. He noticed that she was using her fingers, charade-fashion, to explain something to her avidly attentive companion, and even from the distance could see the fatigue on her delicate features. It wearied her to have to work at charades for long, especially when she had to repeat the motions over and over to make herself understood. "Janette had the bad manners to contract the influenza just as soon as Melissa fully recovered from it. Another week or two and she should be fit for travel."

"Women," Daltry muttered with a shake of his head. "Can't be organized and do these things all at once, of course."

Graydon smiled. "Not in my family, at least. And now

if you will be so good as to excuse me—'' he stood ''—I'll go and rescue Lady Lillian from Seaborne Margate's ever enthralling charms.''

''Before she faints dead away from them, most certainly,'' Daltry replied pleasantly. He lifted a hand to wave him away. ''Go on your way, then, Good Knight Graydon. I should never detain a gentleman from his course of duty.''

She saw him coming, he noted as he neared her, and looked desperately happy to see him. Relieved, almost.

''Lady Lillian,'' he murmured, taking the hand she lifted and squeezing it lightly, ''I hope you're enjoying the day. Good afternoon, Margate.'' Relieved, almost. When she clung to his hand, rather than let him release her, Graydon knew that something was wrong.

''Graydon,'' Sir Margate returned stiffly, openly displeased at having his private tête-à-tête interrupted.

''Marvelous picnic, don't you think?'' Graydon remarked, tucking Lily's hand comfortingly beneath his arm and holding it there. If Margate had been bothering her with any of his usual nonsense, he'd strangle the man. ''Greenwich is ever a pleasant delight, and Lady Strathway always does these things so well.''

''Indeed,'' Sir Margate agreed, gazing at Lily in a manner that made her look away. ''Absolutely…*marvelous*.''

Graydon's smile froze upon his face, while with every ounce of self-control he forced back the anger that flooded him at the other man's meaning. It was fortunate that Lady Margaret appeared at that moment and insisted upon stealing her niece away to introduce her to an old friend. Lily went gratefully, although she held Graydon's hand for a moment longer than necessary when she took her leave of him and, gazing pleadingly into his eyes, shook her head. Graydon merely smiled.

When he and Seaborne Margate were alone, watching the women depart, he remarked, ''A lovely young lady, is she not?''

''She's fantastic,'' Sir Margate agreed, setting his hands

behind his back. "I can't seem to think of anything else, of late."

Surprised, Graydon glanced at him. Perhaps he'd misunderstood the matter. "Your feelings have become involved, then?"

"Oh, yes," was the emphatic reply, and still his gaze moved over Lily as she greeted her aunt's acquaintance. "My feelings and every other part of me."

Graydon let the words pass as typical male prosing. His own feelings for Lily, after all, were hardly as pure as he wished them to be. "You seemed to be having a rather involved conversation." He started them strolling along the river.

"Did we?" Margate left off his admiration of Lily with a sigh, turning to smile at Graydon. "I'm glad it seemed that way from afar. I don't want to look a fool, after all, while I'm pursuing the girl. Of course, I didn't have the foggiest notion of what she was trying to say. Those heathenish motions she makes with her hands!" He shook his head.

Graydon all but gaped at him. "If you couldn't understand her, then why the devil have you kept her company all this past half hour?"

Sir Margate laughed. "Really, Graydon, I'm sure you could tell me better than I could you. If you're able to understand that delicious woman, so much the better. For me, I don't give a snap of my fingers whether she makes a moment's sense. It won't make any difference once I've got her in bed."

Chills shivered up Graydon's spine, followed by a sharp, tingling heat. For a moment the entire world turned a shattering, violent red. His feet stopped moving. His fingernails curled into the palms of his hands. And somewhere over the thunderous din in his ears, he heard his friend say in a purely affable tone, "And if you think that I'm going to wait until you're done with her, old man, then I'm sorry to inform you that you're far wrong. If Cardemore hasn't yet killed you for bedding his sister, then he certainly won't have cause to kill me.''

"What—" he hardly recognized his own voice when he spoke, so low and unsteadily "—makes you think Cardemore would let me do such a thing? To use his sister in such a manner?''

"Gad, man. Everyone knows that the mute are amoral. Born that way, they are. It's a known fact. And Cardemore's not such a fool as to think anyone would actually *marry* the woman, unless it's some desperate fortune hunter after her dowry. Even then, she'll want her needs attended to, and, provided I've managed to push you out of the picture, who better than I to attend to them?'' He chuckled and grinned in a manner that Graydon was well used to. It invited him, as a fellow man, to enjoy the jest. Instead, without thinking upon his actions, Graydon put one hand on Sir Margate's collar to hold him still, and with the other hand made a fist, which he planted squarely in his captive's nose. The sound of bones crunching was gratifying, but it wasn't enough. As Margate began to howl and struggle, Graydon pulled him close.

"*Swine.* If I ever hear you so much as speak Lady Lillian's name again, I'll break more than your bloody nose. And if you want to continue breathing, you contemptuous pig, then you'd best stay far, far clear of her.''

And then, to make certain that his point was perfectly clear, Graydon lifted Sir Seaborne Margate off the ground and, with all of the other picnic-goers avidly watching, tossed him into the Thames.

Chapter Ten

Lily tried to turn and walk away, but Graydon took hold of her arm and swung her back. He looked just as furious as she felt.

"Gather your things, Lady Lillian. We're leaving."

How dared he! Lily thought, glaring at him. He had no right to make himself her champion, to involve himself in matters that were *hers* to care for. Far beyond caring that they were the focus of more than a dozen pairs of interested eyes, Lily jerked free and emphatically made the hand signal for "no."

He seemed not to notice, although she knew that he understood perfectly well. She'd taught him the hand signal, along with a host of others, and he had proved to be an apt pupil.

"I'll speak with your aunt," he said firmly, "and make our excuses to Lady Strathway. Now go and gather your things."

No, she signed again, and felt the pressure of his fingers on her arm increase.

"Lily," he said in a low voice, clearly striving to maintain his composure for the benefit of those watching them, "I realize that I've just embarrassed you beyond repair, and that by this time tomorrow both of us will be the prime topic of Town conversation, but if you don't want the spectacle of Sir Margate and myself brawling about on the lawn being added to the one I've already provided, then I suggest that you gather your things and leave with me. *Now*. Before he crawls out of the river. Because the moment he does, and if he's still able to stand without assistance, I'm going to kill him.''

Lily went to gather her things, and a few moments later found herself being handed up into Lord Graydon's high-perched phaeton. She cast a glance at their stunned audience—at Lady Strathway, who, supported by her two daughters, was weeping disconsolately into a handkerchief, and then at Aunt Margaret, still standing with the acquaintance she had only just introduced Lily to before they were interrupted by the spectacle. Isabel wasn't too far away, standing beside Lord Daltry's large, sheltering person; the girls' eyes met and held, sharing an unhappiness such as only they could. Finally, Lily looked beyond the crowd to where several men had pulled Sir Margate out of the river. He was sopping wet, but alive and well, evidenced by the expression of rage on his face, all of it directed toward Lord Graydon and herself. Seeing it, she was suddenly glad to be leaving the idyllic spot Lady Strathway had chosen for her picnic.

The moment other impeding carriages were moved to clear the way, Lord Graydon started his light phaeton forward. They rode in silence for the first five minutes, with Lily thinking of nothing but that he could have handled the entire matter better than he'd done, and turning over a variety of ways in which to express her displeasure, from whacking him with her parasol—a method Isabel tended to favor when provoked—to not speaking to him at all and, once he delivered her home, never seeing him again.

But that, she told herself more reasonably once her anger began to cool, was an impossibility. She could probably manage one entire day without the sight of him; two, perhaps, if she worked at stoking and maintaining her anger. But three days would be the end of it. She would want him, then. She would be desperate for him. By then, just the sound of his voice would be enough to make her heart turn over with delight.

It was distressing to think upon, but entirely, irrefutably true. Because somehow she had done the most foolish thing, and had fallen in love with a man who already loved someone else. A man who would never deign to look at someone like her with any interest, save that of a friend. And even then had done so only for the sake of his much dearer friend, her own brother.

It was horrible. Awful. The worst thing that Lily could have ever imagined occurring during her one season in London. She had dreamed of a good many things happening to her here, but falling in love hadn't been among them. She had come to the realization long ago that she would never have a husband, for no man would want a wife who couldn't speak to him. She had accepted the fact and made her plans accordingly: if Aaron never married, she would take her place as the mistress of Cardemore Hall and devote herself to managing the estate as he wanted it to be done. It would be a quiet life, but she would find contentment in it. If Aaron did take a wife, Lily would ask her brother to set her up in her own establishment near where her former tutor, Mr. Charles Cassin, had started his school for deaf-mutes. It would seem strange, perhaps, for the daughter and sister of an earl to take up teaching, but for Lily it would be a joy.

Until a few days ago those had been her only options for living out her life. But she had learned that there might be another choice. She might decide to become a man's mistress. Lord Graydon had explained such matters quite fully, making it clear that society didn't particularly seem to mind if a married lady of high birth took a lover, or even many lovers, just as a man was allowed to take mistresses. He'd said nothing about ladies who weren't wed, but it stood to reason that someone in her position, who was *un*marriageable, should be permitted some leniency. And since that night at Vauxhall, Lily had begun to realize that men whom she'd before believed were gazing at her with simple appreciation were, in truth, eyeing her with an altogether different contemplation in mind. She could not only take a lover, but she could choose from among dozens of men. Sir Margate had all but spoken his willingness aloud just this afternoon. Not that she would ever consider him, of course, or any of the others who'd signaled their desire. There was only one man she would become mistress to, if he ever asked her.

The Earl of Graydon.

He wanted her, too, although he was far too mannerly to express it openly. She only caught it sometimes if she looked at him suddenly and found him watching her, or when his gaze settled on her mouth, as it so often did. It had bothered her in the beginning, for she'd thought he was willing her to speak, but once she'd understood, her irritation had vanished. She loved him, and although he would never feel anything remotely similar for her, it was enough—more than enough—to know that she could be something to him.

It was perhaps ignoble to be so certain that she would live in sin, perhaps completely wrong, but she didn't care. Her life was such that every happiness had to be grasped with as little guilt as possible. There were many things that she would never share with speaking women—a husband, a place in society, children—but she could at least know what it was to love. She *would* feel guilty, especially about Miss Hamilton, who had become such a dear and good friend, but Lord Graydon had said that married men took mistresses, and if he was going to do so, it might as well be she as another. Aaron would prove difficult, of course, if he ever found out, but as long as she and Lord Graydon were careful—well, had not he himself said that these things must be carried out quite discreetly? Aaron had been so discreet about his own mistress that Lily had never even

realized such a woman existed until the day when they had
so accidentally met in Bond Street.

But she was far beforehand, she thought as she glanced
at him, at his set face and tightly clenched jaw. He hadn't
asked her to become his mistress, and, because of his close
friendship with her brother, he might never do so.

He seemed to sense her gaze upon him, but didn't look
at her. Instead, he slowed the carriage bit by bit, finally
bringing it to a stop right in the middle of the road. Then
he sat, not turning, with the reins in his hands, and was
silent. A full minute passed before he bowed his head
slightly.

"I don't know quite how to begin to apologize, save to
do it," he said. "I have never in my life behaved so badly,
in such a public arena, and especially not to the detriment
of a lady. I don't particularly care about throwing Sir Margate in the river, because he deserved that, and much worse,
but for whatever shame and embarrassment I may have
visited upon you and your family—and I am not insensible
that this may be great—I deeply regret my actions, and beg
your forgiveness. Please be assured that if matters should
become unbearable for you, I will consider it a great honor
to make amends."

She wasn't quite certain what he meant. If Aaron
couldn't fix matters, she doubted that anyone could. On one
point she was quite firmly fixed, however. The Earl of
Graydon must accept that he could not take on fights that
were her own. He could not change the way things were,
or give her the gift of being able to speak with the ease
that others could. Even if she became his mistress, he
would not be able to shelter her from stares and whisperings and being treated as if she were invisible.

Touching his shoulder to gain his full attention, she
looked patiently into his remorse-filled eyes, and pointed
very firmly at herself. "It whas *mah* truh-ble."

He blinked slowly and straightened in the seat. "You
couldn't have taken care of it yourself," he told her. "I

admit that I should have handled the situation in a much better fashion, but it would have been foolish for you to even try doing so. I shudder to think of what might have happened if that filthy dog had managed to get you into the woods alone. You wouldn't even have been able to shout for help.''

She began to protest, but he shook his head sharply.

"No. You will no longer associate with Sir Margate for any reason, for any amount of time, at any event that you may both attend together. You will stay away from him. *Completely.*''

Lily flipped open the gold case at her wrist and removed a sheet, but he put a hand out and stopped her.

"It won't do any good to argue, Lily. If you won't keep away from Margate because I tell you to, I'll make certain that your brother keeps you away from him. And if I tell Lord Cardemore even half of what that man said in my hearing, you may be certain that you'll find yourself packed off to Cardemore Hall within a half day, and Sir Margate will be fortunate to find himself still among the living at the end of that same time.'' His fist tightened about the reins as he pinned her with an angry glare. "Why did you continue sitting with the man, putting up with his nonsense, when you know very well that one word, even a look, would have brought me to your side?''

Her throat ached and burned, and she was so tight everywhere that speaking was sharply painful. "It is n-hot your c-hon-cern! Ohnly m-hine!''

His handsome face turned to stone. "Not anymore. I'll not allow you to be put in such a circumstance in future.'' Then he turned away and started them in motion once more.

They didn't speak again until they reached Wilborn Place. If the phaeton hadn't been so high, Lily would have gotten down herself, disdaining, in her anger, to suffer Lord Graydon's touch any longer than she must. But he put his hands around her waist and pulled her to the ground, and then held her so.

"Lily," he said, his tone so gentle and filled with penitence that she didn't push away, as she'd wanted to. "Will you invite me in for a few minutes. Please? I want very much to explain to you why I—"

"Lady Lillian?"

Lord Graydon dropped his hands at once and stepped away, the cloak of perfect civility falling on him with the rapidity that Lily had come to expect.

She knew who it was that hailed her, knew at once the familiar voice, and, without thinking of who might hear her, she cried out with joy. Stepping around Lord Graydon's large person, she saw him. He was standing at the open door of Wilborn Place, hat in hand, clearly having only just departed.

"Lady Lillian," Charles Cassin began, "how fortunate that you arrived just now. I had so hoped that I'd not miss—" his breath whooshed out as she raced up the step and threw herself at him full force "—you."

She didn't know why she started to weep. It was terribly embarrassing, and so foolish. But she was so very glad to see him, this man who for years had been her only voice, who had labored so long, so hard against her stubbornness in order to give her a voice of her own. He was her teacher, her dear friend, and in the midst of all the joy and madness she'd experienced in London, being with him again was a relief beyond expression.

"Dear Lady Lillian," he said kindly, patting her shoulder with the hand that held the hat so that the brim knocked against her arm. "How I've missed you. I came today only with the hope of seeing you, and when Lord Cardemore said that you were gone, I was terribly saddened. But here you are, my dear, and all is well."

Sniffling, Lily pulled away and wiped her wet eyes with the tips of her gloved fingers before signing, *Why have you waited so long to come? I asked Aaron to send you an invitation to visit long ago.*

He fumbled around in his coat pocket, drawing out a

handkerchief and pressing it into her hands. "It was impossible until now. I had to have someone to watch over the school and the students in my absence. If it weren't for Lord Cardemore, I doubt I should have been here in time for your ball. He somehow arranged for two students from the French Institute to come and work with me for the next year. It's a tremendous blessing. I can't begin to tell you."

Oh, yes, of course. Lily signed, smiling up at him through her tears. His kind, familiar face was so dear to her. *I know how hard you work, and I'm so grateful that you could come. It wouldn't have been the same without you!* She grasped one of his hands, as she had done so often when she was a girl, and kissed it.

He patted her shoulder again and chuckled. "We'll have none of that, now, my lady. The honor is mine. I'm terribly glad to be here to see my butterfly make her debut. Won't you introduce me to this gentleman who is waiting here so patiently? And then I must be on my way."

You can't leave yet! she told him.

"But I fear I've already imposed upon your brother long enough...."

Please! she begged. *Stay for another hour, if you can. I have so much to tell you. Please.*

His eyes held hers for a silent moment, and then with a nod he said, "Very well, my dear. If you're certain that Lord Cardemore won't mind."

Lord Cardemore didn't mind. In fact, Graydon thought from where he sat across the drawing room half an hour later, as far as Lord Cardemore was concerned, Mr. Charles Cassin seemed to walk on water. The earl and his sister sat on either side of the sainted Mr. Cassin, conversing happily. From the rapid movements of her hands, Lily seemed to have a good deal to say, and for the first time in nearly a month Graydon was the only one in the room who couldn't understand a word she was saying. It made him feel slightly insane. Worse, it made him feel as if he were suddenly invisible. Lily had told him before what that felt like, and he'd sympathized with all the well-meaning sincerity of the ignorant. Now he knew firsthand what she'd meant.

Charles Cassin was a surprise. Graydon had expected him to be a much older man—grandfatherly, even, from the way in which Lily had described him. But in truth he was of an age with Graydon, nearing his thirties, a tall, quite handsome man. And striking, really, if Graydon would be honest about it, with straight black hair that swung back and forth with every movement of his head, framing a square, classically masculine face. His demeanor was calm and mannerly, his dress as plain and unremarkable as that of a Quaker, but on him, with his lean figure, quite appropriate. He spoke in a soft, even tone, smiling at Lily with obvious affection as they conversed. The close relationship between them was clear. Lily gazed at Charles Cassin with open adoration, and Graydon wondered, with a tightening sensation in his chest, if she was in love with the man.

"We've achieved much at the school," Charles Cassin was saying now, "due mostly to the great kindness of Lord Cardemore." He nodded toward the earl, who leaned back in his chair in a relaxed, indolent pose. "Without his patronage, I fear the Cassin Institute would have closed long ago."

"Nonsense," Cardemore replied. "What little I've done would have gone to waste without your vision and effort. You've made the institute what it is."

Charles Cassin flushed at the compliment, which Graydon hardly found extraordinary. Kind words issuing forth from the mouth of the Earl of Cardemore would shock anyone.

"I don't know that that's so, but it is very kind of you to say, my lord. I do feel that we've made strides toward gaining a better reputation for ourselves since Mr. Lockley ceased his denunciations of the sign-language method. It has been our hardest task, as you know—overcoming the old belief held by the scientific community in England that the sign language only encourages amorality among deaf-mutes. I was beginning to feel quite discouraged until a few months ago, when Mr. Lockley suddenly left us in peace. I don't know how it came about, but he has stopped all efforts to have the institute shut down, and, as a result, in the past three months alone we've taken on twelve new students whose families are fully supportive.''

Graydon didn't miss the feline smile on the Earl of Cardemore's face. Seeing it, he had a good idea about what had happened to silence Mr. Cassin's detractors. Whoever the unfortunate Mr. Lockley might be, Graydon felt a sudden kinship with him.

''And so you understand why it was so difficult for me to get away until now,'' Mr. Cassin went on. ''With so many new charges, it would have been quite impossible without Lord Cardemore's intervention in arranging for the two student teachers to come from France.''

Lily's hands fluttered in happy response. Cardemore nodded his agreement at what she was saying, and Mr. Cassin replied, ''As am I, my dear.''

Graydon crossed his legs and sighed. He felt as if he were a foreigner in a land where everyone spoke the language but him.

''You are very kind, my dear,'' Mr. Cassin answered after more flutterings. ''And Lord Cardemore has been so generous as to offer me lodgings, but I've already taken suitable rooms for the short time I'll be in London.''

Lily made a brief hand signal this time, one that Graydon at last, with a measure of relief, recognized.

How long?

She'd asked him that question enough for him to be familiar with it. *How long* would it be before the fireworks started at Vauxhall? *How long* would he be in the House of Lords before he would be free to take her for a drive in the park? *How long* would it take to get from Wilborn Place to Madame Tussaud's?

"Only two weeks, I fear," Mr. Cassin replied. "I'm promised to return to Wroxley at the end of a fortnight."

This news upset Lily so much that she began to protest, and took hold of one of his hands. Graydon unfolded his legs and sat up slowly, not entirely certain what it was he meant to do but thinking that if she kissed the man's hand again, Mr. Cassin would shortly afterward find himself much the worse for it.

"There's nothing to be done, Lily," Cardemore told her, sending a bemused glance in Graydon's direction. "I've already tried to convince Mr. Cassin to change his plans, but he'll not be moved. You'll recall that he's a formidable foe, I hope."

Lily dropped Mr. Cassin's hand and sat back with clear dissatisfaction, and Graydon let himself relax.

"I'm terribly sorry, Lady Lillian," said Mr. Cassin. "I do hope, however, that you'll spare a few hours for me one day? I should like to have a longer visit with you...."

Raised voices in the entryway brought his speech to a halt.

"What the devil is that commotion?" Cardemore muttered, standing. "Isabel must be home."

It was Lady Isabel, as Graydon saw a moment later, when the drawing room door opened to admit not only her, but Lady Margaret and Lord Daltry, as well.

"All men," declared Lady Isabel, shaking at Lord Daltry what was left of the lovely blue parasol she'd taken to the picnic. "*All* men are complete idiots! Uncle Aaron," she demanded, "you tell him!"

"My dear girl, I'm hardly likely to do so, am I?" Lord Cardemore surveyed his niece with a tsk. "What have you done now, Isabel? Tried to kill someone? Your dress is torn."

"Yes, I *did* try to kill someone." Lady Isabel said, clearly unconcerned by her state of dishabille. "Sir Seaborne Margate, to be precise. And I would have done it, too, if Lord Daltry hadn't interfered."

Lord Cardemore looked past his furious niece to Lady Margaret, who was standing calmly near the door. "We owe Lord Daltry a debt of gratitude, I perceive?"

"We do." Lady Margaret nodded. "Isabel was well on her way to doing herself an injury when Lord Daltry kindly intervened."

"Kindly!" Isabel stamped her foot. "Sir Margate wouldn't think so, I vow. The unmannerly beast threw him back into the Thames, didn't he?"

The unmannerly beast, Graydon surmised, must have been Matthew, who was presently standing to one side of Lady Margaret, looking fully out of sorts.

"I'm beginning to think she shouldn't be allowed out of the house," Lady Margaret continued in her usual calm, "especially if she's going to continue attacking peers of the realm in such a violent manner. She clearly doesn't understand what her unfortunate behavior will mean to both her and Lily here in London."

"I understand it very well," Isabel insisted hotly, "but if Sir Margate's behavior is what is considered acceptable in Town, then I should be more than pleased to go home to Somerset and never return! And I will *not* stand by while a member of my family is openly insulted! When Uncle Aaron hears what that disgusting man was saying about Lily and Lord Graydon, he'll—"

"Isabel!" Lady Margaret said sharply. "That's enough."

The relaxed amusement in Lord Cardemore's eyes died, replaced at once by a wariness that he turned upon Graydon. Neither Graydon nor Lily had said why they'd returned from the picnic early, and, in the face of Charles Cassin's visit, they'd not been asked.

"I see," Lord Cardemore murmured softly. After a silent moment, he smiled at his niece. "Indeed, we can discuss the matter later, my dear. Don't distress yourself."

Lady Margaret set a hand on her daughter's shoulder. "Lord Cardemore has a guest, Isabel, if you haven't yet noticed. Go and say hello to Mr. Cassin, and then take yourself upstairs to change your clothes.''

Lady Isabel squealed delightedly at the sight of Charles Cassin, and launched herself at the man.

"Charles!" she cried, hugging him. "How marvelous! Have you come for our ball? Oh, how wonderful! Lily, isn't it the most splendid thing! Now we won't care if the whole Town shuns us and doesn't attend our comeout, as long as Charles is there.''

Graydon was beginning to feel ill. Being in the presence of the wonderful Charles Cassin was almost more than a mere mortal could bear. Making his most polite excuses, he begged leave of the company and promised that he would see the ladies that evening at Lord and Lady Beauchamp's home for the musical supper to which they had all been invited. He didn't particularly want to attend, given the day he'd had, but it was his fault that both Lily and Lady Isabel were going to be the topics of much talk, and it was his duty to do what he could to ease matters. He bowed over the hands of the ladies, ignoring Lily when she squeezed his fingers and made a murmuring sound, as if she suddenly realized his displeasure and wanted to ease it. He assured Charles Cassin of his pleasure in meeting him and expressed the hope that they would meet again soon. He told his *dear friend* Cardemore that he looked forward to seeing him at White's in the near future—a safe bet, since Cardemore didn't frequent any of London's clubs— and was assured, in turn, that they would certainly see each other soon. He began to say something to Lord Daltry, but Matthew mumbled that he should be going, too, and followed Graydon out the door.

On the step, Daltry said, "What the devil was that all about? Who's that man Isabel was throwing herself at?''

"Lady Lillian's sign-language tutor." Graydon began to pull on his gloves. "You tossed Margate into the river again?''

"Had to. Isabel was hitting him with her parasol, and he

tried to defend himself. I couldn't have him accidentally hurting her, could I?''

"No," Graydon said with a sigh, "I suppose not. Where are you headed off to now?"

"White's," Daltry said with a shrug. "You?"

Graydon was tempted to go to his mistress, or to Frances, to any place where he would be cosseted and with every effort appeased. "Just home," he said. "I need to stick my head in a bowl of ice after weathering the divine Mr. Cassin."

Daltry's eyebrows rose. "Indeed?"

"Indeed. Tell me, please. Do I need to present myself at Seaborne's lodgings?"

"No. Lady Isabel was mistaken in the matter, as usual. Sea knew well enough to keep his mouth shut after you'd done with him. It was your dragging Lady Lily off that started rumors flowing. She heard them and mistakenly assumed Seaborne was the source. That's all."

"Gad," Graydon muttered, setting his hat upon his head. "I believe I'll need a bottle of brandy with that bowl of ice. Good day, Matthew."

He took himself home and gave both his butler and his valet instructions that he wasn't to be bothered by anyone, for any reason, until it was time for him to prepare for Lord and Lady Beauchamp's soiree.

Alone in his bedroom, he loosened his cravat, poured himself a large glass of brandy and sat down in front of a highly polished Italian desk to begin a ritual that had become familiar to him in the past weeks.

He unlocked the desk's top drawer and pulled it open. Inside were what seemed to him to be hundreds of little pieces of paper. On each one Lily had written a few words, sometimes a sentence or two; he could recall the exact moment when she had handed every single one of them to him. At random, he picked one.

I think it lovely of them to be so concerned about others!

How can you tease about them? I'm sure they're completely delightful.

His mother and sisters, he thought with a smile. They'd been riding in the park, talking about his family. And of St. Cathyrs. He hadn't meant to tell her anything about his ancestral estate, since through her own brother he had nearly lost it, but somehow, in their first week of acquaintance, he'd found himself talking of little else. She was too well practiced at being a listener for him to resist her gentle prodding. He'd told her St. Cathyrs's history, about the ancient castle there which seemed more welcoming a home than any other he possessed, about his plans for it and for his people.

Talk of St. Cathyrs led to talk of his mother and sisters, and she had laughed when he told her stories of surviving all of their well-meaning care. He closed his eyes now and leaned back in his chair, hearing it all over again. No one laughed the way Lily did. It was a more like a chuckle than laughter outright, deep and husky and disturbingly sensual. She had laughed and enchanted him and finally written him that beautifully scolding note for speaking so teasingly about his family.

With a sigh he set the note back among the others, then spent a few moments picking up a few more at random and recalling when she'd given them to him. At last, he began to go through his coat pockets, emptying them of that day's notes, unfolding and reading a few and finally dropping all of them into the drawer.

Sitting back, he took up his brandy and held it in both hands, contemplating the open desk drawer and all the tiny notes for a long, silent while.

It was impossible, he told himself, that he should have fallen in love with her. Lady Lillian Walford. He was simply enamored of her beauty and charm, and much taken with her manner and intelligence and wit. That was all, and nothing more.

And yet, what he'd felt this afternoon when she'd kissed

Charles Cassin's hand had felt quite distinctly like jealousy…and not the mild sort, either, but the maddened, firebreathing, murderous kind. Graydon didn't think he'd ever felt anything so utterly distressing in his life.

But it was impossible. He was the Earl of Graydon, and the woman he took for a wife must be able to act as hostess in their own homes as well as serve as his emissary in the homes of others. She must be able to run his numerous households with some measure of efficiency, and be capable of organizing the many social functions he would be obliged to hold as his standing in Parliament rose. And, aside from that, he was all but officially betrothed to Frances Hamilton. He couldn't honorably bow out of that no matter how badly he might wish it.

It was impossible. He shoved the desk drawer shut with one forcible movement, then leaned forward to cover his weary eyes with the palm of one hand. Completely, utterly impossible.

Chapter Eleven

In the darkest corner of his library, the Earl of Cardemore waited, watching as his niece and sister kissed his sister-in-law good-night. They had returned early from the musical supper they'd attended that evening, but, even so, he'd been prepared. It was his nature never to let anything run to chance, certainly not when it was something, or rather, someone, as important to him as Margaret Walford was.

The girls moved to kiss him next, and he received them in his dark corner, one after the other. They looked tired, and not especially happy. As he enfolded each girl in his embrace and returned their affectionate partings, he vowed that he would soon put an end to whatever it was that held them so low.

When the girls had left, Margaret began to pull the gloves from her hands, and said, "I believe I'll excuse myself as well. No sense in keeping you from your business."

She never seemed to look at him anymore. She certainly never remained in his company if she could avoid doing so. Not since the day when she had so regrettably seen him with his mistress. He wondered if it was simply the fact that he kept a woman that bothered her, or if it was because that same woman looked as nearly like her as he'd been able to manage. Perhaps the idea that he'd been pretending it was she to whom he made love disgusted her. Perhaps it made her sick with distress. The thought had tormented him for days now, just as her avoidance of him had, until he no longer cared whether she detested him or not. He could not be in the same dwelling without seeing her, wanting her—wanting matters to stand between them at least as they once had, so that they might be comfortable together, and sit together in the evenings as they had used to do before she'd seen him with his mistress.

"Stay," he murmured, slowly pushing from his corner toward her the distance of a few steps. "You said that you wanted to play a game of chess one night, and, as you can see, I've had Willis set the table near the fire." He nodded toward the place he spoke of. "If you're not too tired, of course."

Still she didn't look at him, but gazed at the chess table.

"I did see it," she admitted in a soft voice, "but I thought perhaps you had one of your business associates hiding away to play with you. You do tend to conduct your important matters late in the night." With care, she laid her silk wrap over the back of a nearby chair, along with her gloves. "I'm not too tired."

He pulled out a chair for her, and as he pushed her into place, asked, "May I pour you something to drink? I have your favorite Spanish sherry here." He opened a cabinet and drew a crystal decanter out, along with a small glass. "There is also a French champagne that I recall you used to enjoy." He glanced at her. "I had Willis put it in ice in case you wish me to call for it."

Looking at him curiously, she gave a slight nod. "The sherry will suffice, thank you. It is kind of you to be so thoughtful of my pleasure, Aaron."

It was the first time she'd called him by his Christian name since that awful day in Bond Street. He drew in a slow breath and with an effort steadied the slight shaking of his hand as he poured the sherry.

"Say that after I've beaten you soundly at chess, mad-am." He handed her the glass and then took his own seat opposite. "Shall we make a wager?"

She chuckled and sat back in her chair, regarding him over the rim of her glass. "I should have known you'd have something in mind. Scoundrel. What is it to be, then? Shall I have to be polite to all of your business associates?"

He nearly laughed at that. She'd met one or two of his more unsavory employees in passing, and had openly expressed her distrust of them.

"Nothing so dire, I promise," he assured her now. "The winner may choose his or her prize at the end of the game."

"Aaron," she began, eyeing him with suspicion. "What is it that you want?"

Only to be with you, he thought silently. *To have an hour with you here, each night for the remainder of your time. Nothing more. Would you hate that so very much?* But the words sounded so maudlin and foolish that he couldn't bring himself to say them aloud. She would laugh if he did, but after the game, if he won, she would be too honorable to deny his request, or to laugh at it.

"I'll leave it for a surprise," he said. "If I win, that is. I'll not even ask what you'll want if you win. I trust you completely to be fair, you see."

"Very well." She set her glass aside. "Let's begin, then."

The first few minutes passed in silence as they made their initial moves, before Cardemore asked, "Your evening at the Beauchamps' passed well, I gather?"

"You don't gather anything of the sort, Aaron. Please don't jest. It was perfectly awful. Everyone staring at the girls, and whispering. I wanted to stand upon a chair and give them all a scolding, save that it would have made the matter worse."

"Nonsense," he murmured, contemplating the board. "Your father, the duke, may not come to Town often, but he commands enough respect in this country to keep his only daughter from being censured for any reason. You could probably stand upon your head in Pall Mall in the middle of the day and never hear a word of protest. Was Lord Graydon present at this fiasco?''

"Yes. He brought Miss Hamilton with him. I quite like that young man, but at just this moment I would gladly wring the ears from his head.''

"Indeed? And what did Lord Graydon do to merit such violent feelings?''

Lady Margaret glanced up at him. "His manners were exact, and he treated Lily with distinct, and distant, courtesy. This, after he's made her fall in love with him. And don't look at me like that, Aaron. You know very well that she's developed a very strong *tendre* for him. After spending nearly every day with the man for the past month, why should she not do so? And although I doubt she's given herself leave to dream that anything more might come of it, she has grown to think of him as a dear friend. Tonight he treated her as if she were a complete stranger, and you saw for yourself what that did to her.''

"She did appear rather despondent,'' Cardemore admitted. "She and Isabel, both. Never tell me Lord Daltry behaved as badly?''

"Worse,'' she told him. "He didn't attend at all.''

"Oh, dear.''

"Yes, Isabel was quite downcast. It's the first night he hasn't haunted her since Almack's. She was torn between worrying over his health and wanting to commit murder upon his person.''

"Poor Isabel,'' Cardemore said, adding, almost as an afterthought, "And poor Daltry. What a pair they make. Can you quite like it, Margaret?''

"Oh, I should love the boy for a son-in-law,'' she said, "but I do wish they didn't have to court in quite so energetic a fashion. I don't know that either of them will survive the thing long enough to walk down an aisle.''

Cardemore chuckled. "It makes me feel so old, I vow, to see Isabel and Lily wooed. Can it be that they were little girls such a short time ago? Or have I missed so much being gone from Cardemore Hall these past five years?''

She gazed at him with such sudden and open affection that he had to lower his gaze at once. ''You've missed much,'' she told him. ''They were but girls when you left, and now they've grown into young ladies. And such lovely young ladies they are. We did a fine job with them, Aaron.''

''You did, rather.''

''No, it was both of us. You were a better father to Isabel than George ever was or wanted to be. I won't even speak of how good you've been to Lily.''

He thought of the plans he'd made for his sister, of the shadows and deceit behind them. If Margaret ever knew the truth, she would probably never speak to him again.

''Not as good as I should have been,'' he murmured, moving one of his pawns forward. ''Not as good as I wish I had been.''

''We won't speak of it,'' she returned just as quietly, and he knew that she understood his discomfort. ''I am worried about Lily, though.''

''You needn't be. Whatever malaise Lord Graydon may be complaining of, it will soon be remedied, I assure you.''

''I don't like the sound of that.'' She picked up a knight and placed it with care. ''You're not to interfere, Aaron. I want your promise.''

''Certainly,'' he lied. ''You've nothing to worry over. I shall be as meek and obedient as a lamb.'' He removed the knight with his bishop, and grinned as he placed the piece on his side.

''Meek and obedient aren't words that I associate with you, my lord. I want you to leave Lord Graydon in peace. He's done nothing wrong, and indeed, I think he believed that he was being helpful to Lily this night. And perhaps he was. He understands these matters far better than Lily or I do. Unfortunately, she doesn't care as much for what society thinks as she does for his company. She's come to rely upon him, you know.''

"I know," Cardemore replied quietly, sending a castle forward three squares in an effort to corner her queen.

"If it hadn't been for Miss Hamilton, the night would have passed as a full loss. She's quite the bravest young lady I've ever had the occasion to meet.''

That got his attention, and he lifted his head. ''Miss Hamilton? More so than Isabel? I never should have thought any young lady could be braver than Isabel Walford. She did beat Sir Margate about the head with a parasol, after all.''

"Even so. Miss Hamilton was a sight to behold. She gave a reformative speech to a group of young women who were gossiping about Lily that would equal anything delivered by Hannah More. She nearly had them reduced to tears by the time she was done, I vow, and they were fully repentant for their cruelties, even going so far as to beg Lily's forgiveness.'' With an elegant move her queen found safety. ''Mr. Cassin was quite taken, I fear.''

''Was he?'' Cardemore was beginning to feel trapped. She was too good at this game. ''I wondered if he would find anything to amuse him at such a fine gathering. He looked none too pleased when I asked him to serve as your escort this evening.''

"He was, and he did. And Miss Hamilton was equally taken. They took supper together. She found his work with deaf-mutes fascinating, and he quite admired her dedication to the Orphan Relief Fund. I only know this because Lily and Lord Graydon had to sit through the whole thing, as they all four shared a table.''

"Gad," he muttered. "I apologize for accepting the invitation for you. If I'd known it would turn into such a maudlin event, I would have thrown the thing into the fire the moment it arrived.'' He sent a bishop halfway across the board to threaten her queen.

"The sooner we leave London, the better." Her queen skipped out of his range.

"You don't regret coming, do you, Margaret?"

"I never wanted to come in the first place, as you know. Check." Her castle slid to a stop on the row where his king resided. "But despite my fears for Lily, I've come to think that the time here has been good for them both. However, I do believe it might be best if we left before Lily's heart becomes more involved than it already has. As it is, she's going to suffer for a good long while once we've returned to Somerset. One's first true love is always the hardest to recover from."

He certainly didn't want to hear about *her* first love. With a frown he moved his king forward, out of her castle's aim. "But will Lily agree to returning home early? That is more to the point."

"I don't believe she will," Margaret murmured, tapping her chin with the tip of one finger. "Both she and Isabel will want to stay until the bitter end, barring any catastrophes. Such as Lord Graydon becoming officially betrothed to Miss Hamilton or Lord Daltry losing all interest in Isabel. Otherwise, I believe you're saddled with us, Aaron. And this makes checkmate." She slid her queen four squares to the right and grinned at him in a manner that he recognized all too well.

He leaned forward to examine the board more closely, then sat back with a groaning sigh.

"Indeed it is." He wrestled down his disappointment with an iron will. "When will I learn never to game with you, Margaret? Very well, what do you desire as a prize? A new dress? Something for one of the girls?"

"Well," she said thoughtfully, picking up her sherry glass and sipping from it. "You said that you trusted me to be fair. I suppose asking you to come back to live with us at Cardemore Hall would rather stretch that standard?"

"Rather," he said dryly.

"I thought it might be so. Then, perhaps—" she hesi-

tated "—a dance will suffice. In your ballroom, of course.
We can't have a proper dance in here, with the furniture in
the way."

"A dance," he repeated tonelessly. "In my ballroom."

"Yes."

"At Lily's and Isabel's comeout ball."

She shook her head. "No, tonight. Now."

He was afraid that was what she'd meant. He had never
held her in his arms before, save for those brief, proper
moments when they had observed greetings and partings.
He had never been so foolish as to attempt anything further.

"It's not lit," he said, his facile brain racing for any
excuse to keep from making a complete and utter fool of
himself. "And we have no music."

She slid her chair back and stood. "I don't mind about
the dark. Surely we can take a pair of candles with us. And
I shall hum a tune. Aaron—" she gave him a half smile
"—never say that you're afraid to dance with me."

He was. Bone-shakingly afraid. But it was true: he would
never say so. Instead he made a face of impatience and slid
his own chair back. "Certainly not. But the servants will
be bound to think we've both gone mad. Very well, my
lady. If you wish to waste a perfectly good chance at ob-
taining your heart's desire on a foolish dance, I shall make
no objection." He moved past her to open the library door.
"And if I should step on your toes, I hope you will recall
that it has been a long while since I've attempted anything
quite so inane. In fact, I believe I was all of ten at the
time."

Chuckling, she took up a candlestick and lit it from a
nearby lamp. Striding past him into the hallway, she said,
"If you step on my toes, my lord, you will most likely
break them, and then you'll be the one who'll have to play
chaperon to Lily and Isabel."

"Ahem," he said. "I understand perfectly."

It had been a number of years since anyone had danced
in the ballroom at Wilborn Place. His mother had once held

grand events here, his grandmother, an aristocrat down to her toes, had held even grander ones. When it was alight and filled with people and music, as it would be next week for the ball, it was an extraordinarily beautiful room, but now, empty save for the dust-covered instruments pushed aside to one corner, and silent, its aspect was merely gloomy. Cardemore stood gazing about him, looking anything but what he felt, which was doomed and frantic.

"Margaret, are you certain this is what you want?" His tone was polite, almost disinterestedly so. "This hardly seems a worthwhile prize for your win. I noticed a sapphire bracelet at Rundell and Bridges last week that I'd far rather see you have. At least it would be of some value."

"If you liked it so well," she said, walking across the room to set the candlestick upon the covered pianoforte, "then perhaps you should give it to your mistress, rather than to a mere sister-in-law."

Oh, *gad.* She might as well have poleaxed him. "Perhaps I shall," he returned gruffly.

She inspected the dust cover on the pianoforte minutely, smoothing one hand lightly over it. "Have you ever danced with her? Your mistress?"

"No."

"Then give her the bracelet with my blessing." She turned. "Well, sir. Are you ready to make good on our wager?"

He nodded. "What is it to be? A country dance? A waltz?"

"A waltz, if you please."

"I've only seen it done," he said, setting what seemed to him like the hugest, ugliest hand in God's earth on her tiny waist. "You must forgive me if it is not very exact." He held his other hand up, waiting, beginning to feel breathless too soon and horrified that she might realize it. She set her gloveless hand in his and he thought, with brief amazement, that she seemed to be breathing rather deeply, too.

"I won't care if it isn't exact, Aaron. Shall I hum a tune?"

"Please. Slowly, if you will, or I may never have the nerve to get us started moving."

She began to hum a familiar waltz tune and, after a few seconds, he pulled her into motion, slowly and with care, holding her as distant from himself as he possibly could. But it wasn't far enough. He tried to concentrate on the steps, on how he thought the dance should progress, but all that his senses could register were her scent, and her warmth, and her deep, alluring, feminine voice. She was gazing at him full in the face and he wouldn't allow himself the weakness of looking away.

His body had begun to respond and harden the moment he had realized that they would dance, that he would touch and perhaps even hold her. His was not, as other better gentlemen might aspire to, a merely romantic love. He loved her in the way that a man loved his woman, and with that love came want, and a strong, abiding desire. He knew, as well as he knew anything, that he would love and want her with the same driving passion when they had both turned old and gray. If he had loved her any less—even a little less—she would have long since been his. But *this* love, as he had discovered to his torment, was the sort that wouldn't let a man treat his woman so lightly. She must be kept safe and well, never harmed by the unwanted attentions of a man whose face and form sent young children scurrying and whose past was filled with darkness and violence.

She pressed closer, forcing herself nearer despite his efforts to hold her back. The humming had grown uneven, like her breathing.

"Margaret," he murmured, trying to warn her.

But she either didn't hear him or didn't take note. She kept on humming, gazing at him, moving with him in rhythm to the tune.

He didn't know how long it was that they danced, or

when it was that she finally stopped humming. They were simply moving together slowly in an indistinct circle, nearer and nearer until her body was pressed fully against his own. She had to feel what she was doing to him, how very much he wanted her. But still she held his gaze, so close now that he could feel the warmth of her breath through her parted lips. When he lowered his mouth to hers he told himself that he wouldn't care if she slapped him or shoved him away in disgust. She couldn't consign him to a greater Hell than he already existed in, having her so near again, day after day, wanting her and knowing that he could never have her.

Her lips were soft and warm, damp against his own; he had spent years wanting to kiss her, and the reality far outweighed his imaginings. He felt slightly stunned by the fact that she was in his arms, that he was kissing her. Gently he moved his mouth, and with something akin to pure wonder felt her murmuring response. Her cool hand moved up to stroke the side of his face, once, and then she pressed against him as if she wanted this, and him. When he touched her with his tongue she opened to him, gripped him more tightly, and every particle of sense that he possessed fled.

He took her mouth the way he had always wanted to: hungrily, ravenously, branding her taste and scent and feel upon himself for all eternity. With one hand he held the back of her head captive, while the other slid downward, memorizing the delicate bow of her back, and downward still to the feminine curve of her hips, and lower still to cup her intimately against him. She moaned into his mouth, and he made an answering sound.

It was impossible to get close enough. Her hands roamed his back and shoulders, touching his hair and face with a desperation that matched his own, and she broke their kiss only to say his name, rushed and pleadingly.

"Yes," he said, lifting her in his arms so suddenly that she made a small sound of surprise. He laid her down carefully on the wooden floor, and her arms reached up for him as he came down half on top of her, with his leg pushed between both of hers even as his hand pulled her skirt up to her thighs.

I love you, he thought as he kissed her again, tugging at the bodice of her gown until it slid down one arm. He wanted to tell her out loud, to make her understand why this was so right, that she meant everything to him, more than his own life. But he would show her. He would show her more than words could ever say, and then, when he was deep inside of her, when they were one, he would tell her. His hand had bared her breast to the caresses of his lips and tongue, and she moved beneath him restlessly, stroking his hair and arching upward.

"Aaron," she murmured. "Oh, Aaron."

He kissed her mouth tenderly, then gazed into her eyes as his hand found its way beneath her raised skirts.

"Margaret," he whispered.

He loved her. So deeply that he didn't think he would ever know the end of it. He would never hurt her, or bring harm upon her, or let another do so. He would always keep her safe and loved.

She made a gasping sound as he touched her intimately, through the cloth of her pantalettes, and her eyelids closed with pleasure. He lowered his head again to kiss her, and then, suddenly, he stopped.

Safe and loved. He would never hurt her.

He closed his eyes against the words, willing them away, but they would not go. Safe. And loved. He would *never* hurt her.

He pulled his hand out from beneath her skirt, away from her warmth, and heard her draw in a sharp breath.

"Aaron?" Her voice was trembling and unsteady.

Shaking his head, he pushed up and away, rolling until he lay on his back. He covered his eyes with the back of one hand and decided that death would surely be better than this. He was a *fool.* He should take her and have done with it. She wanted him. She'd given him every evidence of that fact.

But she didn't love him. She couldn't. It was impossible. Perhaps, for some bizarre and misguided reason, she might want him, but that would be the most of it. She was a woman with needs, and passionate as well; he was a handy and familiar source of relief. That was all. Need, and nothing more.

"Aaron?" she said again, reaching out a shaking hand to touch him. "Please, don't. Please. I don't want you to stop."

He drew in a long, taut breath before saying, "I want to." And then, with more control, "Or I don't want to, rather. Not with you." He dropped his hand from his eyes and rested it against the place where his heart was pounding so hard and rapidly that it actually ached. "Not with you, Margaret."

She lay still beside him for the space of perhaps ten seconds before he heard her pulling up the sleeve of her gown.

"You'll go to your mistress, I suppose."

"Yes." It was the simple truth. He was in very great need, and wanted it eased.

With a fluid movement she sat up and struck his shoulder with a fist, so suddenly that he didn't have a chance to prepare for it.

"Margaret."

"*Damn* you, Aaron." She loomed over him, her hair falling loose from its arrangement, down to her shoulders, and her eyes shining with tears. "Go to her then! Go and take your pleasure of your whore, with my blessing!" She gathered her skirts and rose from the floor with something less than her usual grace.

"Margaret," he tried again, unsure of what he could even say to her.

But she walked away without another word or look, shutting the door behind her with loud finality, and left him lying there on his ballroom floor, alone.

Chapter Twelve

"He'll be here, Lily. Please don't fret so. The House of Lords can't hold him forever. He was one of the first to accept his invitation, and he *will* be here."

I suppose you're right, Lily signed to Isabel quickly before turning to smile at the next person who went through the receiving line.

"And he did ask if he could lead you out in the first dance, did he not?" Isabel whispered when she could. "The minuet?"

Yes, Lily answered with a nod. *And he asked for the first waltz, as well.* She gave her hand to a gentleman who bowed over it, and made her best curtsy, just as she had been doing for the past hour and more.

"Then he certainly is coming, despite the fact that he wasn't able to attend dinner," Isabel insisted after she made her best curtsy as well. "Will this line of people never end? I'm sure we didn't invite half so many."

The words were tartly spoken, but Lily heard the satisfaction behind them. Somehow, by some miracle, their comeout ball was a success. So many people had already arrived that there was going to be the most dreadful squeeze, which, as Aunt Margaret had told her, was what every London hostess hoped and prayed for when she gave a party. But her aunt, standing at the head of the receiving

line in her place as hostess, didn't look as if she was glad
for the impressive turnout. Aunt Margaret only looked
rather weary and solemn, as she had done for most of the
past week, despite the fact that she was exceedingly beautiful in the elegant, emerald green gown she wore. Aaron
stood next in line, handsome in his black evening dress,
Lily thought, but he, too, looked somewhat grim and stiff.
She tried to tell herself that it was because he hated such
social events, and hated even more being on display to
people whom he avoided, in general, like the plague. But
it wasn't that. Not at all.

Something had clearly happened between Aunt Margaret
and Aaron—something extremely disagreeable. For the past
week they had acted like perfect strangers, as if they had
little more than a few civil words to say to each other whenever they met. And usually they stayed as far apart as possible. Gone were the smiles and teasing manner they had
always shared, and the easiness that had forever existed
between them.

If only Graydon would come. He would know the way
to ease her mind. She had seen little of him during the past
week, and when she had he'd been polite and distant,
friendly but not overly so, and certainly not as they had
been before. But she had realized what that was for. He
was merely trying, in what he considered the best possible
manner, to ease her fall from grace following the disastrous
picnic at Greenwich. The only trouble was that there hadn't
been any fall from grace. Sir Margate had spent three days
making abject public apologies for his wretched behavior,
and then he had suddenly vanished. Not even his friends
seemed to know where he'd gone to. Even so, Graydon
continued to act coolly, and Lily was beginning to despair.

Twenty minutes later, the house had filled nearly to overflowing and the receiving line had begun to thin.

"I believe it is time for us to join our guests," Aunt
Margaret stated, signaling for Willis to assume the greeting
of any others who might arrive.

Shouldn't we wait a few minutes more? Lily asked.

Aunt Margaret shook her head firmly. "Willis will announce those guests who prefer to arrive fashionably late.
But we cannot leave those who have already arrived to wait
much longer. And the dancing must begin soon or the supper will be unpardonably late. If Lord Graydon has not yet
arrived, your brother may lead you out, which is quite acceptable."

Lily's heart sank, and she noticed that Aaron, too, looked
rather dismal at the prospect, but she dutifully fell into step
beside Isabel as Aaron offered Aunt Margaret his arm and
led her into the ballroom.

Their guests looked anything but impatient. The house
was beautifully decorated in a theme of flowers and fresh
greenery, windows had been opened to let in the blissfully
temperate night air and, in the room set aside for refresh-
ments, the multitude of additional servants Aaron had sent
to Cardemore Hall for had busily been pouring not only
tea, lemonade, punch and ratafia, but also fine Spanish port
and sherry and French wines and champagne. Card games
had been set up in the library, waiting only for the ball to
formally begin for eager players to take their seats. The
musicians, seated on a dais framed with velvet curtains of
dark blue and gold, had been playing music since before
the first guests had arrived. The atmosphere was one of
pleased anticipation, perhaps even of approval. People
smiled, bowed and curtsied, parting to make way for Aaron
and Aunt Margaret. Lily felt Isabel grasp her hand, squeezing for a brief, reassuring moment before releasing it.

They had only just reached the dais when Lily heard the
murmuring behind her, and then a hush. She assumed it
was a silence that anticipated the beginning of the dancing,
and therefore the formal beginning of the ball, but when
she sent a swift glance back toward the ballroom doors she
saw the real cause, and then she couldn't pull her gaze
away.

He was magnificent, standing alone, clothed in stark

black and white evening dress that made his blond hair and blue eyes stand out quite vividly. He wasn't simply Lord Graydon tonight, but the Earl of Graydon, a person of great moment, not to be disdained or reckoned with, but a man, every inch of him, who demanded respect and appreciation.

Every eye was upon him as he strolled in a relaxed and easy manner toward Lily, while she, with her heart pounding loudly in her ears, watched him come. He was so far superior to every other man there that the rest of them seemed not to exist while he held this impromptu court.

"The minuet," she heard Aunt Margaret instruct the head musician, and from the corner of one eye she saw Lord Daltry disengage himself from the crowd of onlookers to approach Isabel. And all the while Lord Graydon advanced, not stopping until he was directly in front of her. He looked away only to make a formal bow to Aunt Margaret, and to greet Aaron, and then he turned back to Lily and, as the music began, held out his arm.

"Lady Lillian, I believe the honor of this dance is mine?"

She nodded once and spoke to him. "Y-hes, mah l-hord."

His eyes came alight at that, and he pulled her forward, out into the middle of the ballroom floor, near where Lord Daltry had taken Isabel. No other couples would join the floor until some minutes later, when Aunt Margaret invited one or two others to begin, after which a flood of dancers would crowd them.

"You're very beautiful tonight, Lady Lillian," he murmured intently as he drew her around to face him, so low that only she could hear. "And I count myself the luckiest man in all of London to be the one to lead you out in this dance."

Then, holding both her hand and her gaze, he slowly, and with great elegance, began the courtly dance.

Strolling through the Earl of Cardemore's gardens with Lily on his arm, Graydon felt a sense of a seldom known unreality. It seemed impossible that this beautiful, well-kept, lantern-lit fairyland belonged to the house he had first visited so long ago, on the night when Cardemore had blackmailed him.

He had realized, during his many visits to the home when he had arrived to collect Lily and Lady Isabel for one of their outings, that Wilborn Place was not quite so dark and dismal as he had originally believed, although that was the manner in which Cardemore preferred to keep it. There was clear evidence of its being a grand and elegant dwelling—he had long since known that it was one of London's older aristocratic homes—but the scope had been completely unimagined until tonight, when he had entered to find every room thrown open, ablaze with light and beauty and packed to the rafters with the most prominent members of the ton. There was little more that the thirteenth Earl of Cardemore could do to satisfy the rampant curiosity about him and his usually dark, ominous ancestral home than to hold that same home, and himself, open for inspection. Graydon hoped, for Lily's sake, that the effort would prove successful.

"Have you enjoyed the evening, Lily?" He patted the hand she held upon his arm and smiled at her. "It has been a great success. I doubt any other young lady this season can boast of such a squeeze for her comeout as you and Isabel shall be able to do. It's quite a coup."

She chuckled in the deep, husky manner that never failed to inspire wicked thoughts in his lately unmanageable brain. Then she set her free hand to her forehead and made an exaggerated wiping motion, along with a face that looked fully relieved.

He laughed. "Glad to have it nearly over, are you? I understand. It must have been quite an ordeal for both you and Isabel, just as it seems to be for every young lady. But you've come through with flying colors. Lady Margaret is to be commended."

Several other couples were strolling along the myriad garden paths, taking a short rest from the ongoing dancing and enjoying the cool, pleasant air, and Graydon inclined his head in silent greeting as they passed one of them. Sitting on a bench not too far away, near a profusion of roses, he saw Frances and Mr. Charles Cassin involved in deep conversation, their heads inclined toward each other and their expressions as serious as if they were taking on all of the world's troubles. He wondered, briefly, what it was that they were talking about, and if he should work up some measure of jealousy, just as he had striven to do during the past week as Frances had so glowingly and constantly spoken of the admirable Mr. Cassin and his good work. But jealousy was impossible. Relief was what he felt, and a certain measure of gratitude that Frances was being attentively taken care of. Dismissing them from his mind, he returned his attention to the woman beside him.

She was especially lovely tonight. Her gown, like the others Lady Margaret had so wisely chosen for her, was simple and proper, yet deceptively so. The color was white, as a comeout gown should be, but it was made ethereal by an airy netting of shimmering silver. Her white-blond hair was swept up in a striking arrangement and fixed with a pretty silver circlet ornamented with silver and white flowers. On her wrist hung one of her little note cases—silver, this time, and quite delicate and fine, and about her neck was a single strand of exquisite pearls. Otherwise she was bare of adornments, but she hardly needed any. Her beauty was such that artificial ornamentation would only prove distracting.

He'd kept away from Lillian Walford as much as he could since the picnic in Greenwich, and on those rare occasions when they had met, he'd been acceptably polite and congenial. It was a conscious effort on his part, not only to stop rumors, but to temper the distressing turn his feelings for her had taken. He'd also made a concerted effort to reestablish his relationship with Frances, taking her to the theater and out riding in the park. She was, as always, a sweet and amiable companion, but for the first time since he'd known her, Graydon hadn't found himself thinking of her as his future bride.

But he was determined to do better, to completely banish Lily from his mind. It had to be done for the best of all those involved. His own wants and wishes had no place in the matter. To be selfish now would be not only unpardonable, but dishonorable, as well.

The particular path they were on was well lit, as were most of them, but Lily touched his arm when they neared one that was much less so, and pulled him in that direction. He should have resisted the temptation, he knew, for if anyone discovered that they had gone off alone together on a darkened path, rumors would begin to fly again, and he couldn't allow that, for both her sake and his.

But she tucked her hand beneath his arm and tugged, and looked at him with such exasperation that he smiled and gave way. Soon he understood why she had chosen that particular path. It led to a delightful alcove, set with a pretty, burbling fountain and an arbor of wisteria. Beneath the arbor was a bench, and it was to this that Lily led him, releasing his arm and sitting down with an audible sigh.

"Are you feeling weary, Lily?" He sat beside her.

She leaned her head back, closed her eyes and nodded.

"So mhuch w-hork," she said. "Ah'm so gl-had it's ahl-mhost oh-ver." She opened her eyes to gaze at him. "Th-hank you for coh-mhing toh-night."

"Where else would I be?" he asked. "I want this to be the most memorable night of your life. The most wonderful, just as you desired it to be. Whatever you want, whatever you wish, only tell me, and I shall do it, if I can." He lifted her gloved hand and kissed it.

An expression of unhappiness crossed her lovely features, and he murmured, "What troubles you so, Lily? Is it the foolishness that I gave you that afternoon after Greenwich? The memory has haunted me, and I deeply regret my behavior. I meant to apologize when we arrived here that very day, but with Mr. Cassin having only just arrived..."

She shook her head. "Oh, n-ho. N-hot that. Ah d-hon't th-hink of it. It's all of th-his—" she pulled her hand free of his light clasp and waved it into the air, toward the noise of the ball "—and A-hant Mah-gret and Ah-rhon." She pressed the same hand against her head, as if it ached. "Ah j-hust d-hon't unnerst-hand...."

"That's enough," he said quietly, possessing her hand and pushing it into her lap, holding it there. It was, he knew, painful for her to speak for very long, and her voice had taken on the grittiness that signaled such pain. "Let's take matters one at a time. And you must write, for that is less tiring for you than charades, certainly than speaking. There's enough light, I believe, for you to write and for me to read. Tell me first, then, about the ball."

She seemed relieved to be asked to write, and sat forward and flipped open the silver case at her wrist.

Why have so many people come tonight? It's impossible that it should be only because of Isabel and me. I know you will speak the truth.

He would, he thought. At least as far as he knew it, and as far as he could without hurting her.

"You're too modest if you think that a great many of those who came tonight did not do so for your benefit, also for Lady Isabel's," he said, folding the note and slipping it into an inner pocket. "But there are those, I admit, who merely came to see and be seen. You're aware, of course, that your family is among the oldest recorded in the peerage, and therefore far above even many of those who possess greater titles. And there has always been a great deal of curiosity about the thirteenth Earl of Cardemore, as he's not socially active. As well, this magnificent home hasn't been opened for viewing in many years. The opportunity to see both it and him could not be passed by. Indeed, those who attend tonight count themselves fully blessed, for little else will be spoken of for the next week, and they'll be able to say that they were here and saw the event firsthand. I daresay only a personal invitation to Carlton House would have been a more welcomed boon than the invitation to attend your comeout ball.''

The answer clearly relieved her; her smile and self-conscious laughter told him that. He wished that he could have told her the entire truth, that her brother's power had coerced some of their guests to be in attendance, particularly those, Graydon guessed, who were of the higher reaches of the peerage. He had counted, among the several dukes and marquesses in the crowd, two of the royal dukes, the Prince Regent's own brothers, happily imbibing Cardemore's excellent spirits in the refreshment room. One of them had even gone so far as to dance with Lily earlier, although he had accomplished the thing without once looking at her face or saying a word to her.

"Now," he said, unconsciously setting his arm behind her as he leaned nearer, "what's troubling you about Lady Margaret and the earl? Does he not like the fact that half the eligible men in London are slavering over her? Lord Kimball has made his intentions very clear, has he not?''

He has, the odious man, Lilly wrote. *But that's not the trouble. It's them.* She underlined *them* twice. *Aaron and Aunt Margaret. Something has happened.*

"Something?" He had an idea of what she meant. It couldn't have been coincidence that Cardemore kept a mistress who looked so much like his sister-in-law. "You mean, something of a personal nature?"

With greater agitation, she wrote, *I don't know! They're hardly speaking, and they avoid each other as often as they can. What can the matter be? I've asked, but they deny that anything is wrong.*

"Perhaps that's so, my dear," he said gently, wanting to soothe her. "Perhaps they've merely been overtaxed of late. Would it be so strange in the midst of the rigors of the season? Your Aunt Margaret has had not one, but two young ladies to chaperon, as well as to launch. And your brother is a busy man, with hands not only in Parliament but in commerce and the monarchy as well. It's said that the Earl of Cardemore wields nearly as much power in England as the Prince Regent, and outside of England much more." Although certainly, he added silently, power of a far different, and darker, sort. "I should think that most exhausting, were I in his place."

She shook her head disconsolately.

"If there is more to their behavior than that, then there is nothing you can do save to leave them in peace and give them time. Any interference would only complicate the situation. You must see the truth of that."

With a weary sigh, she leaned back and let her head fall against his arm.

"Ah th-hink Ah-rhon lohves her."

"Do you?" Graydon asked softly, running one finger lightly over the curve of her cheek. He had long since ceased to experience the small shock that surprised him whenever he gazed directly into the pure beauty of her face. His feelings had progressed rather beyond the reach of the elemental. But he allowed himself the pleasure her features gave, and knew, with a calm certainty, that if she had been his, that pleasure would never fade or change, regardless of how time or illness or accident might possibly alter her. "That may be so. Indeed, I should think that a great many men have fallen in love with Lady Margaret. She's not only quite beautiful, but a fine and well-bred lady as well. And your brother is only human, after all. But if it is so, Lily, then you must leave him, and your aunt, in peace. Love is a strictly personal matter, not to be invaded or treated lightly by outsiders. One day, when you have experienced the emotion firsthand, you'll understand what I mean. Until then, you mustn't dabble in things unknown.

"Now, my good lady—" he set a finger to her lips when she tried to speak "—you must answer a question. If I were to kiss you, would you find it quite offensive?"

Her eyes widened in what he hoped was disbelief, rather than disgust. He had had the honor of her first waltz, of the first dance at her comeout ball, and he would forever hold the memories dear. He wanted one more first, and then he would come away from his summer with her, if not entirely glad, holding at least a measure of contentment.

"It is the night of your comeout, Lily," he murmured. "I only wish to kiss you, as a young lady should be kissed on such a night."

She blinked twice rapidly, swallowed and whispered, "Ess," so softly that it sounded more like a trembling hiss than a word.

He lowered his head and kissed her. It was a brief meeting of mouths, almost, although not quite, as innocent as the manner in which cousins might greet, and just exactly what he had meant it to be. Something sweet and gentle for them both to remember. But for all that, and for all that Graydon told himself that, he still felt fully amazed at the depth of the experience. It wasn't a bolt out of the heavens or a light-headed feeling or anything like he had imagined it would be. It was altogether different. He felt calm and sure in a way that he had never before known, as if he had suddenly left behind every last vestige of his youth and become a man complete. There were no questions now, no fears. This was exactly as things should be.

She must have felt something similar, for her eyes held a look of wonder that he had not seen in them before. She reached up to touch his face, tentatively, and said his name with a wonder that matched her expression.

"An-non-nee."

It was the first time she had ever spoken it. He had never been particularly enamored of his Christian name, but coming from her lips, it sounded like the most beautiful word on earth.

Somehow his mouth was on hers again, and her arms had gone about his neck, and he had pulled her nearly onto his lap. And he discovered, as he reveled in this first intimate knowledge of her, that he had been premature in his assumption that the lightning wouldn't strike. Holding her, learning the softness of the mouth that had tantalized him for so long, tasting her sweetness and knowing her eager response, made him feel as if the top of his head had blown off. A dim, remnant particle of sense warned him that there was danger; they were in her brother's garden, in the midst of a ball, undergoing a public embrace that would shock even the most liberal-minded members of the ton.

"No," he murmured as he pulled away, so dazed that he couldn't manage to untangle the arms they had about each other. "No, Lily."

She gave him a contented, slumberous look; when he attempted to lift her from his lap and seat her on the bench she made a husky, protesting sound that made him shiver with want.

"No," he repeated firmly, unlacing her hands from about his neck. "Good Lord." He released a shaking breath. "We're surrounded by people. It would be disastrous if we'd been seen. We should return to the house." He stood, pulling her to her feet, and realized that, for some unfathomable reason, she was angry. "Lily, I didn't mean for this to happen, and I apologize. No, don't look away." He tilted her chin upward until their eyes met, although she resisted him. "There's nothing for you to be ashamed of. Nothing."

Ashamed? Lily fell still, arrested by his words. She wasn't ashamed. She was *angry*, just as any woman might who'd been told by the man she loved that it would be disastrous to be caught kissing her. The moment he'd said it she'd felt a perfect fool. Of course he wouldn't wish to be caught with her, for then rumors would begin to fly again, and he, being an honorable man, would probably feel compelled to ask for her hand in marriage. It would be a fate worse than death for him or any other fine gentleman. She *knew* that already. He didn't need to say it aloud and ruin what had been the most perfect moment of her life.

She tried to turn away, but he took her by the shoulders and held her fast.

"Don't blame me for this." His voice was intent, harsh. She'd never heard him speak in such a manner before. "God alone knows how I would change matters if I could, but it's impossible. Impossible, Lily. Understand what it is that I say. Too many people would be hurt, perhaps even you—"

"Ah d-hon't c-hare!"

"But I do," he answered softly. "You have no idea what society can do to you. And—worse—what it can do to others who are completely innocent." He tilted his head back toward where they had passed Miss Hamilton and Charles Cassin, and Lily suddenly understood. "Even if we don't care for ourselves, we can't let others be harmed. Lily." His hands lifted to frame her face. "Understand. Please. Understand all I'm saying, and all that I cannot say." He lowered his head slowly and kissed her again, softly and lingeringly, and then lifted away and met her searching gaze. For a moment they stood thus, and then he took her hand and placed it upon his arm, leading her in the direction of the house.

They had only just reached the path when they were greeted by the sight of the Earl of Cardemore strolling languidly in their direction, looking rather bored.

"There you are, my girl," he said as they neared him. "I've been searching you out, as it's nearing time for our blasted dance. Your aunt will never forgive me if I conveniently let you stay lost so that I can sit the thing out."

"We were just coming back," Graydon told him, releasing Lily's arm. He hadn't missed the questioning look in Cardemore's eye, regardless of how uninterested the man strove to appear. "The cool night air has been quite refreshing."

"How nice," Cardemore replied in a tone more sarcastic than polite. "Goodness knows you've taken plenty of it, Graydon. You should be floating with oxygen by now.

Now, Lily, don't fuss," he added when she made a sound of distress and touched his sleeve. "Lord Graydon may be my *very dear friend*, but I don't doubt he understands me well enough and approves that I've got the right of it."

"Indeed," Graydon replied peaceably. "I apologize for keeping Lady Lillian from the ball for so long. It was remiss of me. My only excuse is that while being in such delightful company, the time simply slipped away."

"Yes, that and your wits along with it," Cardemore retorted testily, "what few of them you possess, anyway. Lily, don't fuss at me. Graydon's not an idiot, after all."

"Thank you," Graydon returned dryly, although, frankly, he was amazed. He'd never seen the Earl of Cardemore actually behave like a human being. He couldn't decide whether the man was irate because he believed Graydon had been committing improprieties upon his sister, or because he was afraid to dance. Or, perhaps, both. "Well, then. The dance awaits. I'm sure you don't want to miss the start of it."

Cardemore made a grumbling sound. "There is nothing that I want more, but Margaret will have my head if I don't make a complete idiot of myself. In front of witnesses."

Graydon had to cough to cover his laughter. Cardemore glowered at him darkly before turning to his sister.

"Have you prepared your toes, Lily? I shall strive not to break too many of them."

She had just placed her hand upon his proffered arm when a loud, feminine exclamation broke the relative silence of the garden, followed by what sounded like a hard slap and someone falling into some bushes.

"Isabel!" Lord Daltry cried from the midst of the commotion.

"How could you!" Isabel shouted furiously in response. "You wretch! How *could* you?"

"Good heavens," Cardemore muttered. "Has Daltry taken to slapping Isabel about? I shall have to kill him for that, I'm afraid."

"Isabel," Lord Daltry cried again. "Wait!"

Isabel came running down the path and went straight into her uncle's arms. Weeping, she clung to him, and shook as if she'd had the shock of her life.

"I-his-bel!" Lily said with distress, setting a hand on the other girl's shoulder. "W-hat hap-pen?"

"Calm down, Isabel," Lord Cardemore said gently, patting his niece with a comforting hand. "Tell me what happened."

Isabel was sobbing too hard to answer. It was Lord Daltry, arriving at last, brushing leaves and twigs from his elegant coat, who answered.

"She *hit* me," he said. "That's what happened. Just look at this."

He pointed at his face, where even in the dim light a swelling that was rapidly closing the lids of his left eye could be seen.

"A right hook," he said hotly. "Even Jackson never would have seen it coming."

Isabel swirled about suddenly, fists up, and both Graydon and Daltry quickly stepped away.

"Yes and I'll do it again, you *beast*, if you ever dare to touch me again!"

"You needn't worry about that!" Daltry told her. "I wouldn't touch you if it was my only salvation from the fires of eternal damnation!"

"Oh!" Isabel cried, fresh sobs overtaking her. "You're a perfect swine! I wish I'd really hurt you! I wish I'd broken your arrogant nose!"

"Matthew," Graydon said with censure. "This is too bad of you. Remember yourself and where you are."

"Remember myself!" Daltry gaped at him. "*Remember myself?* All I did was try to kiss her and she *hit* me! And I do *not* have an arrogant nose!"

"This is Lady Isabel's ball," Graydon told him tightly. "You've just ruined it. Entirely. As well, you have caused both her and Lady Lillian unutterable humiliation."

"And he didn't just try," Isabel countered. "He kissed me!"

"What of it?" Daltry bellowed. "You kissed me first! What was I supposed to think?"

Isabel set her hands on her hips and faced him furiously. "You were supposed to think that a lady has a certain prerogative that a gentleman does not!"

"Ahem," said the Earl of Cardemore. "I believe it might be best, under the circumstances, if all concerned would keep their damned voices down. Isabel—" he took his niece by the elbow and turned her toward him "—I want you to sneak into the house through the servants' door and go upstairs to repair yourself. You may return to the ball when you're ready."

"But, Uncle Aaron, he—"

"My dear," Cardemore interrupted gently, "you may be reassured that we shall discuss this matter in full detail. Later. Go along, now."

Isabel gave Lord Daltry one long, last fulminating glare before gathering up her skirts and striding off toward the house.

"And as to you, my lord," Cardemore began, but Lord Daltry stopped him.

"Don't fret yourself, Cardemore. I intend to do the right thing."

"Oh?"

"Certainly." Daltry straightened to full height. "I shall pay my respects on the morrow and request Lady Isabel's hand."

Lord Cardemore looked at him with interest. "I can't see what good it would do you. Surely you don't need or want it."

Daltry blinked at him. "I mean, sir, that I shall ask for your permission to make Lady Isabel my wife."

"I understand very well what you meant," Cardemore told him, "but my answer remains the same. My niece will wed when and as she pleases, not because and if society pleases, and I can't see making her marry any man simply because he's taken to wrestling with her in the bushes. Until you can convince Isabel to accept you on your own behalf, don't make me waste my time in receiving such a tiresome visit.''

''Sir, I insist that you hear me out on this matter.''

Lord Cardemore turned to him slowly, all civility gone. ''Now that,'' he murmured, ''is a mistake, my lad. Never insist anything from me, of me or in my presence. It is a fatal error. Strive not to forget that. Lily,'' he said as she violently pinched his arm, ''don't fuss at me. It is most vexing, especially when all I can think of is that in a few minutes' time I'm going to flatten your feet.''

He ignored her as she furiously signed something at him, and instead turned back to Lord Daltry. ''You'll take yourself off, I trust, and not cause further embarrassment? Those who've listened in the garden will cause enough trouble. There is a side gate to the east. Find it and let yourself out. I shall make excuses if anyone should ask. Graydon,'' he said, holding that man's gaze. ''You'll stay. Of course.''

Nothing, Graydon thought, could make him go. Even if Lily hadn't been looking at him so pleadingly, he would never have abandoned her to what the rest of this night would bring. Rumors were about to start flying—again— and even if nothing could be done to spare Lady Isabel, he, at least, could try to keep Lily safe.

''Of course,'' he murmured, making a slight, very correct bow to his host. ''It is my most ardent intention.''

Chapter Thirteen

The weather had grown unseasonably cool, and the night air was damp and heavy with fog. The Earl of Graydon looked out his carriage window upon the gray mists with little more than vague interest. Despite the fact that it made the going on London's streets slow and life, in general, uncomfortable, the weather suited his mood very well. Eight days had passed since the ball at Wilborn Place. Eight long, wearying days. The House of Lords had been constantly in session, a circumstance he normally would have welcomed, as attending Parliament was his main purpose for coming to Town each season. Now, however, he couldn't find the old pleasure that politics and legislature had always given him. It evaded him, just as every other pleasure did. Lillian Walford had made it so. He had tried— God only knew how hard—but it had been futile. He couldn't stop thinking of her during the day. Or dreaming of her while he slept. It was, he thought, becoming something of a problem.

He hadn't spoken to her in more than a week, although he had seen her from a distance on a number of occasions. It hadn't been *possible* to speak with her, and not simply because the Lords had kept him so busy.

The days following the ball had taken on a nightmarish quality. Fashionable society, being somewhat restrained by both his and Margate's behavior, had allowed the events that had taken place at Greenwich to pass. But the scene that Daltry and Lady Isabel had played out in the Earl of Cardemore's gardens had rekindled the fire, and it had shortly thereafter grown rampant. The Earl of Cardemore had aggravatingly taken himself out of Town for an undetermined amount of time and, without his aid, Graydon had been hard-pressed to contain the rumors that had scurried hither and yon, gathering poison as they went. His only ally had been Lady Margaret, who had done what was necessary to maintain as normal an appearance as possible in the midst of the vultures, taking her charges about Town as if nothing at all out of the ordinary had occurred. Graydon had played his own part to perfection. With society watching all of them so closely, he had done what had been expected of him. He had been polite, and gentlemanly, and distant, and had silently damned the rules that demanded he be so.

The carriage finally pulled to a stop, and Graydon took up his hat. It would be good to spend an evening at White's, dining and gambling and trying to shore up Daltry's spirits. Later, when he attended Lord and Lady Denber's ball, he would be the proper Earl of Graydon; for now he would enjoy a much needed few hours of relaxation.

A footman opened the door and Graydon stepped out, taking a moment to set his hat upon his head and gain his bearings. The fog was so thick that the entrance to White's, only a few feet away, was nearly invisible.

"My lord, stay a moment." A voice halted him as he had begun to move forward. "I must speak with you. It is quite urgent. Please, my lord."

The voice was familiar, and Graydon stopped. He was too near his own servants to feel any danger.

"Come, then," he said, knowing already who it was that approached him. He had hoped never again to see the little man whom Cardemore had hired to follow him. "I warned you once what I would do to you if I ever set sight on you again.''

"I've not been following you, I vow it. I went to your house earlier, but they said you'd gone out, and so I came here, to your club, hoping that you would come. My lord, the matter is most urgent!''

"Speak then,'' Graydon told him.

"It's Lord Cardemore's sister. Lady Lillian. She's been taken. Kidnapped. By one of my lord's enemies. Just this night—''

Graydon reached out and picked the man up with one hand, dragging him near.

"Lady Lillian's been taken? Is it the truth you speak?''

The man was trembling beneath his fist.

"God's truth, my lord. God's truth, though I wish it were not. I came to you because my lord is away from London, and too far to reach in time. I pray that you will lend me aid!''

Graydon shook him. "How did it happen? How do you even know of it?''

"After you had done with me,'' the little man said, panting, "my lord set me to watching over his sister, Lady Lillian. Tonight, as she and Lady Margaret and Lady Isabel made their way to Lady Wyscott's, their carriage was set upon by John Saxby's men. Saxby, I tell you! My lord's greatest enemy. Most of them carried Lady Lillian off in another carriage, and the others commandeered my lord's carriage and went away with Lady Margaret and her daughter.''

"God Almighty,'' Graydon muttered.

"I don't know where any of them has been taken to, but it's Lady Lillian I'm afraid for, my lord. Being my lord's sister and in Saxby's hands, she's in terrible danger. He and Lord Cardemore are sworn enemies. I can't think but that he means her the worst sort of harm!''

"Did you see which way they took her? Lady Lillian?''

"Aye, my lord. I followed behind for as long as I could,

until I lost them. They were heading for the wharf. Right for the docks. I don't know where after that.''

"And Lady Margaret and her daughter. In which direction were they taken?''

"North, my lord. North is all I can say. They might have gone anywhere for all I can tell you.''

"Do you know where Lord Cardemore has gone off to?''

"I've sent a messenger after him already, and I've sent every available man in his employ out to search for the ladies.''

"Good.'' Graydon roughly set him aside. "Get into my carriage and wait for me. I regrettably require your assistance in this matter.''

Striding to the door of White's, he gave the doorman a message. Two minutes later Lord Daltry appeared, bareheaded and without his cape.

"Tony,'' he said. "What's this all about?''

"Come into my carriage—'' Graydon took his friend by the arm and dragged him out of the doorway "—and you'll know.''

"You're certain this is where you lost them, Porter?''

"As certain as can be, my lord.''

Graydon stood outside his waiting carriage, looking about him in the dense mist with a gnawing sense of doubt. They were near the docks. He could hear the river lapping against the wharves and smell the strong scents of fish and oil. A bell sounded in the distance and lights shone dimly beside the waterway—small, almost futile efforts to guide ships in the thick gloom.

"We'll have to go in on foot,'' Porter said, lifting a pistol from beneath the folds of his cloak and checking it. "Your fine carriage will only draw notice, which we don't want. Lord Cardemore's men will be waiting for us somewhere nearby. Perhaps they've found where Saxby's taken Lady Lillian.''

Graydon pushed his own weapon farther into the confines of his coat.

"You believe this fellow Saxby will settle for payment, then? I don't want to run the risk of Lady Lillian being harmed."

"I can't say that he'll settle for anything less than whatever it is that he wants from Lord Cardemore. But one thing's certain. If we'd called in the Bow Street Runners, as you wanted to do, Lady Lillian would be dead before you could shout for help. The only chance we've got is if you can offer Saxby something he wants in exchange for her life."

"Yes, but will he?" Graydon murmured, signaling to his footmen to wait for him to return before following Porter into the gray darkness. They walked side by side, forced into nearness by the enveloping fog. Only the clouded lights that here and there marked the wharf's few occupied buildings gave them direction, as well as the dim sounds of gaiety and fighting issuing out of the tavern that was their destination. It was, Porter had told him, one of the places where John Saxby carried out his business.

They slowed as they neared the tavern entrance, then quickly moved aside as two drunks suddenly, and loudly, came stumbling out the doors, singing at the top of their lungs.

Maaaary Leeee was faaaair to seeeee
On a suuuunny daaaay in Dooooover

Clutching each other, lurching back and forth, the drunkards made their way toward one of the docks.

"God's mercy," Graydon muttered. If Lily was here, being kept by such men, he'd see John Saxby hang from the top of Newgate's highest wall.

"I'll go in alone and see if Saxby or any of his men are

inside," Porter whispered. "Dressed the way you are, you'll only draw unwanted notice. Stay here by the door and keep an eye out. Don't leave this spot. We'll never find each other in this fog. I'll be back as soon as I know something."

Graydon held him back with a hand on his arm. "Where are Cardemore's men?"

"My lord?"

"Cardemore's men," Graydon repeated. "You said they'd be waiting for us."

Porter brushed his hand away. "They're all around us, my lord, hidden and waiting, just as they should be. Didn't you hear the signals as we walked? Although I don't suppose you're used to such things."

"No." Graydon drew in a long breath and released it slowly. "I'm not. Go on, then."

He stood outside the path of light as Porter made his way into the crowded tavern, and listened. There was nothing unusual that he could make out over the tavern's din, only the lapping of the water and the sounds of the boats. And the singular bell, which continued to call out in its lonely manner. Either Cardemore's men weren't interested in letting him know of their presence, or they acted so silently that it was humanly impossible to detect them.

A cheerful whistle neared him, and then the sound of a single pair of footsteps. Graydon moved a little farther away from the door, but when the tavern light revealed a young boy walking past him, he said, not over loudly, "Wait. Boy."

The lad stopped and peered into the darkness. Graydon saw him finger the pocket of his thin jacket, where he probably had a knife concealed.

"Who is it?"

Graydon stepped into the light. "Don't be afraid. I mean

you no harm. I only want information, which I'm willing to pay for."

He'd never seen such a shabby-looking youth, dressed in little better than rags. The boy's face was dirty, his hair long and greasy beneath his cap, and his body thin. He smelled strongly of the sea.

"Od's foot," the boy said, his gaze moving from Graydon's face all the way down to his boots. "We gets fine gents down 'ere times and again, but I never seen one the likes of you. Not lost, is it? Information, you say? It better be that, my fine lord, for I'm not going nowhere wiv' you, no matter what y'say you'll pay, and if you try any tricks wiv' me you'll wish you 'adn't." The small knife was at last produced.

"No, that's not what I want," Graydon assured him. "Only information. I'll pay you well for your trouble." He drew a crown out of his pocket and lifted it into the small light.

The youth eyed him warily, but took a step nearer.

"I'm listenin'."

"A young lady was taken away by force tonight...*my* lady, as it happens...by a man named John Saxby. I want to know where I can find him."

"Find 'im?" the boy repeated with a laugh. "John Saxby? You're queer in the attic, m'lord, if it's him you think stole yer lady. 'E couldn't've done it unless 'e could fly, and even if 'e could, the Black Earl's men would kill 'im if 'e tried."

Graydon stiffened. "What do you mean?"

"Only that yer a loony cull, is what," the boy said with clear impatience. "Listen 'ere, you'd 'ave to go all the way to Jamaica to find John Saxby. 'E's been there two years and more, workin' 'ard labor for the Black Earl. It's a sure thing 'e'll never see bonny England again. Not in this lifetime nor the next, not if my lord the earl has anyfing to say about it.''

"God." A chill swept over Graydon. "The Black Earl. Do you mean Cardemore? The Earl of Cardemore?''

The boy shoved his knife back into his pocket. "Who else *would* I mean? Don't you know nuffing?''

"How do you know about Saxby?''

"You ask a lot of questions," the boy said warily. "You wiv' the Beat?''

"I only want my lady back." Graydon set the crown into the lad's thin, grimy palm. "Tell me.''

The boy pocketed the coin next to his knife, and his features took on a proud look. "'Oo should know better than Jonah Wood? I've sailed on m'lord's ships since I was near to this 'igh." He showed Graydon with his hand, holding it just above his knees. "I was on the very cruise wot delivered Saxby to Jamaica. Saw 'im taken off to m'lord's plantation, in irons, no less." The boy shook his head. "'E won't be coming back to England, *ever*. Not unless it's in a box. Once the Black Earl's done wiv' you, you're finished, matey.''

"Yes," Graydon murmured, staring into the darkness. "I know that truth well." He held up another shining crown in the night air, feeling it glisten with wetness even as he held it. "Answer me one more question, and you'll earn this.''

"Wot is it, then?''

"Are any of Saxby's men still abiding in this area? Are there enough of them to—''

"Hey!" the boy suddenly cried, jumping back, wide-eyed. It was the only warning Graydon had of danger before he felt the stinging blow on the back of his head. He fell to the ground, reaching out and grasping the boy's ankle.

"Get...*carriage*...tell them..."
Another blow, and then darkness fell.

She had tried to reach the window half a hundred times at least, and had rattled the door twice as often. But it was hopeless. The window was too high, and the door was too tightly locked. There was a guard outside, but whenever she pounded on the door he only told her to be quiet and save her strength.

Sitting on the bed, Lily folded her hands and tried to think of what she should do. It was difficult; she was not only frightened, but exhausted and hungry. They had brought food earlier, along with a decanter of wine, but she hadn't yet been able to bring herself to eat it. Perhaps it was drugged. Indeed, it probably was. She didn't exactly know what these men wanted her for, although she had a fairly good idea, but unless she was insensible, they were going to find it exceedingly hard to achieve their goal.

The room was damp and chilly, but not completely wanting. It was surprisingly clean, and the furniture, consisting of a bed, chair and table, was comfortable. What kind of place was this, she wondered, that it should look so mean and rough on its face and yet so acceptable inside?

Merciful Lord, but it was cold! She shivered and tried to warm her arms with her hands. A familiar hot ache had begun deep in her chest, but Lily tried to persuade herself that it was nothing. She couldn't fall ill now. It would be disastrous, when she needed all of her wits, and strength, about her. The men who'd brought her here had said they'd light the small coal stove if she'd promise not to try to burn the place down, but she'd shaken her head firmly. No promises. Not with those men. They'd brought blankets, instead, and told her to stay warm, and they'd left a lamp with the evident hope that she'd not use it for any harm. She eyed one of the blankets now, wondering if it were wise to disdain everything they'd brought her. She would only spite herself now if she fell ill.

Her brother would come for her soon. Or Lord Graydon. Surely as soon as it was discovered that she was missing they would begin searching. Surely they would. Although Aaron was away from London, and Lord Graydon had spent nearly every day and night of the past week in the House of Lords. She didn't know what had happened to Isabel and Aunt Margaret, if they'd been able to get home, or to safety. Perhaps they were prisoners as well, along with Aaron's coachman and footmen. Perhaps more than a day would pass before anyone would become worried. But that was unlikely. Aaron's servants would wonder why they'd not returned from Lady Wyscott's dinner party and would begin to make inquiries. And they would send a missive to Aaron, if one of them knew where he was, or to Lord Graydon if they did not. He would know what to do, and how to find Aaron, and between the two of them she would most certainly be found and rescued. Lily was fully confident of that. Or at least, she thought as she wrung her hands nervously, as confident as she could be.

A loud commotion began outside the room, with the voices of several men shouting. It went on for a long while, and when someone banged on Lily's door, she jumped up from the bed and moved to the table on which the lamp was set.

"M'lady? D'ye hear me?"

Lily picked the lamp up carefully, both surprised and gladdened at how heavy it was.

"I'm goin' t'open t'door now, m'lady, 'nd I don't want no trouble wiv' you. Just stand clear, d'ye hear me? We none of us wants to bring ye any harm." Then, in a lower tone, the man continued, "Georgie, lad, you go first 'nd make sure she don't try nuffing wot might 'urt herself."

With a rattling of keys, the door was unlocked. It swung

creakily open upon its hinges, and Georgie stuck his head in.

"M'lady?"

Lily lifted the lamp higher, ready to do what she must to defend herself.

Georgie saw, and attended.

"Now we'll 'ave none of that, if you please, yer ladyship. We're not 'ere to 'arm you, only to bring in some company."

The door opened wider, and Lily saw him—Lord Graydon—being dragged along by two of her captors. He was completely insensible, or perhaps even worse.

"An-non-nee!" she cried, and nearly dropped the lamp. Georgie moved quickly and took it away from her. They carried Lord Graydon in and placed him upon the bed, roughly shoving his legs upon the mattress until he lay flat. When they moved away Lily knelt beside him, setting her hand upon his neck, feeling with relief that he was still alive.

"An-non-nee," she murmured, letting the tears she hadn't been able to cry for herself start. "An-non-nee." She touched his forehead, where a red and purple bruise swelled.

Her captors, looking on, chuckled and nodded, and Lily swung upon them with all her fury.

"An-mals!" she shouted, stopping on a sob before gathering the voice to speak again. "L-how," she said with disgust. "F-hil-thy. *An-mals.*"

Georgie lowered his gaze and scratched his head, while the others looked markedly uncomfortable, but they said nothing and left the room, closing and locking the door.

She covered Graydon with a blanket, tucking it all around him. There was a pitcher and basin set on the floor beside the bed, and she filled the basin. Wetting the cloth they had brought with her dinner, she gently wiped his face, avoiding his wound as much as possible. He moaned when she passed the damp cloth over his lips, and she wet it again and pressed it to his mouth until he relaxed into a deeper slumber. She untied his evening cape and pushed it from his broad shoulders, then loosened his cravat and undid the top three buttons of his shirt. Removing his gloves proved to be more of a challenge, as they were skintight and his hands quite large, but she persevered until he was free of them. When there seemed to be nothing else that she could do to make him comfortable, Lily pulled the chair near the bed and sat with her fingers held lightly atop one of his hands, so that she might assure herself that he was warm.

He had come for her, just as she had known he would. He had come to save her, but had only gotten trapped in the same wretchedness. And hurt in the bargain. Guilt gnawed at Lily, mingled with renewed fear. It had been bad enough to wonder at what was going to be done to her, but what would they do to Lord Graydon? Surely they wouldn't murder a peer of the realm, especially not an earl? She closed her eyes and tried to think, to convince herself that such a thing would never come to pass, that they would release him without further harm. But thinking was impossible. She was cold and hungry and exhausted to her very core. She leaned forward to the mattress, just far enough to rest her head upon her folded arms and so that she could share some of his warmth, and fell asleep still holding his hand.

"Lily."

Her eyes opened slowly, groggily, and very much against her will. She let them fall shut again.

A hand stroked her hair, her back.

"Lily."

The next moment he was pulling her up onto the bed, sliding her across his body and then somehow beneath him.

He was warm and hard and big, and she felt the heat and heaviness of his body covering her own.

"Lily," he murmured against her ear, licking at it with his tongue so that she shivered. "You're so late. I was worried." And then his tongue trailed upward, across her cheek and suddenly pressed against her lips and into her mouth.

Lily's eyes flew open and she pushed at him in a panic, but Lord Graydon paid no heed. He kissed her deeply, possessively, filling her with the taste and feel of him. She pushed again and he murmured into her mouth, pressing harder and more fully against her until she felt the unmistakable proof of his complete arousal. One of his hands cupped her breast, and she gasped and turned her head forcibly away.

"Mah l-hord!"

"Mmm," he replied, trailing kisses down her throat. His hand left her breast to push her bodice away. He chuckled sleepily as he slid the sleeve down her arm and exposed her fully to his wandering mouth. "You're dressed," he murmured. "Silly." He began to move against her again, his hips against her own, in a slow, rhythmic motion.

"Skirt," he muttered, pulling it up about her waist. "Damned nuisance." His hand slid up between her legs, and Lily tried to clamp them together.

"N-ho," she pleaded. "An non-nee!"

He moved upward again, capturing her mouth and kissing her tenderly.

"I love to hear you speak my name," he murmured against her lips. "So beautiful. All of you. Lily." His fingers stroked gently at her thighs, coaxing her apart. "Let me," he whispered. "I need to feel you. Taste you. All of your sweetness. Let me."

He kissed her again and continued to murmur and encourage, caressing her with gentle care, until she felt all her will slipping away and opened herself to him.

"Oh, Lily." His tongue licked at her open lips. "So sweet." One finger pressed against her most private area, touching so lightly and delicately that she shivered. A feeling of deep pleasure shuddered all the way through her, unlike anything she had ever known before. She felt hot and restless, uncertain of what was happening. "So warm and soft." He kissed her and made a deep groaning sound in the back of his throat. "All for me." Lily instinctively pushed upward and heard her own inarticulate groan rising from her throat.

"*Lily.*" He suddenly moved on top of her again, as if he were in a rush, pushing her legs apart to lie between them. His hand fumbled desperately between them, and she moved restlessly, kissing him, touching his clothed chest with her hands.

He was pushed up on one arm, suspended above her while he worked frantically at opening his trousers, and he laughed in a self-mocking tone and said, "*Why* am I clothed? It's damned silly."

She laughed, too, because it did seem silly, and because she was nervous, and because she almost couldn't believe that he was going to make her his mistress under such strange and daunting circumstances. And then, feeling that unpleasant burning in her chest, she coughed, twice.

He fell still, then, completely still except for raising his head to gaze down at her. In the dim light he blinked, and his eyes widened and focused. He looked as if he were coming awake from a long, deep slumber.

Graydon stared down at Lily and told himself that this wasn't happening. This was only a dream. His dream. Exactly as he dreamed it every night. Except that they were both fully clothed, as they never were in his dreams, and they were not in his bed, either, as they always were. She was warm and real beneath him; her scent was on him. Everywhere, it seemed.

"God Almighty. Lily?"

The delightful smile on her face died away, replaced at once by a mixture of embarrassment and slight perplexity.

"Ess?"

"Oh, my God." He pushed up onto his knees. "You're not a dream?"

She shook her head. "N-ho."

"Oh, God!" He scrambled back on the mattress, away from her, and stared with open shock at her state of undress. "Lily, I—I beg your pardon. Good God." With a swift hand he pulled her skirt down to cover her parted legs and stood, immediately turning his back to her. "I'm terribly—terribly, horribly sorry." What could he say? What could he possibly do *or* say? "I most sincerely apologize, although I realize I have no right. Please believe me when I say that I wish none of this had ever happened."

Her voice was a soft murmur behind him. "Ah unnersthand, mah l-hord." He heard the bed squeak as she rose from it.

"You don't," he said miserably. "You can't. I have these dreams—I don't suppose I can even tell you about them without being even more insulting than I already have been." As each moment passed what he'd done seemed worse and worse. His body ached with wanting her. Her scent was on his hands, reminding him vividly of the fact that he had touched her intimately. With a groan of want and dismay he sat upon the chair, still turned away from her, and ran a hand through his hair. "A fine hero I've been. I came tonight to try to save you, and not only end up a prisoner as well, but have attacked you in the vilest manner possible. I can't even begin to think of a way to apologize. I'm sure you wish me to the farthest corner of perdition."

She coughed, but gave no answer. After a moment of silence he felt something cool and wet being pressed against his aching forehead. He looked up and saw her standing beside him.

"Lily." He covered her hand with his own. She slipped away, leaving him holding the cloth instead.

"D-hon't aphol-ho-ghize ag-hain," she said, and coughed. "Th-here is n-ho n-heed. Ah unner-st-hand."

"Lily," he began, but she turned away.

"D-hoes your head ah-hache?"

"Yes," he muttered, and nearly tossed the cloth away. Instead he used it to try to wipe her scent from his hands. "I'm not much of a hero, as I said. Do you have any notion of who your abductors are?"

She sat on the bed and shook her head, not looking at him.

"They've said nothing to you of their intentions?"

"Ohnly th-hat th-hey w-hon't hurt me." She folded her hands together in her lap. "Th-hey hav-hn't." She shrugged, as if it didn't mean anything.

"Daltry's gone after your aunt and Lady Isabel."

She looked up. "Th-hey were ta-haken too?" She coughed several times, covering her mouth with her hand.

"As best I know, they were." He glanced about the room to gain his bearings. He would get her out of this first, he decided, and then feel guilty about what he had done. He couldn't think now about whether she would ever forgive him. The dismal prospect of her not doing so would only make him feel maddened. "I don't know by whom, or why," he lied, deciding it best not to tell her that one of her brother's minions had apparently been a party to the kidnapping. "Daltry's headed after them. He's sure to do better than I have." He attempted a smile, which she didn't return.

"Wh-hat ab-hout Ah-hron?"

"I don't think we can depend upon him, Lily." It would be unkind to lie to her on that score. "We'll rest here another hour or two, and then attempt an escape. I can reach that window, I think."

She nodded and began to look hopeful. "Oh, y-hes. Ah tr-hied it, b-hut it w-has too—" She was seized by a fit of coughing, so hard that she doubled over from it.

Graydon moved to the bed and rubbed her back with the palm of his hand in a small, circular motion, pressing hard as his mother had taught him rather than pounding as was commonly, mistakenly done. He looked about the room for the source of water she'd used to dampen the cloth with, and instead saw the tray of food and decanter of wine. A moment later he was holding her up by the shoulders and pressing a cup to her lips.

"Drink this," he told her firmly. "I don't care what it tastes like," he added when she tried to turn away. "Drink. All of it." He let her take her time, patiently letting her take it in sips but not taking the cup away until the wine was gone. Beneath his arm, he felt her slender body trembling with cold, and cursed himself for not having thought earlier of her comfort. It was as cold and damp as a cave in their dismal prison. Her weak lungs were certain to be adversely affected.

She pushed the empty cup away with clear relief.

"Hor-hi-bhile," she said with feeling. "S-hour. Prohbbly p-hoisoned."

"I can't think that it is. I don't know that it would benefit our captors any to have you insensible, especially since you can't shout the house down. Don't speak," he commanded. "Your voice has grown raw along with your cough. How long has it been since you've last eaten? Tell me with your hands, Lily."

She held up six fingers and he immediately stood to fetch her a plate of food.

"This doesn't look too bad," he pronounced, having sorted through the greasy offering of meat, fish and vegetables. He selected a slab of beef and two small potatoes for her. "Eat some of this. Our captors apparently want you to remain healthy, at least enough to feed you better than they probably eat themselves. Lily, dear," he murmured as he set the plate upon the table and moved to pull her to her feet. "Don't look so downcast, love. I may not have been much of a rescuer, but I would rather lose my life than let any harm come to you. We'll only rest until dawn approaches. We can hardly see otherwise, with this heavy fog—and then we shall be quit of this place. I'll have you safe soon. I promise you that on all I hold dear. Trust me."

She nodded and let him lead her to the table, moving so stiffly.

"Eat as much as you can," he said as he pushed the chair beneath her. "I'll finish whatever you don't. Then we'll rest. Unless our captors begin to keep a better watch on us, we should soon be quit of this nightmare, one way or another."

Chapter Fourteen

Lily slept badly, coughing and shivering, moving restlessly on the bed despite her deep exhaustion. She'd fallen asleep beneath his watchful eye within mere moments of lying down, even while he'd still been piling every available cover upon her. It had reassured him, somewhat, that she had trusted him enough yet to allow him to do so. It was more than he deserved. Every time he thought of what he'd done—baring her breasts to his mouth, touching her so intimately with his fingers—he shuddered with remorse.

She must think him an animal. A disgusting, lust-ridden animal. Not that it made any difference. She would have to wed him now, whether she was disgusted or not. He'd very nearly possessed her virginity, which was just as good as having possessed it. They would have to marry. There was nothing else to be done.

Of course, simply spending several hours alone together in this dismal place had all but ensured the necessity of marriage. If a whisper of it ever found its way into the greedy ears of the ton, her reputation would be shattered for once and for all—unless they wed. Even then there would be gossip and stares and plenty of unpleasantness, but nothing that couldn't be weathered for the few months it would last, especially if they presented a happy and united front. Before a year was out the Earl and Countess of Graydon would probably be seen as a love match, if Lily could manage to put up such a face. *If.* He'd be fortunate if she so much as spoke to him kindly again, much less pretend to love him. But she had no choices now, just as he did not. She would be his wife.

Lily murmured in her sleep, then began to cough again. Graydon leaned forward to smooth his hand over her white-blond hair, stroking the loosened strands gently until she subsided. In slumber, she appeared more angelic than ever.

She was warm to his touch. Too warm. And yet she shivered beneath the blankets. Her cough was raw and becoming worse as each hour passed in this damp hellhole. He had to get her out, he thought, glancing toward the window and the black fog outside. If they attempted to leave now they would be groping in complete darkness, trying to find their way as blind men. And that fog—it would wreak havoc on her already suffering lungs.

He'd heard nothing from their captors since he'd wakened from his amorous stupor to find himself making love to Lily. Nearly three hours had passed since then and there had been nothing; not even a breath of sound save for the bells and horns that told him they were still by the river. He wondered if anyone was even there, or if, should he manage to get the door opened, someone would suddenly appear.

A pebble fell upon the window, clattering softly. Graydon watched and listened. A moment later another struck the dirty pane.

Standing upon the chair, he found that he was easily able to reach the window. It opened with little trouble and the chill fog seeped in.

"M'lord!" a young voice murmured quietly. "You there?"

"Jonah?"

"Aye. Speak soft, matey, or we'll find all the trouble we want. Can you climb out, then?"

"Are there guards?"

"I've took care of that, but 'e may come to any time. Climb out and be quick!"

Graydon took hold of the sill and pulled himself up to look outside. Jonah Wood was barely visible in the fog, standing on the ground some feet below.

"My lady is here with me," he whispered to the boy. "I shall have to boost her up and let her down. You must catch her. She's quite ill."

"Od's feet!" the boy cursed impatiently. "It'll cost you extra, then. You bear that in mind, m'fine lord. Well hurry up about it! He'll kill me if I get caught."

"Lily." Graydon bent over the bed, patting her cheek to rouse her. "Lily, wake up."

She came to groggily, and he scooped her off the bed and into his arms, blankets and all.

"Mah l-hord?" she murmured sleepily.

"Hush. We're leaving now, through the window. There's a young man on the other side who'll help you down." He carefully stood upon the chair. "Reach your arms up and grasp the sill. I'll push you up the rest of the way. Be careful."

Coughing, she nodded, and put her arms up to do as he said. Graydon easily managed to seat her upon the sill, and she swung her legs over the side.

"Good girl," he murmured, holding her hands as she slowly slid out of view.

"I've got 'er!" Jonah whispered harshly from the other side. "Let go!" To Lily, who was still coughing, he added, "Stubble it!"

Graydon threw the blankets down to the ground, then quickly lifted himself up and out of the window.

"Thank you," he said to Jonah the moment his feet hit the ground.

"Thank me later and make it mean somefing," the boy told him. "Come on. Hurry!"

"Just a moment." Graydon wrapped Lily in the blankets,

swinging her up into his arms. He nodded at Jonah. "Lead on. Don't lose us in the fog."

Holding one end of a blanket, the boy led them through the wharves and docks, going slowly, moving with care. Once or twice he stumbled but each time got up and unfailingly moved forward. It seemed to take forever, but finally Graydon realized that they were leaving the water behind and moving farther into the city. No one had followed them, but whether that was because their escape had not yet been noticed or because they'd been let go, he wasn't sure.

"I had a carriage—" Graydon began.

"Porter sent it away," the boy told him in a low voice. "Gave 'em some good cause to belay their worries. That was hours ago, matey, and yer a long way from 'ome."

"Just find me a hackney," Graydon told him. "You'll be appropriately rewarded for your trouble."

Twenty minutes later, as dawn lightened the yet thick fog, Graydon was lifting Lily into a disreputable-looking hackney, sparing a fleeting moment to wonder what his servants and neighbors would think to see such a vehicle pulling up before his town house.

"Get in," he told Jonah, but the boy shook his head.

"Better not. I'll catch it bad enough when m'lord finds out what I've done."

"The Black Earl?" Graydon said softly, realizing at last that all his suspicions were true. Cardemore was behind the kidnapping, behind everything.

"You'll forget you ever 'eard that name, matey, if you know wot's best."

Graydon reached into a pocket to withdraw a coin purse. "Will you be safe, Jonah? If Cardemore discovers you've helped us?"

"That's my worry," the boy told him with a note of defiance. "I take care of meself."

Graydon removed a crown and put it back in his pocket.

'Just in case," he said, and then pushed the full purse into
Jonas' hands.

"It's yours," he said as the boy gaped at the small fortune he held. "For services rendered. My home is in Berke-
ley Square, and you may come to me there if you ever find
yourself in need of assistance. I should like to repay you
far better than I have with this." He nodded at the purse.
Then he shook the boy's grimy hand and jumped into the
carriage beside Lily.

"Not good," Dr. Patterson pronounced in Graydon's
study some hours later, having just examined Lily, who was
ensconced in the countess's rooms above. "It's a severe
inflammation of the lungs, accompanied by a fever and
chills. I'm afraid it will be a day or two before we know
if she'll fully recover."

Graydon tented his fingers beneath his chin and regarded
the physician from the depths of his exhaustion. He'd spent
every moment since their arrival at Lily's bedside, doing
what he could with his housekeeper to make her comfortable until the doctor arrived. Filthy, wrinkled and unshaved,
he knew he must look quite a sight.

"Fully recover?"

"My lord, she may not even survive."

"God." Graydon bowed his head. "What can be done?"

"I shall bleed her at once, of course. She must be kept
warm and comfortable. There's little else until the fever
passes. In a day or two, we'll know."

Graydon nodded. "I've sent for my mother and sisters."

"Better nurses I couldn't ask for," Dr. Patterson told
him. "Your mother has worked miracles before."

"Yes," Graydon agreed. "I only hope she arrives
quickly enough to work another one."

He accompanied the doctor back upstairs and watched,
grimacing, as Lily was bled. She was too weak to protest
anything now, as she'd done when he'd refused to take her
to her brother's home. She'd pleaded with him to take her

to Wilborn Place, but he wouldn't. He wasn't certain that he ever would. She was his now, completely under his care. Within a few weeks she would be his wife. In his present mood, he was inclined to forbid her to ever again so much as cross Wilborn's threshold. To ease her fears, he had sent a missive there to give word as to where she was, also to discover whether Lady Margaret and Lady Isabel had yet been found and recovered. A similar note had gone to Lord Daltry's apartments. No word had yet come back from either place, but Graydon wasn't worried about that. Word would come, and soon. He had only to be patient.

He pulled a chair next to the bed after the doctor left and sat watching as Lily fitfully slumbered. His housekeeper had been openly distressed when Graydon had carried Lily up the stairs and into the bedchamber that adjoined his own. It was scandalous that she should sleep so near him, despite the fact that she was far too ill for him to bed, but Graydon didn't particularly care. He had to have her near him until he could be certain she would live.

"N-ho!" she mumbled in her sleep, moving restlessly. Her sweat-dampened face turned toward him, and he reached out to smooth away the hair that clung to her.

"Hush, love," he whispered. "All is well."

She reached up to grip his hand, pulling it to her mouth to kiss it. He wondered, as he moved to lie upon the bed beside her, if she was dreaming that he was Charles Cassin. He was too weary to feel more than a fleeting moment of jealousy.

"Sleep, Lily." He let her keep his hand, not minding the painful grip she held it in. He set his other one lightly about her blanket-covered waist. Sleep pulled him down as rapidly as a whirlpool, so strongly that he couldn't resist. His last dim thought was that his servants would be unhappy to find him so improperly sleeping upon the bed beside the desperately ill Lady Lillian, and that he would never be able to explain it to them.

* * *

"My lord?"

The words barely penetrated Graydon's darkness. He wasn't able to do more than register their presence.

"My lord?" His butler spoke a little louder this time. Graydon made the effort to make a sound of sleepy displeasure. Beside him, beneath his arm, Lily burned as hot as a furnace. But she was alive, he thought with numb reassurance, although he could both hear and feel her drawing in breath with difficulty. She was still clutching his hand.

"My lord, please forgive me." A hand touched his shoulder, hesitantly shaking him.

"Go *away*, Crane." Graydon warned, his voice deep and harsh. He felt wretched and ill, battered, as if someone had filled him with poison and then beaten him with a heavy stick.

"Lord Cardemore is below stairs, my lord. I'm terribly sorry to disturb you, but he's threatened to retrieve Lady Lillian by force if you don't come at once to speak with him. And Dr. Patterson has returned as well." Crane cleared his voice delicately. "I'm certain you don't wish him to see you here with...Lady Lillian."

Graydon sat up slowly, blinking. Every inch of him hurt. Lily murmured when he loosened her fingers and slid his hand out of her grasp.

"I'll be back, love," he murmured, leaning to kiss her hot forehead when she turned toward him. He tucked the covers around her with care. "Rest easy. I'll be back." To Crane he said, as he rose unsteadily from the bed, "Ring for my valet. Bring me hot water and a pot of coffee. Send Dr. Patterson in to see Lady Lillian." He moved toward the door that opened into his adjoining rooms. "And tell Lord Cardemore that I shall be down shortly to speak with him. He may wait for me or not, as he pleases. Until then—" he stopped just long enough to look at his butler directly "—set every footman in the house to guarding over this room. Lady Lillian is not to be disturbed by the Earl of Cardemore for *any* reason. Do you understand?''

Crane bowed low, then went to the bellpull.

Cardemore was sitting in the room's most comfortable chair and drinking brandy when Graydon at last opened his library doors. With narrowed eyes Graydon entered the room and shut the doors behind him.

''You've made yourself comfortable, I see.''

Cardemore evidently didn't care to speak pleasantries any more than Graydon did. He set his glass aside. ''I want my sister,'' he stated.

''You can't have her,'' Graydon replied as bluntly, moving across the room to the chair opposite the one Cardemore sat in. He folded himself into it with care, hurting every inch of the way. ''After the circumstances you arranged to occur yesterday, I'm too weary to do to you what I should like. I'll settle for merely telling you. Lily is mine now. We will marry at the end of next month, if her health is sufficiently recovered at that time. Until then, you'll find whatever acceptable excuses you can think of to stay away from her. Afterward, I shall take it upon myself to keep her out of your way. And that, my lord, is all I have to say to you.''

He began to rise; Cardemore stood and shoved him forcibly back into his chair.

''Oh, no, you don't, you foolish puppy—''

Graydon pushed his hand away with a snarl, all of his civility slipping away in the grip of his anger and exhaustion. ''Don't push me any farther, Cardemore, or you'll *never* see Lily again. Sit down if you want to speak to me. I'm done with your threats.''

Instead, Cardemore straightened and regarded him in silence. After a moment he poured another drink and put it into Graydon's hands. Then he sat.

''Then we'll speak on equal terms, if you can do so. You've given me fair warning, and I'll return the favor.

Heed me well. Since the age of four and ten I've bargained for my very life with demons so evil you couldn't begin to imagine their depths. I'm far beyond being roused by a boy like you." He settled back in his chair. "We'll have the truth between us. I'm not unaware that you realize who was behind the kidnappings, both yours and Lily's. Now I only want to know your terms."

"Bastard," Graydon muttered, draining his glass and slamming it sharply upon the table beside him. "You spoke so eloquently of never forcing your niece into an unwanted marriage, yet you readily maneuver your own sister into such a bargain. And have perhaps killed her in the doing. Or don't you know that, yet, with all your powers?" he asked bitterly, seeing the other man's face pale. "You should have found a better way of forcing me to the altar than exposing your beloved sister to the elements, Cardemore. If Lily ever knows the full truth, she'll not forgive you. *If* she survives the fever that's taken her."

Cardemore's left hand curled into a tight fist, the only sign of his deep agitation.

"You needn't wed Lily. It was a grave mistake to attempt to force you to it. I'll have her removed to Wilborn Place at once, where she should and must be. I release you entirely of your debts. You have my word that you will never again be importuned by myself or my employees. If you require compensation for your time and trouble, you need only name your price. "

"Oh, God." Graydon leaned back against the chair and laughed, almost deliriously amused. "I see it all now. Did you think to force me into wedding your sister by guile and hold sway over me with your threats? I was to be the ideal husband, was I not? But that was before matters changed. Now that I know the truth, you're more than willing to set me free, despite what it would mean to Lily's reputation." He gazed at the ceiling and chuckled, a foolish, weary grin on his face. "Oh, no, Cardemore. It will be the other way around. Lily will stay here with me. You will do as I say and keep away from her, as much as possible, until we are wed. And you will do everything that is entirely proper, for Lily's sake. On the day that you walk her down the aisle of St. George's and put her into my keeping, you'll be doing so for good. After that, you may only pray I'll soften enough to let you see her again." He met Cardemore's gaze and held it. "You shall have to pray very hard, indeed."

"I still hold the deed to St. Cathyrs," Cardemore told him softly. "Your mother, and sisters—"

"Only think of how Lily would regard you if she knew that you'd had both her and me kidnapped with the intent of forcing us to wed," Graydon advised with a smile. "Can you not envision it? Can you not see *exactly* what her reaction would be?" He rose to refill his glass, glancing once at Cardemore to add, "I can. Indeed, I can see it quite clearly. I hope you've done nothing to Jonah. I wasn't certain whether he helped us to escape at your command or not."

"He did not," Cardemore told him, his voice perfectly calm, despite the fact that he looked as if he was ready to commit murder. "He had no knowledge of the kidnapping or of my part in it until he accidentally stumbled upon you in the fog. It was unfortunate that Porter neglected to let the boy know what was taking place. Jonah never would have made such a slip, otherwise."

"You'll not punish him?"

"I would never harm Jonah, for any reason. He reminds me a great deal of myself at that age. Desperate. It cost him dearly to betray the loyalty he holds for me, and he knew that he chanced his own life in doing so, but blind desperation drove him to risk it. Did he tell you why?"

"No."

"For the money he knew you'd pay. He wished to redeem his two sisters out of a whorehouse. One is older than he, one younger."

Graydon felt as if he'd be ill. "Younger?" he repeated. "The boy is only thirteen, at the most."

"Twelve," Cardemore told him. "I never knew about the sisters—he was too proud to speak of their circumstances—else I would have redeemed them myself. The boy is dear to me, as I've said."

"You didn't," Graydon said.

"Didn't I?" Cardemore set a hand to his temple and closed his eyes briefly, seeming momentarily vulnerable. "Then I meant to say it. He is, and you needn't fear on his account. Porter, however, is dead."

Graydon drew in an unsteady breath. "I see."

"Do you?" Cardemore regarded him with a disturbing directness. "I doubt that you see very much at all. Do you know, Graydon, I happen to like you, for all that you're a fine lord. I never would have chosen you for Lily otherwise. It wasn't because I thought I could control you."

"Forgive me if I don't quite believe that."

"You care for her," Cardemore went on. "You'll be good to her. I knew it then and I know it now. Lily needs someone who'll be good to her. Isabel can take care of herself, but Lily is vulnerable. I couldn't risk her being hurt by a man who was only taken with her beauty or who wanted her money. Even so, I doubted you would wed her, a mute woman, regardless of your own feelings. I meant to trap you into doing so, I admit, and the plan fell wrong. Porter was responsible, and made several errors. In our world such errors make one...unwelcome. He took his own life three hours ago."

Graydon lifted a hand to rub at the ache between his eyes. "I'm glad I'm taking Lily out of your world. She doesn't belong with you."

"No," Cardemore agreed quietly. "She never has. I've always known that."

"I assume Lady Margaret and Lady Isabel are well?"

"Yes. They were merely driven far enough out of Town to be stopped from alerting any authorities, and set down, unharmed, near a decent inn, where they were given shelter. My men were about to abandon my coach on a side road some miles away when they were unfortunately overtaken by your friend, Lord Daltry. That was another error Porter made, not taking into account that you might arrange for help of your own.''

Graydon had begun to wander toward the warmth of the fire, but turned and stared at his guest. "Is he all right?"

Cardemore shrugged. "A small wound to his left arm. Nothing more serious.''

"A *small* wound?"

"He was shot. There was nothing else to be done. He was intent upon rescuing whoever he believed was still inside the coach, and had to be subdued. The ball did no more than pass through his flesh, here." Cardemore pointed to an area on his upper left arm. "He's perfectly fine, I assure you. I carried him myself to the inn where Margaret and Isabel were, and had a doctor in at once to bind the wound.''

Graydon sank into the nearest chair. "You took him?" He gazed at the man until understanding dawned. "Ah. I see. You were on your way from whatever false location you were supposed to have been at to rescue Lady Margaret and Lady Isabel, and met with your men, and Lord Daltry, midway, is that it?"

Cardemore nodded. "And ended up rescuing Daltry, instead. It wasn't precisely the romantic and heroic image I'd hoped to impress upon my ladies, but Isabel was immensely grateful to see Lord Daltry. He's quite risen in her esteem, as you might imagine. She believes him to be the bravest man presently alive on God's earth. He's at his own dwelling now, probably sleeping like a babe.''

The weariness was beginning to overtake him. Graydon shook it away. "I shall visit him as soon as Lily is well." He couldn't think past that. "Were you to rescue Lily and myself, also?"

"At morning's first light," Cardemore told him. "My men and I were to stage a wonderful scene for your and Lily's benefit, a small war to rescue you from John Saxby and his men. I was not, as you might believe, going to pretend outrage at your having spent the night locked away with my sister. Your own sense of honor would have accomplished the outcome. Just as it has.''

To this, Graydon said nothing. He ran a hand through his hair and gazed at the fire.

"You needn't wed her," Cardemore said. "It's not too late."

"It is," Graydon told him dully. "For you." He looked at the other man. "You thought to get a husband for your sister who would jump at your every command, so that you might forever keep her happiness beneath your control. But it is not to be. Lily will despise you if she ever knows the truth, and so now I control you. If you have any hope for Lily to look at you with love again, you'll do as I say and leave us in peace."

"I won't have it," Cardemore began, but Graydon shook his head.

"You take an unearthly pride in the world you come from, but I won't have Lily tainted by it. She resides in my world now, and will, for the remainder of her life. Her happiness is in *my* keeping."

Cardemore met his gaze directly, his face without emotion. "Let me see her before I go."

The plea didn't move Graydon at all. Compassion was beyond him. He seemed only to feel his deep weariness. "You'll not see Lily now, or even tomorrow. I don't know when. Send Lady Margaret if you wish to know how she is."

Cardemore stood stiffly. "I'll beg, if that's what you wish."

Graydon felt sick to his very heart. His eyes burned with their need of sleep. "The only thing I wish is for you to go. If there is to be a funeral, you'll be the first to know of it. That's all I can offer you now."

Cardemore said nothing. After a moment he turned and left.

Graydon ascended the stairs slowly, ignoring the hot ache of his muscles as he made his way into the room where Lily lay. The smell of blood greeted him as he walked through the doors—Lily's blood. The housekeeper was removing a bowl filled with it from the stand beside the bed. Dr. Patterson finished tying the wound he had opened to bleed her, and looked up. Beside him, Lily lay pale and still, save for the gasping, laborious rise and fall of her chest as her body struggled for air as if she were drowning.

"She's not making the progress I had hoped," Dr. Patterson said quietly, standing. "I'm afraid we must prepare for the worst. Her family should be notified at once."

Graydon felt heavy, everything surrounding him seemed to darken. "How long?"

"She's very weak. Perhaps by nightfall. Perhaps by tomorrow morning. It's difficult to know. I'll send a nurse to tend her, unless you wish me to stay?"

"No. No one. I'll stay with her."

"But, my lord…"

Graydon had already crossed the room to stand beside the bed. "Leave us," he said. "All of you." He didn't even glance at the servants in the room.

He stood a long time after they'd gone, gazing down at her, listening to her labored breaths.

"Lily," he whispered. "You must live. You must. I'll do anything." He slowly knelt beside the bed. "You see? I'll beg God not to take you. Listen." And then he prayed, his words incoherent and muddled even to his own ears, desperate and headlong. He knew it didn't make any sense, but surely God would understand what he meant. Surely he would.

He pressed his face against the mattress and curled his fists into the bedcovers, feeling a sudden and complete hopelessness. He couldn't begin to think of what to do.

"Merciful heavens! What on earth are you doing on the floor!"

Graydon's fists uncurled. He lifted his head and turned to look toward the bedroom doors.

"Mother," he murmured. "You're here."

She was still pulling off her gloves. "Of course I'm here," she said in a chiding tone, moving toward him in her dainty, birdlike manner. "You sent for me, did you not? My dear, you need to be in bed! Come up off the floor, then." She took hold of his hand and tried to pull him up, but he put his arms about her instead, holding her.

"Mother, you've got to help me. Dr. Patterson says she's going to die."

"Oh, my." She patted his head lovingly. "Certainly she won't die, my dear. I'll not have it. Now you take yourself off to your bed and have a good long sleep. Your sisters and I have a great deal of work to do and you must leave us to tend our patient. Lady Lillian, is that not her name? My, isn't she a pretty little thing? Come along, dear. On your feet." She tugged at him until he stood. "I'll call your valet to tend you at once." With one arm about his waist, she guided him to his adjoining room. "It was foolish of you to put her here, next to you, Anthony, but we can discuss the matter later. For now, I must mix a mustard plaster and prepare a remedial tea. And, of course, Melissa and Janette have brought their special pillows. Lady Lillian will be breathing much easier in only an hour or so, I promise you. You're not to come and see her again until I give you permission, love. Shocking, really, it is to have you roomed so closely together, but it can't be helped now." She opened his door and pushed him inside.

"Mother," he said, holding the door open even as she tried to close it, "send me word at once if anything happens. Promise me."

She regarded him from her merry blue eyes, a handsome, blond little bird of a woman. "You must care for this young woman a good deal, Anthony."

"Yes, I'm going to marry her."

"I see," she said, her eyes widening a fraction. "In that

case, I must make more than certain to get her well as quickly as possible. Go to bed, my dear. I give you my promise, but it will not be necessary to call you. I've never lost a patient yet, and my future daughter will *not* be the first.''

Chapter Fifteen

The Earl of Cardemore wasn't used to failure, or disaster. It had been so many years since he'd felt truly helpless that he'd nearly forgotten what the emotion was like. It was hard, now, to make himself know what had happened to him, to put a name to it. It was what a once young man grown old must feel, to look at his aged body and realize that his former strengths were gone.

There were still a number of things he could do to put the Earl of Graydon back beneath his hand. Thinking of them only made Cardemore feel weary. Lily was safe now, in Graydon's care. Word had come only an hour earlier that she was going to live, that Countess Graydon and her daughters had performed one of their miracles and saved her. Dr. Patterson had reported to him personally, having left Graydon's home after having assured himself of Lily's state. Cardemore wondered, with a faint smile, what Graydon would think if he knew that not only Dr. Patterson, but several of Graydon's own servants, were secretly in Cardemore's pay. There was nothing that Graydon did or would do that Cardemore couldn't be apprised of.

But it didn't matter. Not anymore. It was over and done with, the scheming and plotting, and now Cardemore would leave them in peace. Lily would be content with her earl, and Graydon would be good to her. It was what he'd wanted for her, although he'd always assumed that he'd not have to give her up in the bargain. But Graydon had spoken the truth: Lily didn't belong in his world, and never had. His world, which was all darkness and violence. Soon, he must send Margaret and Isabel away from it, as well. He must see them settled, safe and content, and then never see either of them, or Lily, ever again.

The fog had lifted earlier in the day. His room was fully unlit, but he stood near the open window, and gazed outside at the stars and moon. Such brilliant lights they were against such utter blackness, just as Lily and Margaret and Isabel had been his lights, shining against the darkness his soul had ever known. His only lights; he loved them so well. How foolish and empty his life would be without them.

He didn't have a heart, or so it was said. Cardemore gripped the windowsill and bowed his head low. He didn't have a heart, a conscience. Everyone knew it and said it. It had been lived out of him too many years ago—lived and overlived in so many ways, deaths, deceits—he was beyond being human. And well beyond tears—that most telling sign of humanity.

"Aaron?"

Margaret's voice surprised him; he hadn't heard her enter the room, a sure sign that he was losing his touch. At this rate, he'd be a ready target for any and every assassin whose master sought him dead. Cardemore drew in a rough breath and wiped his face with the palm of his hands. His eyes burned and ached and he wished, fervently, that she would go before he proved to be human, after all.

"What is it?" he asked, glad to hear the covering roughness of his tone.

She closed the door softly. He felt as if he'd been closed in a trap.

"Go away, Margaret. You shouldn't be here. In my bedroom. Not unless you're ready to share it with me."

He meant the words to frighten her, to make her go before he hurt her. He felt desperate. He was going to lose her forever, and when she was gone he would no longer care whether he lived or died. Nothing would matter at all, except that he had once kept her safe.

"You've been here for hours," she said softly, still standing by the door. "Lily is going to live, Aaron. There's no reason to punish yourself."

He uttered a mirthless laugh.

She was silent for a long while, utterly silent, and yet he could not summon so much as a word to speak to her. He stood in equal silence, waiting.

"I am ready," she said at last, her voice low and tentative. He wondered if she was afraid of him.

"Ready?" he repeated tonelessly.

"To share your bed."

He didn't know whether to laugh or weep; he barely held a grip on his control.

"I didn't realize you were so desperate, Margaret. I should be happy to oblige, of course, but you'd do far better to ask Lord Kimball to scratch your itch. He, at least, wants you."

He heard her sharply indrawn breath and felt the pain of it as if it were a knife pulling through his gut. He clutched the windowsill more tightly to keep from turning toward her.

"I seem—" she began, stopping on another sharp breath. When she spoke again her voice was light, trembling. He couldn't bear the hurt he'd given her. "I seem to have made a mistake. I beg your pardon."

"Margaret—"

"I'll leave you in your darkness, then, Aaron." Her voice was stronger now. He could hear her anger coming to life, and was glad for it. "But I want you to know this. I don't want—and will not have—any man but you."

She left, slamming the door soundly. Cardemore turned about to stare at where she'd been, and the door suddenly swung open again. Margaret stood there, looking as beautiful as she ever did when her Irish temper got the best of her.

"And you might as well know, Aaron Walford, that I took the liberty of dismissing your mistress while you were away from Town." She lifted her chin and then slammed the door again and walked away.

He stood paralyzed with shock, utter and complete, for all of five seconds. And then he went after her.

"Margaret!" he shouted, swinging his door open. She was halfway down the stairs and didn't even turn to look at him as he followed rapidly behind. "Damn you—" He grabbed her elbow to swing her around to face him.

She wrenched free and slapped him so hard that for a moment his head swam. "You bastard!" she shouted, oblivious of the servants, of anyone. "Don't you touch me after what you've just said! How dare you!"

He didn't know what she was talking about—what it was, in particular, that he'd said that she objected to. But it didn't matter. He bent and slung her over his shoulder and began to carry her back up the stairs.

Her fists on his back felt more like pats than strikes. He hardly felt them. "Aaron Walford!" she screeched furiously. "Put me down!"

"I've changed my mind about your offer. I've decided that you may share my bed."

"Well I've changed my mind, too!" she told him hotly. "Put me down!"

"Mama!" Cardemore heard Isabel cry from the bottom of the stairs. "Uncle Aaron!"

He turned, carefully, with Margaret still wriggling on his shoulder.

"Nothing's wrong, Isabel," he assured her over her mother's loud invective. "Your mother and I are going to have a very long...discussion. Tell the servants not to disturb us. For any reason."

He shut and locked his bedroom door first, and then threw her on his bed.

"I'm not going to bed with you now!" she said furiously, trying to scramble away as he grabbed her, pulling her beneath him and pinning her there.

"Oh, yes, you are. I'm not going to stop this time." He kissed her, ignoring all of her protests, and kept on kissing her until she began to kiss him back.

"Now," he said, panting for air. "Do you want me, Margaret?"

"Yes."

"Good." He reared up on his knees, took her dress in two hands, and began pulling it from her body. "Because I've wanted you nearly every single moment of the past twelve years. Do you understand?"

The look on her face was the most enchanting thing Cardemore had ever seen. "I understand, Aaron. I've wanted you for a long time, too. You're ripping a perfectly good dress, dear."

He tossed the shredded garment aside and tackled her shoes and underthings.

"I'll buy you one to replace it." He struggled to get out of his own clothes. "Whatever you want. Anything you want."

She sat up and pushed his hands aside, opening the buttons on his shirt with ease. "Very well," she murmured, kissing him. "I love you, Aaron."

"Oh, God." He took her face in his hands and made her look at him. He'd never felt so afraid before. "Don't say that."

She spread his shirt wide, pressing her palms against his chest. "I'll say whatever I please. I love you."

He was trembling, shaking with his need. "Love me, then," he muttered. "You'll hate me, later."

"Never." She feathered kisses over his wide, scarred chest while her fingers worked at the fastening of his trousers.

His need for her was powerful, but he made the time go slow. He had waited too long to take any moment for granted. And she—wonderful, generous woman that she was—matched him touch for touch, kiss for kiss, denying him nothing. He caressed her with his hands and mouth, touching, tasting everywhere, all of her. In turn, he held nothing back, for she was just as demanding. He'd never known such an exquisite lover; she touched his ugly, scarred body and made him feel as if he were magnificent.

"I love you." He said it over and over, not meaning to but unable to stop once he started. Because it *was* love, this act between them. For the first time in his life it was love, and nothing would ever be the same again.

Afterward they lay together quietly, his arms holding her near while she rested her head against his shoulder.

They were silent, until he finally began to speak.

"I've loved you since the moment I set sight on you. Do you remember when that was? At my brother's funeral."

She smiled against his chest. "Did you? Does that trouble you, Aaron?"

"It doesn't trouble me in the least. I should think it might trouble you, however, to realize that your husband wasn't even in the ground before his brother began to lust after his widow."

She chuckled softly, her breath stirring across his skin. "I never loved George. Not in the way that a wife should, at least, but our marriage was arranged and love isn't part of what's bartered for. I was as fond of him as I was capable of being and I gave him a child, but nothing more. He wasn't an easy man in that regard."

"No, he wasn't." Cardemore skimmed his fingers lazily down one of her arms. "But I daresay he was easier than me."

"Oh, no. You're wrong, Aaron. Far wrong. Where did you ever come upon such an idea?"

"Perhaps from something my father told me?" he suggested.

"Perhaps," she agreed. "George and the old earl were two of a kind, hearts and minds like ice. If either of them ever loved another soul in the world apart from themselves, I was never able to discover it. They even disliked each other, although cordially." She tilted her head upward to smile at him. "Do you know when I fell in love with you, Aaron?"

"When?"

"It was on the day of Lily's tenth birthday, when none of the children who were invited to attend her party came because that horrid speech doctor had pronounced that she couldn't speak because her tongue was possessed by a demon. Do you remember?"

He closed his eyes. "Yes."

She lifted a hand to stroke his scarred cheek. "She was so hurt, sitting in her pretty new dress on the nursery floor and weeping. You were ready to commit murder."

"I *would* have," he muttered, "if that damned doctor had been anywhere in sight."

"You made a party for her, instead," she said softly, "with Isabel and me and some of the cottagers' children. I watched as you gave the children rides on your shoulders, galloping about the ballroom, and I knew that I loved you. It frightened me so much."

"It should have." He grasped her hand and held it, gazing at her. "It should, Margaret. If you love me, then your heart has made a very bad choice."

"I know," she said. "You're a bad, wicked man, aren't you, my dear? I've always known it, but I can't seem to tell my heart to behave. I love you, and nothing is going to change that."

"You can't begin to know the things I've done—the men I've killed or had killed. The thievery and deceit and illegal dealings. You can't begin to know."

"No, I can't," she admitted. "And I can't say that I won't be angry when I do know. Perhaps I'll be ragingly furious. I probably will be. Indeed, I may bash you over the head a few times—but you know how abominable my temper is. And I'll love you, yet. Always, Aaron. Try me, if you doubt it.''

''I was behind your kidnapping,'' he said. ''I had you and Isabel and Lily taken, and Graydon as well. I did it to force Graydon and Lily into marriage.''

''I know,'' she said gently.

He stared at her. ''You *know?*''

She nodded. ''I reasoned it out from your behavior of late, while Lily's been ill. I prayed that she would live not only for her sake, but for yours, as well. You never would have forgiven yourself if she'd died.''

''I'll never forgive myself, even so.''

''It was a foolish thing to attempt,'' she agreed. ''And wrong, but you know that, and knew it, too, before you did it. You're a bad, wicked man, just as I said. Did Graydon discover the truth? Is that why you didn't bring Lily home?''

''Yes,'' he said wearily, and then told her all of his conversation with Graydon.

''Oh, Aaron,'' Margaret whispered when he was done. ''I'm sorry.''

''I have only myself to blame,'' he said. ''He was right when he said Lily didn't belong in my world. Neither do you and Isabel.''

''But we're here,'' she said, sliding her arm about him and hugging him tightly. ''And we're not going to go away. Including Lily. Graydon will be angry for a while, and rightfully so, but he'll come around in time. You can't think Lily won't insist upon seeing you, not when she adores you as she does. And when she wants you, you must be there for her, Aaron.''

''She'll have Graydon to care for her. She doesn't need her disreputable brother marring her life. Do you know, Margaret? In spite of my regrets as to how matters ended, I'm glad that she's with Graydon. He'll be good to her without my having to make him be. I almost think he loves her.''

"I hope you're right, for she certainly loves him."

"He'll be good to her," Cardemore repeated. "Just as Daltry will be to Isabel, if he ever manages to wed her. And as someone like Lord Kimball will be to you, Margaret."

She sat up slowly and leaned over him. Her long, unbound hair spilled over his chest. "Lord Kimball will never have the opportunity to do so."

"Margaret—"

"I realize that marriage between us is impossible. The laws of England consider us too closely related to allow us to wed. But I'll be more than content to have a less binding relationship. You haven't forgotten that I let your mistress go?"

He began to toy with a few strands of her mahogany hair. "I haven't forgotten. Poor Georgina. She must have been horrified to find you in her parlor. Or wherever it was that you accosted her."

"I was quite proper, I assure you. I went to visit her in the little house you've kept her in, and told her that you would no longer be requiring her services. She was somewhat anxious about leaving Town without telling you first—"

"Poor Georgina," he murmured again.

"—but I was able to overcome her fears with sufficient monetary inducements. Poor Georgina will be quite well off for the remainder of her life, you may be certain. I'll not even ask you to reimburse me."

He chuckled. "You are kind, my lady."

"Well I certainly wasn't *un*kind to your ladybird, but I'll not have gone to the trouble for no good purpose. There will be no more women, Aaron," she said sternly. "Only me. I'll not be a demanding mistress, but on that I will always insist. I'll not share you. And I'll not lose you, either, so please don't look at me in such a domineering manner. You'll not get rid of me, my lord."

He brought the strands of hair that he had wrapped about

his fingers to his lips to kiss, gazing at her the while. "I don't want to hurt you," he said softly.

"Then don't."

"God, if only I could keep from doing so. But it's impossible."

"You're a powerful man. Make it possible. If you want me, then *find* a way. You had best do so, because I'll not be held at arm's length." With her fingertips she traced the line of his jaw, and her voice softened. "Not after this, Aaron."

"Stubborn woman," he said, pulling her down to him. "Stubborn, stubborn Lady Margaret. You're the only reason I wish I'd never left my home. If I'd seen the bride who was chosen for my brother, I surely would have stolen you away before your wedding night."

"And I would have gone," she said, slipping her arms about his neck when he rose over her, pushing her onto her back. "With no regrets."

"Would you, Margaret?" He searched her face intently.

She smiled. "I'll never regret you, Aaron. Never. Not even when I'm angry with you. We've wasted too many years being noble and good. Let's not waste another moment. Let's never regret this."

"I love you," he said, and kissed her tenderly.

"Prove it," she whispered against his mouth. "Show me."

He understood her perfectly.

Chapter Sixteen

"And how is our patient today?" Countess Graydon chirped cheerfully, floating across the room on her tiny feet, which seemed never to touch the ground. The next moment she was plumping Lily's pillows. "My, you've finished all your tea. What a good girl you are." She kissed Lily's cheek with a short, quick peck and then scooped up the empty teacup on the bedstand to take it away. Her daughter, Lady Janette, took her place.

"Her color is much better! Look, Mel. Isn't it better?"

Lady Melissa appeared at the other side of Lily's bed. "Oh, yes, Janie, indeed! Much better! Shall we open a window today? Do you think we dare?"

Lady Janette's brow furrowed thoughtfully. "Perhaps an inch or two, but no more. I'm certain it would be overwhelming to her delicacy, even with the weather so warm."

"But *fresh* air," said Lady Melissa. "It's exactly what those tired lungs need."

"Indeed, I'm sure you're right," Lady Janette agreed. "And it *is* quite warm."

"Four inches, then," Lady Melissa stated with a nod. "It will be more than enough to begin with. Don't you agree, Mama?"

Countess Graydon returned to the bedside and the three ladies, for the next several minutes, held an exhaustive conversation on the merits and demerits of opening the window.

Lily sighed and sank back into her pillows. Lord Graydon hadn't exaggerated his mother's and sisters' love of nursing. She was beginning to wonder if she would ever be allowed out of bed. After two weeks of lying there, she was more than ready to be up and about. She was fully recovered, and hadn't so much as coughed or sniffled in three entire days, yet Countess Graydon and her daughters insistently refused to let her do so much as set her feet upon the floor.

"We shall open one window to one handsbreath," the countess said with finality. "And we shall build up the fire to counter any ill breezes that might occur."

"I'll bring another one of my pillows. Lady Lillian really must sit perfectly upright to exercise her lungs properly and to the fullest benefit."

"An excellent idea, Mel," Lady Janette concurred. "And I shall bring my needlework and keep Lady Lillian company, just in case the weather should turn. We mustn't take any chances."

"Indeed not," said the countess. "I believe half an hour of fresh air should be more than sufficient."

"Most certainly," said Lady Melissa. "We mustn't allow Lady Lillian to overexert herself."

Lily had long since given up trying to make them understand what she wanted. They refused to give her a pencil or paper, fearing that she would do herself an injury while trying to write, and they seemed able to understand nothing more than the simplest of her hand charades. She was invisible again, as she always was.

It was unjust, she supposed, to be angry with these lovely women. While she'd been in the midst of her illness they had done everything for her. *Everything.* On her worst night they had taken turns sitting behind her, physically holding her up hour after exhausting hour so that she might breathe. She surely would have died, otherwise. They had kept her clean and warm, ladled their endless medicinal teas into her and made her comfortable in every way. They were tireless workers, and had refused to accept her gratitude when she had tried, much later, to tender it. They clearly gained a great deal of pleasure from their nursing activities. Indeed, they appeared to be quite content with the idea of keeping her beneath their care for a long, long while.

"Pardon me. I hope I do not interrupt?"

Graydon! Lily sat up and gazed at the door where he stood, so handsome and fine and welcome. He'd rarely been to see her since she'd fallen ill, and she had wanted him so very much.

"Lady Lillian was about to partake of some fresh air, Graydon," the countess told her son as he strolled toward the bed, his gaze fixed on Lily's face. "You may remain five minutes and try not to tire her. How are you, my dear?" She lifted her cheek to receive his greeting kiss.

"Fresh air?" Graydon kissed both his sisters as they fluttered about him.

"Yes," said Lady Melissa, moving toward the window they had earlier decided upon. "It's terribly important for the lungs, you know." She and Lady Janette proceeded to open the window with exceeding care, checking and double-checking the height of the opening.

Graydon watched them for a moment, and then, with a laugh, turned back to Lily. "But my lady looks perfectly well this afternoon, and it is quite warm and comfortable out of doors. Should you not prefer to sit in the garden for an hour, Lady Lillian?"

Yes! she mouthed, nodding energetically.

"Oh, no!" his mother cried at once, echoed by his sisters' horrified exclamations. "Graydon, it is out of the question. Absolutely, completely out of the question."

Lily pressed her hands together and looked at him pleadingly, and he smiled.

"Half an hour, then, if you're so worried, Mother. I shall carry her and keep her in the sun, I promise." He bent to pull the covers aside and scoop her up into his arms. Elated, Lily set her arms about his neck and held on tightly.

"But she's not properly covered!" his mother insisted. "She must have a blanket."

"And a shawl!" Lady Melissa put in.

"Two shawls," said Lady Janette.

"At the very least," stated the countess.

He looked down at the heavy nightgown and bedrobe Lily wore, which covered her more fully from head to toe than her most modest ball gown. He looked down at her feet, and she wiggled them to show that she wore slippers.

"Lady Lillian appears to be very well dressed for a short outing," he said as he swung about and headed for the doors, "but bring whatever you must and meet us in the garden. You may bundle her up as thoroughly as you like."

He carried her quickly down the stairs, ignoring their cries of distress, and when he gave her a conspiratorial wink at having made such an excellent escape, Lily chuckled and grinned.

Servants jumped to open doors as he strode along, and soon, almost before she was prepared, they were outside, in his lovely garden. The sun shining on his blond hair made it look like pure gold, and Lily had to squint against the brightness.

"I'll find a spot with a bit of shade," he said. "And you may rest there until your eyes become used to the brightness. But after that," he warned with mock severity, "there will be nothing but pure sunlight for you, my lady."

He set her upon a bench beneath a lovely oak tree, and sat there beside her.

"Do you like my garden?" he asked, taking one of her hands and kissing it, holding it in his lap afterward.

Lily drew in a breath and looked around her. The day was indeed warm and beautiful, and the feeling of the sun and air was a keen, sensual pleasure that she'd not expected.

"It's bue-tee-ful, mah l-hord." And it was, with several

large trees and a fountain in the middle. She could see several paths from where she sat, some of them lined with neat, tidy low shrubs and some by lazier bushes overflowing with droopy summer flowers. The smell was wonderful, carried by the warm breeze, rich with herbs and sweet flower scents. Bees hummed nearby, and birds chattered in the trees and near the fountain. "Bue-tee-ful."

His fingertips touched her temple, gently, and she turned to him. He was gazing at her oddly.

"It's so good to hear you speak again, Lily."

She made a face. Her voice certainly wasn't anything worth *wanting* to hear. A frog made more beautiful noise than she did.

"It is," he insisted. "You can't know." With a sudden smile he dropped his hand and scooted a little farther away. "You shouldn't be shy to speak with my mother and sisters, you know."

She shrugged lightly, and shook her head. She couldn't bring herself to speak to his family or servants with her ugly, grating voice. Only with him could she do so, and only because she cared so much that he understand her. It was easier, with others, to let them make her invisible. It hurt, but much less so than seeing their revulsion at the sound of her voice.

"Well, then, if there's no changing your mind, I've brought you this." He slipped his hand into a pocket and pulled out one of her little gold writing cases.

"Oh!" she exclaimed, taking the case eagerly. She'd missed not being able to write. In so many ways, with so many people, it was her only voice.

"Lady Margaret gave it to me this morning, after her visit. She wasn't certain, from the way my mother spoke, that you'd be allowed to keep it if she gave it to you directly. You'll have to hide it, I fear."

"Th-hank you," she said, flipping the delicate gold cover open with accustomed ease. "Ah'm so gl-had to have it!"

"Then I'm glad I gave it to you," he said with a warm smile. "Even if my mother should be furious. You'd best hide it now before they descend upon us. I believe I hear them coming. I wonder what they've brought to smother you with, my poor dear."

And smother her, they did, Graydon thought some minutes later as Lily patiently, and silently, sat beneath the bundle of blankets and pillows that his mother and sisters had thoroughly wrapped her in. She looked like a beautiful, fluffy mummy. He doubted she could even move an arm or leg.

His mother and sisters sat near the bench on comfortable chairs, all three of them chatting away happily about their favorite topic: their patients, both past and present. Graydon listened as he always did, with polite and feigned interest. He tried to draw Lily into the conversation, but she merely smiled at him from behind her wrappings and said not a word. His mother and sisters didn't attempt the effort, much to his irritation. They treated Lily as if she were a beautiful doll, rather than a human being, almost as if she couldn't hear. It was a common mistake he'd discovered among society. People commonly assumed that Lily was deaf as well as mute.

And so he and Lily sat side by side on the bench, companionably silent, both of them smiling and nodding as his mother and sisters chatted on and on. It was pleasant, really, although he had hoped to be alone with her for longer than he'd been allowed. Perhaps later he would manage it. What he had to do required only a few minutes, but it must be done today, this afternoon, so that he could proceed with the rest of the arrangements. Two weeks wasn't much time to prepare for a wedding, but it would have to be enough. Already London was rife with rumors and speculations. He'd seen the betting books at his own club, White's, filled with wagers regarding Lily and himself and, most unfortunately, Miss Hamilton.

He'd made his visit to Frances three days ago, and had

been prepared for the worst interview of his life. She seemed to know, already, what he was going to tell her. Indeed her entire family seemed to know. He'd sat with her parents in their drawing room, waiting for Frances to arrive so that he might take her driving, and had endured their misery with silent self-condemnation.

At least he didn't have to worry any longer about breaking Frances's heart. She'd felt almost guilty at being so relieved to be set free of their unspoken agreement. She was in love with Charles Cassin, who had asked her to be his wife before he'd left London some weeks earlier. She had refused him only because she had felt obliged to honor the expectations she had given Graydon, and also because her parents would have been devastated to have her turn her back on such an advantageous match.

"But you see, my lord," she told him as they drove in the park, "I *am* going to marry him, if he'll yet have me. I shall write him this very night and tell him so. Mama and Papa will be disappointed for a time, but I love Charles and mean to be with him."

They had parted amicably. At her doorstep, Graydon offered to accompany her inside to tell her parents that there would be no marriage between them, but Frances had cheerfully insisted that there was no need. She was eager to tell them and then write her letter to Charles Cassin. Graydon had been doubtful that her parents would take the news well. He didn't want her to face their wrath alone, but she had again assured him that all would be well and had sent him on his way.

His mother and sisters talked on, intent upon their discussion. Graydon leaned back more comfortably and glanced at Lily, meeting her amused, blue-eyed gaze and winking. Her eyes were about all he could see of her face, and they were so pretty that he would have been content merely to gaze only at them all day. They would have blue-eyed children, most likely. Blond, blue-eyed children, the whole lot. He liked the idea of a crowd of little golden-headed beings, although he supposed he wouldn't mind if one or another of their forebears raised his or her specter in the form of a dark-haired, dark-eyed babe. Any child of Lily's would be beautiful.

"Anthony? Are you listening to me, dear?"

"Yes, Mother," he said automatically, turning to her with his smile still fixed upon his face. "Of course."

"Then do you agree? I'm sure Lady Lillian would wish it above all things. There, do you see? She wants to go home, don't you, my dear?"

"Of course we must arrange for proper nursing care," Lady Melissa said.

"Oh, yes, we must," said Lady Janette. "I should be most pleased to lend my own services at Wilborn Place for the next month. These London nurses are so unfortunate in their training and habits—well, I'm sure we all *know*."

"Indeed we do," the countess agreed. "We must accompany Lady Lillian for the first month at Wilborn Place, until she's much better. Lady Margaret said only this morning that they should be delighted to have us stay for as long as Lady Lillian will need us. The earl is that grateful."

"Just as he should be," Lady Melissa put in.

"Oh, yes, it's quite right. Quite, quite right," said Lady Janette, nodding. "I'm sure the earl wants what's best for dear Lady Lillian. And we couldn't abandon her at this most delicate moment, when she might suffer a dreadful relapse at any moment."

"Certainly not," the countess said, leaning forward to pat Lily's swaddled knee. "You've nothing to fear on that count, my dear. We shall stay with you every moment until you're fully recovered."

"Yes, Mother," Graydon said quietly, "but if you wish to continue in your care of Lady Lillian, then you must do so here. She is not returning to Wilborn Place." Beside him, even through all her blankets, he felt Lily rivet upon him.

"But, Anthony, I'm sure Lady Lillian would be much

more comfortable in her own home. And it does seem most odd for her to be here, especially now that the main danger has thankfully passed. We must consider her reputation."

"I shall have the keeping of that," he told her. "If you will but leave us alone for a quarter of an hour, I will undertake to do so."

His mother and sisters stared at him; he'd never seen them so silent before.

"You do recall what I said to you on the day that you arrived to care for Lady Lillian?" he asked his mother.

Her dainty features filled with glad understanding. "Oh, yes, indeed I do." She rose at once and kissed him. "How happy you've made me, Anthony." She pulled away some of Lily's blankets to kiss her, as well. "Come along, girls, and we'll give your brother and Lady Lillian a few moments of privacy."

Lady Melissa obediently rose to her feet, saying, "But, Mama, should Lady Lillian be out in the garden so long?"

"It's surely been half an hour, Mama," Lady Janette agreed.

"Nonetheless," said the countess. "We shall let them enjoy a few moments longer." She looked at her son. "Fifteen minutes, Anthony. No longer. You wouldn't wish Lady Lillian to sicken before—"

"I'll not keep her long," he promised. "We shall join you indoors shortly."

He unwrapped Lily as soon as they were gone, pushing the blankets and pillows to the ground until she was left only in her nightdress.

"Have you been heated near to death, yet?" he asked.

"An-non-nee."

The tone of her voice boded him ill. He offered her his most innocent smile. "Yes, my lady? Are you not more comfortable now? I'm sorry that you've had to endure so much coddling from my mother and sisters, but I did warn you some time ago that they were ardently devoted to their nursing."

"Ah'm grr-ate-fhul to th-hem for sav-hing mah l-hife, bhut Ah wh-hant to go home."

"Lily." He took her bare hand in his. "This is your home." He held her gaze. "I care for you more deeply than I have ever cared for any other woman, and can think of no better blessing than to have you for my wife. Will you do me the great honor of marrying me, Lily?"

She seemed to turn to stone, all of her. Even the fingers he held were frozen. Then, with a swiftness that belied understanding, she flung up and away from him, and was suddenly on her feet several steps away.

"N-ho!" she shouted furiously, and he thought that the entire neighborhood must have heard it.

He stood as well. "Lily."

"Ah w-hon't let you do th-his!" Anger poured out in her words and expression. "D-hid Ah-rhon thr-heat you?" She pressed the palm of one hand against her forehead in momentary exasperation. "Thr-rheat-*en* you?" she amended.

"No," he told her calmly. "In all truth, when I told him that I wished to make you my wife, he was not pleased. He said that it wasn't necessary. I assured him that it was. Because I wish you to be my wife."

She was shaking her head. "You c-han't."

He moved quickly, scooping her up into his arms and returning to the bench. "I can," he said, sitting down and settling her upon his lap. "And I will. If you'll only agree to it." When she tried to push back onto her feet he held her fast. "Don't be troublesome, my lady. The countess will never let you out of doors again if you so much as begin to sniffle after being out today. One day I'll tell you all of my horror stories of being kept in the sickroom so often when I was little. I hope we'll never be so nervous with our own children."

"Mah l-hord," Lily said stiffly.

"And I hope we'll have several. Children, I mean. Of both sexes. I don't care what order they come in, either.

I'm not desperate for an heir right off. Lily, love, you've turned completely red.''

"An-non-nee!"

He kissed her, passionately, until her arms slid about his neck and held him.

"I love the way you say my name," he murmured, leaning back against the bench with her resting quietly in his embrace. "I love the very sound of your voice. You'll never know what it does to me. I've dreamed of hearing it when I wake in the morning, with you beside me. No, don't turn away. Have I embarrassed you?''

She shook her head.

"Then what is it? Don't you want to marry me?''

"M-hiss Ham-hil-ton…''

"I've already spoken with Miss Hamilton, and she has wished us happy. Indeed, she is very glad for us." He wished that he could tell her the full of it, about Frances and Charles Cassin, but it was impossible. It would only heap insult upon injury to Frances if any rumors were started before Cassin made some formal announcement regarding his intentions. As well, there was the nagging fear Graydon held that Lily was also in love with the handsome, sympathetic Mr. Cassin. He yet had vivid recollections of the way she had fervently kissed the man's hand.

Lily was looking at him with an equal measure of suspicion and disbelief. "She d-hid?''

"She did." He laced the fingers of their hands together. "I promise you, Lily. She believed that you and I should wed. As do I. Can't you bring yourself to say yes? Am I so bad a match for you? Or so terrible to think of as a husband?''

She pulled her hand free and took out the gold note case from the place where she'd hid it. She wrote for a long time before finally handing him the note.

It's impossible for me to be your wife, whether I wish to be or not. My voice, or lack of voice, makes it impossible. Surely you realize that?

He read the note, folded it and slipped it into his pocket. He had missed having her notes rustling about in his clothes. "I won't lie and say that I've not considered the matter. Yes, there will be difficulties, but nothing that can't be overcome. You and I communicate well enough, and the servants would eventually learn to understand you. I'll not demand that you serve as my hostess for any formal functions, if you feel such a thing would be beyond you. I'll not demand anything of you at all, unless you feel perfectly comfortable with whatever it may be."

But you need a wife who can be a hostess for you. She underlined *need* twice. *You need a wife who will be an asset to you, not a burden.*

"Oh, Lily," he said gently, "you would never be a burden to me. Having you for my wife would give me great joy. I can only hope you might be equally pleased to have me for a husband."

I should like nothing better, she wrote, *but it's impossible! Anthony, only think of what it would mean to you, to your children, to have a wife and mother who can't even go out to shop without an interpreter. Don't you realize how fully dependent upon you I should be?*

"I do," he said evenly, "and I can't think I'll find the duty tedious in the least. And children accept what they know. Our children will love you dearly, regardless of your speech impediment. You'll make a wonderful mother."

I'm deeply sorry to refuse you, Anthony. I'm not unaware of the great honor you do me, and I do wish my answer could be otherwise. But please don't press me. I care for you too much to commit you to such a burden. You must find another, more suitable lady to be your wife.

Graydon was silent for a thoughtful moment, reading and rereading her note. He hadn't counted on this, on having to persuade her into marriage. But he couldn't let her refuse. Her reputation would never survive anything less than matrimony. There was only one way to make her agree, and he had to use it.

"Lily, I don't want to beg, but I will, if I must. If you don't marry me, my reputation will be utterly ruined. My standing in society, perhaps even in Parliament, will be lost to me. I realize that I display the utmost selfishness in asking you to make such a great sacrifice for my sake, but I do ask it. I'm desperate, you see. I've spent the majority of my adult years attaining my place in Parliament, and if I lose that now—"

"An-non-nee!" She sounded and looked completely horrified. The next moment she was furiously scribbling a note.

But that can't be! Why? Just because you saved me? Because I've been staying at your home?

He nodded. "Partly because of that, also partly because we spent several hours locked away in that warehouse, alone together. Along with the other unfortunate events—such as the picnic at Greenwich—rumors have been sent flying all over London, even in the papers. You know as well as I what society expects us to do to. We'll both be ruined if we don't put the best face on the matter and announce our betrothal soon. Even Miss Hamilton won't be unscathed by the poison if we don't move quickly. The longer the cats are given to murmur, the closer they'll come to harming her."

Lily rose, slowly. "M-hiss Ham-hil-ton," she murmured. "Th-hat w-hould be ter-rhib-hle. So un-fhair."

"Indeed, it would be."

She turned to look at him. "Ah-rhon," she said. "Ah-rhon can f-hix it."

"My dear, I only wish he could. But surely you understand that there are some matters even your powerful brother can't smooth over. Our only hope of averting disaster is if we marry."

She wrote another note.

You said that Aaron was not pleased by the idea of our marriage. He said it wasn't necessary.

"Not necessary to save your reputation," Graydon lied smoothly. "And there is some truth to that. He could take you back to Cardemore Hall and keep you there. It's doubtful that your friends and neighbors in Somerset would hear of the scandal, and even if they did, they'd no doubt continue to visit with you socially, since your brother is the Earl of Cardemore. It's my own reputation here in London, and perhaps Miss Hamilton's, which would suffer the most. I shall be seen as the rakehell who seduced and abandoned Lady Lillian Walford. As to Miss Hamilton, if I should marry her, she'll be viewed as the poor second as well as the woman who married a disreputable scoundrel. If I should not marry her, she'll be made the object of pity, a woman cast aside even when I had the chance to wed her. If, on the other hand, you and I are betrothed at once and present ourselves as a love match, society may be inclined to rally to Miss Hamilton's side in her support. It has been known to happen before.''

She sat beside him on the bench, looking fully miserable. He felt like a complete wretch for lying to her, but it seemed impossible to make her do what she must, even for her own good.

"Come, Lily, would it be so bad? For my own part there is nothing I would like better, just as I have told you. And I shall strive to make you perfectly happy, in every way that I can. We shall do very well together, I promise. Say you'll marry me.''

She was silent for a long time, so silent and still that Graydon began to feel unsure, and a little afraid. He was surprised at how important her answer was to him.

"Ess,'' she said at last, staring at her hands. "Ah'll mahry you, An-non-nee.''

"Thank you.'' He covered her hands with one of his own. "Thank you, my dear. You've made me very happy, and I promise you'll never have reason to regret your decision. We'll be content together.''

At last she lifted her head and smiled. "Ess,'' she said, and his heart thumped painfully in his chest.

He gathered her close and kissed her with all the longing

and desire and fear that he'd held in check these past two weeks while she'd been ill. He'd been so afraid of losing her; but now, at last, she was going to be his. Fully and completely his.

"We'll be wed two weeks from now. I'll have an announcement in the papers tomorrow. Shall we have a large wedding, or something small? I'll let you decide, Lily, and you must be certain to do what will be most comfortable for you. We might even go to St. Cathyrs and be wed in the chapel there. It's a lovely old thing, and as we'll be staying at St. Cathyrs until after Christmas, it would make matters more simple."

"W-hill we?" she asked with surprise. "St-hay at S-haint Cat-hers?"

"For the first few months of our marriage, yes." He smiled at her. "Alone, of course, except for the servants. I'll arrange for Mother and the girls to stay here in London until we're ready to return. You'll love St. Cathyrs, Lily. It's always lovely, regardless of the time of year. I'll enjoy so much showing you all of it. And, of course, we shall want to conceive our first child there, will we not? Ah, I've made you turn red again, love." He hugged her tightly and felt as glad as, if not gladder than, he could ever before remember. Everything seemed right and wonderful.

"An-non-nee," she said when he would have kissed her. "Ah w-hant to see Ah-rhon. W-hill you ahsk him to c-home, p-hlease?"

"Of course," he said, thinking that he would put it off for as long as possible.

"To-mho-rhow?"

He managed another smile. "Yes."

"Th-hank you."

"It's my pleasure. I understand that you miss your brother."

"Ess. Verry m-huch. C-han th-hey—"

He set a finger to her lips. "Write, love. Your voice is growing raw."

She nodded and took out a sheet of notepaper.

Can Aaron and Isabel and Aunt Margaret come to us at Christmastime? Or may we go to them?

"Perhaps they would enjoy coming to St. Cathyrs," he replied. "We can go to Cardemore Hall the following year. Now tell me who you'll have to stand up for you," he asked, wanting to change the subject. "Lady Isabel?"

Yes, she wrote. *And you'll have Lord Daltry?*

"Yes. If I can convince him to come out of mourning long enough. He's quite given up on winning Lady Isabel's heart."

But she's been miserable, too! Lily wrote. *She thinks he no longer cares for her company. Ever since the night when he rescued her and Aunt Margaret, he's had nothing to do with her.*

"I'm not certain what the trouble is," he replied truthfully. "I don't think he's yet gotten past the night of your comeout ball, when Lady Isabel made it more than clear that she wanted nothing to do with him."

Lily set a hand to her forehead in exasperation, and Graydon understood her quite clearly.

"Yes, love, we men may be fools, but if we are, then it's women who make us so. Daltry did go to your cousin's rescue, at least. She might take some comfort from that."

She's been worried sick about him. She thinks he hates her now, because he was wounded on her behalf, while she thinks he's the bravest man alive.

"They're both crazed," he teased.

Can't you speak to him? Lily wrote pleadingly. *Will you?*

"He'd not thank me for it. I doubt he wants any interference. And Lady Isabel might not thank me, either."

She'll be glad just to have any sign from him that he still cares for her. I think she loves him.

Graydon sighed. "Very well. I'll speak with him, because you ask it of me, Lily. For no other reason."

She threw her arms about him and hugged him tightly.

He chuckled and returned the embrace. "If you will ever

be so kind to me when I've been good," he said, "then I shall be the most obliging husband on God's earth. But come, I've kept you out far too long. Mother and the girls will be standing by the windows, watching for us to return to the house. They'll be so pleased to know that we're to be wed. They love you already," he said, and picked her up in his arms to carry her back to the house.

Chapter Seventeen

Whether her new relatives loved her or not, Lily wasn't entirely certain. They were glad that their son and brother was at last being wed, and that it was to someone who could lay claim to a noble lineage. For that, Lily supposed she should be grateful. It was far better than being considered a disappointing bride for the Earl of Graydon. Her soon-to-be mother- and sisters-in-law had received the announcement of the betrothal with cries of gladness and plenty of hugs. Even so, she could only imagine how much happier they would have been if he'd married Miss Hamilton. Lily would have been happier, too.

She loved him, and in her more selfish moments she was glad that she was the one who would be his wife, who would live with him and share his bed and give him children, but the rest of the time she only felt a deep, abiding distress. His entire life, from this day on, would be starkly marred. By her.

Her life, too, would be much harder. Now she must be Countess Graydon. She must do what her title required, what her husband would require. There would be parties and balls and dinners and she would have to communicate as best she could, no matter how wearying or mortifying the experience. She owed Graydon that. He was being forced to wed an imperfect wife; the least she could do was make his sacrifice more bearable. She only prayed that he'd not one day come to regret what society had forced him to do.

She had a few consolations. He wanted her physically and found her attractive. That much she could hold on to. But in time she feared that would change. Perhaps he would grow weary of her; her looks would fade with age. Then he would only have a wife with whom he couldn't even hold a normal conversation.

"Are you nervous, Lily?"

In the carriage, sitting beside her, Aaron took her hand and held it. With her other hand she signed, *Terrified*.

He gave her hand a squeeze. "The ceremony will be over before you know it, and then we'll all be on our way back to Wilborn Place."

Wilborn Place. She was so glad that Graydon had allowed Aaron and Aunt Margaret to host the wedding breakfast there. She'd missed being with her family and even with the servants, most of whom understood sign language.

Everything seemed to have changed since her illness. Graydon and Aaron were no longer as friendly as they had once been. Something had happened—although neither of them would admit to it—that had thoroughly chilled their acquaintance. The two men hardly spoke to each other, if they could avoid doing so, and Lily felt that it somehow must be all her fault.

There was something odd, too, about the way in which Aaron and Aunt Margaret behaved toward each other. She couldn't quite put her finger on what it was, but it was there. There were quiet smiles shared, and brief looks. Once, during all of the planning for the wedding, she'd even caught Aaron kissing Aunt Margaret's hand in a far too lingering manner. Isabel had said nothing, but she'd looked as if she were bursting at the seams to do so. But they'd not had so much as a private moment together for Lily to pry the news from her. There had always been Aunt

Margaret or Countess Graydon or Lady Melissa or Lady Janette present.

Isabel was another puzzle. At times she seemed determinedly bright and cheerful, while at others she burst into tears for no reason at all. The only information Lily had been able to get out of her, was that she hated Lord Daltry with a dedicated passion and never wanted to hear from or see the man ever again. Graydon had been a little more forthcoming, explaining that Isabel had sent Lord Daltry several missives, granting him permission to visit Wilborn Place at his convenience so that she and Aunt Margaret might express their gratitude for his attempt at saving them. Lord Daltry had never replied, nor visited. His own heart was broken, Graydon said, and he only wanted to go about letting it heal. It all seemed incomprehensible to Lily. She only hoped that the pair would manage to be civil to each other today, while they performed their duties as groomsman and bridesmaid. She could almost envision Isabel making a dreadful scene in the midst of the ceremony.

St. George's loomed ahead, and Lily gripped Aaron's hand more tightly. It was to be a large wedding, not because she had wanted it, but because Graydon's mother had demanded it. Graydon had said that Lily might do as she pleased, but what had pleased her—a small ceremony at St. Cathyrs—hadn't pleased Countess Graydon at all. The Earl of Graydon was a man of consequence and high standing, both as a peer of the realm and as a member of Parliament. Nothing but half the world watching them exchange vows would do, and Lily, seeing that it would please Graydon as well, had given in, despite the terror she felt at the idea of speaking before half the ton.

It was going to be awful, horrible. They would hear her raw, ugly voice, and before the day was out the other half of the ton would know the kind of wife the Earl of Graydon had wed. Some would say that she was demon possessed, but Lily was used to that. Some would laugh, some would express sorrow, but all of them, she was certain, would pity the Earl of Graydon.

"You're the loveliest bride London has ever seen," Aaron murmured. "I've looked forward to this day for many years. To see you married to a man who will love and care for you. Lord Graydon will do so, Lily. Never doubt it."

She gazed into his much-loved face with tears stinging at her eyes.

"You mustn't be afraid, love," he said softly, taking her chin in his hand. "You'll be a wonderful countess, and will do far better than you think. There may be a few challenging months ahead, but you're not a quitter or a complainer. You're a fighter, Lily. Don't forget that. You fought to overcome your silence, and won. You'll win this battle, too, and come out victorious. Don't cry, love." He wiped her tears away with his fingers. "This should be only a happy day."

But I'm afraid, she told him.

"Of course you are. It must be frightening for every woman to give herself so completely to a husband for the rest of her life. But you're stronger than you think, Lily, and Graydon will be good to you. He told me that you were going to be his wife, rather than asked for my permission. Did you know that?"

She shook her head, sniffling.

"He was determined, you see, even though I informed him that it wasn't necessary." He looked out the window as the carriage pulled to a stop. "We're here. Are you ready, Lily? I'm not. If I begin to weep during the ceremony, you must simply tell yourself that your brother loves his little sister more than his own life, and can't bear the thought of her being grown-up and gone into another man's care."

Oh, Aaron! She kissed him. *I love you so.*

"Just as I love you. I wonder how I shall make it through this day without making a complete fool of myself?" He gripped her hands as the carriage door swung open. "Lily, I'm proud of you for doing this before such a crowd. Don't worry about what the ton may think of your speaking voice. Hold your head high and show them what a brave woman you are, and that you don't care whether they approve of you or not. Keep your eyes on Graydon, and let his be the only opinion you care for. He'll be as proud of you as I am. On that I would stake all I possess."

"Calm down, Tony. You're going to wear a hole in the carpet."

Graydon stopped pacing long enough to glare at his friend, who was leaning against the wall in a relaxed manner.

"It's easy for you to be calm," he said. "You're not the one getting married."

"No, I'm not," Daltry admitted, then sighed. "I don't suppose it would help to tell you that I wish I were?"

"Not particularly."

"Well, then, I'll not say it. Not that it would do any good. I'm sure there isn't anyone present today who'd wish to marry me, anyhow. Is your mama going to weep down the assembly and wash out St. George's, do you think?"

"Probably," Graydon muttered. "Do you suppose Lily is nervous? I wish we'd done this at St. Cathyrs. I never should have let Mother talk us into such a large gathering. Lily can't help but be embarrassed by what her voice will sound like. Damnation! I should have just taken her off to Gretna Green and gotten the deed over with."

"Shocking," chided Lord Daltry. "Relax, Tony. All will go well. How bad could it possibly be, after all?"

Half an hour later, Graydon found an answer to the question. It could be very bad, indeed. He stood before the assembled with Daltry at his side, actually trembling with nerves. Outwardly he forged a perfect calm; inwardly he was quaking. What if Lily couldn't go through with it? What if someone laughed when she began to speak her vows—but that wouldn't happen, surely. Everyone present was too well-bred to commit such a vulgar offense. What if he fainted out of sheer nerves, right in front of God and all those present? What if...what if...what if...his mind was reeling with the words. He wondered if every man about to be married suffered the same awful malady.

The moment Lily appeared with Cardemore and began walking toward him, all of his fears vanished.

He heard the crowd drawing in a collective breath, in perfect measure with his own. She was magnificent. Perfect. Beautiful beyond imagination. He would never again think of what a bride should look like on her wedding day without remembering Lily in this moment.

She stopped before him. Cardemore took her hand and kissed it, then gave it into Graydon's keeping. Behind her, Lady Isabel took her place, and the ceremony began.

He had expected her to be afraid; he had *known* she was afraid. In all of the months since they'd first met at Almack's, she had been utterly consistent in this one thing: her dread of speaking before others. But when the moment came for her to speak her vows, Lily didn't quail or whisper or falter in the least. She lifted her chin, looked Graydon straight in the eye and loudly repeated each and every word so that all of the assembled could clearly hear. Her voice was as it ever was—grating, halting and masculine. Some of the words had the drawn-out gasps and croaks Graydon had become so well used to, which issued forth whenever Lily had to draw in a breath. He was certain, by the silence of their audience, that most of those present were thoroughly shocked and perhaps even disgusted.

To him Lily's words were beautiful. He was so proud of her, and loved her so very much. And he was glad, suddenly, that they had such a large multitude to attend the wedding, so that the ton would know how beautiful and brave the Countess of Graydon was, and understand that her husband was utterly pleased in her.

When she was done he took her hands and kissed each

of them in turn, reverently. Turning back to the bishop, they proceeded with the remainder of the ceremony.

"It was a beautiful wedding." The Dowager Countess Graydon sniffled into her handkerchief. "Absolutely beautiful."

"Indeed it was," agreed Lady Melissa, dabbing at her eyes.

"Oh, truly, the most beautiful wedding," said Lady Janette, leaning toward the Earl of Cardemore. "Don't you agree, my lord? You must be very proud of dear, brave Lillian. I can't think when I've cried more."

"But it couldn't be helped," the dowager countess said. "It was such a *beautiful* wedding."

Graydon, sitting beside his new wife, leaned toward Lily and whispered, "Your brother looks as if he wishes he were on another continent."

Lily chuckled and murmured, "So d-hoes A-hant Mahgrhet."

"And perhaps they wish they were there together," Graydon said in the same low tone. "I believe you were right when you said something's occurred between them. They've exchanged looks several times since we arrived."

Lily nodded and smiled at her husband, thinking that he was the most handsome man alive. He had dressed in blue for their wedding. Blue and silver, so that his eyes seemed even bluer and his blond hair looked more golden.

"If you keep looking at me like that," he said under his breath, "we'll never make it to the inn tonight with our virtue intact. I like it when you blush so prettily." He lifted her hand and kissed it. "If you only knew what I have in store for you, love, you'd turn the most shocking color of red."

"Anthony, dear."

"Yes, Mother?" he replied with guileless innocence, lowering Lily's hand while she strove to regain her composure.

"Have you spoken with Lord Cardemore and Lady Margaret about Christmas yet? At St. Cathyrs?"

Lily felt him tense, although his expression remained perfectly calm and happy.

"I've not yet had the opportunity to do so."

"Oh, you *must* come, my lord," the dowager countess said, "and you also, Lady Margaret, with Lady Isabel."

"And Matthew must come as well," Lady Janette put in. "I'm sure Graydon will wish to have his dearest friend present."

"I'm sorry," said Lord Daltry, sounding rather stiff. "But I've already promised my parents that I should celebrate the holidays with them at Iddington. My sisters and their families will be present, as well."

"Oh, that's a shame," Lady Melissa said, "but I do hope we shall have your company, Lord Cardemore, and Lady Margaret and Lady Isabel?"

Lily looked expectantly at her brother, who was looking at Aunt Margaret.

"That is…very kind of you," Aunt Margaret said haltingly. "We shall see if it cannot be arranged. Thank you."

Lily felt a surge of disappointment. Surely they would come for Christmas. She would speak with them later, just as soon as the wedding breakfast was over and before she and Graydon left. It would be hard for Aaron to give up spending his holiday at Cardemore Hall, for he had always loved being with the family, but he would come to St. Cathyrs for her first Christmas there. She knew he would. And Aunt Margaret and Isabel would come, too. She had only to make them know how welcome, and how wanted, they would be.

She wished that Lord Daltry would come as well. He and Isabel sat in their places, clearly miserable. Even during the ceremony she had caught glimpses of Lord Daltry's somber expression, of Isabel's sad, lifeless gaze. They had looked as if they were at a funeral, rather than a wedding.

"A toast," Lord Daltry said as he rose to his feet. Servants ran to refill glasses with champagne so that all of the guests might join in. "To the Earl and Countess of Graydon. May your days be many and filled with much happiness, and your troubles few. May God bless you and your children to come in all things."

The guests agreed aloud and drank, and Lord Daltry sat down. Beside her, Lily saw Isabel's hand shaking as she set her glass on the table.

Chapter Eighteen

January 18, 1818

Dearest Aaron,

You said in your last letter that you'd not grow weary of receiving so many missives from me, and I pray that is still so. Somehow I can't help but feel guilty for writing to you so often, as I know how busy you are, but I freely admit that it is one of my greatest pleasures, which I look forward to almost as much as I look forward to that time when we shall see each other again. It has been so long, Aaron. I won't upbraid you for not bringing Aunt Margaret and Isabel to St. Cathyrs for Christmas, but I will admit to how very much I missed having you all here, as well as the Dowager Countess Graydon and Lady Melissa and Lady Janette, who found that they, too, were unable to come for the holidays. Lord Daltry arrived at the last moment, coming unexpectedly on Christmas Eve. He was saddened to find that you had decided to spend the holidays at Cardemore Hall, but we managed to have a merry time nonetheless.

Lily set the pen thoughtfully against her lips and wondered if she should tell her brother that Lord Daltry had only made his snowbound journey in order to see Isabel.

She would never, in her life, forget the sight of him walking into their drawing room, dripping wet and red with the cold, and asking, with an achingly hopeful note in his tone, "Is Lady Isabel here?"

He had remained despite his disappointment, and they truly had made a wonderful celebration between the three of them. On Christmas Day, they shared a lovely, cheerful breakfast before attending church together. Afterward they had gone sleighing, the two men singing carols while Lily hummed along, and when Graydon stopped the sleigh at a particularly beautiful spot Lord Daltry had tumbled out quickly and started a snowball fight. Later, as they warmed and dried themselves by the parlor fire, Lily had at last managed to get Lord Daltry to tell what had happened to estrange Isabel and himself.

"It was my haring off to rescue her and Lady Margaret that did it," he admitted, standing near the hearth and staring into the flames. "She hated me before then. You both remember as well as I that dreadful occurrence on the night of your comeout ball. She made her feelings perfectly clear. Then, after I made the attempt to rescue them, she suddenly believed herself to be in my debt, despite the fact that I muddled the whole thing. Still, I had at least made the attempt, and she was determined to be a martyr as a way of showing her gratitude."

A martyr? Lily wrote. *But I'm sure that Isabel's feelings for you are most sincere. She's been terribly distressed by your refusal to see or speak with her.*

She handed the to note to Graydon, sitting beside her, who read it aloud.

Lord Daltry shook his head ruefully. "She tried to express her gratitude on the night of the kidnapping, at the inn, after I'd been shot, and she cried miserably through the whole thing. It was awful. Horrible." He rubbed at the bridge of his nose. "I couldn't bear that I had been the one to make her feel so trapped and...so guilty that she was willing to make the lifelong sacrifice of giving herself to me as a wife. I still can't bear it. That's why I refused to see her in London. I don't want a forced gratitude from Isabel. From any woman.''

"Surely it wasn't that," Graydon said. "Perhaps seeing you come so near death on her behalf made her realize the depths of her own feelings. Lily and I are both certain that Lady Isabel holds you in the highest possible regard.''

Lily nodded, but Lord Daltry remained unconvinced.

"It was the height of foolishness to come here. I was seized by a madness, but I'm glad it's passed. I want Isabel to be happy with the man of her own free choosing, just as Cardemore said she should be. Perhaps that's the only gift I shall ever be able to give her.''

With a sigh, Lily pushed the memory away. It had been the only sadness to mar Lord Daltry's visit, which had been so welcome, especially in the face of her longing for her family. Next year, Lily vowed, they would all be together, either at St. Cathyrs or Cardemore Hall. And surely sometime between now and then they would see each other—perhaps in London, when she and Graydon returned next month so that he might participate in the opening of Parliament.

She bent to her paper again.

In reply to the question you asked in your last missive, of course Graydon doesn't read the letters you send me. I fear that I should be quite offended at you asking such a thing, save that I presume it has something to do with your friendship with Graydon, and I am loath to interfere in anything so private. I can only tell you once more, and promise that it is the complete truth, that Graydon is a wonderful, kind and generous husband. He has been exceedingly considerate to me in every way, especially since we arrived at St. Cathyrs, and has made every effort to make me comfortable and happy here. Seeing the estate through his eyes and words, I've come to love St. Cathyrs as much as he does.

With a smile Lily thought of how true this was. A day

hadn't passed when Graydon hadn't made time to show her something new and lovely about his home and lands. He often took her riding, or for long drives in the surrounding countryside. They'd had lovely, lazy picnics on warm autumn afternoons, and long walks on clear evenings, and several times, on particularly suitable mornings, they had risen early and he'd taken her fishing. At night, in the huge bed they shared, he made love to her, passionately and tenderly, and afterward they lay together, warm and content, while he whispered stories about his childhood, until she at last drifted to sleep. In the mornings, he would make love to her again, more slowly than during the night. It seemed, to Lily, the most perfect way in which to start a day.

Regarding what I said to you in my last missive, about the servants at St. Cathyrs, I pray that you will forget all of it. It was wrong and unkind of me to make such complaints, and I shouldn't have done so. Indeed, when I think of the childish petulance with which I wrote you, I am ashamed. Now that several weeks have passed and I've had time to reflect, I really can't blame Mrs. Hallowby for assuming that I should want her to take charge of arranging the Christmas feasts for both the servants and the tenants, especially as I had not made it perfectly clear that I wished to assume all of the dowager countess' former duties. I'm certain she'll not act without first ascertaining my wishes again.

Although that wasn't strictly true, Lily didn't believe Aaron should know just how often she had attempted to make the matter clear to Mrs. Hallowby and the others, especially since his anger over her complaints had been evident in his last missive. She didn't want him to think that she wasn't happy at St. Cathyrs, or to speak on the matter to Graydon, or, worse, to try and solve the problem in his usual forthright manner.

Lily wasn't certain there even was a solution to the problem. It had been more than a little frustrating trying to convince Mrs. Hallowby that she was perfectly competent to make the major household decisions, and, more, that she *wished* to do so. But Mrs. Hallowby was the breed of woman—like the dowager countess and her daughters—who tended to treat Lily like a child. Lily was well used to it, but she disliked being humored when she tried to give instructions, and then having those instructions ignored the moment she turned her back.

Graydon had at first tried to make the servants obey her, but in the end he'd had to admit that it was beyond even his ability to do so. Mrs. Hallowby and the others weren't willfully disobedient or openly disrespectful, and it was impossible to be angry with servants who were desperately trying to please their lord and lady in the best manner they knew how.

You asked about how Jonah and his sisters are getting on, and I am happy to report that they are all fine and well. The girls, Hannah and Molly, are lovely and so eager to please. Mrs. Hallowby reports that they're learning so quickly they will soon be promoted upstairs.

Lily thought back to the day when Jonah and his two sisters had arrived—in Aaron's finest carriage, no less—fully scrubbed and dressed in new clothes, with a note from Aaron, saying that he was sending them to Graydon in the hopes that they would find useful work at St. Cathyrs. The young girls had looked terrified when Graydon's butler, Tillery, brought them into the drawing room. Jonah had sauntered in behind them, his old swaggering self, taking in the grand surroundings with little interest and speaking in his blue dockside manner. Lily had been terribly glad to see the boy, and was grateful to have a chance to repay him more fully for what he had done to help both her and Graydon, but he informed Graydon right off that he had no intention of staying. He'd only come to make certain that his sisters were taken in, and then he was heading back to London and his shipmates. It had taken Graydon more than an hour simply to convince Jonah to remain for the night, and all of the following morning to talk him into staying for a week. From there they had graduated to a month, and now, four months later, Jonah was as much a part of St. Cathyrs as Graydon, himself, was.

As to Jonah, I can only say, Aaron, that you have never given me so fine a gift, despite the fact that you never have explained how it is that you came to know of him. I suspect that Graydon must have told you about the part Jonah played in rescuing us when we were kidnapped, but that you're too modest to admit to finding the boy and sending him here as a way of repayment. He has been a most wonderful companion to me during the days, and has been so quick to learn the sign language. Indeed, I seldom need to write a word to him, for he understands me so well. It's such a blessed relief to have both him and Jenny to speak to in my own language. I only wish that they were able to have more success with the other servants, but it seems that the same fears we had to wrestle with at Cardemore Hall for so long are equally pervasive here. I've yet to hear anyone at St. Cathyrs whisper about demons, but it's certain that several of the tenants and villagers believe the sign language to be some sort of witches' craft. Jonah's gotten so angry about it that he's ready to start his own war, but I've told him to let matters be. It's enough, for now, that I have him to interpret for me.

We should be returning to London within the next two weeks, as Parliament will be opening and Graydon will need to be there. I'm not certain as to the exact date of our arrival, as Graydon has not yet discussed the matter with me. He seems so much at home here at St. Cathyrs, and I know that he dislikes the thought of leaving. But there is nothing for it, and so we must look forward to our London return as best we may. Please say that you will come to Town while we are there. And please bring Aunt Margaret and Isabel with you. I've missed you all so greatly.

Dearest Aaron, stay well, I pray.

All my love, your most devoted sister, Lily

* * *

The door was ajar, and Graydon stood for a long time, watching through the opening as Lily wrote her letter. He loved watching her. The graceful curve of her neck as she bent over the page enchanted him, as did the feminine way in which her pretty hand fashioned her letters. He wanted to go to her, kiss her neck and hands and fingers and make her forget her missive and her brother and everything in the world save him and her and what they shared together. He had never considered himself selfish, but with Lily he was. Utterly selfish. It was unjust, and sometimes frightening.

But he had come to her now in an effort to be unselfish, to hurt her, aye, but to keep her from hurt, too. It was an unwelcome task that he had to perform, but he could see no other way. The letter he'd had from Matthew three days ago made taking Lily back to London impossible. Old university friends had stopped at Iddington on their way to Bath, and had reported to Matthew that London was knee-deep in gossip about the Earl and Countess of Graydon and their hasty marriage. Matthew hadn't been able to find out from these same friends exactly what the gossip consisted of, but he seemed to believe, from their behavior, that it must be bad. Until Graydon knew exactly what was being said, he didn't dare take Lily to Town. In all probability the rumors were the usual variety, nothing more odd than that he and Lily had anticipated their vows and were expecting a child before the first nine months of their marriage were out. If that was so, he wouldn't waste a moment in damning the ton and sending for his wife. He was beyond caring what fashionable society thought of them in that regard. But if word had gotten out about the blackmail that Cardemore had served upon him—it would be too awful to contemplate. Lily must never know of it. Never.

She finished the letter and sat up, lifting the page to read it through. With a nod, she bent once more to sign her name, then carefully folded the paper and affixed to it a dab of wax and his official seal.

Graydon knocked before she could turn and see him there, and then pushed the door wide.

"Good afternoon, my dear. Jonah said you'd be here in your working room, writing letters, and here you are. I hope you don't mind my interrupting you?"

She rose and came to him with a smile of welcome, lifting her face to receive his kiss. He slid his arms about her waist and held her, thinking of what a fortunate man he was. Lily was everything that any man could want in a wife, and more.

"Ah'm gh-lad to see you. You ahre ahlways whel-come, An-non-nee," she murmured in her husky tone, which had its usual effect on him. She was the only woman who would ever be able to work such magic upon him, and, holding her now, Graydon felt a black despair at leaving her behind when he left for London.

"Have you finished your letter?" he asked, setting her away before he forgot his resolve. "Shall I frank it for you?"

"Ess, p-hlease." She went to fetch the folded missive and placed it in his hands. *To the Earl of Cardemore, Cardemore Hall, Somerset,* he read, forcing himself not to frown. Stuffing the letter in an inner pocket in his coat, he took Lily's hands and led her toward the fire.

"I must speak with you, love, if you've the time to spare for a mere husband. It won't take long, I promise."

She laughed. "Oh, An-non-nee, how fhool-ish! Ah'd rah-ther be wit you th-han ahny-one ehlse."

He wished that she could bring herself to speak so openly to the servants. He understood fully why she was loath to do so, but couldn't help but feel that it would make a marked difference in the way in which the servants perceived their mistress, even if they were shocked when they first heard her.

He seated her in one chair and pulled another close and sat down in it. Leaning forward, he took both of her hands and kissed them.

"First off, I'm sending Jonah away two days from now—"

She gave a violent start and snatched her hands away. *"N-ho!"* she cried.

"Yes," he said calmly. "I know you don't want him to leave, Lily, and that you depend upon him, but I'm sending him to Charles Cassin for training."

Her eyes widened, and he went on. "He's been the quickest one at St. Cathyrs to learn the sign language, and I've asked him if he'd not be willing to learn the language more fully with the help of Mr. Cassin, so that he might better serve not only as your interpreter, but as a tutor to the rest of the staff here. I want all of the servants at St. Cathyrs to understand you perfectly, Lily. It is your due as countess, and as my lady, to be completely understood in all things."

She continued to stare at him in silence, until her eyes began to fill with tears and she said, "Oh, An-non-nee! Tha-hank you!"

The next moment she fell forward to hug and kiss him, and Graydon pulled her onto his lap, receiving her well-pleased accolades with joy.

"There's more," he said, having to admit the full truth of all he'd come to say before she thought too well of him. Even so, he held her tight when she lifted her head and wouldn't let her return to her own chair. "I'll be escorting Jonah to Mr. Cassin's establishment myself, and afterward I shall head for London, in order to attend the opening of Parliament."

"Bhut—"

He hurried on before she could continue. "I'll remain there for the next few months, and will send for you in the spring. You'll be able to enjoy the fullest part of the season without suffering the dismal months that come before-hand."

She was shaking her head. "Ah whant to c-home wit you."

"And I want that, too," he answered sincerely, "but this will be for the best. I'll have the house ready for you when you come. Everything will be in perfect order, so that you'll have nothing to worry over."

She gazed at him solemnly, searching his eyes. Then she pushed from his lap and stood with her back to him before the fire.

"Why?" she asked.

Graydon shifted uncomfortably in his chair. Anything that he said was going to sound bad. The best answer he could give, which was awful as well as a lie, was the one other men he knew gave their wives for wishing to have some time alone. "Because I desire that it be so," he answered softly.

She stared into the fire. "T-hake me wit you," she whispered. "Ah proh-mise Ah'll n-hot shame you."

He was on his feet and pulling her into his arms in an instant.

"God, Lily. You could never shame me. It's bad enough going without you...being away from you...without letting you think such a thing. Love, don't you know how I'm going to miss you? Every moment that I'm gone from St. Cathyrs would be easier spent in Hell."

"Then l-het me c-home."

"Not now," he said, closing his eyes and pressing his cheek against the top of her head, against the silken smoothness of her hair. "In a few months, I'll send for you. Until then, I'll send Mother and the girls home to bear you company, and I shall come to St. Cathyrs as often as I'm able, for as many days as Parliament's schedule allows."

"*Why?*" she asked once more, and he could hear the pain that he'd wanted to spare her.

"It's for the best," he murmured, holding her more tightly, wanting her so badly. "Trust me in this, Lily. You'll be happier here until I've had a chance to put everything to rights in London. Please try to understand."

She was stiff in his arms, standing very still until she at last pushed slowly out of his embrace.

"Ess, An-non-nee. Ah unnerst-hand verry w-hell."

"Lily—"

"Mah l-hetter." She held out a hand, not looking at him. "M-hay Ah have it b-hack?"

He gave it to her.

She took it in both hands and moved to the fire, tearing the missive in two before tossing it into the flames.

"Ah'll g-hive Mrs. Hal-how-by instr-huct-sions to pre-phare for your de-phart-hure," she said, and without looking at him left the room.

Chapter Nineteen

London was dismal, and had been dismal nearly each day since Graydon had arrived. In February it had snowed. In March it had rained. It was now April, nearing Easter, and there wasn't yet even a hint of spring. Not that Graydon cared so much for the weather, but Parliament would be adjourning for the coming holiday, and he would at last be able to get home to St. Cathyrs, and to Lily. He was counting the hours.

He'd once told her that it would be more like living in Hell than living in London to be away from her, but he'd understated the matter. It was far worse than living in Hell. It wasn't like living *at all*. He was dead to enjoyment, dead to pleasure, dead to anything but wanting his wife.

In the past weeks he'd managed to gain a reputation for himself as a surly, ill-tempered, unmannerly brute who couldn't be counted on to behave at public gatherings. If there were any rumors being told about Lily and himself, nobody was telling them in his hearing. Everyone he met in the ton seemed, in his mind, to be responsible for his being parted from Lily, or if not responsible, at least supportive of the idiotic societal rules that had made him leave her at St. Cathyrs. He went to balls and dinners and didn't want to dance or smile or engage in polite conversation. In Parliament he was mean and argumentative, and worse, unreasonable. His own party was about ready to send him down. Or send him home, perhaps, until he came to his senses. He'd been drinking too much of late, not sleeping enough. Nights when he should have been abed after a long day of arguing in the House of Lords, when he was so weary that his very bones ached, he sat up, writing Lily. But she never wrote back, and that only made it worse. It had been weeks since he'd had her last stiffly polite missive. If she was angry and hurt and meant to punish him, she'd chosen an excellent means of doing so. He was wretchedly miserable.

"Is there any way in which I might be of service to you, Lord Graydon?"

Graydon looked up from the book he'd been sightlessly staring at and focused on the face of the store clerk. "I'll take this," he said bluntly, shoving the book into the other man's waiting hands.

"*Lectures on the English Poets,*" the clerk said with nodding approval. "One of Hazlitt's finer works, if I may say so. Would you prefer to wait until it's wrapped, my lord, or shall we have it delivered to your address?" He glanced toward the bookshop's front window. "The rain is still quite strong, I fear."

It didn't matter, Graydon thought. A good soaking wouldn't make him any more miserable than he already was.

"Have it delivered," he told the man, and took his hat and cane from the stand near the door.

"My lord," the man said hurriedly, following him to the door, "allow me to send one of the lads in the back room to fetch your carriage."

"No." Graydon set his hand upon the knob. Outside the storm looked as if it were turning into a gusting hurricane. "I shall tend the duty myself."

The wind rushed at him as he opened the door, blinding him with stinging rain as he pushed out to the pavement. He covered his eyes with a hand and tried to wipe the water out of his face, cursing under his breath as he waited to hear the sound of his carriage pulling up to receive him. He only hoped the horses would be manageable. It had been not only foolish of him to go out in such weather, but inconsiderate, as well. His coachman and footmen must be soaked to their bones.

The wind died down enough for Graydon to peek out from behind his hand, but no sooner had he done so that he was nearly knocked down by a small, darkly bundled figure.

"Oh!" a female voice cried. "I'm terribly sorry!"

Graydon steadied her about the waist, pulling them both back under the small sanctuary of the bookstore's awning.

"Frances?" he asked with surprise. "Miss Hamilton?"

She looked up from beneath her hooded cloak, and he saw her pretty face filled with an equal mixture of shock and distress. "Lord Graydon!"

"What on earth are you doing out in this weather? I didn't even know you were in London." He looked past her into the wet, gray storm. "Where is your maid? Your coach? What could Lady Hamilton have been thinking to let you go out?"

Her face was wet, although from rain or from tears, he couldn't tell. She shook her head with a wretched sob. "She doesn't know I'm out. I didn't bring my maid. Please don't scold." She held onto his sleeve in a pleading gesture. "I know it was wrong, but I had to get out, just for a little while."

He stared at her in disbelief. "In this kind of weather?"

"In *any* kind of weather. I've been so unhappy. I only wished to be alone for an hour."

"Here's my carriage." He took her by the elbow as his coach pulled to a stop. A footman jumped down to open the door and Graydon hurriedly escorted Miss Hamilton inside. "I'll take you home," he said as he settled her into the seat.

"Oh, no! Please don't."

"Miss Hamilton, you're soaked through," Graydon said with calm logic as he tucked a thick blanket about her, "and like to catch a chill. I very nearly lost my wife to such as that, and I'll not allow the same thing to happen to one whom I deem a dear friend." He sat down on the opposite seat, relieved to be out of the rain at last.

Across from him, Frances was shaking her head, looking lost and pitiful, trying to say something. Then she suddenly burst into tears and bowed her head into her hands.

"Frances, my dear!" He leaned forward to touch her knee. "What is it?"

"Please," she managed, sobbing, "don't take me home yet. Not yet."

"Very well. I'll take you to my house for tea, first. Hopefully we'll not be seen, although I daresay the servants will talk. But if you prefer that to being taken home—"

"I do!"

"Then it shall be as you say."

Half an hour later they were ensconced in his drawing room, sipping hot tea before the fire. Graydon had changed into dry clothes and had convinced Frances to borrow a warm dress from Lily's closet. Only their hair remained wet, and the fire was rapidly drying that. It was shocking for them to be together in such a way, but Graydon doubted there was much else he could do to get into society's black graces. For her part, Frances seemed to care even less what anyone thought.

"Your parents wouldn't allow Mr. Cassin to make a formal request?" he asked, sipping his tea.

"Papa wouldn't even allow him into the house," she answered, gazing stonily into the fire. "He threatened to disown me entirely if I so much as spoke with Charles again. I was ready yet to go with Charles and be his wife. We could have gone to Gretna Green. It wouldn't have mattered to me, so long as we were together. My only wish was to be his wife."

"But it mattered to Mr. Cassin, I daresay," Graydon said.

She nodded. "It did. He refused to bring shame upon me, or to be the cause of so great a separation from my parents. I begged him to reconsider." Tears welled brightly in her eyes, and she blinked at them. "But he felt it would be for the best if we simply tried to forget each other. He never—" she drew in a shaking breath "—he never even answered the letters I sent him."

"Oh, Frances," he said sadly. "I'm sorry. Truly sorry."

"There was nothing you could have done to set things to right," she told him kindly. "Although I believe you would have tried. You've always been very good to me, my lord."

"I should have spoken with your parents myself, on that day when we agreed to bring an end to our understanding. I never should have let you do so alone. Were they very angry?"

"Utterly. Papa was furious, and Mama wept and wept. I never expected them to react in such a manner, but I underestimated, I think, their hope that I should wed into a higher title. For a long time, they seemed unable to think of anything but the disappointment I had served them. Even now they speak of it, especially since I've refused so many invitations this season. I know I should put forth an effort to make another eligible connection, for their sake, if not for my own." She touched her forehead in an unconscious gesture of vulnerability. "But I just can't. I have no care for any of it, for the dancing and flirting and other foolishness the ton resort to in an effort to amuse themselves. I shall never marry, and only pray that my parents will accept that and relent and take me home soon. I am mortally weary of London."

Guilt struck Graydon like so many damning blows. He was the one who'd brought her down to this, to such misery. During all the months while he'd lived in such complete happiness with Lily at St. Cathyrs, Frances had been suffering.

"I understand, my lady, for I, too, am weary of Town and the life to be had here. But I would ask you to reconsider. There are a great many fine and decent men who would give all they have to attain the honor of making you their wife. I realize that your heart is with Mr. Cassin, but as he is no longer available to you, would you not rather marry a man whom you can at least respect and like and make your own home with, rather than stay beneath your father's hand for the remainder of your life?"

She closed her eyes briefly, looking weary and sad. "I can't bear going about Town, to parties and balls," she whispered. "The gossips, and the looks. They're everywhere. Just everywhere. And afterward, when we've returned home, my mother weeps as if she had no reason to continue living. It's so hard."

"Oh, Frances." He took her hand and held it. "Frances, what have I done to you? How can I make this better?"

She looked at him, smiling faintly, the kind and sympathetic Frances he had always known and admired. "This isn't your fault, my lord, any more than it is mine or Mr. Cassin's or my parents'. Or Lady Lillian's. This is simply the way society has deemed things be, because we have not fitted into its perfect vision. Please don't worry over the matter. I'm ashamed for even telling you my troubles, when you've so many of your own. How is Lady Lillian? Please tell me."

He sat back in his chair with a sigh. "She's angry with me for leaving her at St. Cathyrs. She won't even answer my letters. I've only had word of her through my steward, and that only to report that she is in good health. I wish, very much, that I'd brought her with me."

"Do you?" Frances asked. "Even in the face of all the horrible rumors that have been flying about Town? The snubs and gossiping are bad enough without that, too. Surely you can't wish to expose her to such venom? Of course I realize that she'll know the truth of why you wed her, purely out of love, but the spite being directed toward her own brother is sure to be hurtful.''

He stared at her. "So it's true," he murmured. "Will you tell me what's being said? Please, Frances.''

"My lord, surely you've heard? About Lord Cardemore blackmailing you into marrying Lady Lillian? Some say that he bought up all your debts, and some go even farther, hinting that he held the deed to St. Cathyrs. Although I'm sure that's quite foolish, as your properties must be fully entailed and the deed safe from any such thing.''

Graydon felt the blood draining out of his face. His mouth, like the rest of him, was stiff with shock. He could barely speak to her. This was far worse than he'd expected.

"Where did you hear these things? Who was it told you?''

Her gaze filled with concern. "My father was the first to speak of it, because he felt better in believing such lies, for then it was not my fault that our understanding came to an end. But there have been others who've spoken, as well. Graydon!'' she exclaimed when he stood with a curse and threw his delicate teacup smashing into the flames. "Never tell me it's true!''

With an effort he controlled himself. "Forgive me," he said tightly, rubbing his eyes with the palm of one hand. "Forgive me. I don't know what to tell you. St. Cathyrs isn't entailed. I wish to God it had been. And I had run up debts—there were so many improvements I wished to make to the lands.'' He laughed harshly, mocking himself. "I wanted to make St. Cathyrs better, and nearly ended losing it altogether.''

Her soft hand touched his sleeve, and he realized that she stood behind him. "Is it true, then? But I know that you love Lady Lillian very deeply. Lord Cardemore couldn't have commanded that from you, no matter what he did.''

He released a taut breath and turned to take her hands in

his. She was so good and kind. He felt like an utter swine for all that he had put her through, for all that she had suffered because of him.

"It's true," he admitted, and told her the whole sordid tale, omitting nothing. "And I love Lily more than I knew it was possible to love. If it's what you feel for Mr. Cassin, then I can only commiserate the more with you, for I should rather die than lose her. Frances." He gripped her hands more tightly. "What can I do? If she hears about this she'll be devastated. She'll think that I only married her because Cardemore was threatening me."

"But surely she'll believe the truth, when you tell her. And, of course, she already knows that you love her. It's her brother's part in this that will wound her deeply. I know you wish to spare her that."

Nine months earlier he'd not have cared in the least whether Lily came to hate her brother or not, but since their marriage, he'd come to understand more fully what Lily felt for her demon brother. She wrote Cardemore faithfully, every week, and sometimes oftener. And she had continually asked Graydon when they might see her family again.

"I want to spare her every pain that I can, but if she hears of this she'll be terribly wounded. How could it have become known? I've not even heard a word of it until you told me just now. No one involved could have spoken of the matter."

"I can't begin to know," she said. "It might have been through anyone, even one of the servants. It doesn't really matter, my lord, now that the rumors are out. If there is any way in which you can spare Lady Lillian, then you must do so!"

"But how?"

She pulled her hands free and turned to the fire, looking thoughtful. "Can you not bring her to Town and let the ton see that yours is a love match?"

He shook his head. "I can't have her anywhere near Town until the rumors have been dispelled."

"Then could not you and Lord Cardemore be seen together, to show that there is no enmity between you? Surely the ton will eventually believe that two men who are so friendly together cannot have been involved in blackmail of any sort."

"That would be best," Graydon concurred, "save that Lord Cardemore is not expected to arrive in London until sometime after Easter."

"Oh, dear. Then I suppose you're right. You must keep her away from London. Perhaps even for this entire season. She may be disappointed, but it would be better than knowing such complete devastation."

"Indeed. But that is my worry, not yours, Frances." He lifted her hand and squeezed it. "You have been very good to me, my dear."

"Just as you have been to me," she said.

They stood looking at each other over the gulf of the ever sobering sadness that had been a daily companion to them both.

"Let me make amends to you as best I may, Frances. Let me escort you to a few events, and be your companion, so that I may make certain of your happiness."

"Oh, Graydon, I don't know," she said, sounding weary again. "There would be so much talk if we were seen together. So much *more* talk," she amended.

"And our lives are filled with such as that now, are they not? But I believe that we can bring some of that to a halt, if we are together and it is seen that we have no care for each other in that sense. We must show the ton that we are only good friends, and not lovers. I shall be perfectly faithful to my wife in every way, and you shall dance and flirt with all of the many men who admire you beneath my approving eye. I'll not let any of them importune you, Frances."

"I know that, my lord, and I am truly grateful. But you must understand that it is only Charles Cassin I shall ever love, and only him that I shall ever wish to marry."

"I understand that perfectly. But I also understand that you will not wish to live beneath your father's roof unless you have made every attempt to appease his wishes. Do this for yourself, for your own peace, so that in years to come, even if you never wed, you will not have to bear your father's reproach for not attempting to find a husband. And," he added, "do it for me. I am more than selfish to ask it of you, but I cannot bear, either, to go into company any longer. At least not alone. If you will go with me, I shall be more than content."

She hesitated, then smiled faintly and nodded. "Very well, my lord Graydon. If it is your wish, then it is also mine. We shall do very well."

Chapter Twenty

Lily celebrated Easter alone, attending church and sitting in the Earl of Graydon's pew by herself, just as she had for so many previous Sundays, and afterward sitting alone at the head of the dining room table, partaking of her dinner, just as she had for so many evenings during the past three months. And on those nights, when she was done, she sat in the drawing room, playing the pianoforte or reading or doing needlework. Alone.

Tonight, she sat beside the fire and decided that she'd had enough. Her husband was ashamed of her and didn't wish to be in her company, at least not while he was in London. That, despite the letters he wrote claiming otherwise, was quite clear. But she no longer cared what he wished or wanted. She hadn't married Anthony Harbreas to be hidden away in the country as he whiled away month after month of the season in Town, and she wasn't going to wait any longer for his permission to join him in London.

He had said that he would send for her, and had promised to come home often, but he had done neither. His letters were filled with longing and affection and remorse, he claimed to miss and want her, but he never asked her to join him. She was beginning to think that she'd been entirely mistaken in the man. She had thought he would never be false, but now it seemed that he couldn't be trusted. If he wasn't handing her bald-faced lies, then *why* hadn't he asked her to join him?

There was only one reason that made sense, and Lily had determined that she would prove him wrong. She would learn to speak beautifully, no matter how difficult it would be. She would work ceaselessly until she spoke with more feminine grace than the most exalted hostesses of the ton, and then she would never let the Earl of Graydon forget how badly he had treated her, or that he had once so cruelly, and carelessly, abandoned her.

It was spiteful, she knew, but Lily no longer cared. She was well past the days when she'd spent all of her time longing for her husband, and waiting for his little offerings of letters and notes to arrive. How foolish he must think her, to believe that she would forever be mollified by such as that! He couldn't begin to know what she had suffered at St. Cathyrs in his absence.

On the day Graydon had ridden out of St. Cathyrs, the servants had ceased to treat her as if she were a sweet, mindless child whose attempts to communicate with them were, at best, amusing. Indeed, without their master present to please, they tried not to treat her in any way possible. Lily became invisible again, and the great house went back to running as it did when no one but the servants were present. Oh, they didn't ignore her entirely. She was fed and dressed and bathed and seen to, almost as if she were some sort of pet to be cared for. She was not spoken to unless she first made an approach, and she was not asked about anything unless she attempted to make her wishes known. Even then, her requests were often ignored or overridden. Once, Lily had given Tillery a note stating that she intended to go shopping in the village, but when she had come downstairs an hour later, dressed and ready to go, the carriage hadn't even been called for. Another time she had written out a weeks' worth of menu suggestions and given it to Mrs. Hallowby, who had chuckled over the list with clear amusement and announced that many of the requested dishes wouldn't be good for Lily's digestion, and that the dowager countess would never approve. Lily had given up and not tried to press the matter. The effort, she knew, would only prove exhausting and probably not worthwhile.

For a time she had hoped that her mother- and sisters-in-law would return to St. Cathyrs to bear her company. Although she knew that they would treat her in much the same manner as the servants did, she'd at least not have to be so entirely alone in the house. Just to listen to them chattering over the dining room table in their bright, rapid voices would be heaven. But she had received word from the dowager countess only days after Graydon had left saying that she and her daughters had decided to spend the rest of the year traveling in Greece and Italy and other neighboring countries with some of their London friends, in the hope of discovering new and unusual cures for common ailments. Dr. Patterson, whom Lily remembered as greatly admiring Graydon's diminutive mother, was to be one of the travelers, and there seemed to be in the countess's letter some hint of romance. Lily was glad to know that her mother- and sisters-in-law were so content, but felt that much sorrier for herself.

Jenny was furious about the way in which her mistress was being treated, but Lily wouldn't let her upbraid the others, at least, she hadn't while she had still believed that Graydon was going to send for her. Graydon had promised that the others would learn the sign language, and once they did everything would change. Surely she could put up with it until then, and until she was with Graydon again.

But he wasn't going to send for her, and Lily wasn't going to stay at St. Cathyrs and live this way. She had made her decision and she was going to stick to it. Steeling her spine, she went to the bellpull, giving it a hard, solid tug.

A moment later the door opened and Tillery entered.

"My lady, did you wish for something?"

"Ess, T-hill-hery," she said, clasping her trembling hands together to keep them from shaking. "Ah w-hould l-hike to spheak to Miss-hes Hal-how-by and y-hourself, right aw-hay."

He stood staring at her as if she were a spectral visitation, and Lily wondered, with a shiver of panic, whether she'd spoken clearly enough or not. Perhaps he'd not understood a word of it. Perhaps he was too horrified at the sound of her grating, manlike voice to give her any reply.

But she had started this, and must go through with it if she ever wished to make her way to London. Straightening, she cleared her throat and added, more firmly. "N-how, if you phlease, T-hill-hery."

He made a rigid bow. "Yes, my lady. I shall find Mrs. Hallowby and ask her to attend at once."

He disappeared and Lily let out a shaking breath. So far, so good. In a remarkably short period of time, Tillery returned with a smiling Mrs. Hallowby.

"Yes, my lady? You wished to see me?"

"Bhoth of you," Lily said, seeing the housekeeper's face fill with a shock that equaled Tillery's. "Ah have des-hided to jhoin the e-herl in Lhon-dhon. T-hill-hery, phlease m-hake the arhange-mhents for mah trah-vel. Miss-hes Hal-how-by, phlease have mah thi-hings p-hacked. Ah sh-hall lheave in the mhorn-hing."

"But...my lady!" Mrs. Hallowby returned in a protesting tone. "I'm sure the earl...what I mean to say is..."

Lily lifted her eyebrows in a haughty manner.

"Perhaps the earl is not yet expecting you, my lady?" Tillery put in, and Mrs. Hallowby began to nod in agreement. "Would you not rather wait a day or two and write to tell him of your intentions? I'm sure he would wish to make certain that the house in London is prepared for your arrival."

"Indeed, my lady, you must write him first," said Mrs. Hallowby, still nodding. "And I shall, of course, need time to pack all that you will need."

"N-ho," Lily stated, certain that if Graydon had given such a command his servants would have scurried to do his bidding without question. "Ah w-hill lheave toh-moh-row. Mhake the neh-cess-hary pre-pah-rah-tions."

"Please forgive me, my lady, but it's impossible," Tillery said. "I shall write the earl first thing in the morning and—"

"N-ho!" Lily slammed a hand down on a nearby table. "Ah am the c-houn-tess of Grah-don! Ah am n-hot a ch-hild! N-hot a p-het! A-hand n-hot a prih-son-her in mah own home!"

Mrs. Hallowby put both hands to her cheeks in distress. "Oh, indeed not, my lady!"

"Certainly not!" Tillery agreed at once.

"Verry w-hell," Lily said more calmly, drawing in a breath. "Th-hen Ah sh-hall lheave toh-moh-row mhorn-hing."

Mrs. Hallowby dropped into a curtsy. "I'll see to the packing at once, my lady."

"And I shall make certain that the carriage is ready," said Tillery, making another bow.

They left the room together, and Lily had to hold on to the table to keep from collapsing. It had worked! They had been shocked by the sound of her voice, but they had *listened* and responded. She felt like shouting for joy! If only Graydon had been here to see her triumph. He had been the one to tell her that she should speak to the servants. Over and again he had tried to get her to do so. If he were to walk through the door at just that moment she would kiss him until he was breathless. Well, perhaps she would break his nose, first, for being so neglectful, but then she would kiss him.

She wondered what kind of reception she would receive when she arrived in London. If he was angry, she wouldn't know quite what to do. But if he was glad—well, she would have to see how she felt. She loved him, missed and wanted him, but she couldn't forget that he had lied to and abandoned her.

She would have two days during which to compose herself, Lily thought, and then, whether he was glad to see her or not, she would be in London with no intention of leaving alone.

Chapter Twenty-One

"Can you believe how quickly the weather has changed? From rain to sun in only two days' time?"

Graydon guided his horses easily through the park gates, glad that he and Frances had decided to go driving before the fashionable hour so that the paths were free of traffic.

"Yes," he said. "It does seem as if spring has at last arrived, does it not? Certainly it was past time."

It was good to see Frances smiling again in her old, cheerful manner. For a while he'd begun to think that she might never smile again, she'd been so miserable over memories of Charles Cassin. But in the passing weeks since they'd run into each other on that rainy afternoon, he'd seen her slowly regain the sunny nature that had so charmed him two years before.

They'd spent a great deal of time together, attending the same functions, dancing and talking, keeping each other from thinking too fully on the ones whom they loved and missed. Together they had pushed away their loneliness, and Graydon would forever be grateful for the friendship and understanding Frances had gifted him with, especially after what he had done to her in ending their betrothal. But even in regard to that the time had been well spent, for they had come to understand just how poorly matched they would have been. Frances had put it into words perfectly one afternoon, while they'd strolled through Kensington Gardens, when she'd said, "How fortunate we are not to have ruined such a lovely friendship by becoming married."

And it was true. He admired Frances for who she was, but she never would have inspired in him the kind of love and passion that Lily alone was able to do.

Thoughts of Lily were less encouraging. She still refused to answer any of his letters, despite the fact that he continued to write her every night. He couldn't seem to make himself stop, and poured every bit of love and longing that he felt for her into each word. But she remained entirely unmoved, and he knew that she would be a long time in forgiving him for what she must deem a complete abandonment. She would think he had lied when he'd promised to send for her, when he'd promised to return to St. Cathyrs as often as possible, and he'd not be able to blame her. He deserved her anger and fury, for it was nothing short of cowardice that had kept him from going home, and nothing less than fear of losing her that had held him back from sending for her.

And so he had stayed in London, even through Easter, writing and sending his letters and praying that they would assure her that his love was constant and unchanged. At least until he could get home and beg for her understanding and forgiveness.

"I shall be leaving London at the end of next week," he told Frances, saying what he'd brought her here to say.

"Oh, Graydon, shall you?" she replied happily. "At last. Lady Lillian will be so relieved to have you home. I know it has been the nearest wish of your heart, for you have missed her so greatly. You've found a representative to keep you informed of Parliamentary proceedings?"

"Yes, and indeed, I wish I had thought of it sooner, to do this the other way around, remaining at St. Cathyrs and coming to London only when necessary, rather than living here and visiting there. Not that I've done any visiting, of course, since learning of the rumors."

"And you should have done so," Frances replied with gentle censure. "When I think of dear Lady Lillian, so alone at St. Cathyrs, my heart goes out to her. I can think of nothing more hurtful, especially to a new bride. She must believe you don't care for her company in the least."

"I imagine that's so," he said grimly. "I can only pray that I shall be able to convince her otherwise and yet keep all of the truth from her."

"You can't keep her safe at St. Cathyrs forever," Frances said. "Eventually you'll visit acquaintances or entertain friends. I fear she will hear of it regardless of your attempts to spare her."

"It is a risk I have no choice but to take."

"Perhaps it might be best if you told her yourself," Frances suggested. "You could ease the pain by convincing her of your love, and that you married her out of your own free choice."

"She might forgive me, but I doubt she would forgive her brother. I don't particularly care for the Earl of Cardemore, but Lily loves the fiend. She would be utterly devastated to know the part he had played in bringing about our acquaintance."

"I suppose you're right," Frances agreed, "but I'm so terribly afraid that Lady Lillian will hear the truth at the hands of others, and it would be so much crueler than if you, or her brother, or both of you together, told her."

"Told her together," Graydon repeated thoughtfully, trying to envision the scene in his mind. "Do you know, Frances, you may have something there. Indeed, it might do very well. I shall have to write Cardemore tonight and ask him whether he might agree to meet me at St. Cathyrs, perhaps at the end of next month, when I've had some time to soothe Lily's present anger with me."

"Oh, I do hope he'll agree," Frances said fervently, gazing up at him.

Graydon smiled and patted her hand. "You're very good to me, my dear, to help me with such tiresome matters. I doubt that I shall ever be able to repay your kindness."

She set her own gloved hand over his. "I only wish to be helpful, especially to Lady Lillian. If she has missed you as much as I have missed Charles, then I am truly sorry for her, and pray that you will never leave her alone for so long again."

"I'll not," he vowed. "Never again." He pulled his hand away and touched her cheek briefly, then turned ahead again to urge his horses forward.

Frances stiffened beside him and gasped. "Graydon!" she cried. "Is that not Lady Lillian?"

It was, and Graydon was paralyzed with shock. She was on horseback, standing in the lane some distance ahead, looking directly at them. Farther behind her, also on horseback, one of his own grooms was discreetly pretending not to see him.

"Oh, God," he muttered, snapping the reins and sending the horses toward her. He could only imagine what he and Frances must have looked like, no matter how perfectly innocent it was, gazing at each other and holding hands.

"Lily!" he called out as they neared her. What in the name of heaven was she doing here? He didn't know whether to greet her politely or demand an explanation. The furious expression on her face boded no good, regardless of what he did or said.

He called to her again as they came nearer, and began to slow the horses, but Lily shook her head and turned her horse about, and within moments was too far away to hear him shouting after her, with the groom fast on her heels.

Lily waited for Graydon in the small sitting room that adjoined her bedchamber, having sent Jenny and the other servants away as soon as she had changed out of her riding habit. He would be home shortly, she knew. Just as soon as he took Miss Hamilton home and bade her good-day.

Miss Hamilton, Lily thought bitterly. She'd believed the woman was her friend, that she had truly wished her and Graydon happy when they wed. But it was obvious that Graydon and Miss Hamilton were still deeply in love. Why, then, had Graydon so insistently wed her? *He* had been the one to insist upon it, despite all her arguments. It didn't make sense. She would have been his mistress, if that was all that he had wanted of her. Surely she had told him so, hadn't she?

A soft knock fell on the door, and she stood just as Graydon walked into the room. He looked disheveled, as if he'd not stopped a moment after coming indoors to straighten his clothes and hair. His cheeks were slightly red, and his breathing uneven, and she realized that he must have run all the way up the stairs.

"Lily."

She had thought everything out very clearly, and was perfectly prepared for him. With a quick movement she flipped open the little gold case at her wrist and wrote him a note.

Good day, my lord. A lovely day for a drive in the park, is it not?

The note trembled in his hand.

"God, Lily."

He took a step toward her, and she very politely turned to look out the window. He didn't come any nearer.

"How long have you been in London?" he asked after a silent moment. "Why didn't you write to let me know that you were coming? I might have saved you the journey. I was coming home to St. Cathyrs next week. For good, I mean."

Were you? she wrote. *How very nice. I believe I would have died of the shock.*

She held the note out to him without turning.

"I was coming home," he insisted. "Lily…darling, I've missed you so." He moved closer, setting a hand upon her shoulder, which she promptly shrugged away. "Didn't you read the letters I sent you? Love, I've been miserable without you.''

She said nothing, wrote nothing.

''You have every right to be angry. I left you alone at St. Cathyrs, and didn't send for you, as I said I would. There are no real excuses that pardon such things. Lily, won't you look at me? At least speak to me?'' With a hand he tried to turn her to face him, but she was as fixed as a mountain.

He groaned and buried his face against her neck; his arms came about her waist to hold her so that she felt the heat and hardness of him all along the length of her back. ''I missed you every moment. I wanted you so badly. I'm so sorry that I hurt you. I'm sorry for everything.'' His lips moved against her skin as he spoke, and she tried to suppress a shiver. ''I love you, Lily. So very much. I was coming home to you.'' He placed gentle kisses along the length of her neck, from beneath her ear down to her shoulder.

She hadn't foreseen how good it would feel to be touched by him again, to feel his mouth on her skin, his arms about her, and Lily felt herself weakening. He must have sensed it, for he murmured again that he loved her and turned her in his arms until they were fitted together. Feeling his body against hers was like coming home again. The rightness of it was something that couldn't be put into mere words. His lips caressed her cheek, her eyelids, her nose, and with every breath he said her name, until his mouth found hers at last and he was kissing her as she had so often dreamed of him doing during the past lonely months.

The taste, the feel of him, made her light-headed. Her arms slid up about his neck, her hands into the soft silk of his hair.

It all happened so quickly that she could never after remember how they had gotten down to the floor, with her skirts up about her waist and his trousers unfastened. All she could remember was the overwhelming need to have him inside of her, hard and deep, and that they made enough noise to provide the servants with months of gossip. Their hunger was a fire, all-consuming, and even when it was over it wasn't enough.

They lay on the floor, dazed, breathing hotly against each other's skin. He gripped her by the waist and lifted her, keeping her joined to his body, and carried her that way into her chamber beyond, laying her on the bed and loving her again without parting from her or stopping to undress either of them. This time he made it last longer, moving more slowly, more purposefully, until the ache was a sweet, burning pain that flooded over her in a strong, lavish tide, draining her so completely that she was insensible for some minutes afterward.

And still it wasn't enough. She was dimly aware that he at last lifted himself away and undressed her, that he put her beneath the covers and joined her there shortly, as naked as she. He roused her with soft kisses and loved her again, murmuring of his love and of the loneliness he'd suffered for her and promising, while he moved deeply inside of her, that they would never be parted for so long again, because she was his very life. Afterward, she fell asleep in his arms, contented beyond measure. Lying beside him again was as near to heaven as she could imagine anything being.

Slender shafts of the late-afternoon sun coming through the window woke Graydon. He stretched and let pleasure flow through him, feeling, for the first time since he'd come to London, at peace. All of the worries and anxieties that had hounded him were gone, evaporating the instant that Lily had so sweetly and wholly given herself to him. That she had done so could only mean that she had missed him, too, and needed him. He was relieved beyond measure, knowing that everything was going to be all right. Lily had forgiven him, and he would make certain that she never had cause to regret it. He would take her back to St. Cathyrs as soon as possible, and they would put this entire dismal period behind them and get on with their lives.

Opening his eyes, he reached for Lily, only to find that, except for himself, the bed was empty.

"Lily?" he mumbled, sitting up and stretching.

She was sitting by the fire, fully clothed, her white-blond hair still loose about her shoulders. She glanced at him, a direct and lingering look, then turned back to the flames.

"Have you been up long, love?" he asked. "I'm sorry to have slept on like that. Rude of me when you've only just arrived. But, Lord, how I needed it."

He slid out of bed and found his trousers and pulled them on. Bare-chested, he went to kiss her, bending over the back of her chair to turn her face up to his. She received the affectionate caress stiffly, and then pulled free of his touch.

Warning bells began to sound in Graydon's head, and he took the seat opposite hers.

"Are you still upset, Lily?" It seemed unbelievable to him that she should be, after what they had just shared. But his sins were many, he was ready to admit, and her hurt most likely great. "Is it about seeing Miss Hamilton and myself in the park this morning? How is it that you came to be there?"

She wrote a lengthy note and handed it to him.

I arrived in Town this morning only to find that you had gone driving, and thought to surprise you by meeting you in the park. It was terribly foolish of me to think that you might wish to see me when you already had such amiable company.

"Oh, Lily," he murmured. "I know what it must have looked like, but I assure you that there has been nothing between Miss Hamilton and myself save friendship. I have been completely faithful to you in every way, physically and otherwise. I give you my word of honor upon that."

Her blue eyes slanted up at him in a contemplative gaze,

as if she wasn't sure whether his word of honor meant anything.

"Miss Hamilton is my friend. Nothing more."

She wrote another note.

It doesn't matter. We married for propriety's sake, to save your reputation and mine and Miss Hamilton's. I'll not question you on such matters now. Perhaps I never will.

The reply hurt him. He had begun to hope that she might be coming to love him.

"I've committed no improprieties with Miss Hamilton," he repeated, then asked, more softly, "Why didn't you answer any of my letters, Lily?"

Why did you leave me behind? she wrote. *Why did you never come home, or send for me?*

Graydon let out a sigh and sat back in his chair. "I left you at St. Cathyrs because Matthew wrote and warned me that there were rumors regarding us in London, and because I wanted to smooth the way before you came. I didn't tell you before I left because I knew you would insist upon coming."

I don't give a snap of my fingers about gossip! she wrote furiously. *What is it this time? The fact that we spent the night together in a warehouse before we were married?*

"In part," he answered truthfully, glad for the excuse she gave him. "Forgive me, Lily. I believed that you would be happier at St. Cathyrs, at least until I could make repairs here. But I haven't been able to do so, and that's why I never sent for you."

Why did you never come home, not even for Easter, when Parliament was out of session?

He didn't really have any good reason to give her, and was loath to give her the truth, that he knew she would want to return to London with him and he was determined, even more so now, to keep her away from it.

"I spent part of the time searching for a representative to sit in my place in the Lords, so that I could come home for good. And then Miss Hamilton has been having a difficult time this season, and I felt that I should do what I could to make her time here happier." He was in miry ground, he knew, but lies, at the moment, seemed preferable to telling her the truth. "Part of her unhappiness has stemmed from our broken understanding."

She wouldn't look at him, even when she handed him her reply. He had already realized that, as part of his punishment, she was not going to speak to him.

I sat alone in church Easter morning. I sat alone in church every Sunday morning. And ate alone at each meal. And sat alone each night, and through every day.

"I know," he whispered, aching to wipe the pain away in any way that he could. "I won't ask your forgiveness for that, because I don't deserve it. I can only promise that I shall never leave you alone again, and that I shall do whatever I must to make it up to you. We'll return to St. Cathyrs, tomorrow and begin again. I'll not leave there without you, unless you give me permission to do so."

I don't wish to return to St. Cathyrs. I've plans in London that will require me to remain for the rest of the season. You may return to St. Cathyrs, if it pleases you.

He ignored this last part and asked, "Plans?"

I have contacted and hired a speech tutor and we are to begin lessons tomorrow. You will soon have no further reason to be ashamed to take me anywhere.

He muffled a groan. "It wasn't for that. I'm not ashamed of you, and never have been." He crumpled the note in his fist. "I love the way you speak, and the sound of your voice. Everything about you is dear to me, just exactly as you are."

She clearly disbelieved this.

Nevertheless, I will have the lessons.

"If it means so much to you, then I suppose you must give it a try. But we shall return to St. Cathyrs. This…speech tutor may come to us there."

She firmly shook her head.

*I will not return to St. Cathyrs until the end of the season.
I wish to remain in London.*

Graydon's heart sank, and he felt an infinite sadness.
How would he be able to keep her from hearing the rumors
about Cardemore blackmailing him? From being hurt? It
would be impossible, just as it was impossible, in the face
of the pain he'd already given her, to force her back to St.
Cathyrs.

"Very well, Lily," he said wearily. "It shall be as you
wish. Only promise me that if these speech lessons become
too demanding, or if they exhaust your voice, you'll give
them up. I don't wish you to damage yourself further, or
become ill again."

She said nothing, but gazed straight into the fire. The
stubborn expression on her face filled him with foreboding,
and he wondered at how he could have awakened so short
a time ago with a feeling of such happiness and contentment. There seemed to be nothing now in his and Lily's
future but disaster, and no foreseeable way of avoiding it.

Chapter Twenty-Two

In late May, the Earl of Cardemore returned to London in his usual way, in the dead of night with a flurry of midnight black horses racing through London's streets, pulling behind them an ominously black carriage. Those of the ton who beheld the sight as they made their way home from a variety of balls and parties agreed the following day that it was just what was to be expected from the demon earl. The man—if he *was* a man—was genuinely perverse to travel in such a way, especially when his station demanded that he make a more sedate, visible entrance to Town in the middle of the day, when everyone could see what he was about. Was it any wonder that his own sister had been abandoned by God? Certain very reliable sources even claimed that the mute were without souls, and perhaps it was so, for what was speech but a gift from God to those who were His own?

But the Countess of Graydon clearly meant to gain a soul, for she had retained England's most lauded speech instructor, Sir Benjamin Hatton, to help her learn to speak. Day in and day out for over a month, Sir Benjamin had been seen coming and going at the Earl of Graydon's town house, but he never had anything to say to his acquaintances about his student's progress, and Lady Lillian had yet to utter a word in public since her return to Town. The whole matter was highly unusual, just as everything surrounding Lady Lillian and Lord Graydon had been unusual. London was filled with talk of little else.

The Earl of Cardemore knew about the rumors in Town, and, despite his unease, he had come to London with the sole purpose of removing Lily from their touch. Graydon had written that she'd not yet become aware of the truth; a small miracle, due only to the fact that she spent most of her waking hours working with Sir Hatton. But Graydon wouldn't be able to keep them from her forever, and it would be better, he had argued in his missive, if she heard the truth from the two of them, rather than from one of society's sharp-tongued matrons.

Cardemore couldn't have agreed more. And aside from that, he'd had enough of being exiled from Lily's life. If she never forgave him for what he'd done, and never wished to see or speak to him again, he would find a way to accept that. But to have her weekly letters, begging him to come to London, filled him with a sharp ache of guilt that he was sorely sick of.

She came to see him on his first morning in Town; he'd never been so glad, or so distressed, to see her. It had been hard—so hard—to let her go away with Graydon on the day of her marriage. Now, after so many months of worrying and fretting and wanting to know if she was happy, he had the unpleasant task of pretending that their time apart had been, for him, simply busy and content. If she could only know how much he and Margaret and Isabel had missed her, especially during Christmas, she would know that it had been no easy thing to be away from her.

But he received her as if all was well, as if everything was the same as it had ever been, and when she asked why he'd kept away, he replied that she and Graydon were newly wed and should have as much privacy as possible, away from the prying eyes of both friends and family. Next year, he promised, they would spend the holidays together. Next year, everything would be perfect.

The following day, the Earl of Graydon arrived, and Cardemore met him in his study. One look at the other man's face told him everything he needed to know.

"I should kill you for what you've done to my sister," he said. "But I can see that you're just as miserable as she is, so I'll hold off."

"Indeed," Graydon murmured, accepting the glass of brandy Cardemore pressed into his hands. "Death would probably be too kind. For either you or me."

"Very true." Cardemore seated himself behind his desk. "I wonder if two men have ever loved one woman so poorly as we have. I should have done as Margaret said and left her at Cardemore Hall. Perhaps her dreams might not have been realized, but she should never have been so badly hurt."

"The worst is yet to come, I fear."

Cardemore regarded him curiously. "Do you think she'll leave you when she knows? Is that what made you ask for my help?"

"She'll hate you, too," Graydon pointed out.

"But I've already lived through Hell these past many months. Her hatred would at least be honest, while her every word of love and longing only adds salt to the wound."

"I realize that," Graydon said grimly, "and accept my part. I'll not ask your forgiveness for anything that I've done, but I'll admit that I regret keeping you and Lily parted. It hurt her far more than it helped. I'll not interfere in your relationship again. You have my word on it."

"Little good it will do, once she knows the truth."

"I asked you to help me to spare her any more open humiliation. It isn't just that she should know the truth, but I hope to prove to her, in the doing, that she is loved by us both. It may not mean much, but surely she'll realize that we've done it to spare her as best we can."

Cardemore contemplated this with a thoughtful frown.

"Perhaps," he said at last. "We should be prepared for

the worst at the beginning, however. I should like to have a week with my sister before we make our dire confessions.''

Graydon shook his head. "A week may be too long. We've three engagements in that time, and she might hear the whisperings at any one of them.''

"Can you make certain she does not? I should like to have a little time of peace with Lily, after being away from her so long, before she comes to hate me, perhaps forever. Surely you'll grant me that.''

Graydon's gaze sharpened. "I don't owe you anything, Cardemore.''

"No, you don't,'' Cardemore admitted affably, "but if you want me to help you in keeping Lily from falling apart at the seams, you'll give me time with her. I was once the man she loved most in this life. I only want seven more days to know that love. In the face of having her hatred for the rest of my years, it's not much to ask.''

"Seven days,'' Graydon granted tightly. "On the eighth, we tell her and take what comes.''

"Agreed. There's another reason why it would be best to wait. Although I did not ask them to join me here, I believe Lady Margaret and Isabel will be in London shortly.''

"You believe?'' Graydon appeared surprised at this. "Did you not make arrangements for them to follow you?''

"I did not. Lady Margaret and I had a... misunderstanding—'' he said the last word with care "—and I left Cardemore Hall rather unexpectedly. Knowing her, I've no doubt that she and Isabel will arrive within a day or two. Being women, however, and prone to pack every garment and shoe in their possession, I'm not exactly certain when. I should like Lily's aunt to be here when we speak with her. Lady Margaret has been as a mother to her, and will be able to lend comfort where we may not.''

"Very well,'' Graydon said. "I want Lily to have every

support possible, and Lady Margaret is indeed a sensible lady. Has she been well? And Lady Isabel?''

Cardemore thought of the argument he'd had with Margaret before leaving Cardemore Hall. She'd been sharing his bed almost nightly since they had first made love—it was impossible for him to give her up, especially when she was just as eager and willing as he. But they could never come to any agreement on the topic of a more permanent union. Marriage was out of the question; not only was it illegal, but it would make Margaret a complete social pariah. And he refused to make her his mistress, or even to call her such, because he'd be damned if the woman he loved would ever bear such an ignoble title.

''Lady Margaret is in perfect health. Isabel is another matter. I suppose young Daltry is in Town?''

''He's been here since late February. Lady Isabel has not been ill, I hope.''

''Oh, aye, indeed she is, and has been. As sick as a body can be without actually contracting any real disease.''

''Lord Daltry has been rather unwell in that regard, himself.''

''Has he?'' Cardemore found this encouraging. ''I promised Margaret I'd not interfere in Isabel's life, but I admit that I'm tempted to get those two together and see if some sense can't be gotten into their rock-hard skulls. Love, you know, Graydon. It's a damned nuisance. Tell me about the lessons Lily's been having with Sir Hatton. She seemed happy enough with him when she visited yesterday, but from what she's suffered with such men in the past, I have my doubts.''

Graydon's expression grew distinctly unpleasant. ''I dislike Sir Hatton and his methods. He's a pompous, self-righteous, long-winded ass who had the effrontery to tell me on the day he arrived that my wife cannot speak because she is under a curse from God. I very nearly threw him out on his ear, and would have done so if Lily hadn't begged me to be patient. How she can abide such utter nonsense is far beyond me. The man starts each of their lessons with Lily upon her knees, begging for God's forgiveness and deliverance. For what crime, I cannot say. But she is determined to speak, and works toward that goal night and day.''

"Has she made any progress? We used the sign language yesterday, and she did not speak.''

Graydon shook his head. "None at all. In truth, she seems worse at the end of each day. Her voice is so raw she can barely make a sound. I'm beginning to worry that she'll take ill again.''

"And with your good mother and sisters out of the country, there'll be no one to perform a miracle to save her,'' Cardemore told him. "I'm well aware of who the vaunted Sir Benjamin Hatton is. He was in league with the same Mr. Lockley who sought to have Charles Cassin's Institute for Deaf-Mutes closed down as a pagan enterprise. They subscribe to the common opinion that all of those who are deaf and mute are amoral, and that their only road to salvation lies in forcing them to speak, whether they wish it or not. I advise you to go home, take Sir Hatton by the seat of his pants, escort him from your home with good riddance and never let him or another of his ilk past your door again. I spent a full year dealing with such men, and watched my sister suffer just exactly as you have said. She was often in tears, utterly wretched and made to feel like some half-human devil child who'd been born beneath Satan's hand. If you love her, as you claim to do, you'll keep her from such hurt and harm at any cost.''

"I am not like you,'' Graydon told him hotly. "If Lily wants to make this attempt, she must be allowed to make it. I'm done with forcing her to do things my way.''

"Pity,'' Cardemore murmured.

"That isn't to say, however, that I'll not try to convince her to choose a different course. I've sent for Charles Cassin, and have asked him to bring Jonah back to Lily as soon as possible.''

Cardemore stared at him for a silent moment, then stood suddenly and extended his hand to Graydon. "I offer you my hand, sir, which is no small thing. With it I tender my apologies for the many ways in which I have offended you, and ask for a concession between us. You have proved yourself to be a man of honor and understanding. If I never believed it before, I do now. Lily is safe with you."

Graydon held the other man's gaze. "I will gladly accept what you offer, on one condition. I have a very great favor to ask of you."

"Ask it, then."

Graydon did, and when Cardemore had ceased to be shocked, they came to an agreement. Graydon lifted his own hand, accepting Cardemore's, and the two men sealed their pact.

Chapter Twenty-Three

Graydon spent another two hours in the company of the Earl of Cardemore, and then went to his club, where he found Lord Daltry, and sat down at a table to share a glass of wine with him. When he mentioned what Lord Cardemore had said about his niece, Lord Daltry's gaze riveted upon him.

"Ill? Lady Isabel? Is she all right?"

"How can I know?" Graydon said with studied disinterest. "He only said that she was as sick as a body could be."

All of the color drained out of Lord Daltry's face. "She's not going to die, is she?"

"Indeed not," Graydon assured him. "I was given to understand that she and her mother will be in London shortly, to enjoy the remainder of the season."

Lord Daltry sat back in his chair. "I see. She must be more fully recovered than Lord Cardemore gave word to."

"My thoughts exactly," Graydon concurred. "Will you give the poor girl another chance, Matthew?"

Lord Daltry began to look miserable. "She wouldn't wish it," he said. "She'll be coming to Town to find a husband. I'll not make a nuisance of myself, as I did last year. Perhaps I'll take myself off to Iddington."

"What, and give your parents such a shock?" Graydon

teased. "No, no, my lad. You stay in London and face Lady Isabel straight on. You wouldn't wish to offend her by your conspicuous absence, I'm sure."

They spent an idle hour discussing the matter, until Lord Daltry at last agreed to stay in Town long enough to make a gentlemanly greeting to Lady Isabel, and then Graydon gathered his things and departed for home.

His butler met him at the door with the unhappy expression that Graydon was becoming used to from all of his Town staff, especially whenever Sir Hatton was there.

He could hear Hatton's sharp, impatient tone all the way down in the entryway.

"Again, Lady Graydon. You must apply yourself if you wish to overcome your defect."

"An*th*-hony." Lily's voice sounded raw and weary.

An audible sigh was heard from Sir Hatton.

"I'm beginning to think that you don't truly wish to speak in a normal manner, my lady. It is not so difficult, if you will only make the effort. An*th*ony. It is quite simple. You do wish to speak your husband's name to him in the way that God meant for it to be spoken, do you not?"

"Y-ees," Lily said.

"Not y-ees!" Sir Hatton cried with an angry slapping of his cane upon the floor. "*Yes.* Only a heathen would speak the word otherwise. Now, again. An*th*ony."

"An*th*-hony." Now she sounded as if she were on the verge of tears.

"My lord," Cranc said, stopping him just as he was heading for the stairs to bid Sir Benjamin Hatton to the devil. "Mr. Charles Cassin and Master Jonah arrived over an hour ago. I've put them in the blue parlor."

"Thank God," Graydon muttered, and ascended the stairs two at a time. He walked past the parlor where Hatton was bringing Lily down to tears, and pushed into the blue parlor, where Charles Cassin greeted him with something very like a snarl.

"How could you allow her to suffer such as that?" he

demanded without preamble. From the redness of his face, Graydon imagined that Mr. Cassin must have heard quite enough during his hour-long wait. "I don't know whether to break your neck for being such a poor husband or send Sir Hatton out the nearest window for being such a self-righteous brute!"

At this, Graydon surveyed the other man with some admiration. "I intend to put a stop to it. That's what you're here for." He glanced past the furious man to where Jonah sat by the window, looking at Graydon as if gutting and skinning were too good for him. "Jonah, it's good to have you home. You've neither of you seen Lady Graydon yet?"

"Not seen, no, but heard!" Charles Cassin stated tightly.

Across the hall they heard Sir Hatton's hard, punishing tones. Lily's weary voice came more softly through the closed door, clearly straining to do as she was told.

Graydon looked at Charles Cassin. "I believe she's had enough of Sir Hatton's lessons. Come with me."

Graydon opened the door to the first parlor without knocking, and both Sir Hatton and Lily looked at him. Lily's face was white with exhaustion, and her eyes red from keeping tears at bay. She was perched upon the small, high chair which Sir Hatton insisted she use during their lessons, her hands clenched tensely in the folds of her skirt. Sir Hatton stood over her, his cane held in one hand as if it were a weapon, his face red and angry. Before him, Lily looked as small and helpless as a child. The moment she saw Charles Cassin, she burst into tears and covered her face with both hands.

"Lady Graydon!" Sir Hatton remonstrated fiercely.

"Stay away from her," Charles Cassin shouted, pushing into the room and taking Lily off the chair and into his arms. "Lady Lillian, what has he been doing to you? This is madness!"

"I'll not stay in the same room with an unholy advocate of amorality," Sir Hatton announced, shaking his cane at

Charles Cassin. "You shock me, my lord," he said to Graydon, "to allow such a man beneath your roof."

"Sir," said Graydon, "I shall have no advice from you, who are here only because my lady insists upon it. Another word and I shall escort you outside."

"Very fine!" said Sir Hatton, and when Lily began to plead with Charles Cassin by the use of sign language, he added, even more haughtily, "And I'll not be exposed to such demon works as this. Lady Graydon, if you use that witch's craft in my presence again, then our association comes to an end, and I will give you over to Satan entirely."

"You're the only evil here!" Charles Cassin said furiously. "Leave her be!"

"Bloody low bastard!" cried Jonah. "Flatten 'im, m'lord!"

Graydon had already crossed the room and taken Sir Hatton by the collar.

"You do not speak to my wife in such a manner again, you filthy swine. I'll kill you if you do."

"*N-ho!*" Lily cried, horrified, pushing away from Charles Cassin. "An-non-nee! Phlease! Phlease!"

"That's the end of it then," Sir Hatton declared, struggling free of Graydon's hand. "Lady Graydon, I am quit of you."

"N-ho!" She grasped at Sir Hatton's sleeve with pleading hands, sobbing now in a broken way that tore at Graydon's heart.

"Lily, let him go."

"S-hir Hat-hon, phlease! Ah b-heg you!"

All the way down the stairs she followed him, crying and pleading, until he slammed out of the house and left her kneeling before the door, weeping.

"Lily." Graydon hurried down the stairs. "Let me take you upstairs."

He tried to lift her in his arms, but she struggled free and turned on him, furiously wiping her wet face with one hand.

"Mhake him c-home back! You mhade him g-ho. You *mhake* him c-home back!"

"No," he told her firmly. "Never."

She flew at him in a flurry of movement, striking him over and over, hitting his face and chest in a sobbing, childish rage. Graydon held her, suffering the small blows until at last she fell against him and wept. He picked her up in his arms and carried her into the blue parlor, set her on a small sofa and gently dried her face with his handkerchief. Then he stood.

"I'll send Mr. Cassin in to you." He turned to leave.

"An-non-nee," she said tearfully, stopping him. He looked at her. "Ah'm sorree," she whispered.

"As am I. Very much, Lily."

Lily waited up late into the night for Graydon to come home. He had left immediately after the horrific scene she'd made, and had given no indication as to where he was going. She assumed he had gone to his club, or perhaps out with Lord Daltry to play cards at the home of one of their friends. She hoped that he had done so, and that he'd not gone to see his beloved Miss Hamilton. But even if he had, Lily knew that she had only herself to blame. She'd as much as driven him away with her childish behavior, with her foolishness. Sitting by her bedchamber window, watching for his carriage, she wished, very much, that she could live this day over again.

Charles Cassin had stayed with her in the parlor for a long while, angry at first and then, after she had tried to explain herself, finally softening.

"I cannot believe that you would have that man here to torture you so needlessly," he said. "Don't you remember what you went through before? With all those other voice teachers?"

She'd been too weary to speak any more, her throat was hot with pain, and so she had signed, *I've only been lazy. I can learn to speak if only I try harder.*

His tone grew so serious, so somber. "Lily, you know what the doctors have said. Your vocal cords are permanently damaged, and by speaking so much you may be damaging them even more. You will never be able to speak as others do, and you must accept that, just as you used to do."

But she couldn't. She had to learn to speak. It was the only hope she had of holding on to her husband, and of being a part of his life. Now, she was only able to please him in their bed, which, thankfully, he still shared with her each night save those when she suffered her courses, which came with awful regularity. Even there she had failed, not even able to give him a child. Was it any surprise that he had sought out Miss Hamilton's company in London, or perhaps had even come because of her? He must regret, so very much, that he'd not married her.

She stayed at the window another hour, and then, full weary, went to bed alone. Sometime in the night he came to her, smelling of smoke and brandy and waking her with soft, warm kisses.

"An-non-nee," she murmured, gladly letting him pull the nightgown from her body.

"I'm sorry," he whispered. "Sorry for everything."

Tears pricked her eyes, and she pressed against him in her own silent apology.

"Don't cry any more, Lily," he said as he kissed the tears away. "I can't bear it. Just let me love you. I need you so."

She murmured his name again and welcomed him gladly, wholly, needing him just as much.

Afterward they lay together, warm and replete, and Lily felt a sense of amazement that here, on their bed, beneath their covers, twined in each other's arms, even in the midst of so much unhappiness—here, everything seemed perfectly right.

* * *

In the morning, Graydon woke to the sound of Lily's voice coming from her sitting room.

"An*th*-hony. An*th*-hony. An*thhh*ony."

His name. Nearly perfectly said. He didn't like it at all.

Rising, he slipped into his robe and made his way into his own chamber without disturbing Lily's practice. There he poured himself a cup of the hot coffee that he found waiting, and sat down at his desk.

There had been a great many additions to his note collection in the past few weeks, since Lily had come to London. During the months he'd been alone in London, missing Lily, he'd spent a great many nights organizing the hundreds of notes she'd given him. He'd eventually gotten them put into perfect order, so that if he read them from the beginning he could recount each day they'd spent together since they'd met.

There was a difference between the open, friendly missives she'd written him nearly a year ago and the formal, precise notes she wrote him now. He wondered if she would ever again write him in such a teasing, humorous, and trusting manner again. Or if she would ever again speak to him on a regular basis. Despite the fact that the dwelling was filled with the sound of her voice day and night, he still felt as if he were missing her, as if she were far, far away from him.

Chapter Twenty-Four

One week later Lily sat beside Graydon in their carriage, both nervous and excited as they made their way to the first ball that they were attending together for the season.

She felt as ready as she possibly could be, and prayed that all would go as she had planned. Tonight she would prove to Graydon that she could be the kind of wife he needed. Tonight, she would prove herself to the entire ton.

He hadn't wanted to attend the gathering, one of the largest balls of the year, Lord and Lady Orchard's annual soiree, but Lily had insisted, despite the fact that she understood Graydon's reticence. He'd not wanted to take her anywhere since she'd arrived in London, except to the opera and theater, and had accepted very few of the many invitations that had arrived for them. This, in fact, would be the first large event they would attend since they'd married, and she could sense his increasing tension even as they neared their destination.

She smiled up at him reassuringly, and he took her gloved hand in his. Sitting in the seat across from them, unhappily dressed in a suit of burgundy velvet, Jonah rolled his eyes and pointedly looked out the window. Graydon chuckled at him before giving Lily his attention.

"Are you certain you wish to go through with this, Lily? We can yet turn back and spend a quiet night at home, which is just what I, myself, should prefer. You've been so weary of late, and you know how demanding these things can be. It's sure to be hot, and a dreadful squeeze."

She tapped Jonah on the knee and signed to him. He was a marvelous interpreter, despite his misery at having to attend such a fancy function and his tendency to adorn her words with street cant. His sharp, quick eyes never missed a movement, even in the dim carriage light.

"Her ladyship sezs she's fine as sixpence and don't want you worryin' 'bout nuffing."

Graydon sighed with resignation. "Very well, my dear. If you're quite certain. Have I told you how lovely you look?"

"Only half a hunert times," Jonah said dryly. "My lord."

She was glad that he approved of the gown she wore. The colors were vivid—bright gold and royal blue—and designed in the latest French fashion, rather daringly cut yet not immodest. For once she wanted to draw attention to herself, to dress with pride as the Countess of Graydon.

Graydon was dressed very fine, too, in formfitting, dark blue evening clothes. He would surely be the handsomest man at the ball, and she the one whom other women would most envy.

She set a hand upon his sleeve and tugged lightly, nodding, and he understood the compliment and thanked her, then covered her hand and held it there.

Lily turned to look out the window, wondering if Miss Hamilton would be at the ball. It was ironic how differently things had turned out from what she had once supposed, when she had believed that she would be Graydon's mistress, and Miss Hamilton his wife. Now it was the other way around. Every afternoon during the past week Graydon had disappeared without saying why or where he was going to, and every evening he returned looking both tired and a little guilty. It wasn't hard to imagine where he'd been.

But she had reason to hope, and reason to believe that

whatever Graydon and Miss Hamilton did together, they did not also share a bed. He still came to Lily each night with the driving, needy passion that she had always found in him. Perhaps she was naive, but she couldn't believe he would have enough of such energy to expend on *two* women. He was quite as worn-out as she was after the lovings they shared.

She was confident that she was the only woman he desired physically; all that remained now was to capture his heart, and Lily was fully optimistic that it was possible. Even if he had married her out of a sense of honor, he had at least done so willingly. He had wanted her for his wife—he'd told her so countless times—and so he *must* feel some measure of affection for her apart from mere desire.

"Here we are," Graydon said as the carriage pulled to a stop before a large town house glittering with light. "Jonah," he added more sternly, "remember your manners."

Jonah gave him a look of adolescent disdain. "I know wot's wot. Don't get in a taking, matey."

"He'll have tongues wagging within an hour," Graydon said with a grimace as the carriage door opened and the boy hopped down to the ground with light agility. "I hope you were right to bring him, love. I used to interpret for you very well, once."

He sounded wistful, Lily thought with surprise. Almost as if he wished he still had the task of being her voice, when she had believed it must have been such a burden for him.

Lord and Lady Orchard's town house was somewhat smaller and less grand than Wilborn Place, but it had been magnificently fitted out for the ball, and was already filled to the rafters with guests.

Graydon led her through the receiving line, with Jonah following close behind. Every eye seemed to be upon her, and Lily wondered if perhaps the ton was well aware of the affair that Graydon and Miss Hamilton had been carrying on. The idea was mortifying, but Lily pushed it aside. She had work to do tonight, and must concentrate solely on that.

The first challenge came all too soon, and Graydon was introducing her to their hosts. Lily's usual habit, when she had used to attend such functions in the previous year with Graydon as her escort, was to curtsy, nod and smile, and then move along, but when Graydon, well used to playing his part in this, would have guided her forward, she pressed her hand lightly on his arm to make him wait. Then, when she had his full attention, Lily gathered up her courage, lifted her chin and said, loudly and clearly, "Thhhank you f-hor invhit-hing us, L-hord and L-hady Orch-hard. We ahre s-ho phleased to be here." With a hand she pulled Jonah forward, setting her arm about his shoulder. "Th-his is mah inter-prhet-her, Jon-hah. Ah hope it whas all rhight to br-hing him?"

Lily cringed a bit at the sound of her voice. She'd tried so hard to make it more feminine, but it had come out just as horrifyingly grating and manlike as ever. The seconds that passed as she waited for the utter silence, and shock, to end, were the longest of her life. Beside her, she saw Jonah clenching and unclenching one fist.

Suddenly, Lady Orchard's face broke into a smile that seemed, to Lily, as beautiful as a heavenly angel's. She moved forward with both hands and grasped Lily's free one.

"Of course it's all right, my dear Lady Graydon. Perfectly all right. We are so very glad that you came to our home tonight. May I even say that we are grateful? You've not been about London much this season, and your presence has been sorely missed. That you have come to us tonight is indeed an honor."

The tension broke all around, with so much relief that several people laughed, including Lily. She had done it, and the rest would be easy. She caught a glimpse of her husband's face, and the shining pride that his gaze held for her was more than enough to repay all the misery she'd suffered in preparing for this night. He took her hand and placed it upon his arm, and led her into the ball as if she were the very Queen of England.

"I only wish," he murmured as they made their way, "that your brother had been here. He would have crowed with pride at you, just as I feel like doing."

They danced the opening minuet, and then a waltz, while Jonah wandered off to find the supper room, and afterward made a circle of the room to speak with acquaintances. By the time Jonah had returned, Lily's confidence had soared, and she sent Graydon away to visit with his particular friends, especially Lord Daltry, who had only just arrived.

Jonah seemed to be as much an object of interest as Lily was, with his canting talk and forward manners. Fortunately, the ton was easily amused. Lily could see that her young interpreter would soon become the rage at balls and parties, and that, because of him, her own popularity would increase. What Jonah thought wasn't difficult to tell. It was clear that he was unimpressed with the fine personages attending the ball; indeed, he looked at each person Lily conversed with as some unbelievably bizarre sight.

"Bloody odd fish," he muttered to her when they moved away from a particularly loud and cheerful group. "If me old mates was to see me now, they'd laugh 'til they was right sick wiv' it."

But he continued to perform his duties without further complaint, and did his best not to embarrass Lily with a poorly chosen word.

Aunt Margaret and Isabel arrived at last, and as Lily stood speaking with them, both Graydon and Lord Daltry approached.

"Lady Margaret," said Lord Daltry, bowing over her hand. "Lady Graydon." She received the same gentlemanly treatment. To Isabel, however, Lord Daltry merely gave a stiff nod. "Lady Isabel. It is a delight to see you all again. I hope this evening finds you well?"

"Perfectly well," Isabel replied tightly, and Lily's heart went out to her. The past many months had not been kind to Isabel. She had lost weight and color, and was so unlike the bright, vivacious girl she'd been a year before.

Lord Daltry's mouth thinned into a straight line. "I'm glad to hear of it. Lady Margaret, would you do me the honor of accompanying me in this dance?"

Aunt Margaret smiled warmly. "Thank you, my lord, but I believe I shall not dance at all tonight. I've something of the headache threatening to come on."

He turned to Lily. "Lady Graydon?"

"Sorry, old friend," Graydon said, his hand closing about Lily's. "My wife has promised this one to me, already."

He pulled her onto the floor as the pairs for the coming dance took their places, leaving Lord Daltry standing alone with Isabel, who looked about as approachable as an angry asp.

Lily couldn't help but watch as Lord Daltry at last asked Isabel to dance, and Isabel's reaction was hearteningly like her old self. She slapped Lord Daltry so hard that the sound could be heard throughout the entire ballroom. In the ensuing silence, only Jonah's low whistle of appreciation could be clearly heard. Isabel and Lord Daltry stood staring at each other, until she turned and stalked away, toward the terrace doors. Lord Daltry, fingering his reddened cheek, followed directly behind, and their arguing voices could be heard through the open French doors until the musicians began to play.

Graydon watched his wife winding her way through the other dancers with a feeling that neared arrogance. She was, as always, the most beautiful woman in the room, for which he was always proud, but that wasn't the reason why tonight he felt so conceited that she was his.

She had done it. After all this time, after all his pleading, she had at last found the courage to speak in public. She had done so on the day of their marriage, of course, but until now had refused to do so again. It had been very well done—he'd been so shocked and pleased that he'd wanted to pick her up and kiss the breath out of her right in the midst of the receiving line.

He doubted that she realized with what perfect timing her act of bravery had been performed. The ton had been on tenterhooks while she'd had her lessons from Sir Hatton, wondering whether, and when, Countess Graydon would at last speak again. Descriptions of her manlike voice had been rampant in London during the days following their marriage, but now, having had the lessons, what would it be like? There had even been wagers registered in the betting books of several men's clubs regarding when and where Lady Graydon would speak and about what she would say and whom she would say it to. Lady Orchard hadn't lied when she'd spoken to Lily of her gratitude; Lily had just made her the most successful hostess of the season.

But it didn't matter how or why her speaking had gone over so well, it only mattered that it had, and surely now Lily would know that he had never been ashamed of her, and never would be. One day more and she would have the truth of what had transpired between Cardemore and himself. If she could but remember tonight, and their happiness, perhaps she might be more ready to forgive him the part he had played in so many deceits.

When the dance ended he escorted Lily to her aunt, with whom Jonah was patiently waiting, and then excused himself to fetch them both some punch.

"Good evening, Graydon," Lord Hanby hailed him. "You've brought your wife out of hiding, at last, I see. May I say that Lady Graydon is enchanting?"

Graydon, remembering a time when Hanby couldn't even bring himself to look Lily in the eye, said, "Indeed, is she not? I count myself the most fortunate of men."

"Sir Hatton has worked a miracle, I hear. Spoke to Lady Orchard, did she? And quite clearly, too."

He made it sound as if Lily were some circus animal, performing a trick. Graydon tamped down the urge to plant his fist in the other man's face.

"My wife has always had a voice," he said tightly. "And even though she has not often chosen to use it, I have always found it quite beautiful to hear. Sir Benjamin Hatton is a deceiver and a fraud, and had nothing to do with anything that has happened here tonight. Lady Graydon wished to speak, and she did. That's the only miracle that occurred."

Beneath Graydon's steady glare, Lord Hanby cleared his throat uncomfortably.

"Of course. Certainly," he said. "Didn't mean to offend. I must say that I've always believed Lady Graydon to be one of the bravest women I've had the pleasure to know. If I suffered the same affliction...well, I doubt I'd be half so game as she."

This mollified Graydon a little. He understood the feeling quite well, and knew that it was the basis that generally caused others to be uncomfortable with Lily or anyone else who was different. It was, after all, only human to fear such things.

"Did I see Lady Margaret and her daughter, Lady Isabel, earlier?" Lord Hanby pressed on. "I should like very much to make them my bow. I was quite taken with Lady Isabel last season, as you know. Pity that Daltry had to make such a mess of things. But he's quite out of the way now, I understand, which gives me reason to hope."

Graydon gave him an unpleasant smile. "I shouldn't hope too long if I were you, Hanby," he said. "If you will excuse me, I believe Miss Hamilton wishes to speak to me."

He hadn't realized that Frances had arrived at the ball until he had seen her standing with a group of young women her own age. The moment she caught Graydon's eye, she motioned with her fan for him to come to her.

"Hello, my dear," he greeted warmly, taking the hand

she offered. "I was just on my way to fetch Lily and her aunt a glass of punch. May I take you to them and bring some for you as well?"

"Not just yet," she said, gazing up at him anxiously. "Graydon, I must speak with you. Privately. Only for a moment. It's quite urgent."

"Frances, you sound almost panicked. What's happened? Have you seen Mr. Cassin since he's been in Town? He has not distressed you, I hope."

She gripped his arm, but, as aware as he of the close scrutiny upon them, released him at once. "Please, Graydon."

He looked about, knowing what it would look like for them to be seen alone together. Too, he didn't like the idea of leaving Lily for very long. But something was clearly troubling Frances, and he couldn't bring himself to turn away her request. "Very well. Wait for me by the terrace doors and I'll meet you there as soon as I've delivered the punch. We can speak in the garden."

"Lady Graydon sez that she had the dress from a modiste in Bond Street," Jonah interpreted patiently. "The name is Madame Yvette, wot makes up rigs like this fer lots of fine ladies." Then he added, by way of personal experience, "'Nd I can tell you it's the driest place I've ever 'ad to bide my time in. Nuffing but women and clothes. I'd rather pick oakum fer a whole week than go back there."

The ladies to whom he told this laughed with delighted amusement, and Lily smiled and tried to regain the sense of equilibrium that had carried her throughout the night. Half an hour ago she had watched Graydon escort a very unhappy-looking Miss Hamilton out onto the terrace, and since then she'd been frozen with a feeling halfway between panic and fear.

Lord Daltry and Isabel had returned to the ballroom shortly after that. He had taken Isabel to Aunt Margaret's

side, made his bow to their host and hostess and left the
ball altogether. Isabel wouldn't tell them what had transpired out in the gardens, but her mouth was rather swollen
and her cheeks flushed, and there was something of the
defiant old sparkle back in her eyes. She looked, to Lily,
as if she'd been well and thoroughly kissed. Still, if anything hopeful had transpired between herself and Lord Daltry, Isabel wouldn't reveal it, and Lord Daltry had looked
particularly grim before his departure.

As soon as she could, Lily disengaged Jonah and herself
from the crowd of ladies, and took him aside.

Are you hungry, Jonah? she asked. *Thirsty?*

He tugged at the collar about his neck with exaggerated
discomfort. "Both. And 'ot, too. Ain't a breath of a wind
in 'ere, I vow."

She hesitated before asking, *Would you like to go out
into the garden for a few minutes? It will be cooler there.*

He looked as if what he'd really like would be to leave,
but he nodded and grandly offered her his arm, as Lord
Graydon had taught him to do.

They sat on the terrace, and then Jonah leaned closer to
Lily and whispered, "Want me to find 'is lordship 'nd spy
'im out?"

Jonah! she signed with surprise.

"I *know* wot 'e's about. Only a blank'eaded nimrod
wouldn't 'ave the drop on it. Brought 'er out 'ere, didn't
'e? Bloody *fool*," he added with open disgust. "She don't
'old no measure to you, m'lady, 'nd that's God's truth."
He made a fist and slapped it into an open palm. "I should
teach 'im wot's wot."

Lily set a hand upon his shoulder. "You d-hon't un-ner-
stand," she told him. "It's verry…dhif-fhi-cult."

"Not to me," he declared angrily. "I know a ruddy
bounder when I see one."

She couldn't think of what to tell Jonah to make things
right, for it was clear that Graydon had offended the boy's
sense of honor. She didn't know if he would understand

that sometimes things weren't a matter of right or wrong, or that a person couldn't always help whom they loved, or what they might do for that love.

"Lily?"

She lifted her gaze to see Graydon leading Miss Hamilton up the terrace steps from the garden. He looked perfectly miserable, and Miss Hamilton, strangely, looked almost angry.

"We came to get some air, yer grand lordship," Jonah stated rudely, and Lily poked him.

Graydon released Miss Hamilton as he brought her forward.

"I'm sure that's perfectly fine," he told the boy before saying, "Lily, you remember Miss Hamilton, of course."

"Of c-hourse." Lily stood. "How n-hice to see you ag-hain."

"I'm so glad that you've finally made it to Town, Lady Graydon. Lord Graydon has been quite lost without you."

Lily wanted to grind her teeth in anger, but managed a tight smile. Instead of speaking, she signed to Jonah, *Please tell Miss Hamilton that I'm sure she's done her utmost to keep my husband from being too lonely.*

With a wicked grin, Jonah repeated the words.

Both Graydon and Miss Hamilton began to look rather uneasy.

"I fear it's been the other way around," Miss Hamilton said at last, hesitantly. "Lord Graydon has been kind enough to lend me his company, and to make certain that I've not been left to flounder on my own. He has been as good as a brother to me, and I shall ever be grateful."

That took some of the wind out of Lily's sails, spoken as it was with Miss Hamilton's usual honest tone. She looked from one to the other, and wondered what she should believe. Miss Hamilton continued to look agitated, and Graydon continued to look grim.

"Forgive me," Miss Hamilton said suddenly, "but I fear I must take my leave. Lady Graydon, it's wonderful to see you again. I do hope your time in London will be enjoyable. My lord,'' she said to Graydon, ''I do thank you for being so good to me. I shall make every effort not to importune you further.''

''Frances…Miss Hamilton—''

''I'm sorry,'' she said quickly, ''but I must hurry. Thank you again.'' She turned and walked back into the house.

Graydon watched her until she had gone from sight, and then said, ''I believe we should go, as well.'' He turned to Lily. ''Have you had quite enough dancing and merriment for one night, my dear? Jonah looks as if he'd kill to get away.''

''Hallelujah,'' muttered Jonah. '''E's got eyes in 'is 'ead, if nuffing else.''

Graydon ignored this and set his arm about Lily's waist. He was looking at her, but she could tell that his thoughts were still with Miss Hamilton. And they remained with Miss Hamilton all during the drive home, and even after, when they had arrived.

''I must go out again,'' he said after he had escorted her and Jonah inside. ''I won't be long, love, but don't wait up for me.'' He kissed her cold lips quickly, then took her face in his hands and gazed into her eyes. ''If I haven't told you yet, Lily, I was very proud of you tonight. You were magnificent, just as you always have been, and just as you always will be. I'm the most fortunate man alive to have you as my wife.'' With that he left her standing in the entryway, with Jonah muttering curses by her side.

Chapter Twenty-Five

He got into bed later than he expected, and even then wasn't able to sleep. Lily lay beside him, soft and warm and resting so contentedly that he couldn't bring himself to wake her, especially not for his own gain. He wanted to make love to her; he wanted to talk to her. He wanted to tell her again how wonderful she'd been at the ball, and how proud he'd felt. He wanted to tell her that he loved her, and that no other woman would ever hold his heart the way she did. It had been an awful moment the night before, when she had clearly believed that he and Frances had been trysting. Somehow—certainly before he and Cardemore made their confessions—he had to make her understand that her suspicions were unfounded.

She lay on her side, away from him, one hand tucked up beneath her chin. Gently, he stroked her silken hair away from the side of her face, and kissed the warm spot beneath her ear.

"I love you, Lily," he murmured, lightly, not wishing to wake her.

His body ached with wanting, and he decided that he had better take himself away before he selfishly acted upon that desire. Sliding silently from the bed, he eyed the coming dawn with a grimace. Later, he would be sorry that he'd not gained any slumber during the night. For now, it seemed best to join Lord Daltry on the daily, early-morning vigil at Hyde Park that had resumed as soon as he'd learned Lady Isabel was back in London.

Matthew was already there, in his usual spot, by the time Graydon arrived.

"Has she come yet?" he asked as he joined his friend.

Lord Daltry shook his head. "Not yet. Perhaps she'll not go riding today. I can't see how she does, when she's been so ill."

"She looked well enough last night."

Lord Daltry gaped at him. "She looked as if she's been bedridden for a year! She's lost weight, and her face is pale as death. I can't think what Cardemore is about, letting her go to balls and parties when she ought to be under a doctor's care."

"She looked quite well," Graydon insisted. "She danced every dance after you left, and was in high spirits by the time Lily and I left."

"Danced every dance?" Daltry repeated in a low tone.

"Twice with Hanby. I think he's going to make an offer for her."

"Hanby!" Daltry's face turned red with rage. "I'd sooner see her shipped off to the colonies than shackled to that pompous, addlepated fool!"

"Well, really, Matthew, he's not all that bad."

"He's *worse*. He ought to marry one of his horses, he loves the bloody beasts so much. He'd not be good to her, as she deserves, or kind and generous. And he'd never be able to control her, either. She'd lead him about as if he had a ring in his nose." He made a disdainful humphing sound. "Hanby, my foot. She'd be wretched with him."

"Somehow," said Graydon, looking past his friend, "none of what you've just said makes much sense. Either she'll be miserable or he will—and I'm not sure which one it is who you think is such a brute. Ah. Here she comes. Flying like the wind, as usual. I've never seen such a magnificent horsewoman."

"Indeed," Lord Daltry agreed in a more reverent tone, turning to gaze at his beloved. "She *is* magnificent, isn't she?"

Something about the way she was holding on to her horse caught Graydon's eye.

"Is her foot out of the stirrup? What's the matter there?"

Lord Daltry brought his stallion's head up to readiness. "I don't know. She's...something's not quite right. Where's the blasted groom?"

"She's lost the reins!" Graydon shouted, but Lord Daltry had already jumped out of the bushes and into the clearing, racing headlong after Lady Isabel and her runaway steed.

The chase didn't last long. Lady Isabel's horse leaped over a low fence and continued on its way, and Lord Daltry, following, somehow managed to fall off his stallion in a jump that a ten-year-old child would have found simple enough to clear.

Graydon was there in but a few moments, jumping down to the ground and running to his friend with his heart in his mouth.

"Matthew! Matthew, are you all right?"

He knelt beside him, taking his hand and finding comfort in the fact that blood still pulsed there.

With a dizzy shake, Lord Daltry opened his eyes.

"What...did I fall?"

"Yes, but it doesn't look too bad. I don't think you've broken your neck, at least. Are you able to move?"

"Did Isabel see it?"

Graydon looked and saw Lady Isabel approaching them at a full-out gallop. The fact that she had her horse under her complete control didn't pass his notice.

"Ah...yes. I'm afraid she did."

Lord Daltry groaned. "Oh, Lord. I wish I were dead."

Lady Isabel hopped down from her horse in an admirably graceful leap, shouting at Matthew the entire while.

"You idiot! You fool!" she cried, throwing herself down

on her knees beside him. "You might have broken your neck! I hope you did break your neck, you senseless lack-wit!"

And then she burst into tears and pitched forward, tossing her arms about his massive shoulders and crying into his neck.

Lord Daltry tentatively patted her back. "It's all right, Isabel. I'm all right."

"I thought you'd k-killed yourself," she sobbed, shaking with her tears. "Oh, Matthew, I would have wanted to die."

"Would you?" Lord Daltry said wonderingly, his arms tightening about her. "Would you really, Isabel?"

She sat up suddenly and pounded his chest with a tiny, gloved fist. "Of course I would have, you idiot! How can you be such a thickheaded fool?"

"I don't know," he replied stupidly, grinning from ear to ear. "I'm beginning to think I don't know much about anything." And then, realization began to dawn. "Isabel Walford, did you...? You *did.* You lost your reins on purpose." The grin had turned into a frown.

"Of course I did," she said furiously. "How else was I to get you to stop being so foolish? If you weren't busy being so blasted noble about everything, I wouldn't have to force you to take notice of me. You've only got yourself to blame!"

"Why you empty-headed little idiot!" he said angrily, pushing into a sitting position with Graydon's help. "You might have gotten hurt, or even killed. I should turn you over my knee for trying anything so dangerous."

"Me!" she cried. "I'm not the one who fell off my horse over a jump that a *rabbit* could have made without difficulty."

"Ahem," Graydon interjected loudly, bringing their tirades to a halt. "Forgive me for being so bold, but do you not think, my lady, that it might be best if we get Lord Daltry to his home before any other early riders arrive and see him in such a state? We wouldn't want a panic, would we? Do you think you can ride, Matthew? Cerberus appears to be unharmed.''

Lily woke to find herself alone. Sitting up, she looked about the room to see if there was any sign that Graydon had even returned home in the night, and found nothing, except perhaps the general disorder of the bed, which she alone might have been the sole cause of. She couldn't remember whether he had joined her or not. If he had, he certainly hadn't waked her.

A sick feeling washed over her. Had he remained the entire night with Miss Hamilton? Oh, God. Could he have done so?

The morning passed in a blur of dread and waiting. She let Jenny dress her and arrange her hair, then went downstairs to pick at her breakfast. She was too embarrassed to ask any of the servants if they knew where his lordship was, or whether he had come home, and so she simply waited.

At half past eleven, as Lily paced in the drawing room, Crane scratched at the door and then entered bearing a silver tray, upon which there lay a single card. Lily read it with a groan. Graydon's godparents, Lord and Lady Barton, were outside in their carriage, waiting to see if they might be invited inside for a visit. Graydon hadn't said a word about them having returned to London, although perhaps they had returned so recently that he didn't yet know. They'd been traveling on the Continent for all of last year and hadn't been able to return to celebrate their godson's wedding. But they'd sent Graydon regular missives, detailing their adventures, and every time Graydon received one he read it aloud to Lily and then mused, with obvious affection, on his unusual godparents. After all he'd told her of them, she had looked forward to meeting this interesting pair, but to do so when Graydon wasn't even present was most awkward. Still, she couldn't just turn them away, and surely Graydon would arrive soon.

Ask them to please come in and take tea with me, Lily wrote. *And find Jonah at once. Please explain to Lord and Lady Barton that my interpreter will join us.*

She handed the note to Crane, who nodded gravely and disappeared. He returned a few minutes later with a handsome, elderly couple, introducing them to Lily in his usual perfunctory manner. When this was done he added, to Lily, "Master Jonah is changing his attire, my lady, and will join you shortly. I shall bring the tea in at once."

Lily nodded that this was fine, and then extended her hand to both Lord and Lady Barton and, with an expansive gesture, offered them the best seats in the room.

The elderly pair looked at her with curiosity, then exchanged nods.

"She's not bad-looking for a deaf-mute, is she?" Lord Barton told his wife loudly, patting Lily's hand as she began to shake her head. "Now, now, my dear." His voice took on the tone that Lily was all too used to, speaking to her as if she were an ignorant child to be indulged. "Yes, I understand. You want us to sit over here, is that it?"

"She doesn't appear to be dangerous, if that's what you mean," Lady Barton said as she took her seat. "And it seems that she allows the servants to dress her in the manner of normal women, for which I'm certain our dear Anthony must be grateful. Some of these people are quite uncontrollable, you know."

"Yes, indeed," Lord Barton agreed. "Very much like the heathens we've heard so much about. But she does make a nice presentation, don't you think? I wonder if Anthony's able to take her out of the house at all?"

"I'm sure he does," said Lady Barton. "Just to be kind to the poor thing. Anthony's always been a thoughtful boy."

Lily stared at the older couple with a measure of horror, not so much for her own embarrassment, but for theirs when they at last discovered that she could understand every word they spoke. She prayed that Jonah would appear soon, and, in the meantime, began to open her little gold case to write them a note and correct the misunderstanding.

"Yes," Lord Barton said more somberly, "and that's what makes it such a damned shame, to know that he was forced into marrying such a woman. I suppose one can't entirely blame Lord Cardemore, but did he have to choose Anthony to blackmail? To have ruined the life of such a fine and promising young man is criminal, especially when there are so many others of lesser quality who would have gladly married the chit for her money alone."

Lily's fingers froze in the midst of writing. She lifted her head to gaze at Lord and Lady Barton.

"But what else could poor Anthony do?" Lady Barton asked. "It was either marry the girl or lose everything he possessed, even St. Cathyrs. Oh, that Cardemore's a devil, all right. I should love to see him suffer the very same consequences."

At this, Lord Barton uttered an unamused laugh. "Who would be brave— or foolish—enough to buy up all of Cardemore's debts and hold them over him, I wonder?"

"Poor Anthony," Lady Barton murmured. "It must have been horrible to be caught in such a web, and then made to marry such a woman. I'm sure he did it only for the sake of his mother and sisters. Didn't you tell me that Cardemore threatened to throw them out of St. Cathyrs without so much as a farthing?"

Lord Barton nodded. "That's what all the rumors say. Cardemore would have ruined Anthony completely if he didn't marry the sister, without a care for dear Anabella and the girls. They would have been utterly destitute."

"And I had so hoped that he'd marry that lovely Miss Hamilton," Lady Barton said. "Such a nice girl, with perfect manners and of a fine family. Goodness knows that he was desperately in love with her."

Lord Barton nodded. "She would have been the ideal

wife for him. It's such a pity." He poked a long, bony finger in Lily's direction. "This one will never be able to help Anthony achieve all of the potential he has, certainly not in Lords. He'll probably have to give up his political career altogether."

"Oh, dear, me." Lady Barton looked even more distressed. "It's so unfair. But I suppose he must put the best face on the situation that he can. He is married to the girl, after all. Do you know, Edmund, she almost looks as if she can understand what we're saying."

"Nonsense," said his lordship. "Not a chance of it. Deaf and mute, she is, and probably of a low intellect, in the bargain. You can dress these people up and teach them some manners so that they're fit for polite company, but you'll never change the nature of the beast. I doubt the girl's got more sense than a trained monkey."

"Oh no, don't say that," Lady Barton pleaded. "Only look at her expression. It's almost as if she understood every word you said. She appears quite stricken. Poor little thing. I do feel sorry for her. Such a pretty child."

A scratch fell on the door and Lord Barton said, "At last. Might as well have some tea while we wait for Anthony to put in an appearance."

The door opened and Jonah walked in ahead of Crane. Lily stared at him as he drew nearer.

She was stunned, completely numb from it, unable to move or think. If she continued to breathe she wasn't aware of it, though the beating of her heart was so loud it was deafening. Aaron had blackmailed Graydon into marrying her. Graydon had only wed her to save his lands. He would rather die than lose St. Cathyrs. Instead, he had married her.

Jonah stood directly in front of her, speaking, and although she could hear the concern in his tone, she couldn't seem to make out his words over the throbbing thrum of her heart. His hands began to move, and he signed to her, *What's the matter?*

She felt weak and faint and forced her shaking legs to work, to support her as she stood.

"My lady!" Jonah cried, tugging at her sleeve, but she pushed free and moved to the door, insensible to all but the need to know the truth. She ignored all of them—Crane, two of the maids, a footman—as she made her way to the front doors, and then, suddenly, she was out on the stoop, in the bright, clear, cold day.

She knew which way Wilborn Place was, and started in that direction, dimly aware that Jonah trotted along beside her, silent now. After several minutes of fast walking, Lily suddenly fell still. What was she doing? She looked down at herself and realized that she wasn't properly dressed for being outdoors. She wore only a simple morning dress, nothing more. Her hair wasn't even covered.

Jonah moved to stand in front of her.

"Where do you want to go?" he asked.

"W-hil-born Phlace." Her voice was rougher than usual, strangled with emotion.

He nodded. "I'll find a cab, then."

Lady Margaret stretched luxuriantly in the Earl of Cardemore's wide bed, yawning and shifting into a comfortable position to return to her slumber. Watching her, Cardemore felt a sharp desire to rejoin her, but it was already midday and both Isabel and the servants would surely realize what they'd been about. Despite the fact that they shared this very bed on a shockingly regular basis, Cardemore was not insensible to the fact that he and Margaret should at least attempt to maintain some sense of decorum. He finished tying a loose knot in his neckcloth and sat beside her on the bed.

"Up with you," he murmured, leaning with one arm on either side of her to kiss her soft, warm mouth. "Isabel will be finished with all her urgent missives soon and demanding your presence to discuss wedding gowns and trousseaus and every other tedious detail for her upcoming marriage.

It almost makes me wish Daltry had simply taken her off to Gretna Green.''

Not opening her eyes, Margaret smiled. "She was terribly happy, wasn't she? I'm so glad she and that young man have come to their senses at last. Lord Graydon is to be thanked."

"Not if Isabel's going to go about sighing as she was an hour ago. I may be more tempted to shoot him." He bent and kissed her again, and Margaret slid her hands about his neck.

"She won't be bothering us for another hour, at least," she murmured. "Isabel's going to write every acquaintance she has with her good news, I believe."

"Margaret Walford," he said huskily, "you could tempt a monk. Now, come along and behave yourself. There's something I wish to speak to you about."

She opened her eyes at last. "I don't like the sound of that."

He smiled. "It's nothing so dire, I promise. Only something I want you to consider."

"What is it?"

"Becoming my wife. I want to marry you, Margaret."

She stared at him. "We can't," she whispered. "You know it's impossible."

"In England, yes," he admitted. "But not on the Continent. I realize that we might find it necessary to live elsewhere, perhaps in America or on my plantation in Jamaica. I don't really care where, as long as you're with me. You and our child, of course." He pulled the covers back and let his gaze move meaningfully to rest upon her bare stomach, which he touched with his fingertips. "For his or her sake, I believe we should wed. Don't you?"

"Aaron," she said with disbelief, "how did you know? I'm not fully certain of it yet, myself."

His smile was tender. "I know every inch of you intimately, my dear. Even the slightest change is noticeable."

"I had thought myself too old," she murmured. "I've

been so afraid that it might be true—" she skimmed his cheek with a loving hand "—but so hopeful, as well. I'm not certain what we can do about it."

"We'll marry," he stated, "and have our child. You can't think I'd let my son or daughter be born a bastard?"

She shook her head. "You could lose your title. Cardemore Hall. Everything. And even if we should marry, the child will still be considered a bastard in England."

"It doesn't matter. The child will know the truth, that he or she was born out of love, and that we married for his or her sake. I shall miss Cardemore Hall, I suppose, but the title means less than nothing to me. Let it go," he said with a wave of his hand. "Let it go, for pity's sake. If I have you I have everything that matters to me."

"But Lily, and Isabel—"

"Will be settled with their husbands and children of their own. We'll visit them often, never fear. I'd never wish to stay away from them simply to spare England the ignominy of having a banished couple step upon its fair shores."

She was in the midst of opening her mouth to speak when the sound of footsteps pounding up the stairs alerted them to an imminent intrusion.

"My lord!" Willis said urgently from the other side of the bedroom door. "Forgive me for disturbing you. It's Lady Lillian."

The tone of his voice said what the rest of his words didn't. Cardemore and Margaret exchanged glances. She slid out of bed as Cardemore strode to the door.

"I'm coming," he said, waiting until Margaret had slipped through the adjoining door and into the rooms meant for the Countess of Cardemore. Willis was waiting for him, his expression worried.

"She's in the entry hall. She refused to wait in the drawing room."

Cardemore knew, even before he began to descend the stairs, what had happened. His heart was in his mouth with each step he took, and then, when he saw her, standing

there at the bottom, looking up at him, it fell directly into
his feet.

"Lily," he said, held frozen by her expression, so pleading and afraid. Tears coursed down her cheeks, and she
gripped the banister as if to keep from falling to her knees.
Behind her Jonah stood, as still and silent as a statue.

"True?" she demanded, sobbing. "Is it tr-hue, Ah-rhon?"

"Lily." He took a step nearer. "Let me take you into
the drawing room."

She shook her head violently. "T-hell me! D-hid you
bl-hack-mhail him? Grah-don? To mar-rhy me?"

He drew in a shaking breath. "I blackmailed him. But
not to marry you."

"Wh-hat, then?"

"To be your escort. To take you about London and make
your time here perfect."

She blinked as the tears blinded her. Her weeping shook
her slender body.

"N-hot to mar-rhy?"

He clenched his hands into fists, punishing, until he
could feel the nails biting into his flesh. His servants had
disappeared completely. At the top of the stairs, he heard
Margaret begin to descend.

"I meant to make him wed you, also. The night you were
kidnapped—it was my doing. All of it. I had Graydon taken
as well, and put in with you so that your reputation would
be compromised. I never expected that you might find a
way of escape." His gaze fell fleetingly upon Jonah. "Or
that you would fall ill."

Lily bowed her head, shaking it and saying, between the
great sobs that racked her, "Oh, n-ho. Oh, n-ho." She
swayed, as if she would fall, and then slid to her knees,
pressing her forehead against the great column of the banister and giving way to her misery.

"Lily." Lady Margaret moved quickly down the stairs,
sitting on the bottom step and enfolding Lily in her arms.

Lily clung to her, weeping like a child. "Don't, my dear," Lady Margaret soothed, stroking her hair. "You'll make yourself ill. Everything will be all right."

Lily shook her head and said, mournfully, "Nev-her aghain. R-huined. All."

Chapter Twenty-Six

Cardemore Hall seemed different, somehow. Lily couldn't quite put her finger on what it was that she found lacking, but there was something. Perhaps it was because she caught herself suddenly comparing her beloved lifelong home to St. Cathyrs, which she had admittedly grown to love, or perhaps it was because, for the very first time, she was alone here, without Aunt Margaret or Isabel or any other family member.

She wandered the massive house alone each day, walking in and around rooms she'd known all of her life, remembering other days and times when she had been in them, events that had taken place in them. The long gallery, for instance, where Aaron had arranged races between her and Isabel and himself on rainy days—races that he'd always lost, despite his bigger size and ability to run faster. And the library, where her father had used to sit in the mornings and evenings, talking to himself in a low voice. She had stood outside, pressing her ear to the doors when the servants weren't about. It was the only time her father ever sounded kind. After his death she would go into the room and sit in his chair and stare at the paintings of him and her mother on the wall, him so stern, her so gentle. When Aaron came home after his long absence, the first thing he'd done—the very first thing, right upon entering

Cardemore Hall—was to go directly to the library, stand upon her father's chair and pull her father's portrait from the wall. It had been stored in the attic ever since. Lily wandered upstairs one day during one of her lonely walks to see it again, and had been profoundly surprised at the reaction that the stern, unbending face had wrought upon her. She knelt before the portrait, a lantern glowing dimly beside her, and wept with a deep, aching sense of loss and regret. He hadn't loved her, and she never would have realized that fact if Aaron hadn't come and loved her, instead. All that she knew about a father's love was because of her brother. He had been everything most precious to her, until she had met Graydon.

There were other rooms at Cardemore Hall that held special memories for Lily. Aunt Margaret's sewing room was one. It was one of the smallest and least remarkable rooms in the entire, monumental house, and yet when Aunt Margaret was there, working on one of her particular projects, it was also the place where the rest of them seemed to be. Lily could remember many a happy afternoon during her childhood spent sitting by the fire with Isabel, playing with dolls while Aunt Margaret sat in one chair, working, and Aaron sat in another, reading aloud. Now it was only empty—so empty and lonely that Lily couldn't bear to do more than stand at the door and gaze into it.

She had Jonah for company, of course, and Jenny and all of the servants who had raised her since she was but a child, and there was a measure of comfort in being fully understood and treated like an adult by people who spoke her language. But for all that she was as lonely at Cardemore Hall as she'd been after Graydon had left her at St. Cathyrs.

Aaron had promised that he'd leave her alone for the rest of her life, that he would never try to see her or contact her. That was what Lily had wanted then, in that most horrible hour of her life when pain and betrayal had been all she could feel. She could remember vividly saying the words, not deigning to sign them to him, not even looking at him, and hearing his promises given in turn, his voice flat and void of emotion. And yet she knew that she had hurt him. He had asked her to forgive him, begged her, but it hadn't been possible. Not then. Now, spending each day alone in the place that had once held all her happiness, Lily didn't know what was possible or impossible.

She was lonely. She wanted Aaron and Aunt Margaret and Isabel. She wanted life to be easy and pleasant again. And most of all, she wanted Graydon.

Inside of Cardemore Hall she thought of her family, but when she wandered through the estate lands, by the lake and through the dark, shady forest trees, she thought of Graydon. In her bed at night, with the darkness hiding her tears, she wept for him, utterly miserable.

But there was no good in it. He was free of her and would be glad of it. He would divorce her and marry Frances Hamilton. And then he would be happy. The entire past year, from the time that Aaron had blackmailed him until the time that Lily had finally set him free, would eventually be nothing more than a dim memory to the Earl of Graydon. For Lily, the days—and nights—that she'd had with him would serve as the most precious she would ever have.

"'E's goin' to come fer you," Jonah told her repeatedly, having been out of patience with her since the day they'd left London. "Mark my word. You'll least 'spect it 'nd 'e'll be standin' there, right before you."

But Lily knew that he was only voicing a hopeful, never-to-be realized dream. A full week passed, and then another, and there was no word. Lily had gotten exactly what she'd asked for from both her brother and her husband. They were going to leave her in complete peace. Perhaps even Aunt Margaret and Isabel would stay away, especially after the distressing scene she'd played out at Wilborn Place. Thinking of it now made her wince with regret. She'd not even stayed long enough to say goodbye to Isabel.

At the end of the second week, after finishing dinner in the company of the ever effusive Jonah, Lily decided to go to the music room instead of the drawing room, where they usually retired to play a game of dice, which Jonah was teaching her. It was the one room she'd not entered yet, perhaps because it held memories more frustrating than pleasurable. She'd not inherited any sort of musical talent, though she'd striven to become at least marginally accomplished on the pianoforte. Isabel had been far more talented.

Jonah gave a low whistle as she opened the music room doors. A footman had already lit the fire and the lamps, and the room looked as beautiful as Lily remembered it being.

"This is near as grand as that fancy dancing room next door," Jonah said admiringly as he walked about. "Shame everyfing's like ghosts." He picked up the edge of an instrument cover, peeked beneath it, then dropped it again. "S'pose it keeps 'em dry."

With a laugh, Lily removed the covers from the pianoforte and set them in a heap on the floor. Then she sat down and began to play a familiar waltz, slowly and haltingly at first, with all the faultiness of long-absent practice, but eventually with greater ease. So absorbed was she in improving her performance that she not only lost track of time, but of Jonah, as well. Thinking of him suddenly, she glanced up to find where he was, only to be met by the sight of her husband, instead.

The music came to an abrupt halt, and Lily stood.

He was dressed for riding, in muddied breeches and tall boots. His handsome face was flushed with cold and his bare head was slightly disheveled. Over his shoulder he held a large leather bag, looking for all the world as if he were delivering the mail. Even in his most elegant evening dress, he had never appeared so wonderful. Lily's heart constrained painfully at the sight of him, and at the steady, somber gaze he held upon her.

He gave her a civil nod. "Good evening, Lily. I apologize for intruding without an invitation, but I've ridden a long distance today with the express purpose of seeing you, and didn't wish to wait another hour in the drawing room. I hope you don't mind.''

The words were polite and evenly spoken. If he had missed her at all, there was no hint of it in either his tone or demeanor.

She slowly sat back down upon the pianoforte bench, uncertain of what she should say. Behind Graydon she saw Jonah, a satisfied grin on his adolescent face.

Graydon took a step nearer. ''You instructed me in your parting missive to leave you in peace, but I fear that was impossible. There were some few important matters that we have yet to discuss. Personally.''

Of course, she thought as her heart began to pound with painfully hard thumps. She had asked him for a divorce, and there would be legal matters, perhaps papers that she must sign. She should have thought of that.

She looked beyond him to Jonah, and signed, *Ask his lordship to wait for me in the drawing room. I shall attend him presently, and we may have tea.*

''She sez—'' began Jonah.

''I'm not in the mood for tea, if you don't mind,'' Graydon said, holding Lily's gaze, ''although a brandy would be welcome. And I believe we can discuss everything necessary here. I'll not take up much of your time.''

Lily nodded and rose from the bench once more, signing, *Ask the footman to bring his lordship a decanter of brandy here in the music room, please, Jonah.*

''And while you're at it, Jonah,'' his lordship added, not unkindly, ''go and find some other spot to amuse yourself in. Lady Graydon and I wish to speak alone.''

Jonah shrugged and left the room, and both Lily and Graydon moved toward the warmth of the fire. She unconsciously clasped a hand about her wrist, remembering too late that she never wore her note case at Cardemore Hall.

''I'll not tax you,'' he said, as if reading her thoughts.

Lily lifted her chin. "Ah d-hon't care ab-hout that."

"Don't you?" he asked softly, looking at her more closely as they took chairs facing each other. He dropped the leather bag from his shoulder to the floor. "You should, Lily. Especially if you're going to be so eager to get rid of me. I won't be here to make you rest your voice when it's needful, if you do."

She looked at him sharply. "You ahre the one who is eag-her. To be fhree."

He shook his head slightly. "You wouldn't be so certain of that if you'd been the one to come home and find your house in an uproar and your lady wife gone. My godparents were frantic with apologies, although I suppose you know that already, as you were at least kind enough to spare *them* a few moments before you took flight." His gaze narrowed. "I realize that your anger is fully justified, Lily, but I wish you had at least given me a chance to make an explanation before leaving. I would have let you go if you'd still wished it. To simply leave that missive for me to find was—"

"I th-hought you w-hould be glhad to have me g-hone," she told him curtly. "You l-hove Miss Ham-hil-tohn."

"Indeed, I do," he agreed. "Almost as much as I love my own sisters. She's been very good to me, especially when I was away from St. Cathyrs and missing you so badly. She kept me from going insane."

"You l-hove her!" Lily charged hotly, glaring at him. "Ev-hen when Ah whas in Lon-dhon, you w-hent to see her. Ev-rhy day!"

A moment of bewilderment crossed his features, and then he smiled. "I went out every day, my dear, but I didn't go to tryst with Miss Hamilton. I promise you that on my very honor. There is nothing between Miss Hamilton and myself save friendship."

Lily didn't believe that for a moment. "D-hon't lie to me, An-non-nee," she murmured, hurt that he would do so. "Phlease."

"I'm not lying to you, love."

At the sound of the meaningless endearment, which he had so often, and so carelessly, used, tears filled her eyes. She had cried buckets of them in the past many days. She was beginning to wonder if they would ever stop.

Graydon looked equally grim. "Does it distress you so much to know that I love you? There was a time when I came to hope—" He shook his head. "But it doesn't matter now."

She wiped her eyes with the edge of her sleeve and said, "There is n-ho nheed to pre-tehnd. I know ever-thing. All of it. Ah-rhon told me." She sniffled loudly, and felt as foolish as a child. "You d-hon't nheed to feel hon-hor-bhound. Ah will-hing-ly rel-hease you."

A footman scratched at the door, and in a moment Graydon was pouring himself a large glass of brandy. He poured one for Lily, as well, but she shook her head when he tried to offer it to her.

"You'll want this later," he said. "Your voice will be raw." He settled back in his chair and took a long sip before speaking again. "Your brother told you the part he played in bringing us together, I know. About blackmailing me into being your escort and about having both of us kidnapped to force us into marriage. It was wrong of him to do so. I also admit that, at the start, when he held St. Cathyrs over me, I was angry and resentful of both you and him. I even toyed with the idea of making you fall in love with me and ruining you so that I might have revenge upon him, but that died the moment I set sight on you, Lily. I don't know that I fell in love with you then, but if not, it was very shortly afterward."

She shook her head sorrowfully. "It whas j-hust des-hire. No-thing mhore."

"I wanted you. I admit this also. I wanted you so badly that I was dreaming about you. That night when we were kidnapped, I thought I was having one of those dreams."

"Ahnd then you f-helt hon-hor-bhound to wed me."

"I told myself that was why, also because I wanted you.

But the truth is that I loved you and was ready to go to any lengths in order to make you mine. I wouldn't admit the truth of that to myself at the time. It seemed easier to pretend that I was merely being your knight come to the rescue, but I doubt that I would have so readily sacrificed Miss Hamilton's reputation for anything so simple. If anyone has truly paid for the folly created by Cardemore and myself, it is she.''

"You whill m-hake it up to her," Lily said bitterly.

"I'm afraid that's impossible. You see, dear—'' his voice softened "—she married Mr. Charles Cassin yesterday, by special license.''

Whatever Lily had been expecting him to say, it certainly hadn't been that. The shock was so complete that when he said her name twice, sternly, she wasn't able to respond.

"I'm sorry,'' he muttered, picking up the drink he'd poured for her. "I should have found a better way to tell you.'' Kneeling, he placed the glass to her lips, and made her drink a little. She coughed and sputtered at the bitterness of it, but he seemed somewhat reassured. "That's better,'' he said, patting her back.

"*T-hrue?*'' she stammered. "Is it?''

"Perfectly true,'' he assured her, returning to his chair and pulling it a little closer to hers. "I stood up for Mr. Cassin as his groomsman. Your cousin, Lady Isabel, stood for Miss Hamilton, or rather, Mrs. Cassin, I should now say, although Frances privately declared to me that she wished it might have been you. She's quite fond of you, you know. It was to keep Frances from committing a grave error that took me away from you on the night of Lord and Lady Orchard's ball. She had determined to run away to Gretna Green with Mr. Cassin, you see, and I left you as I did in an attempt to prevent the assignation and the complete finish of her reputation. Fortunately, Mr. Cassin was of much the same mind, and only met Miss Hamilton at their agreed-upon spot in order to tell her that he would only have her as his wife with her father's consent. I accompanied them to Lord and Lady Hamilton's home to lend whatever aid I might in convincing them to accept Mr. Cassin's suit. The results, as you perceive, were most satisfactory.''

At this, Lily burst into loud, uncontrollable tears. Graydon was on his knees beside her in an instant.

"Darling! What is it?"

She gripped his sleeve. "Ah'm sorree," she cried. "S-sorree for you, An-non-nee."

"For me?" he repeated angrily. "Lily, you little fool! Do you think I'm pining away for Frances Hamilton? I was never so glad in my life to know that she was happy and well settled. What will it take to make you understand that I love you?"

She hiccuped and sniffled and let him wipe her face with his fingers.

"Mah voh-hice. You c-han't whant me."

"I love the sound of your voice," he said fervently, holding her face in his hands and making her look at him. "I love everything about you. But we've been far too long in speaking honestly of the matter. I still curse myself for letting you have Sir Hatton in to torture you for so long, every day—"

"He help-hed me!" she said. "The b-hall—he help-hed me…"

"It *wasn't* him!" Graydon told her. "Don't you know how grating and hoarse you sounded that night? He nearly ruined it for you, with all his pompous self-righteousness and brutal methods. It was *you*, Lily. You alone who made that night a success. You spoke of your own free will, in your own voice, and with all your own sweet charm. You made them see you, made them *accept* you. And once they knew that you weren't afraid of your own shortcomings, they weren't afraid anymore, either. You weren't invisible, Lily, because you wouldn't let yourself be invisible. It was you, and only you, who made it happen."

She shook her head, but he stopped her, made her look at him again.

"We'll speak the truth. It's far past time. You can't speak as others do, Lily. You will *never* be able to do so."

Fresh tears blurred her vision, and she tried to pull away.

"Listen to me," he commanded. "I don't want to cause you pain. I'd rather do myself an injury first. But we must get past this if we're to have any kind of happiness together. I know Charles Cassin has spoken much the same thing to you, because he told me so. What made you begin to doubt the truth of what you had always known and accepted before?"

"Whant-hing." She sobbed, bowing her head, setting her hands over his and making him release her. "Whant-ing."

"To speak like others? It's never going to happen, love. You might as well wish to fly. You have to accept for once and for all that you will never have a normal speaking voice. It's not fair, but there's nothing that can be done to change it. You must learn to live around it, just as I must. It's not so very hard, if we do it together."

"N-hot that," she whispered brokenly. "Did-hn't wish for th-hat."

"For what, then?" he whispered.

She sobbed, horrified to tell him the truth, unable to keep from doing so. "F-hor you to l-hove me."

"Oh, Lily." He lifted her head and kissed her on the mouth, long and fully. "I do love you."

"N-ho," she said, lowering her face once more. She couldn't look him in the eye. It was impossible, in the midst of all her shame. "N-ho, An-non-nee. You nheed—" she drew in a gasping breath, feeling her voice begin to go "—bhetter whife. Phar-lah-ment—"

"Parliament is a price I'm willing to pay to have you for my wife. A price I'll gladly pay."

"Nhot fair for you," she whispered.

"Just as your being poisoned when you were but a child was not fair. But ask me, instead, Lily, if it would be fair for me to lose you, when I love you more than my own life? Do you think I could sit in the House of Lords and be glad, knowing you were lost to me? Can you think I'll ever, even once in my life, regret choosing you over that?''

''An-non-nee—''

''There's more,'' he said, stopping her. ''We must have the full truth between us, and then you must decide whether or not to send me away. I knew, almost while it was happening, that your brother was behind our kidnapping, and I knew what his goal was, that we should be forced to marry. He wanted you settled in a good marriage to a man whom he knew cared for you. But knowing the part he had played, I was suddenly the one in command, instead of the other way around. He knew that you would hate him if you ever discovered the truth, and because of that, I held sway over him.''

''You threat-hen Ahr-rhon? Th-hat you w-hould t-hell me?''

He nodded. ''If he didn't stay away from us—from you. I was angry, and wanted him out of our lives forever, or as much as possible without you becoming suspicious.''

Her eyes widened. ''Th-hat's why…Christ-mhas?''

''Yes. That's why. I'm the one you have to blame for the misery you suffered in missing your family so. They wanted to come, for they missed you just as fully. It was my doing that they did not, and I regret it more than I can say. Seeing how you wanted them, especially your brother, I regretted it all during the Christmas season, and knew myself to be a fool. You have every right to be furious with me, Lily, for that and for a hundred other reasons. There will be much for you to forgive if we're to go on together.''

She sniffled and touched his cheek. ''Ah for-ghive you, An-non-nee.''

He took her hands and kissed them. ''Thank you.'' He pressed nearer to her. ''Lily, do you love me? Please, you must tell me, and speak the truth. I'm willing to set you free if it's what you truly wish, but if you love me—if there's any chance that you might one day love me—then I beg that you will tell me now.''

She set her shaking fingers against his lips and met his searching gaze. Tears rolled down her cheeks. ''Ah love you, An-non-nee. Ah've loved you for a l-hong, l-hong t-hime.''

''Lily,'' he murmured, and pressed his face against her neck, holding her. ''Lily.''

She slid her arms about his shoulders. ''Ah love you,'' she said again. ''S-ho mhuch.''

''Why did you never tell me? Why did you leave me?'' he asked, pulling up to look at her again. ''It nearly killed me, Lily.''

''Ah didhn't th-hink you c-hould ever l-hove me. Ah whanted to s-hct you free.''

''It's impossible,'' he told her, and stood. ''And I'll show you why.''

He took the leather bag upon the floor and opened it, and then tossed the contents into the air. Lily found herself pelted by a blizzard of drifting notes, and then Graydon was before her again, pulling her out of her chair and into his arms, so that they knelt together on the floor. The tiny bits of paper drifted all about them as he laid her down on the parquet floor.

''Do you know what that is?'' he asked.

Her face was still wet with tears, but she knew, and she smiled. ''Mah n-hotes,'' she said with wonder.

''Your notes,'' he repeated, and kissed her. ''I kept every single one, and know them all by heart. Now, sweet wife, tell me that you love me again. I need so much to hear it.''

She told him, over and over again while he kissed her, until he lifted up and grinned down at her.

''You haven't realized yet. The very reason that kept me from you for two entire weeks.''

''What?'' she asked, dizzy from his kisses, from the entire past hour.

He lifted a hand and signed his response to her—*I love you.*

She stared at him, and he continued, slowly, *I'm not good at it yet. You will have to be patient.*

Awe possessed her features. After another moment of silence she lifted her own hand. *You understood what I told Jonah. You understood all of it.*

He chuckled. "I caught a few words and guessed the rest. I had hoped you would notice. I've been taking lessons for over a month now, from your own brother. Then, after you left me, I pressed Charles Cassin into service, at least until the day of his wedding, when I finally took pity on him. You shall have to be patient with me, love, for I fear I'm rather a slow student. In time I'll know the sign language perfectly, if you'll but give me the chance. Indeed, I'm hoping you'll become my teacher."

But why? she signed.

"Don't you know?" he asked.

Because you love me?

"Because I love you," he murmured, lowering himself to her again. "Because it will be our own language, together, and because I shall always love you."

* * * * *

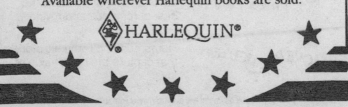

Presents Extravaganza

25 YEARS!

It's our birthday and we're celebrating....

Twenty-five years of romance fiction
featuring men of the world and captivating women —
Seduction and passion guaranteed!

Not only are we promising you three months of terrific
books, authors and romance, but as an added bonus
with the retail purchase of two Presents® titles,
you can receive a special one-of-a-kind keepsake.
It's our gift to you!

Look in the back pages of any Harlequin Presents® title,
from May to July 1998, for more details.

Available wherever Harlequin books are sold.

◈ HARLEQUIN®

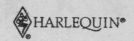

Not The Same Old Story!

 Exciting, glamorous romance stories that take readers around the world.

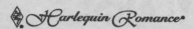 Sparkling, fresh and tender love stories that bring you pure romance.

 Bold and adventurous— Temptation is strong women, bad boys, great sex!

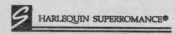 Provocative and realistic stories that celebrate life and love.

 Contemporary fairy tales—where anything is possible and where dreams come true.

 Heart-stopping, suspenseful adventures that combine the best of romance and mystery.

 Humorous and romantic stories that capture the lighter side of love.

Welcome to *Love Inspired*™

A brand-new series of contemporary inspirational love stories.

Join men and women as they learn valuable lessons about facing the challenges of today's world and about life, love and faith.

**Look for the following April 1998
Love Inspired™ titles:**

DECIDEDLY MARRIED
by Carole Gift Page

A HOPEFUL HEART
by Lois Richer

HOMECOMING
by Carolyne Aarsen

Available in retail outlets in March 1998.

LIFT YOUR SPIRITS AND GLADDEN YOUR HEART
with *Love Inspired!*™

**Steeple
Hill**™

MEN at WORK

All work and no play? Not these men!

April 1998

KNIGHT SPARKS by Mary Lynn Baxter

Sexy lawman Rance Knight made a career of arresting the bad guys. Somehow, though, he thought policewoman Carly Mitchum was framed. Once they'd uncovered the truth, could Rance let Carly go...or would he make a citizen's arrest?

May 1998

HOODWINKED by Diana Palmer

CEO Jake Edwards donned coveralls and went undercover as a mechanic to find the saboteur in his company. Nothing—or no one—would distract him, not even beautiful secretary Maureen Harris. Jake had to catch the thief—*and* the woman who'd stolen his heart!

June 1998

DEFYING GRAVITY by Rachel Lee

Tim O'Shaughnessy and his business partner, Liz Pennington, had always been close—but never *this* close. As the danger of their assignment escalated, so did their passion. When the job was over, could they ever go back to business as usual?

MEN AT WORK™

Available at your favorite retail outlet!

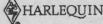 

Look us up on-line at: http://www.romance.net   PMAW1

DEBBIE MACOMBER

invites you to the

HEART OF TEXAS

Join Debbie Macomber as she brings you the lives and loves of the folks in the ranching community of Promise, Texas.

If you loved Midnight Sons—don't miss Heart of Texas! A brand-new six-book series from Debbie Macomber.

Available in February 1998 at your favorite retail store.

Heart of Texas by Debbie Macomber

Lonesome Cowboy	February '98
Texas Two-Step	March '98
Caroline's Child	April '98
Dr. Texas	May '98
Nell's Cowboy	June '98
Lone Star Baby	July '98

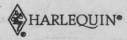

HARLEQUIN®

New York Times
bestselling author

Jayne Ann Krentz

will once again spellbind readers with

A Woman's Touch

When Rebecca Wade inherited land her boss, Kyle Stockbridge, considered his, she absolutely refused to sell out. Especially when he used a declaration of love as a way to convince her.

Despite Kyle's claim that their relationship—and his feelings for her—were independent of the issue between them, Rebecca knew that selling the land wouldn't solve all of their problems. For that to happen, Kyle would have to prove his love.

Available in April 1998 at your favorite retail outlet.

MIRA

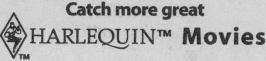